I0575157

Tales From The Night Garden, Vol. 1

Lemon Balm

Artemis Quinn and Auden Eris-Everen

The copyright and collaboration info:

Control number for the Library of Congress is currently pending.

Copyright © 2025
Conquer Thy Fear Studio, LLC
Artemis Quinn Burnett
Auden Eris-Everen Cline

All rights reserved. No part of this publication may be reproduced, stored or transmitted in any form or by any means, electronic, mechanical, photocopying, recording, scanning, or otherwise without written permission from the publisher. It is illegal to copy this book, post it to a website, or distribute it by any other means without permission.

ISBN: 979-8-9997538-0-9 (E-Book)
ISBN: 979-8-9997538-1-6 (Paperback)
ISBN: 979-8-9997538-2-3 (Hardcover)

No part of this book has been created, edited, illustrated, or otherwise altered using a large language model (LLM) or as part of any generative AI or neural network architecture. No part of this book may be used as data for training any large language model (LLM) or as part of any machine learning or neural network architecture (generative AI).

This novel is entirely a work of fiction. The names, characters and incidents portrayed in it are the work of the authors' imagination. Any resemblance to actual persons, living or dead, events or localities is entirely coincidental. Real places are mentioned, but the areas in the book may not align with how those places actually are.

All of the artwork, including the cover design and formatting, is done by Artemis Quinn Burnett AKA VampireAntihero of Conquer Thy Fear Studio, LLC,. You can find more examples of their work and commission info at: https://www.vampireantihero.com/

Our developmental editor is Julian Greystoke. You can find them on Fiverr here: https://www.fiverr.com/juliangreystoke

Our line and copy edits were done by Keegan Burnett and Artemis Quinn Burnett.

https://www.conquerthyfear.com/

Join our discord community!

https://discord.gg/dK7H6htPFt/

Author's Note

Whoa there, traveler!

A small location note: Real places are mentioned in this novel, but the descriptions may not align with the actual localities. Most of the settings are fictional, set within the real world.

A small formatting note: There is telepathy in this story. In order to avoid confusion, thoughts that are internal are *italicized*, whereas thoughts that are shared with people are ***"italicized, bold, and in quotes."***

Triggers: We want you to dive into the story, but we also know that it's a dark fantasy. Please note that the story contains some difficult topics, and we want to make sure that you're prepared for it while reading. The story has more lighthearted moments than not, but just in case it is an issue, here is a list of common triggers woven throughout the story:

Mental health struggles, Suicidal ideation, Self-harm/neglect
Disordered eating
Implied (off-page) past abuse
Vicious animals
(very slight) homophobia/transphobia
(very slight) mentions of animal death
(slight) Mentions of drug use
(very slight) Mentions of prostitution
(very slight) mentions of child neglect

To frogs and otters, for the fun and feedback.
To grizzlies and dragons, for giving us both time and space.
To bats and wolves, for being the helping hand that kept the other going.
To a little wolf who dared an older wolf to dream.

And in loving memory to a very special fox who believed in the bat before the bat could.

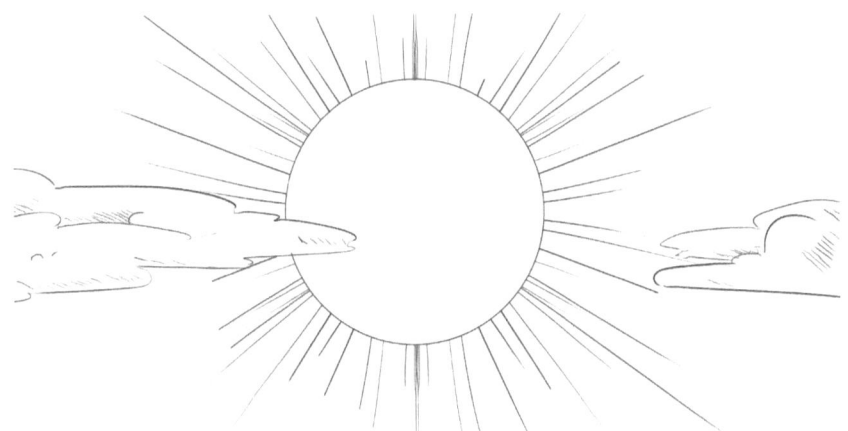

That Time That Life Was Mundane

Cypress

Okay, stop me if you've heard this one before — I am sitting in a dark room with a vampire. The setup sounds like a joke, but there's no punchline. But, if you don't laugh, you cry, right? So, let me spin you a tale of a vampire and a werewolf sitting in a dark room. I know, I know — Vampires, Werewolves? Sitting in the same room, and not killing each other? It's quite amazing.

I'm Cypress, and I'm one part of this story. My vampire friend over there? That's Acanthus, and I think you'll find we have a lot to say. This story is kind of about us, and some stuff that drew us together, but it's also about things way, way bigger than us. Things that I didn't know existed until I met a vampire, rotting in a coffin and hoping to die. Acanthus is here with me because this story isn't just mine to tell. From now on, I think we'll switch back and forth on telling the tale of 2022.

It sounds stupid because it's just a year, right? But honestly, the events have turned my life into the opposite of a joke. I've been kind of bobbing along in the World of Shadows, with my Vampire companion holding the guiding lantern through the dark. But, the story doesn't work if I start in 2022. I need to start at the beginning — at least, the beginning for me — so let me take you back.

⸱ ⸱) ꭰ꭫ ꭲ ꭲ ꭲ ꭲ ꭲ ⸱ ⸱

"Cypress! Did you finish that report I asked for?"

Lemon Balm

My head was resting on my desk when my boss Anita rounded the corner. I shot up from the surface, the fluorescent lights mixing with the bright monitor back-light in an awkward, overstimulating mash of blue "high definition" light that made my eyes ache. My gaze landed on her gaunt, angular face, peering with a scowl beneath furrowed eyebrows. Her brown corkscrew curls flew wildly away from her face, and her almost black eyes screamed disappointment at me as I put on the cheeriest tone I could muster, glad for the fact that I didn't have to fake a smile under my brightly-colored mask. The soft cotton fabric had a cartoon-ish splatter of white clouds across a bright blue sky; the pattern made me happy in the morning, but the joy it brought was sucked out of me within five minutes of being in the office. Anita was a hawk; terrifying at the best of times. I happened to not finish the report she was questioning me about. "Sorry Boss, I had a few other things I had to get done first."

Even with the mask perched on her angular face, Anita's jaw clenched and I could see the gears grinding in her head as she gritted her teeth. She sighed and pinched the bridge of her nose. "Cypress. I asked for this report at 10 AM."

I didn't need to see her mouth to picture the sour-lemon frown. I was already busy with the IT tasks I needed to do, and lately I had been wearing another hat for data entry because the entire department was in shambles. The report that she had asked for wasn't something that either department I was covering was responsible for. "I know," I replied quickly, trying my best to sound sympathetic without giving her room to berate me. It was easy for me to slip into that corporate, cold mask to placate her. "We had more pressing matters."

Despite the importance of a spending report in Anita's world, we had to fire three people today for not showing up to the office. Cutting our losses. The height of corporate capitalism. It's not like there was a pandemic or anything. Not to mention, my *actual* department — IT — was being tasked to set up Work From Home for eighty percent of the employees while I was busy trying to please my toxic boss. Anita was unsympathetic to my plight. "I need that report first thing tomorrow morning Cypress, even if you have to work all night to finish it!"

I get it. I get it. No need to bite my head off. I tried my best not to let my irritation show. "Yes Anita. You'll have it." I smiled my most pleasant, award-winning smile, pleased to hear that it slipped into my voice rather than the budding headache at the base of my skull, but this woman was a stone tower.

"Tomorrow. Morning." She hissed this through gritted teeth as she stormed out, the cloying scent of Freesia in her wake.

I sighed, hit print on the report I was working on, counted to thirty in my head, and shut down the computer. She would already be in the parking lot by the time the report printed. "Can't yell at me from there," I grumbled at my stony-faced reflection in the dull shine of the fake wood desk. The name plate in front of me reflected upside down. *Cypress Borne. He/They. IT Specialist.* I reached for the hand sanitizer to its left and pumped it into my palms for good measure. In case the masks didn't clue you in, the year is 2020. Yes, *that* 2020, with the lockdowns and the trauma surrounding it that no one wants to talk about. To be fair, I *also* don't want to talk about it, but I need you to know, Reader, that it was a thing. And, unfortunately, I lived in New York City at the time.

Mundanity didn't exist in our lives during that fever dream of a year. This is really when I started to wish for things to be more mundane, but I had no real scope of just how wild my life could get at that point. Mundane. Mundane? Muuuuundane. You ever say a word so much that it no longer sounds right? Yeah. Totally Mundane, all the time. In fact, if you say mundane fast enough, it sounds like "Monday." We crave routine. It's human nature to blend in. That's... normal, right? Right.

And yet, when you really boil it down, there's so much that we take for granted in the mundane. When we blend into the crowd, we want nothing more than to stand out. When we have a routine, we want nothing more than to break it and to do something exciting. Mundanity is something that we crave, but our normalcy can be so overwhelming. And sometimes, when your life gets crazy... that becomes the new normal. I wanted to be able to stand in a crowd without getting heart palpitations over the thought of some disembodied cough. I also wished, more than anything, to be able to leave this job, but what was I going to do? It's hard to interview for something that would let me work partially remotely with a six figure salary. Here I was, trapped by my 401k as a prisoner to my own comfort. What a paradox.

Actually, this position kind of fell into my lap. I'd been a data entry grunt for a few years, trying to pay my way through school and live on a shoestring budget when I landed this job by fixing Anita's computer. She had accidentally downloaded a virus from a phishing email, and thankfully, I was in her department and there was an opening in IT. I was really lucky, but it was something that caused me an extreme amount of stress and anxiety at the time. The new degree helped matters. Looking back at who I was at the start of all this, I kind of miss when dealing with my job stress was the worst of my problems.

I was a social twenty two year old guy, freshly graduated from college with a Computer Science degree and a minor in Finance. I'd managed to finish school in June of 2019, and I'd only had a few months of catching up with life before the lockdowns hit. I missed my friends, my gym routine, and my ability to go somewhere other than my apartment. I remember that my confidence was high despite being scared a lot of the time. I had a good job with security. No one would do the amount of work that I was currently handling, coupled with Anita's impulsive and verbally abusive management style. The salary was too good to pass up.

All of these are echoes of the mundane; the simple, routine life that I craved before the pressure of COVID hit. I even kind of fit into that nice mundane box with my appearance. Lined up with anyone else on the street, I could probably be mistaken for just about any other standard, vaguely-attractive brunette white guy. And, really, I don't care much about what I look like. I just don't want people to run away from me because I'm tall or intimidating. This is why Anita gets under my skin so much; I care a lot about what people think about me. Pretty much the only thing about me that doesn't fit into a conventional cis- white American male box is that I'm non-binary, but I mean, there's nothing out of the normal about being queer, either.

Hopping out of my chair, I grabbed my travel mug and briefcase, and opted for the stairs over the elevator. If I started cardio now, I wouldn't have to work so hard at the gym later. That meant I would be walking home, and walking there. No taxi! The gyms had just reopened the week before, and I was craving the bright cheery athliesure outfits and the smell of chalk. I was willing to work out with the mask on my face if it meant seeing an area that was different from my studio or my office. Besides, working out alone at home was incredibly lonely.

I slowly descended the stairs from the 4th floor where the IT core team was located. I still craved a life that was simple, positive, and kind. I wanted the stereotypical American life: a job that paid enough to keep me comfortable, a partner that loved me and enjoyed my company, maybe two and a half kids and a white picket fence. The kids, honestly, were negotiable, and the white picket fence, well. You can't very well find those in the city, and I don't quite consider myself a country kind of person. But, it circles back to the mundane, right? Nice. Easy. Normal. Calm.

When I got to the first floor, I scanned the lobby looking for familiar faces. There were none — my hope to see a friend was naive. New York City doesn't allow for familiarity. Sighing, I resigned myself to another night alone. Dreaming of white picket fences and meeting an eventual lover in New York City at the height of a global pandemic may have been the inner delusional romantic side of me. I wasn't remotely looking for a relationship at the time, anyway; the thought of dating, of kissing someone, made me physically ill in those days. The concept of a lover was way more palatable than actually finding one.

My friends had been super nervous to leave their respective homes, and honestly, I couldn't blame them. I wasn't about to bother someone to come to the gym with me. Kennedy and Kassidy weren't really into the gym scene and lived all the way in the Bronx, and Junior was a friend that I could only really take in small doses. I don't think I really wanted to reach out to him and put a sour note on a space where I felt safe. Vic and

Frankie were the most likely to come, but Vic's sister had some autoimmune disease that I could never remember the name of, and no one had seen him since the shutdowns. Most restaurants and bars were really restricted, and it was our age group that was mostly getting sick. Even with being careful, I couldn't honestly say that the disease wasn't terrifying.

It was the end of August. The air was heavy and hot, and it felt like my clothes were soaked the second I walked through the door into the baking concrete jungle. One woman stood next to a street sign, balancing against it as she switched her pumps to far more comfortable walking shoes. I was already pulling at my tie, my suit jacket casually thrown over my arm. The mask stayed safely on my face despite it being itchy and damp against my skin, and I was already regretting my decision to walk home and then to the gym. People avoided each other, carefully flowing like water throughout the streets but keeping as much distance as possible. I watched one guy follow my lead, loosening his tie as if it were a noose, huffing and puffing as he pulled off his jacket. *Why does anyone walk in this weather?*

The seven block walk from work to my tiny studio apartment was pretty uneventful. Small groups of people carefully measured their distance from others, most wearing masks and most being miserable in the heat. I thought about the little 400 square foot paradise waiting for me. I had grown up in the Catskills north of the city, and I still wasn't used to how cramped everything was even after living here for a few years. The apartment wasn't much, but it got me through the day. A small part of me knew I wanted more, but a large part of me was terrified of losing the comfort and complacency that my routine and high salary provided.

Living in the city, even in areas outside of Manhattan, was astronomically expensive. I didn't need much in terms of space, and being surrounded by people was oddly comforting. I personally preferred my little pocket of neighborhood in Brooklyn over the skyscrapers in the city proper. It wasn't as if I needed all of the luxuries the city had to offer. At least I have a coffee maker. I remember when Junior was surviving on a mountain of discarded paper cups from cafes.

It was a comfortable twenty minutes before I hit the fences in front of my apartment complex. Tasha, my neighbor, was in the apartment on the ground floor on the left end of the complex. Because she was on the corner, she had the privilege of accessing the small, three foot by three foot fenced-in yard for her dog Carlton. The Dachshund in question barked at me in greeting as I walked past their gate, his brown tail wagging ferociously as I paused my journey. "Hey Buddy, Good to see you!" I leaned down over the gate and scratched him behind his beige speckled brown ears.

Lemon Balm

I always stopped to pat him when he was out. He was a sweetheart; I think the "Beware Of Dog" signs plastered all over the chain link fence were a bit overkill. My door was technically two doors over from Tasha's, because the access to the upper floor apartment was between us, but that was alright. Dogs were worth the patience it took to spend extra time in the heat.

The neighbor glared at me from the doorway, her dark green eyes flashing. She was a firecracker of a woman, a solid foot or more shorter than me, her dark brown hair always in a bun and usually clad in scrubs. She rolled her eyes in a typical New York kind-but-not-nice sort of way. "Don't touch my dog."

We got along well enough, but our banter made onlookers feel as if we hated each other. Truth was, she was a trauma center nurse and asked me to feed Carlton when she worked doubles. I gave her an award-winning smile and flipped my damp, curly brown hair out of my eyes. "Hey, Tasha! Always good to see you, darling."

Tasha rolled her eyes, fiddling with a little amethyst point she wore around her neck for 'protection'. I'd never call her out on it, but I couldn't understand how someone that worked in a scientific field could put stock in crystals. "Cypress, you idiot. Get inside before you have a heat stroke."

I laughed and struck a pose that was guaranteed to make Tasha crack a smile, playing up the goofy stance with obnoxious overconfidence. "What. Don't like what you see?"

In those days, my confidence and ego were even bigger than the skyscrapers of the city. I was safe in my little world, all things considered. As expected, she laughed. "You cocky bastard."

She walked out to the gate, scooped up Carlton, and brought him inside. I watched as one of the "Beware of Dog" signs fell on one side, dangling from a corner and threatening to fall to the concrete, before pulling my keys out of my slacks and making my way up the sidewalk. I hopped up the little step to my door. A moment of jingling keys, and then I was greeted with a blast of precious air conditioning as the door swung open and I was met with the large, spacious ground floor studio.

Back in my apartment, I threw on athletic shorts, a gray undershirt, and some running shoes. The stress of the day was already melting away as I anticipated the burn in my muscles from lifting the free weights. The thought of going to the gym filled me with a joy that mirrored a kid on Christmas, and gave me back energy that had been sapped away during the work week. It was a Friday, too, which meant that classes would be happening and more people would be there than usual.

I work out, mainly because it's a hobby that helps me to both focus and burn off the anxiety that sticks way too heavily to my rib cage. I don't want to veer too deeply into self-deprecation, and keeping fit helps me curb that into something positive. The way I bulk doesn't help how big I am, sitting at a healthy 6'4" on a standard day. But, my smile keeps me approachable. Dimples make me cute, and I can slouch to be less intimidating. That was one thing that I missed about pre-COVID the most -- I couldn't disarm someone with a smile, and more people acted scared of me.

I didn't need the gym to work out, and I did body weight exercises at home when they were closed down, but nothing quite hit the same as a hard workout. There was a type of euphoria that set in once it was done, and I felt both better about myself and the life that I was living after a good bout of exercise. It also helped that there were people around. I poured more coffee into my travel mug, and away I went, armed with a gym bag filled with all of the things that I might need. The gym was about a mile from my apartment in the opposite direction of my job. If the traffic behaved, I could jog there in about fifteen minutes. The traffic gods were thankfully on my side today, and I won the crosswalk war.

It wasn't long before I was inside of the tackily-painted yellow interior and making my way through the lounge, towards the workout equipment. The gym was a lively place even with the restrictions still in place, and people stood a respectable distance apart, most of the patrons with earbuds in their ears. I was surrounded by people doing their own thing, but working on themselves and aiming to be the best thing that they could be. One girl had a timer going on the treadmills, and she was running at top speed as the timer blazed "35 minutes" in cyan blue.

I had to pass the machines to get to the free weights. There were a few people, one man doing lunges with a 25lb plate and one on the barbell with a spotter watching intently. Working out with other people around felt far less lonely than trying at home. I was elated to see a spot in between the lunger and the barbells. At a respectable distance, of course, marked in a neat, even square of yellow tape.

Walking over, I nodded to the lunger, who nodded back, lowering the weight to the floor and letting out a huge sigh through an anime mask. Soon, I'd be in the same state of hyper focus, counting my repetitions and feeling the burn in my muscles as sweat dripped from my neck and back. There's this weird sense of friendly camaraderie with other gym-goers, like having company, without having company.

The familiar whistle of one of the fitness coaches sounded, signaling the start of a calisthenics class. I tipped my head towards the classroom, setting up with a few 20lb weights. The buzz in the gym inspired me, and made me feel better about my day. If you ignored the masks that rested on people's faces, the energy levels in the gym were at an all time high. Since it had been a few months since I had worked with free weights, I figured that it would be better to go easy on myself.

Lemon Balm

After my final set, I sat for a moment with my gym towel draped across the back of my neck, heart pounding. I was giddy; panting through my mask as the endorphins flooded me. Racking my weights, I debated on what to do next. I was too tired to move on to another type of exercise, and it was nearing seven o'clock. It wouldn't be a good idea to only do endurance training for arms, though. A well-rounded workout was the only workout to have. Chugging half of my coffee, I decided to hit the machines.

The calisthenics class was wrapping up, and by the time I did my last set on the leg press, the gym was starting to clear out. It made sense to me; it'd been a hot day, and a lot of people would rather be getting ready to go clubbing rather than working out on a Friday evening. Because I walked here, I missed a bit of the optimal people-watching window, but I didn't mind. I'd still had a great workout and experienced a bit of that shared camaraderie.

Pulling a fresh towel from my bag, I made a beeline for the showers. I'm aware it didn't make sense, when I'd be running home again anyway, but why should I have to wear three layers of sweat along the way? Looking back on it now, it kind of surprises me how comfortable I used to be, being in a semi-public area and dealing with nudity. I'd never shower at a gym, now. After the shower cooled me off, I made my way to the lounge at the front of the gym, where the built-in smoothie bar was calling my name. It wasn't guaranteed to be open due to the food restrictions, but it looked like there may have been someone in the back room when I walked past earlier. I was surprised to see it open, but not surprised to see sealed cups and wrapped straws on the counter.

The girl behind the counter, Joanna, was one that I knew fairly well from before the gym had closed. She was a stunning woman; bright hazel eyes in a hooded almond shape that left me captivated in her kind warmth. Her straight blonde hair was cropped short in an angled bob, and I don't think I'd ever seen her with it longer than her chin. She was fit, and though she was shorter than me by at least eight inches, her confidence made her seem ten feet tall. She'd worked there for at least two years, though I had never seen her outside of the establishment. I didn't expect to see anyone I actually knew tonight. "Hey, girl, what's up?"

"Oh! Hey, Cypress! I almost didn't recognize you with the clouds." She pointed up towards her face, indicating the mask.

I laughed, winking at her. "You could say my head's in the clouds. How you doing?"

"I'm good," she replied, her blush visible over the line of her black mask. "You know, glad to be back here. My other job is kicking my ass." She looked up towards the menu and abruptly changed the subject. "You got an order for me, hotshot?"

I leaned against the counter, my shaggy brown curls falling into my face. I needed a haircut. "Your number, preferably," I replied, "I'd like to catch up sometime when I'm not smelling like sweat and gym chalk."

She sputtered, and I laughed, shaking my head. "I'm joking, Joanna. A green smoothie with peanut butter, please." I wasn't the type to flirt with waitresses and baristas while they were on the job.

She laughed, though it was a bit breathless. "Gotcha, coming right up."

After a few minutes of pulsing blenders, clinking of ice crushing together, and the sloshing of juice, I had a delicious smoothie sitting in front of me on the black and gray speckled counter. I swung my gym bag around my shoulder, grabbing for the zip. "How much do I owe you?"

"Forget it," Joanna replied as she handed me the thin thermal paper receipt, "It's on the house."

"Oh no," I frowned, rubbing awkwardly at the back of my neck. "You sure? I feel bad taking it for free."

"Nah, I got it!" Her voice was cheery. "I haven't taken my free one yet today, and I probably won't. You get kinda sick of smoothies after a while."

I laughed, noticing writing on the receipt as I grabbed the smoothie from the counter. "Alright, well, if you're sure. Thanks, Joanna!"

When I flipped it over, her neat cursive was scrawled across the thermal paper. I felt a little guilty, she must have written it when I wasn't watching. Her neat print said under the numbers, *Let's catch up away from the gym chalk, yeah?* The attention flattered me, but I wasn't exactly interested in a relationship, despite my teasing. Imagine trying to start dating during Covid. All the same, I thanked her for the smoothie and pocketed the number. I wasn't going to outright shoot her down, you know? It was nice to know she was interested, and maybe I'd take her up on it when I was a little more comfortable.

She said a quick goodbye as I turned and made my way out of the gym, pulling the straw up between the mask and my face to sip at the smoothie. I added Joanna's number to my phone one handed, then pocketed the machine to rip up the receipt and threw it away. Don't need some creep getting a nice girl's number. A cool wind blew through the street, and I tilted my head up into the feeling. Looking up to the sky, there was an endless expanse of dirty gray-brown above me, just beyond the freshly illuminated streetlights.

The stars were non-existent in the city that never sleeps, and it was one of the things I missed the most about living in the Catskills. I closed my eyes, picturing the thousands of glittering silver stars studding the navy, purple, and black sky. The endless din of car horns and sirens couldn't touch the night, there. It wasn't worth it to think about the country; I needed to start my jog. The streetlights were harsh, though the park usually offered some reprieve from them. I start walking, deciding to take the long way back to my apartment. As I jogged to the street corner with my smoothie still in hand, my phone began to ring. *Who let the dogs out?*

That ringtone was only set to one person on my phone — Tasha. I grabbed it from my pocket and flipped the call on, not breaking stride. "Hey, hun, what's up?"

"Cypress, sweetheart," her thick Long Island accent came through the receiver. "Work's yanking me by the leash, the ER department is overwhelmed and I was called in. I gotta be there in about half an hour and I don't have time to stop home, can you watch the dog?"

"As if you have to ask. I've got Carlton. Go take care of business."

Tasha laughed. "I knew I could count on you. Listen, I left already and Carlton's outside. It's cooling off and he was having fun, but I don't want him out too much longer. You still got my key, right?"

"Yeah, it's on my ring. Don't worry, I'll bring him inside. Does he need food or anything?"

Tasha hummed a negative. "I fed him an hour ago. He might need breakfast in the morning."

That was good. That gave me time to relax at the park, so long as Tasha was alright with it. I'd never owned pets myself, but I'd watched Carlton enough to know he would be alright for an hour. "I'm stopping by Saratoga before I come home so he'll be out for about half an hour, is that okay with you?"

I didn't want to leave the Dachshund in the yard longer than Tasha wanted him out there. I was already halfway to the park, and getting home would take about twenty minutes. Tasha sucked in a sharp inhale, and my stomach panged. I distracted myself by sucking at my smoothie. "Y'know, sure. He can stay out. But you better get your ass there by like, eleven," she said sharply. "You know he's a digger and I don't want him loose."

"Yes ma'am. I'll have him in by ten, even."

She laughed again, and we said a quick goodbye before hanging up. By then, I was on Halsey Street. I made it to Saratoga Park in record time, and found a spot to spread out comfortably under a tree. I resumed people watching as the air began to slowly cool.

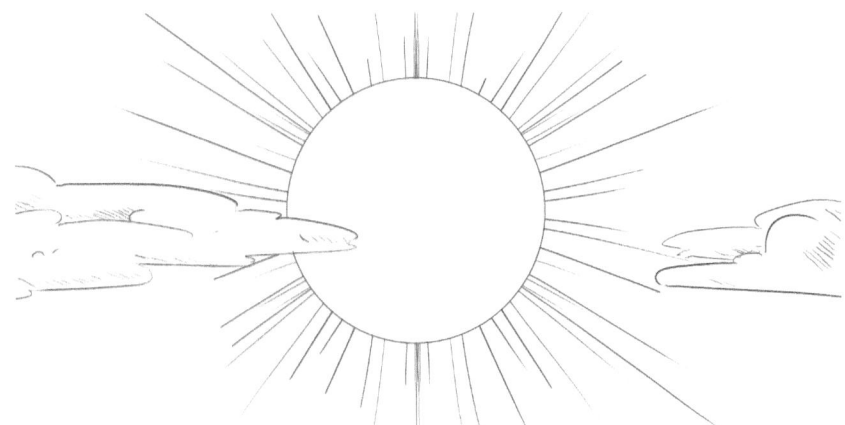

That Time I Was Bitten By A Dog

The sun was fully set by the time I had settled. I shot Joanna a quick text — *hey, just so you have it, this is Cypress :)* — before throwing my phone into the gym bag and flopping under a tree. The dark wasn't as oppressive tonight as it could be. It was mellow; a lazy lull setting into the park as a nice breeze blew through the trees. The evening was moving quickly and it was coming up to 8pm, and people on the sidewalks were riding bikes and walking their dogs. There was even a kid who couldn't be more than sixteen skateboarding. He pulled off a kick flip, cheered, and pumped his fist. I laughed as he skated out of the park. As I was sitting there, one of my acquaintances from work spotted me, and we chatted for a few minutes before I took my leave. The rest was rejuvenating, and I was ready for the eight blocks home.

Most of the park had gone quiet. It didn't take long for the dark underbelly of the city to slide into view once the sun had set. *Oh, fuck, Carlton's out!*

I rushed to stand, hoping that Tasha was right and that the Dachshund hadn't dug out of the fence. Outside was his favorite place to be, and even though anxiety gnawed at my gut, I knew the dog was well-taken care of and Tasha definitely left him with water. I found myself going at a leisurely pace through my little corner of the city, despite my anxiety.

Unlike Manhattan, where all of the offices, suits, and rich people were congregated, this part of the city was bustling with the residential life it held. It seemed impossible, but everyone treated each other like a neighbor, and I'd never had a bad experience here. Everyone says that the city is dangerous, but as long as you keep your nose out of trouble and don't act like a tourist, most people will leave you alone.

New York is full of people who have had hard lives, and will take no shit. But, in my experience, very few are cruel. They'll call you a moron if you mess something up, all while getting ready to help you out. This particular part of the neighborhood had smaller buildings than a lot of the city, as well, but it still had that feel that only New York could give. We were a stone's throw away from a city bus that could take us to La Guardia if we needed to fly, and I could walk literally anywhere I needed to.

My apartment was rent controlled, so I wasn't hit with astronomical raises in pricing, and all in all, it was a good place to be. The only downside was that I had to leave my car at my mother's house in the Catskills — but that'd be the same anywhere in the city. It was expensive to park here, and the traffic made a car basically worthless unless you were outside of the city entirely, north of Tarrytown. I was thinking about selling it, but I was attached to the thing. It had gotten me through most of college.

It was an easy trek back home, and I whistled as I walked, my steps light and my spirit lighter. The people milling about were chatting and laughing around me. We were still avoiding each other in our own respectable bubbles, but the energy had shifted. The walk took less time than I expected, and soon I was rounding the corner on my empty street, a smile playing on my face beneath the brightly colored sky print. I walked comfortably beside the squat brick buildings. However, I paused in front of the chain link fence by Tasha's gate when I heard Carlton growling ferociously. I peeked over the fence to see him backed into the corner, his teeth bared.

Instantly alert, my skin prickled in the night air and my stomach dropped like a lead weight. Carlton never growled. A part of me worried that I messed up by leaving him unattended, and a cold guilt gnawed on the inside of my ribs. "Hey little guy! What's the big deal?"

The loud warning bark he responded with made me flinch. This was incredibly out of character for the dopey little Dachshund. It's not like he didn't know me; he had never even so much as grumped my way before. I watched him for a moment as he let loose, bark after bark in my direction, teeth bared and caramel brown eyes wide enough to see the whites. It was unnerving; Carlton, typically a happy little brown thing with small areas of beige in his ears, was usually always panting and frolicking on his short little legs throughout the tiny yard, his long brown tail whipping wildly as he played. Now he was wild and it almost looked like he was staring past me rather than at me. I was way out of my depth, here. I looked around the yard, and then behind me towards the street, seeing nothing. Carlton's hackles were raised as he growled, barked, and snapped. "Ooookay?"

My gut told me that I should leave the poor dog alone. Maybe something had bitten him. Either way, he was beside himself, and I was worried for him. I was tempted to pick him up and bring him inside of my apartment with me, but I didn't want to chance a bite. In my mind, a cartoon-ish flood of dollar bills rushed out of an open city window into the air at the thought of the doctor bills that would spawn. But, this was a lot of noise for the city, and Tasha was careful to keep the neighbors off of her ass for noise ordinances. My veins were buzzing with adrenaline as I tried to decide what to do, agitated with being stuck between multiple useless options.

I needed to make a decision rather than just standing here. Maybe it'd be better to change and spend some time with him at her place. I kept walking past the fence, my gait a bit quicker and back tense as I adjusted my duffel and put my hand on the door knob to my apartment. "Relax, buddy, I'll come grab you in a second," I said aloud. The Dachshund's bark grew more frantic, the dog whimpering as I fumbled with my keys.

I heard a growl that was very near, and very, very, deep. That's definitely not a Dachshund. My heart dropped into the pit of my stomach, dread chilling me to the bone despite the lingering heat of the summer night. Suddenly, Carlton's growling made so much more sense; he must have picked up on the danger I missed in my comfortable, mundane familiarity. My skin crawled and for a moment, I debated whether or not I should just open my apartment door and slip inside without looking to see what was stalking me. But knowing something dangerous and threatening was out there, I couldn't leave Carlton to face its wrath. The dog didn't do anything wrong, and I'd rather get attacked than let him get hurt. Maybe it was a misplaced sense of confidence that made me turn around. Maybe it was my size and general fearlessness. Maybe I was just angry that something upset a dog I was close to. Dear Readers, I'm an idiot, and chose the wrong option.

I smelled it before anything else — the heavy, nauseating scent of a wet and dirty dog filled my nostrils, and I gagged. The guttural growl had been replaced with harsh, intense huffs, and I wondered if an animal maybe escaped the zoo or something. Slowly, with the uneasy burning of eyes boring into my back, I turned around, only to meet the gaze of the biggest, ugliest dog I've ever seen. And I mean this thing was massive, and standing far too close to me for my liking. It was like a mastiff, but its features didn't match. If anything, it looked more like a husky.

If I turned back around and tried to rush into my apartment, I'd risk it following me in. The eyes were sunken into their sockets, the right one green and left milky white and icy blue with blindness. A scar raked through the blinded eye. The beast was covered in other scars, bald patches, and dried blood. It had white and gray tipped fur, but you could hardly tell between the missing chunks and the dirt and grime. It totally had rabies, or mange, or something. My breath caught as I paused, trying to think of what to do. I spoke in a placating voice, though even now I couldn't tell you whether or not I was trying to calm myself or the dog.

"Whoa... Hey now. Easy boy."

The dog snarled and snapped its jaws. I could see its teeth from where I stood, even though the dog was a few feet away, its maw glistening. Time seemed to slow, and my heart hammered against my sternum. I'm a big guy, and pretty strong; I didn't get scared by much. I think that's why this near panic clung to me so completely. I still have nightmares about this moment. My actions, as deliberate and quick as they were, slowed to a crawl of step-by step moments. Each one felt as if it took forever.

I had to make a move. I reached behind me, twisting the handle to my apartment. Suddenly the dog was on me. It clamped down on my leg as I turned to run inside. I wasn't fast enough. I'd never seen anything move so damn fast. I screamed, pain spiking through my calf as the dog pulled, and it yanked me from the door, dragging me down the sidewalk. "Help! Rabid fucking dog, somebody help me!"

My leg sang with pain, stabbing through me with each jerk and movement. There was no time to react. At one moment, I was scrambling with my door, and in another, I was dragged halfway down my block. Carlton's frantic barking and whimpering followed us. I started kicking the dog in the face, screaming, switching between telling it to fuck off and calling out for someone to come help me. Any noise. Those nature documentaries always told you to shout at bears, right? Or maybe my kicking would make it drop my leg, like punching a shark in the nose. Maybe these things would work with a dog, too.

Nothing I did would make it stop. It wouldn't let go. My gym bag was still slung across my chest, and the weight of it around me gave me a weirdly detached comfort at the back of my mind, like a life jacket. It's funny, the details that wind up sticking in when you're panicked. "Help, please! Fucking anyone! Help!"

I kicked the dog harder, starting to twist and wriggle to free myself from its teeth. The muscle on my leg tore, and nausea flooded through me as I lurched. All of the warmth of my body flooded to my calf as it shook me. I kicked at its nose again and started yelling louder, agony searing through me. "I'm gonna die!"

The more I yelled, struggled, and kicked, the harder and more aggressively the dog shook me. I kicked it countless times before it finally dropped my leg. Slowly, menacingly, it stalked towards my face, hovering over me as spittle and blood dripped from its maw.

My scream echoed off of the buildings as it ripped from my raw throat. Adrenaline pulsed through me, and I shook as I panted in short, quick bursts. Balling up my fist, I tried to figure out the best angle to punch at its throat or muzzle. Somewhere weaker than its nose. I still don't know if it was out of quick thinking or out of instinct as I swung the gym bag. I tried to crawl backwards. There was enough room between us that I could punch it in the throat if I could aim the hit. Something about its eyes made me pause before I threw my punch; the one that wasn't mangled had an intelligence to it that felt human. No way... this isn't happening.

This dog seemed to nod in acknowledgment. Before I could fully react to what was happening, it jumped away from me and lumbered off. Adrenaline pulsed through me as I tried to process what had just happened. The whole altercation couldn't have been more than five minutes. Why would such a vicious dog attack me, only to run away a moment later? My entire leg from the tip of my toes to the joint of my hip pulsed, hot and aching, and my arms shook as I fought to unhook my fingers from the gym bag. I couldn't breathe. My lungs were raw like they had been scrubbed with sandpaper.

I stared down the road, frozen and terrified. If I tore my eyes away, I was certain that it'd come back. Tears streamed down my cheeks, and I heard a sputtering sobbing noise that I dimly registered as my own voice. I was oddly connected, but also was watching this scene play out from ten feet above my body, and three feet to the left.

Hot wetness touched my uninjured leg, and I realized with a start that I needed to stop my own bleeding. I looked down at my mutilated calf and groaned, my stomach lurching again as the smoothie from earlier threatened to replay at the back of my throat. Every movement made my entire lower body pulse with pain, and the way the chunk hung from the bitten part on my calf made the world far away and shrouded in blackness as I fought the urge to faint. I was fine with fake gore like on movies and TV, but nothing prepares you for seeing a piece of your own body dangling like that.

Where was everyone? I needed help, and I needed it now. I had cried out so many times. So much for that neighborly feeling. My chest heaved in short, breathless bursts, and I looked around the street, disoriented. I had to call the hospital, or the cops, animal control... anyone. I tried to get my brain to connect with my body, to remember where my cell phone was. Pulling the towel from my gym bag, I wrapped it around my leg, swaying with the effort to stay present.

I fumbled to keep it there, my hands not fully cooperating with my body as I reached for my pocket, only to find it empty. "Goddammit," I muttered, my voice hoarse and raw from screaming, and rough with pain. "Of all the times to keep that in my bag..."

As the stress began to take over the adrenaline, there was a small part of my mind that was already thinking of the medical bills, and the fear of being in a hospital at the height of a pandemic. I tried not to think too hard of rabies as I worked on finding my phone. I pivoted, reaching behind me for the side pocket zipper without losing pressure on my leg.

Then I saw my hands... Covered in stark white fur, my nails sharpening into long fearsome claws. That was about when I started screaming again, and the world went black.

This, Readers, is where mundanity well and truly died for me. (Turns out, Lycanthropy is just as contractible as rabies.) The next thing I remember was waking up at the lower end of Central Park, my back tickled by the grass and skin covered with dew in the early morning. I frowned, confused. *When did I wind up in the grass? The last thing I remembered was trying to find my phone. And then...* And then what? I had started to hallucinate; my hands weren't my hands anymore. And then, I had no recollection of the night after that. I did remember, however, that I had been bitten by a very big, very ugly dog, and that my leg had been mangled. My chest tightened, my breath coming in short, quick bursts as fear spiked through me and my skin went cold and numb. Why couldn't I remember anything? Where exactly was I, and how did I get there?

There was also the fact that the grass directly tickled against my skin, and the more that I came into consciousness, the less that made sense. I sat up quickly, and my leg screamed in protest, the skin taut and tender. It dawned on me that I was naked, with a badly injured leg. Luckily, I was in a fairly secluded portion of the park, in between a bush and a tree. I groaned softly in dismay. "No... What the fuck..."

I whipped my head back and forth, asking myself again, *how the hell did I get here?* Central Park was in Manhattan. I lived less than eight blocks from Saratoga Park. I was eight miles from where I had started. Moving to stand, I was hyper aware of my injured leg, and tried to be careful as I shifted my weight. Something tugged at my chest and forced me back to the dirt. I looked down and found the woven nylon of my gym bag still somehow stretched across my chest. My clothes were completely gone, but my bag was snugly slung over my shoulder. A tuft of white fur clung to where the strap clipped to the bag. Nothing made sense. Now that I knew my bag was still around me, I knew that my phone and wallet were likely safe. *Well, thank fuck for that...*

I remembered the teeth that had sliced through skin and muscle in my leg. With the amount of blood I lost, I should not have been able to be awake right now without medical help, let alone worry about anything other than my wound. The towel had mysteriously disappeared, just like the intense pain I imagined I should be feeling. My gaze shot down to my injured leg, and I twisted it to try and see the damage.

No issues moving. That was really odd with the severity of the bite, but my shoulders sagged in relief. Then, I processed what I was looking at, and my jaw fell open. The bite was there, yeah, but it looked like it was weeks old. Irritated and dirty, my leg was swollen as if I'd sprained it at the gym, but it seemed like just a surface bite. There wasn't anything to indicate that it was infected. The chunk that had been hanging off less than twenty four hours ago was neatly woven back into place. There's no way this was the same dog bite that I had suffered the night before. I lifted my leg, carefully extending my foot. Pain shot up my calf and into my knee, but the muscle contracted fine. There's no way that dog hadn't taken an entire chunk of skin. "How long have I been out here?"

Dread once again filled my stomach like a lead weight. Shifting the gym bag off of my shoulders, I dove into it and grabbed my spare clothes. I swung my head, eyes darting around to double-check that the coast was clear before I pulled the tank top over my head, satisfied with the emptiness of the park. The basketball shorts followed just as quickly, and I desperately wished for more cover than the single tree I was using for support. I was glad that no one was there to watch me bouncing on my uninjured leg while fighting with a pair of shorts. Besides, it was Central Park; there was no way that I had been out there for longer than a few hours. If I had, I'd have been in a body bag or a hospital. The thing about living in a big city, is that there's not a lot of opportunities to lay around injured and unnoticed.

After I was uncomfortably dressed, I pulled my phone from my bag and stared at it in confusion. August 31st, 4:49 AM, the screen blinded me in its unfeeling blue light. It hadn't even been six hours. How in the hell had I made it eight miles away from home on foot with no memory of it, in less than six hours? My skin prickled once again as if someone had thrown ice water on me, despite the temperate morning. I tested more weight on my injured leg, and found that I could stand without help from the tree. Phone still securely in hand, I stared at it for a moment, debating on who to call before dialing a number and lifting the device to my ear.

That first blackout was just one of many. The number I called was the Non-Emergency line for the police. The fact that I was in Central Park and couldn't remember the night scared me, and my way of dealing with fear was to ignore it. So, I did what I could control, and I reported a dog acting strangely near the Saratoga Park area, and hung up before they could take my information. I was embarrassed and anxious; something stopped me from going to the hospital. Maybe it was that I couldn't explain the way I had healed so quickly from such an extreme bite. Maybe it was that I just wanted to go home. I realized with a jolt that Carlton was still outside. *Please, whatever gods, luck, or spirits that be, let Carlton be safe…*

Lemon Balm

Tasha would probably be home before I was. At best, I was going to get an earful for leaving him out all night. At worst, I was going to come home to a devastated neighbor and a lump of meat where a loving, dopey dog once lived.

I wish I could describe the ride home. If I'm being honest, the whole thing was a blur. From the time I stepped out of Central Park into a taxi, to the time that I stepped out in front of my apartment. I think I was in my head for most of the ride, my fingers absent-mindedly picking at the fur stuck in the nylon strap of my bag as my stomach twisted itself into knots. Or, should I say, what was left of the bag. It looked like it had been dragged through the underbrush of the park; covered in grass stains and mud, with twigs sticking out of various places. The strap had little polyester threads sticking out of a slash that had nearly ripped it in two. The ride was short, and I wasn't even fully out of the taxi before Tasha's voice cut through the air. "Alright, Cypress, what the fuck?"

I whipped my head towards her and held up my hands. "Wait, Tasha, let me explain —"

She stomped up in all of her 5'2" glory, her dark green eyes flashing over her burgundy mask. It was kind of comical in hindsight how someone that only came up to my chest could be so intimidating. At the time, I was terrified of her anger. "You're damn right you're gonna explain, you big fuckin' oaf! You left my dog outside all night," she yelled, going up on tip-toes as the taxi sped away. "What, a morning joyride is more important than my dog?"

"No, that's not it," I hung my head, averting my gaze as I clutched at my elbows. "You know I'd never leave Carlton out if I could help it. Listen, please, calm down and let's go inside? Something's wrong with me."

She glared at me, crossing her arms. The silence went a beat too long for my liking, and I held my hand out towards the apartments. "Look, Tasha, I'm serious. My door's open and the keys are in the lock. I'd never leave my place like that, right?"

Her eyes went blank and she turned to glance at the door to see that I was telling the truth. The blood that spilled from my leg the night before still stained the concrete, dark and foreboding, further down the block. Small lines and drips of it led from my stoop towards the sidewalk. I could see it over her shoulder, and I shuddered, flashes of the night before playing in my mind. As she turned back to me, her eyes softened, and she sighed. "Alright, fine. Come inside, let me give you a once over."

"Yeah, sure," I nodded, keeping my voice soft. "Just let me grab my keys, and make sure I wasn't robbed in the last seven hours."

She shook her head, fiddling with her amethyst point in unease. "Carlton's fine. I'll just follow you to yours."

18

I fought the urge to roll my eyes at the sight of the crystal. I nodded, leading the way to my door. Pushing it open, my shoulders sagged in relief as I was greeted with my perfectly normal-looking studio apartment. I took a moment to soak in the details of the plain white walls and chrome appliances, my eyes slowly scanning the space as I stepped into the large room. The black granite counters of the kitchen were neat and spare of any clutter, just as I left them. The plain gray linoleum floors were the same. I was half-expecting to see the place ransacked, but not even a single blanket was out of place, my collection neatly stacked in a wicker basket by the black and chrome futon. Everything felt so strangely normal; undisturbed despite the door being open all night.

I grabbed my keys from the lock, thanking my lucky stars that I hadn't gotten robbed on top of everything else. "Start explaining," Tasha's voice cut my relief short. "Carlton was fine when I got home, but I was pissed when I saw him outside. I hadn't noticed your door was open. What happened?"

My mouth was dry. I licked my lips, anxiously distracting myself by going to the fridge and grabbing a water bottle. I uncapped it, slamming half of it back before I leaned against the fridge and stared at the tiled floor. "I was attacked by something," I said hesitantly. "A dog, I think. A big dog. I got home and Carlton was growling and barking his head off, and I paused by my door because I heard a growl behind me…" I scrunched my face, closing my eyes and trying to focus. "It grabbed me and dragged me down the street, and then… I don't remember."

"You don't remember? You got dragged down the street by a dog? Cypress, I haven't seen another dog larger than mine in this neighborhood outside of the park in years."

I opened my eyes and stared at her, frowning. "Yeah well, I don't know what to tell you. I lost time, and I swear, Tasha, my calf was mangled, but now it looks like I barely have a scratch. I don't know how a dog bite could just disappear," I took another few hearty gulps from the water bottle.

She crossed her arms again and huffed. "I'll check you over. I can tell something happened, but I don't believe for a second that you had a dog bite just up and disappear."

I stared at her. It made sense that she was rejecting my story; I *lived* it and I couldn't explain it. Wordlessly, I slid into one of the black breakfast bar stools and stuck my leg out for her to see. "Carlton is fine, you said? The other dog ran away, but I didn't get a chance to check on him before I blacked out."

She had bent down to look down at my leg, but her gaze shot up to mine. "He's fine," she said, her eyes sliding back to my wound, inspecting it. "Not a scratch on him."

19

Lemon Balm

The divots in my skin were deep and scabbed in thick, uneven layers. Not enough time had passed for it to heal like that, but a bite was definitely there. Tasha looked at the bite closer and shook her head. I could tell that she was still skeptical of my story. "This looks weeks old. You said it happened last night?"

"Dead-ass. I'm not lying to you."

She straightened up, reaching to place her wrist on my forehead. "Christ, you're burning up. Did you go to the hospital, Cypress? You could have gotten rabies, distemper... A whole host of diseases."

Anxiety spiked through my chest. I had thought of diseases, but that was once again scary and I once again opted to ignore that fear. Was I warm? I didn't feel feverish. At least I knew I didn't have rabies. I was chugging water, after all. "I didn't," I said, tacking on a white lie for good measure. "I was worried about Carlton, and my apartment. I didn't want to take more time away."

Tasha sighed. "Listen, sweetheart, I dunno what happened to you, but forget about it, okay? I'm not mad. Just... Do me a favor and get to a doctor, alright? I don't like this loss of memory shit, any more than I like the look of that bite or the weird story surrounding it." She held her finger in front of my eyes and I watched her fingertip as she slowly moved it back and forth. "Did you hit your head?"

"Not that I know of," I replied, my voice small. "But, you know, it's possible."

"I don't like that. Not at all. You can track my movements..." She pulled a pen-shaped flashlight from the pocket in her scrubs and shone it into my eyes. "I don't think you have a concussion, in any case."

I looked down to the floor again, fidgeting with the cap of the bottle. "I'll get to a doctor, and see if I can't get rabies shots, just in case. This thing was massive, and was missing most of its hair... I don't know, it was the size of a lion. And it *smelled*."

I wrinkled my nose, tossing the empty bottle towards the recycling bin. It bounced off of the rim, hitting the wall before it fell back into the bin. If the circumstances were different, I might have cheered. Tasha turned, heading towards my door. "I'll check with the neighbors, see if anyone's seen anything. In the meantime, get yourself looked at, alright? I don't want to see you foaming at the mouth in a week."

"Yeah, I hear you. Thanks, Tasha," I replied to her as she walked out of the door.

She didn't look back, but one thing was crystal clear — I wouldn't be able to tell anyone about the dog bite and be believed. This was something I'd need to hide, and hope that things went back to normal.

So, I did.

That first blackout and waking up in the park was the beginning of a nightmare. I kept trying to work and maintain a life similar to that of a mundane human. I hadn't told anyone in my inner circle about the dog bite. The police never did find it. I, however, had to go through a series of intensely painful rabies shots, and this started my foray into an endless train of medical and mental health professionals failing me completely. The blackouts continued to happen well after the rabies treatments.

In the months after the dog bite, I tried to go back to normalcy. I lost many nights to blackouts and hallucinations, always waking up alone and without clothes somewhere far away from where I started. My hands and feet would be covered in mud. Despite the black outs and lapses in memory, I did my best to keep to my routine and work schedule around medical appointments; distracted, exhausted, and in a fog most of the time. The blackouts began randomly, at first. I'd realized after the fact that I lost a stretch of time, and it terrified me. I started writing down what I was doing when they happened to track what caused them.

I began to lock myself into my apartment, withdrawing from anyone who asked to spend time with me. It was getting harder and harder for me to function in a normal life, even as the effects from the lockdowns started to wind down. As things began to open up, I tried to find more doctors and specialists to help me. A part of me kept trying to rationalize what I had seen the night of the bite, and trying to tell myself that the shock of it all had maybe made me hallucinate. There was no real reason for me to be losing time, but I had started thinking maybe I was suffering from seizures. Maybe it wasn't seizures, but blackouts caused from a mental illness of some kind. They found nothing worth noting, no matter how many doctors I tried.

As time went on, desperation tugged at me at every turn. As my friends became more comfortable going out, I began to make excuses to avoid being in public. I was terrified that I was hurting people or myself in these blackouts. I had sparks of memories that made no sense to me and that I couldn't explain; a flash of a white paw here, a glimpse of the woods there. I spent countless hours talking to various medical professionals, to no avail.

I was never one to talk to my friends about my problems in the first place; I didn't want to burden them with what I was feeling. If the blackouts weren't seizures, and if they had no medical reason to happen, then that meant that there was something fundamentally wrong with my brain. Maybe the dog bite was causing stress issues, or maybe a therapist would have answers that medical doctors didn't.

Lemon Balm

Sometime around March of 2021, one of my best friends, Kassidy, reached out via text while I was on lunch at work. *Cy, we miss you!* ♥ *come to the secret pour tonite?*

I found myself staring at the text for a long time. I don't remember how Kassidy and her twin came to be a part of my friend group. They lived in the Bronx, so even pre-COVID restrictions, I didn't see them as often as I'd like. I met Kassidy first, and she was hilarious. She started bringing around her twin Kennedy a short while later. Kennedy was a fireball, and punched Junior in the nuts the first time he hit on her.

I was close with Kassidy; we flirted with each other incessantly, and had tried to date on and off throughout our college years. It'd never go anywhere, but she found me charming. If anyone could convince me to break my isolation, it was her. I chewed on my lip. *I dunno, K. You know I haven't been feeling so hot.*

Come on, Cypress. I'm starting to feel like ur avoiding me.

She was good at guilting me into doing what she wanted. The guys of my friend group weren't very different. Looking back, my entire support group was pretty superficial. Maybe I was, too. I'm not sure. It's easy to fall into bad behaviors when that's all that you see around you. You could say that I was hanging out with six idiots, but the people looking in were seeing seven. Even if I knew what she was doing, the guilt still gnawed at my ribs. "Fuck," I muttered. *Not avoiding you, just been stressed. What time?*

It took a minute for her to respond, and I watched the little ellipses animation as she typed. When it popped up, my guts twisted again. *Junior, vic, n frankie were saying around 6. does that work 4 u? sorry works busy*

Could I really handle everyone in a loud place? Knowing Junior was coming especially stressed me out. We had the type of friendship that depended on taking pot shots at each other, and I'd been avoiding him since I came out as non-binary. I didn't have any evidence that I hurt anyone in my blackouts, but I had started to correlate them to high stress, and I wasn't sure if it was the smartest idea. "Ah, what the hell... I deserve to have fun. Maybe it'll help."

I decided to chance a night out with my friends, and I sealed the deal with a single text. *Then I'll see you at six.*

It was supposed to be a good time. Drinks were flowing, and they were already kind of tipsy by the time I got there. Kennedy and Kassidy were flirting with the bartenders and twirling their long blonde hair. Junior, the only friend I kept from senior year of high school, was speaking with some redhead that was hanging on his arm. He stopped mid-sentence and looked over at me, scanning me from head to toe. "Damn Cy, I see why you've been avoiding us. You look like shit, man."

I cringed at the 'man'. I didn't mind male-gendered terms, but Junior used it as a weapon. Anything between us that was seen as a weakness was fair game to our banter. (And yes, dear Readers, I'm aware how toxic this sounds. That's because it was toxic between us; I don't claim to be proud of this.) I shot a huge grin back at him over my beer, hiding my wince. "Yeah, Junior. You look the same as before quarantine. I guess you didn't take the time to work on yourself."

Frankie, (his real name is Franklin, but don't call him that, it's a good way to get punched) laughed and joined in. "Yeah, I see where you're coming from Cy, that's a face only a mother could love."

Junior laughed again. "At least my mother hugged me as a child."

The air in the bar suddenly got tense, and I glared at Junior, my jaw aching from how quickly I clenched my teeth. "That's a fucking low blow, Junior," I replied, deadpan, and Kassidy wrapped her arms around my chest.

"Aww Cy, why are you so sour today?" She whined. "Bad day at work?"

I shook her off and stepped back. "I told you, hun. I've been stressed lately."

Victor clapped me on the shoulder. "Well, that's why we're here. Take a load off, Cy. Settle in. We'll be here for a while."

And that's what I did. Or, tried to do, anyway. Usually Junior's comments about my mom wouldn't get to me so badly, but I found myself on a hair trigger, unable to laugh off the disrespect. And he kept it up all damn night. Eventually I had enough and snapped. Junior was well into his fourth beer, and my jaw had been aching from biting my tongue. I watched him as he threw an arm around Kassidy, laughing outlandishly at something Vic said. His hand wandered, and Kassidy pushed him, standing up to move seats. "Oh come on, baby, you know you like the attention," he laughed, and Kassidy started to tear up.

"You're a real fucking jerk, Junior!" Kassidy yelled before she stomped away.

I barely had time to see Kennedy slide out of her chair to follow her sister before I grabbed Junior by the collar and dragged him outside. "Hey Vic," I called over my shoulder. "I'm calling the twins a cab, let 'em know for me."

I didn't look back as Junior cussed and struggled against my hold. "Cypress, dude, what the fuck?!"

Lemon Balm

I didn't answer, calling the cab company, and getting the operator on the 2nd ring. "Yeah, I got two ladies at the Secret Pour. Kassidy and Kennedy Steadman. Yep, I'll pay the tab ahead."

As I gave my card information from memory, I shoved Junior out of the door and watched him stumble onto the sidewalk. By the time I finished the phone call, Junior had recovered and stumbled towards me with a sloppy swing. I sidestepped, swinging my own punch and landing square in his gut. He stumbled, winded, before sloppily throwing a punch again. I sidestepped him and growled, low and dangerous, as he stumbled. "Don't ever fucking touch Kassidy like that again, you piece of shit."

"Fuck you," he screamed back. This time, when he swung, the hit landed on my jaw. It was about then that Vic, Frankie, and the twins came out. The next few minutes were a blur, but there was a scuffle as Vic and Frankie broke us apart.

"Why the fuck do I still call you a friend?" I shouted at him as I was dragged away. The two of us were bloodied and battered. Sometime during the scuffle, Kassidy and Kennedy slipped into the cab I had paid for. Frankie dragged Junior across the parking lot, and we were glaring at one another over their shoulders. "You're a fucking shithead," I spit at Junior.

"Real big words coming from a druggie's son!" Junior shouted, and I lunged again. Victor pulled my arms behind my back and hauled me away.

"Okay Cy, enough is enough. Go home, sober up." I let Victor pull me away, and I thought about what he said as the tension fell from my shoulders.

"You know what Vic, you're right," I replied, though I remembered thinking, I wasn't that drunk. I'd only had one beer. "I'll go and cool off. Probably best I don't talk to Junior for a while though."

My entire body was an exposed, frayed nerve, like I had lost all of my thick skin and self control. My friends stopped calling after that. A single text from Kassidy thanked me, but she didn't try again when I didn't respond.

I began to see myself as a monster. I craved, more than anything, some form of connection. The dog bite had completely turned my life upside down, and I wasn't sure what I could do to solve it. I was descending in a spiral. I actually got desperate enough to put my pride aside and seek out help for the trauma the bite had caused, or maybe awoken as a trigger. After that night, I threw everything that I hadn't tried yet at my stress and blackouts. I tried new counselors, psychiatrists, and meditation. It didn't work. I tried journaling, EMDR, sleep studies, hypnosis… Hell, I tried everything.

Then one night, I woke up in a cold sweat, but it felt like my skin was blistering at the same time. I groaned, preparing for another black out, but it never came. I got up, hoping a shower would soothe this discomfort. I caught my reflection in the little mirror on my way, and I thought I was dreaming; having a nightmare or a flash back to the incident with that dog.

My eyes, still perfectly human, peered at me behind a snout,and a face covered in white fur. My actual hair, typically curly and brunette, was matted and stuck to my skin, slick with sweat. I watched in terror as it pulled back and started to go stark white. I was stuck between man and beast, unable to deal with the horror and panic, faced with the literal monster I'd become. It's a hellish spot to be. *The fur in my gym bag... it can't be...*

The realization made the fear burrow its way straight down my spinal cord and fracture my reality. I remember destroying my small apartment in a fit of rage, as if I had no control over my body as my clawed fingers ripped my haven apart. Tearing the futon and bedding to shreds, pulling panels from the walls, tearing the carpet from the floor; I was a monster, and I was inconsolable.

I think it was that instance that made me finally get over the last shreds of my ego. As I stood in the ruined chaos of my apartment, I thought, *I can't do this. I need answers.*

Since every medical professional I saw had failed me, I decided to take things into my own hands. There was something bigger happening, and the white fur was a hint. I bought cameras that I could control from my phone, hoping to record myself going into a rage, or something like sleepwalking, or at least acting delirious. I was to a point where I was starting to look into astral projection and possession.

The cameras lasted for only one use. I set them up in various areas of my apartment and pressed record on my phone when I felt the effects of a blackout start to come on. The footage that I had caught scared me so bad, I rejected it instantly. *This makes no fucking sense.*

Rather than deal with my cracked sense of reality, I tried to rationalize everything away. Maybe I was hallucinating what I was seeing on that footage. When I brought it to my therapist, she laughed me out of the office. But, if she saw what I was seeing... no. I was so frustrated with the outcome that I deleted it and threw the cameras away. It must have been tampered with. Someone had to be fucking with me. Maybe the cameras had been hacked. I think deep down I knew it was real, but the experience reinforced that I was alone. I had nowhere to turn, no one would believe me.

After that, nothing seemed to matter anymore. My work performance suffered to the point of needing to rely on FMLA to cover my absences. I lost my job. Out of work, and out of luck, I relied heavily on my savings and odd jobs that I could do alone and away from people. I marketed myself as a handyman. I knew enough about carpentry and simple electrical to be able to follow code on repairs, thanks to my upbringing. I had a good amount saved up, nothing to brag about, but enough for, say, a year or two if I couldn't figure this out. Thank you, six figure salary.

I gave up on all of the mental and medical professionals, and told myself that I was having garish, frighteningly life-like hallucinations. They'd happen frequently, and never around people. When I felt my skin start to tingle and burn, I'd leave and wait them out in that destroyed apartment. In late August, I finally went back and asked one of the therapists if I should go on an inpatient psych hold. She gave me the number to a facility, and I actually went; no hallucinations happened, and I left after the mandatory three days.

I threw myself into body weight exercises and cleaned my home to a spotless husk of a living space, filled with dumpster dived furniture or unbreakable, soulless pieces. The futon, bent too out of shape to unfold, got replaced with a camping cot. An end table, busted beyond repair, got replaced by a sturdy cardboard box that someone's TV came in. Nearly everything else was either the same broken crap I'd destroyed in my rages or tossed into the dumpster. I was in the mindset that I didn't deserve comfort.

I was entirely antisocial, never letting myself get close enough to anyone for them to invite me out. Flirting with the smoothie barista? A thing of the past. After the psych hold, I pushed away anyone left clinging to me. Joanna had tried a few times to meet, but I kept making excuses. The first week of November — I'm not sure which day, because I'd lost track — I lay doom scrolling social media with a splitting migraine in my temples when a message notification from her popped up. *Hey you...*

I ignored it. Another message popped up, and I stared at it for a moment before clicking it to read the whole thing. *I don't think this is going to work out, Cypress. I'm tired of missing you. You seem to ignore me more often than not. I don't even see you at the gym anymore. I don't know what's up, but I think we're best as friends.*

I didn't bother to respond, instead deleting the entire text chain. *Who would want a monster like me?* I resigned myself to a life of being alone and apart from the society that I had once so easily taken for granted.

One night in early February of 2022, I found myself completely out of options and desperately craving some form of human interaction. The cell phone had become a brick in the corner, rarely charged and never ringing. Some impulse made me reach for it and I dialed the number before I thought through what I was doing. After three rings, my mother's slurring voice came onto the other line. "Cypress?"

"Hey mom," I said quietly. "I didn't wake you, did I?"

I heard laughter in the background of her silence. I nearly went to speak when her voice came through the line. "No, sweetie, I'm not at home," she replied, her words slightly distorted and jumping unevenly, as if she was struggling to focus on her words. "What's up?"

I closed my eyes, beating down my disappointment. She clearly was partaking in something. *Not my problem...* I sighed. "Look, ma, I lost my job, and... I don't know if I want to stay in the city. You still have my car, right?"

She laughed. "Of course I have your car! I'm sorry you lost your job, sweetie. Need me to pick you up and take you home for a bit?"

I glanced around my destroyed apartment. Leaving and breaking the lease would probably be the best option. I'd be sad to lose the controlled rent, but it wasn't like I could keep this charade up much longer. My mom's voice broke through the receiver again, sharper and a bit less light. "Cypress, honey?"

When I say I went to my mother, I was well and truly out of options. "Yeah, mom, I'm here," I said, before swallowing back a lump that had mysteriously formed in my throat. My face burned with shame. "Sorry. I need you to come get me. I promise I won't intrude for too long."

When she finally spoke again, she sounded much more sober. "I'll be there first thing in the morning. Text me your address, baby, I'll be on the road as soon as daylight hits."

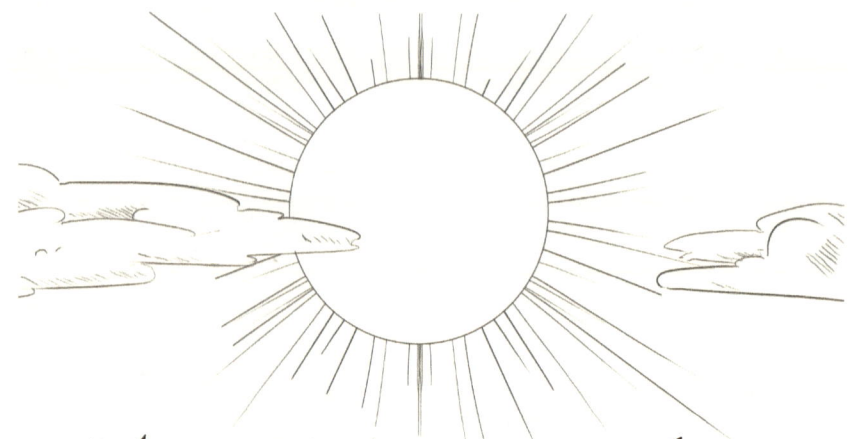

That Time I Tried To Break The Cycle

True to her word, my mother drove to get me in my 2015 Volkswagen Golf. She showed up dressed in a black party dress with ripped stockings, gigantic bug-eye sunglasses set on her narrow nose and wincing at every noise slightly above a whisper. Hungover, or strung out, I couldn't tell, but one look at her gaunt face told me that she hadn't been eating much again. I didn't talk to her about her demons anymore. She'd been sober on and off since I was a kid. My heart twisted, and I promised myself that I'd cook us a big meal when we got to her house, even if I didn't feel much like eating, myself. I filled the car; a few trash bags of clothes and the red camping cot. Slamming the back hatch shut, I glanced towards her. "Can I drive?"

"Be my guest." She threw the keys.

The house was haunted with so many memories of the past. Everything was exactly the same as I remembered; except older, dirtier, and with a decidedly sad air of defeat lingering. The smells of cigarette smoke, mold, and dust weighed the air down. The walls, once brightly colored and a source of joy, all held the ugly yellow cast of tar. I remembered picking the saturated teal for the dining room with glee at seven years old — a reward for getting A+'s all year — and the laughter that came with splattering paint everywhere. The pang in my chest lingered as I walked through the hallway to my old room. I wasn't sure if the ache was nostalgia, or just longing for a time where I didn't know my mom had problems.

She hadn't changed a thing in my room when I left. The door still hung crooked from when I tried to replace it and bent a hinge. A plain twin bed with a sapphire blue comforter sat in the corner. The walls matched it. There was a bookshelf full of poetry, art books, and how-to manuals on various carpentry projects and workout regimens on the opposite wall; the bottom shelf a chaotic, cluttered mess of old yellowed sketchbooks and notebooks. A small wooden desk sat under the window, and I watched the dust motes float in the air through the early morning sun. *The more things change, the more they stay the same*, I thought glumly as I wrenched open the window.

Originally, the plan was to stay with her for a few days while I researched new jobs in the city. I'd filled her in on everything that had happened in the last two years, from the doctors and therapists all the way to the mysterious illness and hallucinations, but I left out the things I couldn't explain. She didn't believe how bad the hallucinations could get until around the third day. The burn started in my arms and I locked the door to the basement, and barred it shut with stacks upon stacks of disintegrating cardboard boxes and yellowing plastic bins. No one could get in, and more importantly, I couldn't get out. I sat in the dark stone room, waiting for the burning to overtake me while simultaneously begging for it to end.

It was four hours later when it stopped. It looked like a tornado had ripped through the old papers, toys, and other random things hidden sloppily away in bins. Boxes lay exploded apart, and the white ghost of nails scratching across the foundation stood out starkly in the gloom. Shattered glass from picture frames mixed with scraps of torn paper and splintered pieces of wooden beams. It looked like a beast had torn through, and my arms were bleeding from the fray. I unstacked the remaining pieces by the door and emerged from the wrecked cellar, purging my stomach of the breakfast my mother had so painstakingly made.

She stared at the wreckage of her basement. Her arms trembled, and she held back tears as she slowly turned around the room. Her voice was a broken whisper as she took in the broken boxes and old furniture. "Oh, Cypress... don't be me, honey. Please, please, don't be me."

I gritted my teeth at the unspoken words. *You're on drugs.* But, being the good child that I was, I bit back the anger and tried to hear the core of what she was saying. The tears started to fall as she said, "You gotta leave that fuckin' city, baby, it's changed you."

If she only knew. I spent the next two months in the sad little time capsule of a room. Most of the time that I was in the Catskills, I wandered hiking paths and stayed out of her hair and her house. When I could, I was working odd jobs and gigs. The longer that I stayed, the more that I wanted to leave. I found myself surfing the internet more often than not, looking for places that I could afford with what was left of my savings. I only had about $30,000 left, so a lot of my scrolling happened on auction sites advertising foreclosures. It was during one of these auction site doom scrolls in the early morning that I struck gold.

An abandoned house in the middle of nowhere sat proudly at the top of the auction site, marked, new listing! in bright red font. It was in Peekskill, only a little over an hour from the city in a clump of forest; nearly 40 acres attached to the property. It had been converted from a church, so there were some really cool features like a big rose window in the front. It was far away from the noise and chaos of the city, but close enough to head there with my car if I needed to. It was perfect. The listing showed several pictures of the charming little brick building from the outside, but there weren't any of the interior. I found myself lingering on the listing, scrolling through the photos. "Huh," I wondered. "This place looks promising."

I read the blurb that was beneath the pictures, looking for any red flags. *This charming brick building was built as a church in 1847, and converted into a comfortable home in the 1910's by the Sylene family. Abandoned since the mid 1980's, this church needs substantial repairs before it can be considered livable by today's coding standards, but it has potential to be the perfect home if you're willing to put in the work! Comes with 40 acres of forested land. Contact our Realtor office today to schedule a showing. Plumbing? Yes. Heat? Forced air. Basement? No. Attic? No. Currently priced at $20,000, or best offer.*

My heart sped at the thought of owning this place. Did I dare hope? It was within my price range. The repairs didn't bother me; I'd spent more than enough time fixing up my mother's house as a teen, and my recent odd jobs as a carpenter had sharpened my skills. I had nothing but time these days. A little elbow grease never hurt anyone. Besides, it'd give me an excuse to work hard and maybe feel something other than apathy. I missed moving my body and getting that endorphin rush. I stared at my phone screen for a long while, before clicking the number to call the realty office and schedule a walk through.

I pulled up to the church just before noon on a Wednesday in the middle of a particularly stormy April. Despite how much rain we had gotten that month, the sun was strong, and it was warm and bright. The air in the forest was sweet with the smell of new growth, and my breath was clean and bright with every inhale. The building looked bigger than I had expected, and the nice day had me feeling lighter than I had in months. I got out of the car, leaning against my door and waited for the Realtor to show. As I waited, I soaked in the details of the property.

There were four stairs leading up to a small concrete porch in front of heavy, dark-stained oak doors, splintered and weathered with age. The small gravel path leading up to the stairs were laid in multiple colors, a strange motif of bats and moons in the patterning that left a whimsical feel to the front. The bricks were two different colors of beige, the lighter beige rimming the stairs, the rose window, and the door. Stained glass was also nestled in a vanity window above, mirroring the pattern of the rose window above that. Neat wooden garden boxes were crafted on either side of the steps, surprisingly well-kept despite the church being abandoned. I made a mental note to ask the Realtor if the bank was working on the lawn and maintenance.

Just as I was debating on whether or not to walk around the building, the sound of gravel crunching under tires on the driveway caught my attention. An overweight, balding man with a navy blue blazer and khaki pants climbed out of a gigantic, wide and low car. As he straightened, huffing and puffing, I stepped forward. "Mr. Hall?"

The man smiled, dabbing at his sweaty forehead as he grabbed a small folio from the passenger's seat. "Mr. Borne!"

I cringed inwardly at the honorific, but I didn't correct him. "Hey."

"I apologize for being slightly late," his expression matched the sentiment. "I took a wrong turn and almost made it to the next town before I realized."

I laughed, shrugged, and shoved my hands into my pockets. "Hey, it happens. Besides, you're exactly on time. I haven't been here long."

The man held his hand towards the steps as I pushed off of my car. "Well then, shall we?"

I grinned. I didn't want to seem too eager, but this was the most excited I'd been since the dog bite. "Please!"

The first thing that I noticed when we walked into the church was that it was all one large room, except for a single door to the right that led to what I assumed was the bathroom. The whole room was painted a neutral white. The colors of the stained glass danced playfully across the scratched and damaged hardwood floors, and there was a set of stairs leading up to a loft across the room. There was also a lingering floral smell in the air. I thought it may have been roses, but I wasn't sure where the scent could be coming from. I hadn't noticed any bushes in the front. The smell wasn't off-putting, but it mixed with something earthy that I couldn't place. My nose had been more sensitive since the dog bite, so I didn't mention it aloud.

The church itself was smallish, but bigger than my studio apartment. The kitchen was beneath the overhang that the loft caused, creating the illusion of a separation. A fully stocked bookshelf sat against the wall that separated the bathroom from the living area. Two sad, faded, lumpy couches sat in the middle of the room in an L shape, with simple end tables at either side and one in the corner made by the L. The only other piece of furniture in the large room was an old secretary-style writing desk, coupled with a comfortable-looking green armchair. I found myself staring at the ornate railing leading up to the loft. "Can we start up there?"

I pointed to the stairs, and Mr. Hall nodded. "Of course, Cypress, of course. You're the interested party; I go where you want."

He didn't have to tell me twice. I climbed the rickety wooden steps, noting how the planks creaked and groaned under our weight. The actual supports seemed solid enough, but the planks themselves were bowing, splintered, and in rough shape. I'd have to refinish the floors, or at least cover them, if I wanted them to be nice. Thinking about that made my stomach fill with butterfly wings, warm and hopeful and fluttering. *Stop it, you've barely seen one room. I shouldn't be thinking of ways that I could make the space comfortable while I cleaned it up. At least finish the walk through, first.*

The floors of the landing were just as ruined; scratched, uneven wooden planks warped and creaking beneath our feet. The colored glass from a second rose window cast greens, blues, and yellows across the floors, and the sunlight made a spotlight effect from overhead. I looked up to see a drop-down ladder overhead, leading straight up into a small bell tower that was open to the outside. It hung open by about an inch, the breeze fighting its way in through the prominent crack. *That's going to be a problem, come winter. But, maybe I can cap it with a trap door, or replace the hinges... I'd have to look into it.*

As I thought, I let my eyes wander around the loft. The church was surprisingly clean, for an abandoned place. I didn't see any signs of animals living in the space, despite the roof having an open and easy access point. My thoughts came to an abrupt stop when I noticed a simple wooden casket shoved into the corner of the loft against the railing. "Why is there a casket?"

"Pay it no mind," the man said, laughing.

A casket in a church; go figure. Other than that, the building was ordinary. The kitchen housed some old appliances that frankly terrified me; the stove looked like one of those cast iron deals that they hadn't used since the forties. The fridge had a similar outdated feel. It wasn't one of those that housed a block of ice, but it might as well have been that old. Honestly, that wasn't a game changer, but I made a mental note to make the appliances the first thing I fixed. I think I had already decided to buy it before the walk through had started.

"So... I'm the first person you've had who has any interest in this place?"

"The place has been abandoned for quite a while. The bank bought the property from the city as part of a bounce back program, and here we are. There shouldn't be any troubles for you, Mr. Borne. Most people think this place is too much work to polish up, but I think it's a charming little church that has a lot of potential."

"And the land is included in the price?"

The Realtor nodded. I took one more look around and smiled. "So, where do I sign?"

And so, I began on my venture to move into this house, carefully avoiding my mother as I packed my belongings. I'd been out to the church a few times to start cleaning up, but only with the Realtor in tow during the day. I wasn't able to start actually fixing or changing anything until the deed was officially in my name. It took three weeks, give or take, for the bank to get all of the paperwork together and for the inspection to pass. The closing paperwork was signed in the late afternoon, and the key was comfortably in my pocket by 5pm. I drove out to the church just past dark on May 2nd, 2022, and when I pulled up the gravel driveway, there were candles burning in every window.

"What the…" I sniffed the air, and the smell of rose petals clung to my throat and nose. The sweet floral played with that kind of earthy smell I'd noticed during the walk through. The smooth scent of sandalwood added a richness to it all. It had to be squatters. Maybe they were hippies, meeting to discuss ways to end global warming, rather than cultists here to sacrifice goats. *That'd be nice. Drop acid… Not Bombs.*

Lemon Balm

It was a still night, and I couldn't really see any movement within. The air was moist and heavy, promising oncoming storms. I wasn't sure if I wanted to throw the door open and announce myself, or just wait it out until morning. My breath quickened, and I glanced at each window, my eyes darting from flame to flame as I tried to figure out what to do. *I could call the cops...? No wait, my phone's dead. Fuck.*

There was an eerie calmness to the woods that made my skin tingle as if creatures of the forest were watching me from the trees, and it was quieter than I would expect on a late spring evening. It was actually uncanny how silent the woods were. I expected to at least hear crickets, or birds. Something. It was like the animals sensed danger around this place, and I didn't care to linger on that thought. My guts twisted; I didn't need another uncanny animal attack under my belt.

Sighing, I made my way from the car, leaving the headlights on and steeling myself for a confrontation. The smell of rain hung in the air, and it mixed with the candles in a sharply sweet haze. Tell me why I own this church, and I knocked on the door. The windows were open, and the quiet scratching I have now come to identify as a quill pen came to a stop. My shoulders were near my ears, tight and square, and I slouched low, throwing my hands into my pockets. There was a very long pause, almost as if the presence inside was deciding whether or not to show themselves. "Fuck it," I muttered and reached for the door.

The second my hand settled on the antique knob, the creaking wood swung open. "Can I help you?"

Their voice was neutral, but with an untrusting and cold edge just beneath the surface. There stood, I shit you not, one of the most beautiful beings I've ever had the pleasure to be in the presence of. Their thin, lithe form blocked the light from inside. Their heart-shaped face was partially hidden in shadow from the hood of an emerald cloak. Their hair tumbled in chaotic rolling curls from beneath the hem and down to their waist; the color of autumn leaves, rich wine, and tarnished copper. But, from what I could see, their skin was incredibly pale and smooth, their thin lips a perfect petal pink. They had tight, dark clothing that clung to them. Something about them immediately grasped my attention in a way that I wasn't fully used to.

I didn't know it at the time, but this mysterious, ethereal stranger was Acanthus Sylene. I can describe this being now with as many adjectives as the thesaurus holds, both in English and French. Eternally 21, and eternally beautiful. Non binary in the way that gender means absolutely nothing, my vampire companion is anything but mundane. At the time, I was stuck gaping at them as if they were a mirage.

Assessing my car and the key I held in my hand, they flipped their hair out of their face. I was taller than them by several inches, and I instinctively hunched my bulky, 6'4" frame down even further. They couldn't have been taller than 5'10". Their eyes were sharp, intelligent, and analyzing; a haunting green, rich brown and gold flecks encircling their pupils in a chaotic mash of hazel color that feels like the same energy as an ancient, haunted forest. They were a stark contrast to my tired and dull steel and storm gray. Those eyes held me captive, blazing from their pale white skin in a magical fire. I hadn't spoken to them, far too distracted by their beauty to find words. Their voice was cold, the neutrality all but gone. "You could catch flies, you know."

When I picked my jaw up off the floor, they were openly glaring at me. "Umm... I apologize, I don't mean to bother you. I — uh —" It wasn't like me to trip over my words, but I had fallen out of the habit of interacting with people. "Shit. I own this place now, so you need to find a new place to, uh, hang out," I finished lamely.

They started laughing at me, to my utter confusion. They clutched at their chest, doubled over and heaving with their mirth as the joke sailed fully over my head. "Oh you silly little Pup. You nearly had me."

If I'd been more aware of myself, I would have been offended by this person. I raised my eyebrow at them, unimpressed. "Pup?"

The nickname was patronizing. What was I supposed to even do, here? I expected a confrontation, but this just didn't make sense. I shook my head to clear the fog that seemed to settle over it. "Excuse me? I don't understand."

They looked me up and down again. Their coldness threw me off. I knew that I was polite for a New York-er, but I don't think that I had ever dealt with someone so overtly entitled and rude. I was being far too polite to someone literally squatting on my property. Their voice cut through my inner struggle, and I found my attention captivated again. "You made no effort to hide your scent," they said through a scowl, their voice neutral with a very subtle sneer beneath it. "You are a brave soul, walking into my domain like you own the place."

What in the ever-loving holy fuck were they talking about? "Umm... Well..." I casually sniffed the air, seeing if I could tell what they meant by 'hiding my scent'. All I could smell was the candles, the scents complex and layered and sending my head into a spin. I showered today, right? Suddenly extremely self-conscious, I doubled down on my point. "Actually, I do own this place."

The laughter began again, and followed me through the air until I stomped to the car and pulled the deed from the passenger side. I cut the lights, locked the doors, and made my way back to the church. "I'm serious," I said flatly, as I held the deed out to the stranger at the door. The laughter stopped.

Lemon Balm

"Give me that," the stranger commanded. My body betrayed me, and I did. They looked me up and down. "Sit," they commanded again, and I tried my damnedest to fight it.

I sat on the concrete landing, cross legged and stared up at them, waiting. They were treating me horribly, and yet I wanted to hang on every word. What the hell is wrong with me?

I tried to ask a question, literally anything. I couldn't. I definitely wasn't in control of my actions, and the strange eagerness that I had to please this person felt wholly outside of myself. I wondered if this is how a marionette felt. At the time I was a stark skeptic, unable to put aside reason to consider the supernatural. And the fact that I didn't have control of my body already had me thinking about whether or not I should call poison control in the morning. Maybe there was a carbon monoxide leak in the church, or maybe the candles had some sort of drug that they were releasing into the air. I didn't know.

If this person was aware of my discomfort, they didn't care. They were scanning over the deed. "This is real," they muttered. "It's… It can't be." They looked back into the church.

"Yes," I managed to choke out. "It's real…"

From where I sat on the ground, they seemed impossibly tall and intimidating. They looked down and studied me. "Who is your Alpha?"

"Alpha?"

Apparently one word questions were okay. They huffed and rolled their eyes, and I gritted my teeth, a spark of irritation making my face flush. Wasn't I the one who held the deed to this church? Honestly, they could go kick rocks. Feeling bad or not, they were trespassing. "Ah yes. A progressive one? Have they done away with that Archaic Alpha/Omega system? Who is your leader?"

I scrunched my face in confusion as I shook my head. There was a pause. The silence was heavy, and I wished they'd talk again, if only to hear their voice. This also irritated me. Why was I hanging on to their every movement? They were a squatter in my home.

"You… Are pack-less…" they murmured. "Young Pup. How long have you been pack-less?"

I tried to bite my tongue in a stubborn attempt to avoid submitting to their will, but there was no choice. "I have no idea what you are talking about."

Their eyes went wide. Right about then, the sky let loose. An instant downpour began and wet the concrete around me, my shirt soaking through as thunder rolled in the distance.

"Oh my," they assessed the sky. "I suppose you should come in, so we can discuss this matter." They waved the deed. "Come in Pup. Do not shake out your fur."

I wanted to yell at him. I was absolutely incensed, and yet, it was as if I was disconnected from my anger. Was I drugged? I cannot believe I was listening so intently to this guy. I wanted to punch his haughty face. My fingers moved reflexively with the strength of the urge, but I couldn't move more than that. My heart was thundering in my ears, and my jaw was beginning to ache with how tightly I clenched my teeth. I spoke when they asked me. I listened when they talked. I must have been drugged.

They were detached and analytical; I had the distinct impression that I was just something to study. Their gaze made me wonder if this is how rats felt when they were forced to wander mazes for cheese. The haughtiness had slipped from their voice just a bit. "Young Pup, what is your name?"

I wanted to say something biting. Something witty. Something sharp. None of the above happened, and I screamed internally. "Cypress. Cypress Borne."

"Hmm. Mister Borne. I'd say it's a pleasure to meet you, but it seems there's been a misunderstanding," they replied.

The tension in my throat loosened for a moment. There my anger was. I tried to hold onto the feeling. "Don't call me Mister."

They tilted their head to one side. "Amazing."

I rolled my eyes, my curls falling into my face. "Are you going to talk in riddles all night Mister...?" Great. Awesome. They knew my name, and I don't even have a clue.

"Acanthus," they replied, their voice aloof and distracted as they flipped through the deed again.

I shook my head as the fogginess set back in. Acanthus? What was that, was that Latin? I'd certainly never heard a name like it before. Not that I cared, I just wanted the guy to leave. "Look, Mister Acanthus. Edge-lord Supreme. Can you please stop burning whatever the hell you are burning? I feel like I dropped acid or something. I don't care what is happening here, but you need to go."

I'd never dropped acid before, but I heard stories. And man, whatever was happening certainly felt like it could be a trip. They waved their hand in the air, stopping the words in my mouth. "I can sense you are upset with me, while this should be the other way around. I should have at least ten years before I inherit this land from myself. So, how have you come to be the owner of it? Keep it brief, Pup. My patience wears thin."

"Stop. Calling. Me. That," I snarled. The condescending nickname was pushing me towards my limits at mach speed. "I don't understand what you are talking about. This place was foreclosed on. It's been over 110 years since there's been any sort of communication. They've sent letters, and notices, and they've all been returned to sender. I. Fucking. Own. This. Church."

Cursing in his presence felt wrong. It almost hurt me, like the word had turned into a material blade, scratching across my esophagus like broken glass. I had no problems cursing in normal circumstances. *What is going on?*

"I'll beg you to watch your mouth," they hissed as they turned back to their desk, searching through papers. "Politely now, what is today?"

"Wednesday," I bit out.

They took a deep, calming breath, flipping their hair over their shoulder and beginning to braid it. "You are really trying my patience. What year is it? 1986?"

"It's on the fucking deed!" The familiar burning of those hallucinations started in my fingers. I was even further disconnected from my body as I began to lose myself, both to my anger and to the burning. What fucking right did this person have to tell me I'M trying HIS patience? What fucking right did this guy have to mock me, 1986? Really? I held my hands up, trying to find a way to warn this stranger... Back off, now.

"Pup," He shifted into a more defensive stance, hands in front of him in a soothing gesture.

"STOP IT," my voice was animalistic and crazed. I've let it go too far, and now this stranger will see a beast I've done my best to escape.

That Time I Forced A Werewolf To Turn

Acanthus

It is amusing to me that Cypress talks about the mundanity of human life at the beginning of their journey. Perhaps that is because my human life was very much the opposite of what Cypress would consider mundane. His crashing into my world completely killed the careful mundanity that I had both craved and crafted in this portion of my afterlife. The tale of our meeting ends from Cypress' point of view where it does, I suspect because they don't remember. You see, as dramatic (and, albeit, mocking) as Cypress may be in the way that they kicked things off, they're harmless. A young Pup, with little to no experience of the world.

I thought of the way their human form looked when I first saw them, gaping and awestruck on the concrete landing of the top stair. Bulky and big, but clearly malnourished, their frame towered over me, their slate and steel eyes large and expressive. Their lips were thin, and their jaw full and wide; dimples in their cheeks and chin creating a charming boyishness. They slouched, and even when they were irritated, an easy-going smile lifted the corners of their mouth and deepened those dimples. Their insecure politeness had been endearing. I almost felt bad shutting down the conversations the way that I had.

I will say, at the time I felt justified in my behavior. After all, a strange Werewolf had appeared on my doorstep with not even a hint of a warning. There is a long history of war between Vampires and Werewolves. I was only protected by a tenuous verbal treaty with the

Eastern territory's Alpha. Cypress had no way of knowing this at the time, but I was defensive of my home. I am the founder of The Night Garden, and most everyone knew it; though I hadn't been in charge of it since the early 20th century.

I'd owned the little church since it had been built in the early 1800's. It was one of the sanctuaries on the Night Garden paths before I claimed it to be my own domain. Technically, it was still a stop on the paths; refugees still came through for a night or two at a time, but I was largely undisturbed. I had "inherited" it from myself several times throughout the years. I'd noticed small changes recently, but I had written it off as daytime visitors. Perhaps travelers on the Garden paths, making themselves comfortable. Where this may not make sense at the moment, you will come to understand, soon enough.

I had taken a slightly sadistic joy in how easily they had fallen under my spell; a talent I otherwise try desperately to mask when I'm around others. I am not nefarious. I am not cruel. Up until I heard the warnings of Cypress' transformation, I thought that the Wolf had been put up to this. I thought maybe they were a new member to a local pack that I didn't recognize, and were being hazed. One of the unfortunate realities about Wolf society in the Americas is that it would be natural for the Wolves in the area. They knew that I was dangerous and would defend my home if need be, and an attack on a Pup would be a perfect reason to reinstate the war between us.

I watched the naive interloper start to shift and went on guard. I had meant to antagonize, yes, but never to push them past their point of control. I have quite the time pulling back and mitigating my powers — they often get me into trouble, especially when I lose my temper. I must admit that my patience is as thin as frayed wire these days. It was even worse at the time. I also genuinely did not know the year. I hadn't ventured away from my little church since the last time I had transferred the property to myself in 1913, short of necessary excursions. There were only three reasons that I ventured into society; sustenance, Night Garden business, and rare occasions of social graces with some of my Witch friends.

I am an Anesh, a vampire clan that is prone to periods of madness, especially when starved. I have not cared for myself much in the last several decades. Endless swaths of time run together in kaleidoscopic hazes. To me, the 37 years between 1986 and 2023 had felt like maybe six months. This is only made worse by the strength of my powers. I am unfortunately a being who has worked to hone my magic, and the stronger your magic is as an Anesh, the more susceptible to periods of madness you are. Our first meeting was a recipe for disaster. Cypress has a weakness for magic when being caught unaware, and I struggle with keeping my powers at bay.

So, when the stench of slobber and wet dog began to overpower the calming smell of oud, sandalwood, and roses, I readied myself for combat. I knelt down close to the rough-hewn wooden floors and slowly crept away, keeping my eyes trained on them. I calculated the amount of force I would need to counter an attack from such a tall, bulky figure. The silver ring on my left hand and the crucifix chained around my neck would prove to be effective weapons if the wolf chose to attack. I cursed the fact that they were the only silver within reach. Anything else, I would have to either summon or lunge for, and that would leave me wide open to an attack. (No, silver does not hurt me. And I'm quite fond of crucifixes.)

Cypress towered over me. The tufts of white fur started to rise from their skin. Their nails lengthened and blackened as they curved into claws. My heart jumped to my throat. All it took, however, was one scathing glance in their direction. They let out a loud, frustrated snarl, before they erupted into a series of distraught whines and fell to the floor in full wolf form. Their Wolf was massive, a hulking beast covered in white fur tipped with gray, a deep scar raking across their left eye. The expressive steel and stone of their irises caught the candlelight and blazed. Even from across the room, I could tell that they came up to about my chest. They were about the size of a lion, and that surprised me. Most wolves mirrored their animal counterparts in size.

With how easy Cypress was to subdue, it became clear that perhaps I had misjudged the situation. "I wonder what am I to do with you? You must feel so lost and alone."

The wary look I received from those gray eyes had more story than words would have conveyed. I may as well have kicked the Wolf. Exasperated, I crossed the room to look out the window, my mesmer spell breaking with our eye contact. I sensed nothing; this person had truly come alone. "Come, Pu—... Cypress, was it?"

Normally, I wouldn't dare turn my back to a Werewolf. Where the myths are correct when they say that Vampires and Werewolves are mortal enemies, they aren't a threat when we have the upper hand. This was confirmed when I felt warmth emanating from my right. They had come to sit beside me, their fur dripping rain onto the ruined wooden floors. Peering out of the ornate window once again, I took note of the sky, oddly brown with the night storm. Staring at the dark expanse helped me to think about my next steps.

There are two types of Werewolves in our world, both bound by magic and will. The Shifters can control their transformations with innate nature, and learned to do so in the sixteenth century. The Lunars cannot control their shifts, and are at the mercy of the moon. We were at a quarter moon on this night, not that I could see it through the clouds. This was not a shift caused by the planets, though I already knew that; I'd pushed them to this point. Their aches would be my fault, and I would soothe them in the morning. "I believe, through a series of unfortunate happenstances, we have gotten off on the wrong foot. I apologize for my poor first impression. You can stay, and in the morning, we shall try once more to settle this dispute like rational beings."

Cypress huffed, and I bit back a bemused smile. I had a sense that this young Pup couldn't control their shifts, despite being a Shifter. By morning, they'd likely be back to their tall, muscular human form. Perhaps saying this was a bit presumptuous; they had, after all, every right to kick me off of the property. And, I did have other places to stay. But, this was one of the outposts of The Night Garden, and I am nothing if not a competitive, headstrong, and stubborn individual. I would not give up my home so easily. My little church may have been run down, but it was a beacon for people in need and I would not let a clueless dog run me out.

Finally turning my eyes away from the window, I looked down at the young pup and took note of their appearance. The exhaustion wore on them far worse in this form. Their fur was shaggy and unkempt. Their head hung, and they stared at their paws with vacant eyes. A pang of guilt hit me once more. In my complete paranoia and lack of patience, I had nearly broken one of my very core tenets — never turn away one who comes to you in need. My Night Garden friends would be ashamed of me. "Pack-less, and likely unsure or even completely unaware of what is happening to you. Indeed a lost soul has come to me when I least expect it."

I stroked my fingers through their thick coat. At first, there was a little warning growl in the back of their throat, and I paused. I waited for the growl to taper and gently patted their massive head. My attempts to soothe were successful; they leaned up into my palm, and their eyes drooped, still unsure, but much more trusting than before. "There, there. Sleep, and we shall speak in the morning. I promise to let you be as you are, and not to use my tricks. I am nothing if not a being of my word."

I reached up with my free hand and untied the ribbons of my cloak, letting the deep emerald crushed velvet fall to the floor. I, like many Vampires, am a creature who is bound by both magic and moral duty to truth. To date, I have not ascertained whether or not this is because of my human origins as a Catholic priest, or if it is because of the type of Vampire that I am. We Anesh feel things exceedingly deeply. Lying and untruthfulness cuts me to the core; it feels worse than the physical pain caused by sun damage. (There are things that harm us, but I would be a fool to lay out what those are. I do not need some overzealous Hunter finding themself on my doorstep with an intent to harm. It would not be the first time.)

Pulling my hand away from their coat, I sat on the uneven wooden floor and pooled the fabric into a makeshift bed. Cypress' eyes tracked my every move, alert. "A peace offering," I explained. "Though we met in opposition, I assure you, I mean you no harm."

I could see the gears turning within their mind, trying to decide whether or not to trust me. It took patience and quiet on my part, and I waited for what seemed like a lifetime before they finally relented and curled up onto the cloak. I didn't dare to move until the Wolf's sides began to rise and fall in the slow, easy rhythm of slumber. Even if they did not trust me, I think they knew that it was one of those situations where, if I left, they would no longer have any access to answers. They had questions regarding the church, if not about what was happening to them.

In the entire time they had been within my home, I never sensed another; Wolf or otherwise. They weren't lying. "Of all the reactions I could have had," I murmured, my shoulders slumping as a strange tightness settled into my chest, "I had to settle with animosity. Come now, Acanthus, you know better than this."

I moved with a quiet grace that only a Vampire could, away from the sleeping Wolf and towards my writing desk. Fumbling across the mess on the surface, I unearthed a new piece of parchment, and my quill from beneath the deed. *Could people still read cursive?*

With quick, deliberate strokes, I wrote in messy print.

Cypress Borne,

I apologize for my behavior upon your ~~intrusion~~ arrival to my home. I suppose that you are looking for answers, and I must admit that I wasn't ready to listen last night. This whole situation feels like a massive misunderstanding. Though I know you likely have no trust and an overabundance of anger towards me, I have stayed so that we may speak.

At first, I thought you were a threat from a neighboring Pack, though it is clear to me now that I was mistaken. I will explain when we speak. I know you must be sore and your mind fogged; please find beside you a medicine that can help soothe your aches. The drink is herbal tea to clear the fog. Should you want something, there is food, water, and cold brew coffee in the refrigerator.

I introduced myself as Acanthus, which is indeed my name. Acanthus Sylene. Though, on the deed you produced upon my interrogation the name would be listed as Johnathon Harker Sylene. I am quite old and lost track of the years, which seems to have placed us in quite the predicament.

I do not want to lose my home, and nor do I want you to have to find elsewhere. I have reasons that are both good and weighty, and these reasons are bigger than myself. When you wake, and should you be willing, find me upon the loft. I will answer any questions and try to engage in any conversation you may want to have, whether it be of your Wolf, me, or our predicament. I hope my words find you well.

-A.

Signing the letter with a flourish, I sat back in my chair and reflected over the night's activities. A small clock on the top of the desk proclaimed that so much of the night had already passed. Cypress had come just after 9:30, and it was shortly after midnight. If I were to make good on my promise in the letter, I needed to go and gather ingredients now. I'd wasted enough time. *I haven't had a multi-day visitor in at least fifteen years... There's no fresh food here. What is he going to eat?*

I hoped the Wolf had thought ahead far enough to bring some shelf-stable items, or maybe pack a cooler. I had very few things available, thanks to Witches that would visit sometimes. I was careful not to make any sound as I stood from the desk and dropped the letter on the sleeping Wolf's paw. It would be cold without my cloak, but I never quite minded the temperature. Besides, the rain had stopped. This was the least that I could do to make up for my rudeness. Without another thought, I blew out the candles with a soft burst of wind from my powers. Satisfied, I crept out of the quiet room and into the night.

I got to work. First, I found and gathered the herbs I needed and prepared a salve. When that was done, I sat still in the garden and listened, until I could hear the speeding heartbeats of a den of rabbits. Closing my eyes, I lifted my hand and lunged, spearing two with my fingernails. I created a small, meat heavy breakfast and placed the stew in the refrigerator. By the time it was all said and done, the pinks and oranges of the dawn had started to creep into the sky. Cypress had shifted back to their human form in their sleep, and the cloak was now draped around them like a blanket. There were purple shadows beneath his eyes. Guilt ripped through me as I placed the food in the fridge. I turned at a speed only Vampires can, quickly making my way up the stairs and into my casket.

I do not need to sleep in a casket, though I must admit that coffins and caskets are some of the most comfortable beds. Like a giant silk hug, carrying you to the clouds of your dreams in soft arms. There was little reason for me to keep a large bed in my chambers, and I liked the darkened closeness when the lid was closed. It was private and secure; a miniature cocoon away from the world. I lay there, hoping that my efforts to smooth over the bad beginnings would work. Pulling a book from beneath my pillow, I began to read with the help of a small, battery-powered book light, waiting to hear the shuffling of a clumsy Wolf on the stairs.

☽ ☾☽☉◐◑☾

I would like to take a moment to deviate from the tale of our meeting here, dear Reader. Cypress' thought of the mundane — the normal, the daily grind of human life, the simple, detached way that we distractedly go about our days, wishing for something more, or less, or *different* — has been so far removed from my life that I have forgotten what it was like. I don't remember the paltry little squabbles, the worries of tithes or anxieties surrounding food or drink. I don't remember the fear of plague and of pestilence. But, I can relate to the sudden stopping of those things. My turning had directly correlated with Cypress' — it was traumatic, and awful, and made me question my sanity.

You see, vampires are achingly lonesome creatures. We are regularly harmed by those we care for, and have no tolerance for those we don't. There are also elements to my life that have driven me to my solitude, and many of those things are still painful for me to talk about. For now, I shall leave them aside. Such things make it hard to connect to people outside of our small bubbles and, even then, the mistrust of others can last eons. Do you know the old adage; you need to invite a vampire in, in order for them to take you as their prey? That's hardly the case — instead, we usually need to be invited at least thrice, otherwise we feel as though the welcome is not extended. It's a matter of propriety, not of magic.

I admit, where I do fully enjoy the creature comforts of the modern era, I am fairly comfortable existing on the fringes of society. I have been alone for a very long time. In order to find my own sense of mundanity, we must both travel across the oceans to France and take a step back in time. My human life had been deeply entrenched in trauma; night terrors still plagued me of gore and viscera from a time where I could not yet speak but could remember the sound of a sword slicing through the flesh of a loved one.

The last whispers of the now forgotten Cathars had been traveling through southern France in my child years. My parents were part of the sect; victims of the Albigensian Crusades. I remember the steel against my throat and looking up at cold blue eyes through the blur of tears even still. For reasons unknown, a tall, dark-minded man with a stone heart took pity on the child sitting within the pooled blood of his parents.

I became the son of the Marquis de Serré, known for his cruelty. From that young age I was surrounded by faith and the faithful, and was allowed to study only because of my station. I may have reminded the Marquis of a child who had passed; the living replacement. My red hair had been the sign of a Hellion; perhaps this interested him. Maybe his son was murdered for his red hair. After all, when taken under his wing, I had also taken the deceased child's name. How oddly painful it is, to think of being a replica of someone's preferred company. At the age of 16, I was ordained, despite my hair. From that time forward I was no longer under the care of the Marquis (who treated me well despite his nature), and was instead pulled into the fold of the Catholic priesthood.

These old living memories feel like they're hidden behind the black glass of a scrying mirror now. They are of an age so far and forgotten beneath the sands of time that it's nearly impossible to remember what humanity was like. However, I do remember getting very little sleep and preferring the solace of the night. The day was entrenched in responsibility and duty. Darkness has always brought me comfort.

Being favored by the Pope, I was allowed to shepherd one of the newest cathedrals in southern France. The gilded altar had a *memento mori*. For those not well-versed in the Catholic faith, a *memento mori* is a piece of a holy saint's corpse, kept to ensure the sanctity of the hallowed ground. The hand of a saint encased in thick glass stood in the center, behind a prop for the heavy illuminated manuscripts that we would proselytize from in the pulpit. In those days, the Word was written in Greek and Latin, and I was fluent in both (at least in reading; you cannot fluently speak a dead language).

In the year of 1263, I was a robust young man of twenty one years old, well into adulthood for that time. On my way to becoming a bishop, I was in a position of great power and greater inner turmoil. I was known for my impassioned sermons and fervent belief. Many do not realize that the harrowing events of the Spanish Inquisition actually began in France. My diocese was not free from the blood of heretics that stains the halls of the Catholic faith. I shall spare you the details, but perhaps this is why my maker chose me as a victim. I still fall ill at the thoughts of my own willing participation.

I can distinctly recall the summer scream of cicadas through the long, open windows of the newly built Gothic cathedral. Human memory and thought is strange that way; I can hardly remember most of my living years, but I can remember that. Details like names have faded to the weather of time, but I can still picture the moist warmth. The soft kiss of the breeze would come through the windows from the nearby lake. Such a vision, and one that still brings whispers of comfort from ages past.

The moon was full, and we were in the throes of late August's languid heat. The day had been sweltering, and I was thankful for the crisp night air. The silvery light refracted off of the gilded sanctum and fought the warm, orange firelight of the candles for dominance. I held the confidence that only a young man could as I walked between the pews, sweeping up dust with a corn husk broom. I was at peace; newly recovered from a mysterious illness and fervent in my love for God.

The time that we are speaking of was rife with war, torture, and fighting within the church. It was rare to feel peace those days. Once I finished sweeping the sanctum, I slowly made my way back to the center window, looking out past the columns of the buttresses to the lake. I have always loved the beauty of the night, and back then, the stars were brighter and the moon was stunning enough to make you see visions. And yet, my human eyes could only see a fraction of the true beauty within the darkness.

Closing my eyes, I let the breeze caress me as I thought of my adopted brothers and the Marquis. I wondered about them often in those days. I hadn't seen them in months, and I missed them terribly. My youngest brother was soon to be wed, and the eldest was with the Marquis on a bloody campaign. *They must be alright, they have my prayers and the Lord on their side.*

A whisper broke my reverie, barely a noise at all. The hairs on my neck stood up as though a lover's kiss brushed against me, and I whipped around to look through the sanctum. Everyone had left the church hours ago; I was the only one with the key to the massive cast iron and oak doors at the end. Straining my eyes against the dark of the candlelight and the ethereal refraction of the moon, I scanned for any signs of movement. What felt like an eternity passed before I forced my shoulders to drop and turned back to the window. *Just the wind. Devils like to play with your mind in the dark.*

I gasped at the laugh that followed, gripping the broom tighter and whipping around. My pulse quickened and my breathing became shallow as fear gripped my chest, snaking its clammy fingers through my flesh. The laugh had come from everywhere, and yet nowhere at all. "Hear me, demon!" I began, trying desperately to ignore how my voice shook. "You cannot stalk the halls of this sanctum, I am protected by the Lord our God!"

Another laugh ripped through the air, echoing off of the vaulted ceilings and marble columns. My throat tightened as a scream threatened to erupt from my lungs. I tried to move my shaking legs, but I was frozen. Time seemed to stutter, the crying of the cicadas slowing to a deep, grinding lull. I heard from within my own mind in a voice that was not my own, *there is no God here, my naive little one.* The next thing that I remember is darkness, and a sharp pain as teeth ripped into my neck.

What, would you like more? I apologize, dear Reader, but that snippet is about all that I am willing to share; after this moment, only terror remains.

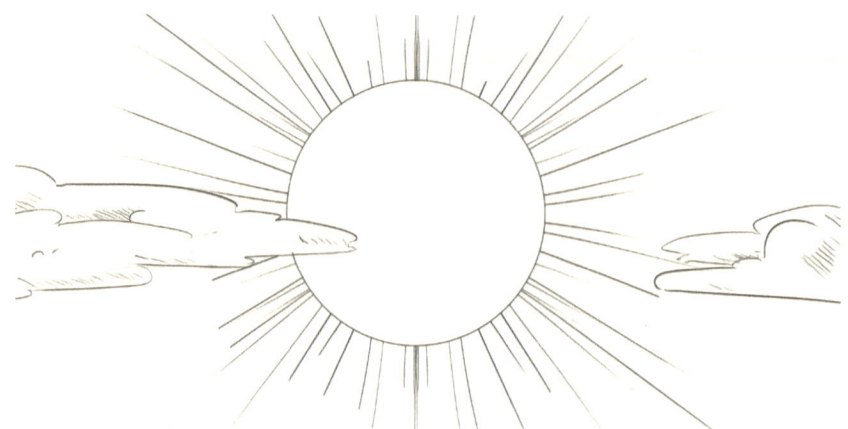

That Time I Asked, "What The Fuck?"

Cypress

None of what happened after I lost my temper is clear. And while I can't confirm if what that pompous bastard tells me is true, I did wake up with their cloak wrapped around me like a baby blanket. I felt oddly comforted by the scent, but quickly shook that thought from my head. Groaning, I sat up, my muscles aching. I must've somehow fallen asleep on the floor. After stretching, I was hit with a terrible clarity. *Wait, what happened last night? What do I remember?*

I was missing my memory. I had lost my temper, and I was *missing my memory*. Again. My heart battered itself against my sternum, and my breaths shortened. Fuck. Fuck, fuck, *fuck*. Did I go off and hurt a complete stranger? This wasn't good.

The more I panicked and came to my senses, the worse it got. I was naked under this cloak. That stranger had been wearing it. Was there blood or tears? Did I take it? With shaking hands, I smoothed the cloak across my lap, looking for signs of a struggle through the piles. I still didn't know what happened when I blacked out, in general. When I blinked, flashes of the monster I saw — *hallucinated* — on that camera footage came into my mind. My rages were bad enough when I was alone, I couldn't imagine what I did when someone was around.

I gulped past a lump in my throat, trying to clear my mind and focus on my breathing. In. Out. Inhale. Exhale. Slowly, I ran my hands over the cloak, my fingers trembling. There were no dark spots or stains that I

48

could find. When I was satisfied with its condition, my shoulders sagged, and I glanced warily around the room. *Is that guy still here?*

Setting my hand to the side of my thigh, the soft crinkle of paper caught my attention. *That's odd, I don't remember bringing anything in, other than the deed...*

I reached under the cloak, grasping the paper. I paused when a hint of the strange, layered smells brought fresh memories from the night before. The frustration of being frozen, losing control of my body, and the irritating way the stranger kept calling me Pup. My chest tightened and my breaths started getting shallow again, but I forced the panic down. I was trying to get my life back in order; the last thing I needed was to find out I had assaulted a stranger. *Should I call the cops? How would I even explain this? Would they even be able to help, what if I murdered the guy? I should — fucking stop.* I focused on the neat print of my name, covering the folded paper in front of me. A letter.

The tension melted from my shoulders, and I let out a long exhale as I processed that I hadn't, in fact, killed the stranger. All I could guess is I had somehow been drugged. How else could you take complete control over someone like that? And, if I had been drugged, then how could the stranger have resisted the effects? I wanted answers. Unfolding the paper revealed the neat, crisp scrawl. *Christ.*

Any thoughts of being drugged or controlled sloughed away under a landslide of guilt and awkwardness. I read the letter a few times, squinting as I still struggled with the contents. *He mentioned Wolves...*

But they couldn't have known about my hallucinations. I wasn't ready to accept that there may be something supernatural happening to me. *If they saw me...*

What? If they saw me transform? Had I transformed? Even thinking about it made me imagine Junior's voice in my head, laughing and calling me a dumb-ass. *Alright, Cypress, think. Are there any clues to anything?*

I glanced around the sparse room again, looking for shredded pieces of clothing, muddy paw prints on the floor. White tufts of fur. I saw nothing. I shifted my attention towards my side, all tension and panic gone from my chest. *This is ridiculous...*

I sighed. I might as well trust this guy. After all, if I had hurt them at all when I blacked out, then I should probably at least hear him out before I start seeking out a lawyer. I was stiff from spending the night on the floor, and my bones wouldn't let me forget it. Stretching my neck and lower back, I caught the singular word in this letter that my heart will always beat for: Coffee. Hopping up, I held the cloak in front of me. I'd never get used to this naked situation. Gritting my teeth, I sucked in a deep breath through my nose. *Don't think too hard about it, Cypress.*

I tied the fabric around my waist, leaving my chest bare. As my mental health had slipped, I started to hate being naked and vulnerable; both things added to the beastliness. I also connected nakedness with my lost memory and rages. My mind wandered towards the car. I had extra clothes in the trunk, but did I really want to walk out there in a makeshift toga? Then again, facing someone else like this was worse than the possibility of seeing someone outside.

I wandered into the kitchen, a little concerned because I, one, did not know what was in this meal that was supposedly waiting for me, and two, did not see a coffee maker. After a bit of searching, a pour-over drip pot revealed itself in the corner of a counter. I had no idea how to use them. I walked to the refrigerator and pulled it open, searching for the food. There wasn't much in the fridge; a crystal pitcher of ice cold water was there, as well as a pitcher of a dark brown liquid. I could only assume that this was the coffee. At least these things backed up the contents of Acanthus' letter. Sniffing it, the bitter undertones of a good dark roast made my mood lift.

Turning back to the fridge, I dipped my head in once more, spotting a small take-away bowl of what looked like a stew on the bottom shelf. *That looks delicious.*

I pulled the bowl from the fridge and looked around. I didn't exactly have a way to heat it, unless I wanted to take a chance with the ancient stove. Sighing, I resigned myself to eating the stew cold. At least the stranger had thought of me. I grabbed a spoonful, and balked at the gamey taste. "What the hell is this, roadkill?!"

It was terrible. I could only eat about half of it before I gave up, putting the meal aside. I wasn't about to waste food; in any case, I could finish it later. Maybe it'd be better warm. I told myself that I may as well accept the olive branch they extended. Back to my original quest — some sort of container for the coffee. I didn't want to drink directly from the pitcher; besides, it'd only be polite to bring Acanthus some, as well. It only took a little bit of searching before I triumphantly found two glasses, pouring equal amounts of coffee in them.

I left them on the counter, searching for my keys. "Fuck yes," I muttered when I finally found them, along with my wallet, neatly placed on one of the end tables. I rifled through my tri-fold, satisfied when I found nothing missing, and then ran out to the car. A moment later, I was way more relaxed and confident in an old t-shirt and ratty, stained jeans. I grabbed a few of the bags from the back and made my way inside.

The bags were fine in a pile behind a couch, for now. Making sure I had a handle on my anxiety, I squared my shoulders and grabbed the cups from the kitchen counter. I walked up the stairs to the loft, halting when I saw the old, derelict casket in the corner. I was almost tempted to back down the stairs again. From the casket I heard a muffled, "You brought me coffee too?"

"Umm…" Glancing down at the cups in my hands, I look back up at the casket. Knowing Acanthus was in the casket set my stomach twisting into knots, and I deflected the fear with a joke. "It's your home. So technically didn't you bring you coffee?"

A soft chuckle erupted as Acanthus pushed open the lid. A small book light was shining from the book in their hands. I was once again disarmed and distracted by their beauty. "The young Wolf is humorous." Their whispery tone carried despite being so quiet.

Confusion twisted my face, and I squinted at them. The nickname felt like an insult, and I tried my best not to take it to heart. I'm a monster echoed in my mind as I asked aloud, "Why do you keep calling me that?"

The irritation from the previous night was well and truly out of the building. I guess I wanted answers more than I wanted a fight. Acanthus' shoulders drew in and they swallowed, their face falling. They set their book aside and sat up straighter, letting the casket's lid rest against the loft railing. "Cypress…"

"Yes?"

I kept my voice carefully neutral, doing my best not to judge. Do people really sleep in caskets like that? I saw it during the walk-through with the Realtor, but I couldn't imagine anyone sleeping in there. How did they keep from suffocating with the lid closed? Their soft, whispery voice cut through my thoughts again. I guess my skepticism would have to wait. "You are aware… You're a Werewolf, correct?"

I snorted. "That is absolutely ridiculous."

I don't know who they thought they were kidding, but it wasn't about to be me. If Werewolves existed, then you could call me The President. I stepped forward, holding out the cup of coffee to them, and stood there. They paused, gauging my reaction before they reached for the cup, a distant look in their eyes. It was like I was a puzzle they were trying to solve. I guess they settled on simplicity. "Ridiculous? How?"

I scoffed, and took a big gulp of the cold brew. It was surprisingly easy to fake confidence when you were chugging coffee. "It just is," I responded after a pronounced swallow. "Werewolves aren't real."

Acanthus frowned. "You don't believe in Werewolves? What about Vampires? Witches? Demons, Fae?"

I laughed. I wasn't that gullible. "Werewolves are just a story that people tell their kids to stop them from going into the woods. Vampires were a way to get out of cutting censored content in old school

Hollywood, and Witches are just people who really like crystals and believe in tarot cards and that their cats can talk to them."

Acanthus choked on their coffee. "I beg your pardon?"

The offense in their tone shook my confidence just a little bit. Maybe I had misread the joke. Crossing my arms, I huffed as the heat rose in my cheeks. I stared them down, losing my patience. "What?"

Anger flashed briefly in those hazel eyes. They closed them, and pinched the bridge of their nose, taking a calming breath. I was reminded of a priest, or maybe a teacher trying very hard to keep their patience with a child. This was so very different from the conversation I had hoped for. I wanted to maybe talk about the church, or why they thought it was theirs. Or, maybe, even, how Lemon got in when I had the only known key. But instead, I was met with this childish fairy tale banter. I distracted myself by holding their cloak out to them.

They dropped their hand and stared at me, their voice tight and clipped. "Okay. Think, have you been bitten by a dog recently? Maybe you have night terrors, cold sweats, and random muscle pains? How about lapses in memory, or blurred spots?"

How did they know? The frantic breaths from when I first woke up came back full force, my heart pounding against my rib cage as if it were a prisoner begging for freedom. I dropped the cloak to the floor, swallowing. How many professionals had I seen, with how many differing uncertain diagnoses and failed medicine regimens? Two minutes after meeting this stranger, they laid out all of my symptoms without so much as batting their pretty eyes? I found my voice, but my confidence was all but gone. "Well, not recently…"

"Not recently? What's that mean?"

Their tone was getting more and more clipped, and their narrowed eyes pierced me. They tapped their long nails on the side of the casket.. The rage that was all too common after the dog bite bubbled up. *Give me what I want to know, Dammit.*

Biting my lip, I closed my eyes, counting to ten before I spoke next. "You said you'd answer my questions."

"You've not asked me any."

I snapped. "No fucking mind tricks, okay? I don't need whatever happened last night to happen again. Was it drugs or some—"

In an instant, they were standing in front of me. *What the fuck?*

That was way too fast for me to see. I gasped and stepped back, and I was stuck against the wall. "Be careful, Pup. I don't tolerate being cursed at in my own domain." Their fists clenched at their sides, and they glared up at me. "Not to mention, I take great offense to the drug comment. I've never drugged anyone in my life, much less touched them."

"Acanthus... I-I'm sorry."

The pathetic whimper fell from my mouth. Why was *I* apologizing? I had a solid six inches on this person, and yet they were terrifying. Standing my ground, I towered over them and forced myself to take up space. I had an overwhelming desire to make myself smaller, to cower from their might. It was an odd combination, and I pulled my arms tighter around me.

Their eyes flashed at my apology, and they stepped back again. They took a few deep breaths, and I was struck by the thought that I'd done the same exact thing downstairs. Was this impatience or anxiety? Something else? They set the coffee on the railing and pulled their hair over their left shoulder, braiding it as they once again derailed my thoughts with another question. "Okay. How long ago, if not recently, did you experience this dog bite?"

I wasn't liking the answers that I was getting. I could leave them in their rotting casket and go. I could get the cops and forcefully evict them, and never talk to them again. I could forget their pretty face and deal with this myself, but then... Well. They had named all of my symptoms, and they didn't even know me. There was something about the way Acanthus was talking that rang true. Maybe I could cut through the crazy and find a nugget of truth in their words. If I left, I'd lose the only hint I'd found about what exactly happened to me. They had to know something that was useful. I was staying for more than just a property dispute.

Literally backed against a well, I resigned myself to the conversation and sighed. "It's been a little over two years."

Acanthus' voice was shrill. "Two *years?*"

I flinched at the sudden change in tone and grinned at them as their jaw dropped open. I couldn't help but mock the way they had responded to me the night before. "You could catch flies, you know."

They stared, snapping their mouth shut. I was left to my own devices, awkward and still painfully aware that I was speaking to a stranger about preposterous things. "Acanthus?"

I think they were in shock. The seconds stretched on. What was with this guy?

"Hello?" I grabbed their wrist to take their pulse as a joke. They were cold. Ice cold. Colder than anyone could possibly be at the end of May with a cloak and long sleeves on. And, I couldn't be sure, but I didn't think there was a pulse. A pit of dread formed in my stomach, and I moved my fingers to find one. Every point I knew of to check, there was no pulse. I gulped, and dropped their hand. "Oh, shit, what the fuck?"

Their gaze snapped back to mine, and understanding blazed in that hazel fire. I held my hand to my chest as if their skin had burned me, and they let out a tiny joyless laugh in response. They murmured, "Vampires aren't real, huh?"

Suddenly, I was very aware of how close they were standing, the scent of decaying leaves flooding my nose as I noticed how sharp their teeth really were. Their canines seemed to lengthen as I was watching, and my heart jumped into my throat. There was no way. There was *no* way. I pressed myself against the wall, looking away. I could rationalize what I was seeing as a hallucination, but what about their ice cold skin? *There's no way this is real...*

"You've not seen the things that I've seen, young Pup. You've not seen Witches burned at the stake, not seen them drowned in rivers, or pressed with stones. You've not seen your own people driven to the hollow point of extinction over a fabricated blood feud," Acanthus continued to talk in cool measured tones. Their eyes captured the light and glowed, shining from their face like a cat's in the dark. The room dropped in temperature. I couldn't tell if that was because of how close they were to me, or if it was the sudden change in their demeanor. Their black frosted nails seemed to lengthen, though their arms stayed at their sides. Their entire presence was a force to reckon with. I almost felt like I was pressed against my studio door again, staring down a giant mangy dog with a frothing maw. "You have no *ide*a what it's like to see the people around you sputter and die."

"No, I can't say I do." I whispered, inwardly screaming at my heart to still and my legs to stop feeling like frozen jelly. This was nothing like the burning of the hallucinations; I was shaking where I stood. *How are you a walking corpse?*

They tilted their head to the side. "You are terrified of me, and yet, you really don't believe you're a Werewolf?"

"I uh…" I gulped. With a short intake of breath, I spoke honestly, trying to knock away this icy fright. "I'm not certain what I believe. And that's the truth. My senses have betrayed me before."

"Your senses, or society?"

I hid my fear with an aloof indifference. "Are you going to continue to ask me questions I don't know the answer to?"

I looked down at the cup of coffee that sat forgotten in my hand. They backed up, and I pushed away from the wall and downed it in a quick, calming gulp. Their voice was back to whispery, full of remorse. "How rude of me. Of course. I invited you to come to me for information."

I closed my eyes again. This entire conversation mirrored the night before... Mirrors. "So, can you see your reflection? Do mirrors affect vampires?"

I guess I was asking the right person. It was like I had gotten onto a roller coaster, and now I couldn't stop the ride. I needed to focus on the conversation in front of me, but my sense of reality was slipping with each and every thing that I couldn't explain. Acanthus blinked at me. "This is the first thing you ask? I can see myself fine."

I don't know if I was surprised or disappointed that their answer was sincere. I couldn't help it; I laughed, a small laugh that I cut short. I didn't know what way was up; I guess that was the best place to start. "Sorry, I uh.. I laugh when I'm nervous. Why can't I think around you? Why is everything so... Cloudy... Hazy? Foggy...?"

"On an experienced Werewolf, this wouldn't be so easy. I do apologize, I try my best to suppress it. It's a power I have, called a mesmer. Because you're pack-less, it's affecting you even though I'm not actively engaging it."

"Pack-less. You keep saying that." I frowned. "But the things you're telling me, I didn't even believe in until two minutes ago. And I'm still not entirely sure of their existence. Like, you could just naturally run cold."

Acanthus huffed at that, crossing their arms. "That's by design, Cypress. You're not meant to know of the World of Shadows. We tend to keep humans in the dark about our existence, because they naturally want to experiment on anything different from them. Witches spent years getting ripped apart for protections and sold on the black market, not to mention Vampire fangs. It's not that hard to keep an open mind, now, is it?"

I didn't appreciate that. "Say I do have an open mind, like you say... I didn't even know... What, I'm going to howl at the moon?"

"Take this seriously, Cypress, of course not," Acanthus snapped.

"Well, I don't know! I don't know the first thing about — what do I even ask?"

Acanthus was quiet. I stared at them, increasingly uncomfortable with every passing minute. When they didn't speak, I sighed. "I guess... I guess I need resources. Weaknesses? Anything I should avoid? Where does one find a pack? How does one?"

"That's one thing that I'm having trouble trying to figure out. You said it's been two years? And you haven't been talked to by anyone that asked odd questions, especially someone dressed as a police officer, or a doctor?"

I shook my head. The only night I'd been questioned by a police officer was the night Junior and I got in a bar fight. It was mutual, so neither of us pressed charges, but we were trespassed from the bar. "No. Not that I can think of," I admitted. I'd also written off doctors after the idiot parade. I was tired of being mocked.

Acanthus shook their head, their shoulders sagging. "You are in a very peculiar situation. Usually, the one who changes you assumes a sense of responsibility. There's very much a parental type of pride when one of you changes another."

"Then, there is no 'one of us' Acanthus. I'm not a Werewolf," I huffed. "This wasn't anything like that. I can't help feeling like it was random. I'd never seen this dog before. It—"

"Wolf."

"I'm sorry?"

Acanthus smiled, and I found my eyes darting to their canines again. Had I hallucinated them growing? "Don't apologize, just call it what it is."

The comment irritated me, but I let it slide. If I corrected this douche each time he irritated me, I'd never get answers to what they thought was going on. Taking a deep breath, I exhaled it slowly before I continued. "This, uh, Wolf… It had never been in the neighborhood. The only dog in the neighborhood I lived in was Carlton. A dachshund."

Acanthus hummed at that knowledge, their eyes sliding off to the side as their brow furrowed and they tapped their chin. "So, because you've never seen this Wolf, you thought you were picked at random? Not to mention, not a singular strange interaction with a doctor or an officer." They paused, and I found myself twisting the coffee cup in my hands, fighting the urge to bite at my nails. When they spoke, their eyes slid back to mine, self-assured and confident. "No Cypress, that's not how it works. Every Wolf is picked for a reason. And if they aren't, then there's a cleanup crew to take care of it. Think, there's got to be something we're missing."

We. That we brought my irritation back, and I huffed. As if they knew what I was going through. As if they were there. They were picking apart my trauma and using it for a campfire story. Did they think that this was helping? Maybe it was a mistake to open up to this stranger, even if they did list off my symptoms. It had to have been a stroke of luck. I narrowed my eyes, crossing my arms once more. I couldn't keep the bite out of my voice as I spoke. "Then what was my reason, huh? I've turned over every minute of that dog bite in my head, trying to make sense of what I've been through. I was standing on my doorstep. There is *nothing* I missed."

I think my irritation threw them off. "I don't know." I rolled my eyes. " We'd have to find your maker. We could ask them then."

Oh what the fuck ever, I huffed, my voice getting loud as I pushed off of the wall, moving towards the stairs. Fuck this. "Hey, Acanthus, I got bit by a rabid fucking dog." I stopped and whirled back to them, gripping the glass in my hand tightly and ignoring the urge to toss it to the floor. "I don't have a maker. I don't know what fantasy land you live in, but honestly, I don't have time for this. Unless you have some form of evidence you can show me, I'm about ready to drop this conversation."

"Evidence to what?" Acanthus gave me a long-suffering look. The utterly calm tone they spoke with didn't match their expression.

"I don't know, something," I fought the urge to stomp my foot like a child. "If supernatural creatures are real, how can you prove it to me without me chalking it up to a hallucination? I can't just push my disbelief aside, especially when you're talking about fairy tale bullshit like werewolves and vampires."

Acanthus didn't answer. At least, not with words. Instead, they tilted their hand up, pointing their long nails towards the ceiling. The empty coffee cup flew out of my hand and, with a gasp, I watched it float towards them. Then, it darted to the side, over the railing of the loft, and clattered into the sink below. A moment later, the water turned on, and I blinked in surprise, shaking my head. The full cold brew Acanthus held followed a moment later. Then, they crossed their legs, hovering in midair in front of me.

"I've grown tired of your disbelief. Focus, please. Have you felt a connection to anyone? Heard a voice in your head? Anything?"

I balked, my mouth dropping open. *Holy shit.*

I couldn't explain away the dishes floating down the stairs. The levitating could be a hallucination, but… I let the thought drift off, unfinished, as I took a step forward and leaned down, waving my arm beneath them where their knees should be. *This is definitely real.*

I guess that's one way to give me evidence. This person knew what I'd been going through. Suddenly, so many things that hadn't made sense before clicked into place. My heart was racing, and I straightened back up to stare at them, breathless. I wasn't going to tell a complete stranger that the first genuine connection I've had in two years was with them. This sudden kinship I'd felt would be immediately gone if Acanthus was being honest about connecting me with resources.

Acanthus sighed again, pinching the bridge of their nose. "Look. I want to help. But this won't work unless you're being entirely honest with me."

Lemon Balm

I didn't know what else they wanted from me. I mean, I told them everything that I could remember from the last two years. "I am. I haven't heard anything. I haven't talked to anyone. I've been on my own. I've tried every form of medicine and therapy that I can find, both scientifically backed and holistic. All they could find was an elevated blood cell count, and they told me to try and de-stress."

"That makes all of this very challenging," they trailed off. "How about this? I shall contact the local packs, let them know there's a homeless Pup. We'll find a place for you."

"Hold on," I said, a bit dazed. This decision was very quick, very upending, and very much just about my life. "I'm still caught up on the fact that you just made the coffee fly downstairs and are currently levitating. Can we talk about this before we make a plan?!"

Acanthus laughed, leaning back in the air. "I'm listening."

This arrogant, pompous asshole. All of my questions were up in the air. I grasped for any stray thought that seemed relevant. "Well, you're a Vampire, right? We're in a church, how are you not on fire? It's sunlight, too, aren't you supposed to be like, catatonic?"

"Of all the questions you can ask," Acanthus replied with amusement, "You again ask about me? What about the Wolves?"

I blinked. They had a point. My heart was pounding in my ears as they answered my questions. "No, and no. The type of Vampire that I am can handle small amounts of sunlight. I'm of an age where it's not entirely detrimental to me, but I do need to stay careful, is all. All of that is besides the point."

"What about like, dirt? You're not sleeping in dirt inside that coffin, are you? Does silver hurt you? Can you handle garlic? What about, like, crucifixes? Holy water?"

The questions tumbled out of my mouth like a toddler, rapid fire. Vampires were real. Vampires were real. If they were real, that meant that werewolves were real too, and that I'd been bitten by one. That was the only logical explanation as to why Acanthus knew my list of symptoms. All of the professionals had shrugged their shoulders and told me to keep up my workout routine. I wasn't ready to handle the conversation about werewolves, or even that train of thought, so I kept coming back to *vampires are REAL*. It was easier to handle a stranger's predicament, than it was to think too hard about my own.

Acanthus held up their hand, stopping me. My heart and mind were both racing a mile a minute. "Slow down, Pup. It's a casket, not a coffin. No, I don't sleep in dirt. Silver has no effect on me, and I am quite fond of crucifixes. Does it make any amount of sense that I'd be allergic to a random piece of food or water?"

All of this was way, way more than I bargained for. I was starting to lose my cool, my responses still rapid fire."How do I know I'm not in a coma somewhere? That I'm not just dreaming all of this? Maybe I had some horrific accident two years ago, and my brain's just taking me on this epic adventure to prepare for death?"

Acanthus' eyes narrowed. "Excuse me? Don't be daft."

I laughed, incredulous. "Acanthus. I'm the daft one? Part of my worldview just entirely shut down in all of five minutes. But, I'm the daft one. In any case, I own this place now, whether this is a dream or not. I don't want to be that guy, but I don't have the funds to purchase elsewhere. So..."

Part of me hoped that this was a dream. At least then I could explain the supernatural bullshit. It was like one half of my brain was desperately reaching for connection with this person. I felt like I'd finally found someone who understood what I'd been through the last two years. The other side of my brain wanted to press delete and restart the day from the moment that I woke up, *sans* vampire talk. Maybe I could figure out the 'Motherlode' cheat code in this brain worm and make myself comfortable that way. Acanthus hummed, pulling me out of my mind. "That is somewhat problematic."

"Problematic, how?" I sat on the floor, and they lowered themself in front of me. "I own the church. I'm trying to hear you out and come up with a solution."

"We can talk about the church in a moment," Acanthus replied flatly. "You must know *something* about wolves."

If I couldn't get them to humor me, then I guess I'd have to face the reality of what they were suggesting. My chest was tight as I struggled to recall what I knew about them. It wasn't like I was super into horror or even fiction. "The only thing I know about Werewolves is that silver burns them, is that true? I know that the moon doesn't do shit. If these blackouts are transformations then they seem to be entirely at random."

"This is good. This helps," Acanthus impatiently pushed some hair out of their face, tucking it behind their ear as they spoke. "There are two types of wolves in our world. You seem to be an at-will shifter. This gives me an idea of who to contact. However, the myth about silver is so prevalent because it actually is true. It won't poison you, or burn you, but you will drop like a lead weight if you so much as grab a silver chain."

Did this mean other fantastic creatures were real? What about fae? Demons? They had mentioned those, right? I wondered if there was a database of supernaturals somewhere. Acanthus said something about black markets; is this really why humans had no idea about this? My head was spinning as more and more questions popped up. When Acanthus finally broke the silence, their voice was far more gentle than before. "If you've got no more questions, then I think I should reach out to one of the Big Five. Within the next few days, you may stay here, as we wait for a response."

I had a lot of questions, but I was getting exhausted. "Wait, wait, the Big Five, what's that? Also, there is no, 'you may stay here', I should be the one saying that."

Acanthus shook their head. "You don't understand. This church is important for more reasons than I can explain at the moment. Perhaps I will tell you as we await a response, but the short answer is that I cannot leave it for reasons outside of myself. As for the Big Five, they are the five Werewolf Alphas that rule over various territories here in the United States. The one that rules the Eastern territories is Nekane. She has a network spanning several states and over seventy smaller packs. If anyone can find you a fitting Pack to get in touch with, it would be her."

That actually made sense. If they couldn't lose the church, then the only way that I could think of solving this was to give up my right to the church that I had just bought. I wish I was a crueler person, because it would be way easier for me to tell this vampire to fuck off. Talk about a $20,000 disappointment. This would leave me homeless, whether this Pack gave me resources or not. In a last ditch effort to try and figure out the more believable aspects of this situation, I chewed at my lip before finally answering. "Well, we could be roomies if need be? "

"Roomies?" Acanthus stared at me blankly, lost.

I shrugged. "Roommates?"

"Ah." They went quiet for a moment. "No. That is not suitable. I don't particularly care for company for extended periods of time. Besides, I tend to have many visitors, and I wouldn't want to interrupt your life in that way."

"Oh. Uh, then I guess we're at an impasse..." I looked down at the floor. Something in me wished that the dog — wolf — had finished the job two years ago. "Help set me up with Nekane's "Pack", I guess. I'll just get out of your hair."

Acanthus blinked. "You have no questions or demands? Nothing at all?"

I didn't think I could handle any more conversation about the supernatural world. My thoughts turned to Tasha playing with her amethyst point. "Of course I have questions. I have millions of questions. But I know when to call it quits."

Acanthus shook their head. "No, no. That's not acceptable. It will take a while to hear back from any packs, and clearly you are both skeptical and completely unaware of anything about the supernatural world around you. I will answer the questions that I can while we wait for a response. You have paid money for this place, and where I cannot lose it, I could always buy my home back from you."

Their voice and expression were both earnest. Despite feeling like either one or both of us were bat-shit crazy, it was a comfort to hear them offer. It gave me a cautious sort of hope, and their smile reassured me. "You'd do that?"

"Of course," they replied matter-of-factly. "This has been my home for two centuries. And, I know that you do not know me yet, but I'll have you know that I've made a pact to never turn away someone in need, regardless of the circumstances."

"Of course," I replied, both relieved and completely confused. I went back to staring at the floor. I didn't really get how their pact mattered here, but I guess I was a person in need, in a way. Really, they were the one in need, and just pretending to have control. But, maybe both sides of that were true. I clearly didn't know the whole reality of the situation. "Yeah. You can buy back your church. Help me set up with the Pack, figure out what all of this means for me, and I'll be okay then. I'm sorry for the trouble."

Acanthus grabbed my chin, directing my eyes to theirs. I tensed, startled by the sudden movement and the intense cold of their touch. Flinching, I stared at them, but I didn't pull away. "It was no trouble, Pup. I would tell you if that was so."

I was quiet for a moment, feeling weirdly shy and taken aback by the forward, confident touch. It was as if I couldn't look away. I shivered; they were cold. Turning my head, I broke whatever spell I'd made up in my mind. Did I make up the strange hold they have over me? They had admitted earlier that there was something they found hard to control. My brain was starting to buzz. All of this was so far over my head, and I needed to think. Acanthus lowered their hand from my chin, and my shoulders fell in relief. Licking my lips, I brought my gaze back to theirs. "I think we can absolutely come to an agreement, but I'd like to wait until I'm settled. Is that agreeable?" Despite my reluctance to touch them, I stuck out my hand. "Those are my terms. Help me settle in with a pack, and you can buy back your church. Deal?"

Acanthus eyed me warily, but shook my hand anyway. "I shall write a letter to the local alpha, forthright."

That Time I Wrote A Letter To An Arch Enemy

Acanthus

Even when they tried to withhold from me, I could read Cypress like a book. I'd met so many different people who held the same demeanor as him; lost, alone, begging for answers and desperate for a connection. The Night Garden was full of straying souls, caught in the tangled web of secrecy and glamours that the World of Shadows at large demanded. Humans caught in the crossfire of petty and stubborn immortals. I was not about to pull away the safety that I brought to Cypress. I wasn't in a position to tell him outright about the Night Garden — It was, after all, one of the only escapes from bad actors in the World of Shadows, and one can never be too careful — but I could at least try and right the wrong I had caused by letting my ownership of the church lapse.

I'd been alone for so long. The Night Garden happened around me and through my paths, but I hadn't been connected to it directly for decades. My sharp edges and quick jump to offense through our last few conversations alone was a testament to how uncomfortable I was with letting people close. This church was one of the strongholds of the Night Garden Paths, and where I hadn't had anyone stay for long periods of time, I regularly guided people along to the next stronghold with patience and solemnity. It was lucky that none had come in the night while Cypress slumbered; visitors could come sometimes as often as twice a week or as rare as years apart, and I had no way of knowing who would show up, when.

Cypress was a special case in the World of Shadows. Wolves were rarely left by their makers, and it was even rarer to see a Wolf on the Garden Paths. So, to have this young Pup in my care, thrust into the World of the Shadows and in need of guidance, was extremely odd for me. It was rarer still that Cypress had found a Vampire and not run away screaming. If I could handle this like just another Night Garden refugee, then guidance was something I could give. I was already in my head, trying to draft a letter to Nekane; an enemy, but also the leader of the Eastern territory and one of the Big Five.

In order for you to understand the gravity of the situation, I must elucidate some of our history. Long before I was made, the World of Shadows was integrated into society. This was in the bloody days of endless war and conquest, back in the golden era of civilizations such as Egypt, Babylon, Rome, and Mesopotamia. Vampires, Witches, and Wolves all were known to humans, and we were all distinctly hated and hunted mercilessly. Vampires are notoriously difficult to kill and their fangs are stronger than steel. People would lust over our teeth, claiming them as life lengtheners, and steal our blood for immortality and baneful magic. Wolves at the time could only shift with lunar cycles, and a Wolf pelt was said to heal the wearer and give them magical protection. A Werewolf foot would also be used to keep evil spirits from the home. As far as the Witches went, people regularly made up all kinds of uses for various parts of them. Witches were impossible to spot compared to humans, but humans made up all kinds of signs.

Wolves originally protected Vampires during the day (or so I was told), and Vampires would do the same for Wolves at night. Vampires and Wolves both had extreme strength, but Wolves were stunted when they could not control their shifts. Both would do their best to protect Witches, but the Witches were more connected to Wolves due to a mutual need. Because the Wolves were shackled to the cycles of the moon and unable to shift at will, they needed the Witches to help protect them against the Hunters. Witches lacked the speed and strength of the Vampires and Wolves, and so they needed someone to help when their powers failed. Witches and Wolves were terrified of the Vampires' powers; even the Nosferatu, who would burst into flame at the slightest bit of light.

I was told all of this by my maker, and later found confirmations in the archive my fledgling Corbin keeps. As we hit the ages of Kings and Conquest, when the Carolingians established France, Vampires distanced themselves from Wolves due to an aggression that began within a cluster of packs. These Packs called themselves the Uprising. Apparently, somewhere along the way, Wolves had stopped looking at their relationship to other supernaturals as mutually beneficial. They started to look at themselves as slaves. This began a heated string of disorganized battles and skirmishes that left Witches torn in the middle, and ultimately led to a lot of unnecessary bloodshed. Some Wolves rejected the notion of fighting, but we largely were divided along species lines. The names of these individuals are lost to history and time.

When I was turned in the thirteenth century, the war had calmed into an uneasy agreement within the World of Shadows, and the existence of monsters was hidden from humanity and had slowly begun to fade from the public eye. Alphas and coven leaders from both Witch and Vampire factions were appointed as political leaders from all of the species involved, and rules were drawn up about treaties and land. This was all in the boundaries of Europe. Sometime between then and now, there was a fundamental shift of power. The Wolves began to learn how to shift at will sometime in the fifteenth century. Now, Wolves basically run the World of Shadows in the West.

Vampires have all largely either gone into hiding or become extinct in North America. Not all vampires are created equal; there are different factions of Vampire that are divided among effects of the blood curse. We have a legend, called the Kingdom of the Four, that explains such factions. Nosferatu were the most stunted; they were disfigured by the Blood Curse, which made it hard for them to become close to others, and any stray sunlight would set them aflame. Chiara needed to find the correct type of donor at the correct celestial situation; they could only turn someone during a full solar eclipse, and it was impossible to know whether or not the curse would take, or the blood would reject the fledgling and boil them alive. Alphosine had the easiest time making Fledglings, but their strength left their young cocky and far too willing to tempt danger. Anesh, like me, had no issues turning. The problem lay in whether or not the fledgling would survive the change with their mind intact. It left us unwilling to try to make more like us.

Thanks to Wolves and Hunters alike murdering us, many of my fanged brethren have fled. The ones that I had kept contact with now are across the pond in Europe. My dear fledgling Corbin resides in my old Château in Grabels, and holds a lot of our histories and legends in his library. Before I turned him in the sixteenth century, all of what I've spoken of was passed down by word alone. But, the story of Corbin is best left for another time.

After Wolves at large learned how to shift at will, Witches were largely stuck by their own alliances and held under pressure by the Wolves, in servitude. Where they had once been on level playing ground, the Wolves became terrifying to the Witches. Emboldened by their newfound power, Wolves also fought Vampires regularly for land. It became common practice for Wolves and Vampires both to force Witches into using their powers as 'clean up crews' and glamours to hide from the humans. The Witches would lose their protection if they refused. There are no bad species, just bad actors within.

Our politics left a lot of people ostracized from the "expected" stations of our lives — supernaturals being hunted by humans for parts throughout history, Wolves abusing their Pack mates or Witches to show their strength, Witches going out of control with their powers and attacking the nearby peaceful people, acts of revenge or hatred… Name it, and it has been done in the World of Shadows. We have no laws to speak of outside of what is commonly agreed on by the supernaturals at large; stay hidden from humans, prevent any more needless death, and hide supernatural happenings from being found. Everything else in our politics surrounds these tenets.

This is where I came in; several hundred years ago, I, along with several other Vampires and Witches, and even a Wolf or two, had created an underground called The Night Garden in order to discreetly funnel people away from trouble. It was all we could do to right the wrongs caused by the rigid camps of supernaturals. So, who would I be, if I put all of that context aside and tossed out the opportunity to help this poor Wolf?

Little beams of light bounced off of the velvet from the cloak on the floor and played on the off-white walls. I raised my hand, pointing towards the wall, and the cloak floated itself to a hook beside its brethren. Quietly, I spoke in the gentlest tone that I could muster. I wasn't certain if they were happy or not at the thought of joining a pack. "It shall take at least a week to hear back from the packs after I send the letter. Might you want to bring your luggage in…? My home is yours, quite literally as it were, and you are welcome to it. I only ask that you stay out of this loft without express permission."

It wasn't that I didn't trust them. Rather, this was the easiest way to keep my carefully constructed barriers in place. The way that we had been speaking in the last several hours felt too close to be strangers, but it was still very much a tenuous connection; acquaintances, at best, and any tenuous connection was enough for me to run far away. Solitude, like it or not, was the last grounded part of me that kept me from floating off into the void (or so I told myself).

"Alright, cool. A deal's a deal…" They stood, and then slouched, their impressive height falling and their broad chest slumping inward.

I looked towards the rose window, watching the glass glitter as the sun's intense rays filtered in. Deliberately, I stretched, easing the tensions from my back. My bones creaked in a way that relieved some long-standing aches, and I groaned softly. Tossing my hair out of my face, I relaxed and started towards the stairs. Making my way down to the main room, I heard the careful thump of bare feet behind me and a small part of me relaxed. At least they were respecting my wishes of vacating the loft.

I thought of the coffee that had gone untouched into the sink. Sometimes I would sip coffee, despite the risk of flu symptoms, but the bitterness burned my throat as it went down. All human food tasted horrible, but I liked coffee for the warm aroma and the heat that permeated my frozen skin. Even cold coffee seemed to bring a warmth with it, pleasantly tingling through me in waves. Liquids were easier than solids when it came to food, but if I chanced too much, it would leave me writhing for hours.

Down in the living room, the curtains were open to let in the day. The light stung my skin immediately where it kissed. I didn't mind the pain, but I closed the curtains with a pulse of my power. Magic is interesting; I take it for granted most of the time, but to use it is the most fascinating sensation. Picture energy laying latent in your body, like particles of white light. To use the magic feels like drawing that light into a concentrated ball, tingling and bright in your chest, before directing it to its destination. It leaves a faint tingling in its wake, like a limb falling asleep. When you use too much of it, it's less of a fatigue and more of a hollow emptiness that rings in the darkness of your bones.

Cypress went to the door, then paused. "Is it okay if I go outside?" I tilted my head and furrowed my brow, and they clarified with, "The sun."

I nodded. "It is fine for you to open the door,"

I moved so that I was out of the direct line of light that would pool in the doorway. They slipped out, and I sat in the puffy-cushioned chair in front of the secretary desk, to the left of the door. Cypress being here had put a wrench in my plans; I needed to head into New York. My personal supplies were running low, and I'd been planning a trip before they showed up on my doorstep. This letter would give me an excuse to run my errands without having to explain my absence.

Cypress was back a moment later, carrying a camping cot, a singular box of personal effects, a cooler, a pillow, and a badly shredded blanket. As they placed the things behind the couch with their duffel bags, my heart twisted. They likely didn't have anything else, or left everything else behind because it was either ruined, or wouldn't fit into the car. The lack of items weighed me down with their tale of sorrow. They are a fitting person to have found me, of all people...

Cypress dropped the cooler, and the top went askew. "Fuck — "

They scrambled to readjust it before any ice fell to the floor.

"Language, Pup," I responded, though my eye twitched in annoyance at the disrespect — I never did like curses. They grabbed their cooler and rushed to the kitchen.

Holding my hand up, I summoned a notebook and a pen to my hands. It was time to draft a letter. It took me a moment of thought before I could begin. There was no love between Nekane and I; a river of blood separated us, and both had lost beloved companions and family at the other's hand. I claim no innocence in previous wars, though our politics kept us safe. The red tape and bureaucracy an attack would cause in this age was enough to keep her at bay, so long as I behaved within my own designated territories. For her to attack me would mean mobilizing a new war.

In a few minutes, I had scrawled out a quick message to my arch enemy that I hoped was civil and forthright. After all, I wanted Cypress to be comfortable; putting the past aside was the best thing that I could possibly do for both myself and for Cypress. The treaty we had also gave me confidence that I was not opening myself up for an attack or aggression. It was written that I was to contact the Big Five if there was a lost wolf; my hands were tied. I reread my neat, tight cursive closely once more.

Nekane,

I hope that this letter finds you well. I know you have no love for me, but I hope to appeal to your better nature. Not for me, but for a lone wolf that had found their way to my doorstep. It seems he was bitten by a stray two years ago and knows nothing about the World of Shadows. I will do what I can to teach him of our current situation, but you and I both know I cannot teach wolf nature to a Wolf. I am reaching out to you to honor our treaty, and because you are one of the Big Five, I trust that if you cannot fold them into your pack, you know of another lesser pack that can.

Please respond with grace and haste.

-Acanthus

As I folded the letter in thirds, Cypress made his way back into the living room and flopped onto one of the couches. It was nice to see that he was starting to settle in. "Comfortable?"

"These couches are in better shape than they look."

I laughed. "Indeed. Now, where were we?"

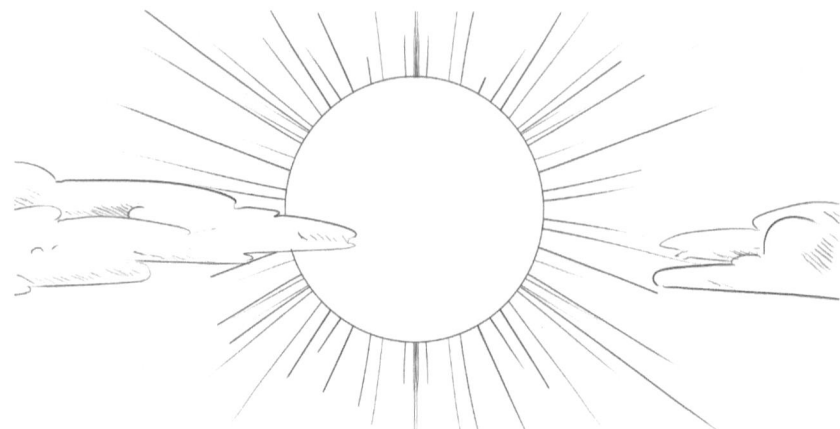

That Time We Decided to Train

Cypress

"Well, we were talking about the plan with the church, I guess, and about the supernatural stuff." As I spoke, my eyes slid towards the clock on the top of the writing desk. "But, it's almost eleven."

Despite their laid back posture, Acanthus looked exhausted; they had dark purple rings beneath their eyes, and their whole body sagged. I hadn't noticed the night before. The vampire shrugged, but a yawn betrayed them. I laughed and shook my head. "Listen, any questions I have can wait until the evening. We're both tired."

Acanthus hesitated, then relented with a nod. "Very well. I will get this letter out to the postbox first thing in the evening, and then we'll start to prepare."

"That's cool."

Acanthus rose from their writing desk with another extended yawn, crossing their legs again in the air. They rose straight up to the loft, not bothering with the stairs. Watching them still made my stomach flip over itself, admiration and fear fighting to dominate my senses. Everything about them felt like it both belonged and didn't. They were beautiful, like a walking statue carved by Michelangelo. But, they used all of these fantastical powers with such ease and grace that it made my knees quake. I was terrified, like a kindergartner watching a horror movie. It was unsettling to watch someone so frail and young-looking wield such insane power without a second thought.

When they disappeared over the side of the railing, the soft *thump* of their feet hitting the floorboards knocked some dust loose from the ceiling. I shook my head and stood, my eyes darting to my small pile of belongings. At least this allowed me to settle in and rest. I set up my cot in the corner of the room, not wanting to use any portion of their loft. They had set a boundary, after all; every therapist I'd ever had always stressed that boundaries were important to respect.

I didn't get much sleep that day. My mind was flooded with more questions, plaguing me each time I closed my eyes. *What am I going to do with a fucking Pack? What IS a Pack? Where am I going to go, will I be able to have some semblance of control over my life? I have no idea what I can do, what powers I have. Can I levitate like Acanthus? No Cypress, that's dumb. What is Acanthus' deal, why are they so eager to help me?*

I tossed and turned on my cot in the main room, and when I got tired of that, I tried to move the cot from the corner, up against the back of the couch. The hours passed slowly, and I alternated between glaring at the window and hiding my face in the blankets. As the pinks, purples, and oranges of dusk started to creep into view through the crack in the curtains, I gave up and searched out some food in the kitchen. Quiet, cat-like steps sounded from the direction of the stairs, and I turned to face them with a mouth full of banana. "Hello," Acanthus spoke, their whispery voice barely audible over the sound of my own munching.

I waved in response. Seconds passed in awkward silence as I fought the food in my mouth. They hung back near the stairs, and we stood in silence for far too long before I finally disappeared the banana with a loud swallow. I shrugged, trying to play it cool. "Hey."

The vampire looked paler than the previous night, the dark circles still under their beautiful hazel eyes. *Are they hungry? What do they even eat, am I going to find fangs in my neck soon?*

I tried not to let my mind linger on these thoughts for too long, but Acanthus' eyebrow was already raised expectantly. "Come on, Pup, out with it. I can see the question written directly on your face."

"You're hungry, aren't you? What, uh… What goes into that? Do you have to drink blood, or like, what? You drank coffee yesterday."

"I'm not going to eat you, if that's what you're asking," they replied flatly. "I do, however, need blood." They leaned against the wall, using their right shoulder as a rest and crossing their legs at the ankle as they inspected their fingernails. "Next question?"

Taking another bite of the banana, I stalled. I tossed the peel towards the trash and watched as it arched through the air and perfectly fell into the open bin. Satisfied, I pulled out a small pack of ready-made tuna from the cooler and ripped it open without much thought, grabbing a spoon and resting against the counter. It wasn't until I had a spoonful of the stuff in my mouth before a tart flavor made me pause. Turning the pack around, I stared at the font sprawled across the front. *Lemon Garlic* was the flavor. They had mentioned they weren't allergic, but I was working with what little horror movie knowledge I had.

Acanthus snapped, dropping their hand and rolling their eyes. "I know you don't know anything about the World of Shadows, and don't fully trust me yet, but don't be ridiculous. Let me ask you, you're allergic to the capsaicin in peppers, everyone is, but do you not still crave the spice? I can handle garlic fine. Eat your tuna."

I snorted softly. "Am I that obvious?"

"About as clear as glass, Pup. Ask about wolves, about Packs, about, I don't know, anything that actually pertains to you."

I blinked. "I don't know what I don't know," I grumbled as I took another bite of tuna, forcing Acanthus to wait and think about that for a moment. "I guess, just tell me about Wolves and packs and whatever? I don't know what to expect."

Acanthus hummed. "Yes, that sounds fair. How about we do it as a game?"

"A game?" Acanthus hardly seemed like the type to play games.

"Yes. How about I try and train you through your shifting, and we can test your memory with questions."

I thought about that for a minute. My mind flashed to a time that felt like a thousand years ago, where I was lifting weights in the gym and feeling the burn in my muscles. I wondered if shape-shift training was like working out; a challenge that would make my physical form burn and feel the work. That actually did sound like a lot of fun. "Yeah, sure. Just let me finish eating."

"Fair enough," they pushed off of the wall. "I need to drop off that letter, so finish your meal in the meantime, and we shall set up the rules when I'm back."

They didn't wait for a reply as they turned on their heel and stepped towards the door. It creaked open on its own and I shuddered. They grabbed a gray and black parasol from a large planter pot in the corner. Making sure they were clear of the jamb, they opened the parasol and then the door closed, hiding them from view. I finished eating in silence.

When I was done, I tossed my trash into the bin and laid on my cot. *I should make a list of questions for them.*

It wasn't too long before they had returned. Or, at least, it didn't feel like it. I must have fallen asleep, because the next thing I knew, I was waking up to the sound of the door opening in the pitch black of our main living space. When Acanthus walked in, their hair was pulled into a messy bun. The candles scattered around the room burst into life, and I blinked, ignoring the way my skin crawled. "Alright, Pup. Are you ready to train?"

I actually don't remember much of that first night. The start was innocent enough; Acanthus returned from delivering the letter to one of the little blue post boxes that are littered throughout America. Where they went, I have no idea. But, I think the completion of a task did them well; they looked younger and more awake, and there was a welcoming vibe that they were giving off. My muscles relaxed, and I grinned at them. "So, what's this training like? I used to lift weights when I was a functioning human, is it the same idea? Working out the muscles, or whatever?"

Acanthus' eyes lit up with mirth, their lips stretching into a shy smile, their fangs poking over their bottom lip. I fought back a shudder at the sight. Come on, *Cypress, scary fangs or no, this is Acanthus. At the very least, they're helping you.*

"Silly Pup," Acanthus shook their head. "It's nothing like weightlifting. Magic, including shifting powers, resides in awareness. You can equate it more to studying, but adding a physical element to it."

That made absolutely no sense to me. "How am I supposed to study what I don't know, with no material or textbook? This isn't a college course, Acanthus."

Acanthus laughed, and the sound was musical. "Hardly. I won't claim it to be easy, but also, I'm not certain how it will feel for you. I'm not claiming to be the best person to teach you about Wolves; I don't know much, myself. I do know that to get you to shift, I'll have to be rude."

My face scrunched in confusion. "How does being rude make me learn to shift?"

Acanthus tilted their head. "Do you remember how you felt, when I was pressing you for information about the deed?"

I thought about the way that I pushed them back, the feeling of losing control at the start of a blackout, the strange burning and buzzing of what felt like electricity in my veins, and the disorientation of waking up after the lost time. I shuddered, and nodded. "Point, taken and noted."

Acanthus sighed, and I reached up to tousle my own hair, glancing at them. They had a look in their eyes — something not quite pity, but close enough to where it irritated me — and I stubbornly averted my gaze as they answered me. "Whatever that feels like, that's the signs of the shift."

I stood, shrugging. "Alright. You're gonna insult me, and I'm gonna shift. I can't say that sounds like the best time, but I guess if you think it'll help me."

"I don't want to insult you," Acanthus protested quickly, "But I don't really know of another way to make you start to gain control."

I shook my head. "Don't worry about it. If it's gotta get done, then it makes sense. Just like… I guess, how does this help?"

Acanthus stepped towards the front of the main room. They glanced towards the door, then turned to look at me. "I want you to pay attention to the way it feels when you are about to shift. Think about how it would feel to gain control over that power, and remember the way you feel when you call forward your Wolf. It would be easier outside, but I don't suppose you're comfortable with that?"

"No," I shot back, a spike of anxiety ripping through my chest.

I was stubborn, but I think I believed them subconsciously about being a Werewolf. The fact that every time I'd black out, I woke up naked, was a fact that I couldn't ignore. Sometimes the smells of wet dogs or bruised grass clung to me. Sometimes, I felt like I hadn't drank anything in a year; tasting nothing but drool and mud. It was the only thing that explained the tufts of white fur that appeared every time I'd lost memory. The tufts of fur haunted me; from the first time with my gym bag, to the time where I glanced at myself in the mirror.

"Very well," Acanthus' soft voice cut through my thoughts, and I found myself relieved at the interruption. "Inside it is. If you don't want to rip your clothes, you're going to want to lose them."

That was incredibly blunt. My cheeks burned with a blush as I crossed my arms, looking down at myself. "Do I… Do I have to?"

Acanthus once again hit me with one of those compassionate looks. This time, I held their gaze, insecure. I trusted them as well as I could trust someone I'd just met. They reached their left hand into the air and twitched their fingers. The velvety, soft emerald cloak rested on my shoulders. "Wear this," they said softly, "It will protect your modesty."

I sagged, woozy from the sudden release of tension that came with the relief. It was agonizingly embarrassing to think about standing there naked, and the gesture highlighted Acanthus' kindness. "Okay, yeah," I said, fidgeting beneath the cloak. "I'm still going to ask you to turn around."

They laughed, before turning on their heel in a fluid motion. "Very well. Prepare yourself, and then we shall begin."

72

This is one of the last things that I remember. Outside of that, the blackouts stole most of that night away.

Acanthus

Cypress may not be able to remember much of the training during that first night, but I do. I'd taken my time delivering the letter, and made sure to hunt before I returned. I'd flown into the city, and stopped at one of my various locations. They didn't have a donor available, but they did have blood bags. I drank two, asked for more to be delivered the next night, and then liberated a poor unfortunate squirrel from their life on the way home. I was far less irritable when I walked back into the church.

When we started training, I floated in front of them, and they watched me awkwardly as I spoke of things I thought would make them angry. I'm not proud of my methods, but I can confidently say they worked. Floating in the air was strategic on my part; if Cypress lunged, I could speed away quicker in air than on foot.

"I don't suppose you have a plan for when you go to Nekane's?"

"How can I plan, if I don't know what to expect?"

I snorted. "I don't know, Cypress, I told you to ask questions. Can you not think of any?"

A lot of the night was compiled in these snarky back-and-forths, and they got irritated enough to shift very quickly. Once the shift would happen, I'd tell them something important — something about Wolves, Nekane's pack, vampires, or the like — and then I'd reach for them once they calmed, pressing a spot towards the base of their neck below their ear to force them out of the shift. They'd lay there, panting, with sweat dripping from their hair.

This first training session, I'd ask the same few questions. "Come now, Cypress, what year is it?"

No answer. "What did I just tell you about the Pack bonds?"

No answer. "How often should a wolf shift in order to avoid body pains?"

No answer. "Do you remember anything I said about the Big Five?"

No answer, at first. Then — a weak little whine. "No…"

And so, I would go back to goading, and repeat myself once they were back to being a Wolf. This method of training felt more like interrogation than help, but I was working with a limited toolbox. Most of the people who came through The Night Garden paths were already established and comfortable in their supernatural abilities. Cypress was a special case. My closest trusted ally of the Werewolf variety was in Wisconsin, four states away from my little haven. I highly doubted that

Cypress would want to uproot their life even further just to be properly trained in a Pack.

Not to mention, that ally was another of the Big Five. She would be taking a large public risk, accepting a stray pup into her pack that was found outside of her territory. It was safer for the Night Garden that I wrote Nekane, despite our differences. And so, I did what I could; goad, then question, then goad, then question. And through it all, I tried my best to ignore how much each shift wore them down.

Cypress

I can't recall details about the conversations throughout the process. In the portions I did remember, it was choppy and dulled, like looking through a colored piece of thick glass.

I could recall bits and pieces of being on all fours. I remember twirling around and seeing evidence of my own tail, feeling the ache of my bones, and the disorientation when I would shift back. I ended the night exhausted, only remembering bleary, confused blips between large swaths of nothing. I crashed hard around dawn, and slept straight through the day and a little past sunset.

When I awoke, Acanthus was leaning against a counter in the kitchen, their fangs sunk into a blood bag. My skin prickled, a deep disgust somewhere low in my stomach. A sour taste bloomed in my mouth, but I bit it back, my gut twisting. *Where did that even come from?*

"Hey," they greeted me after pulling their teeth from the silicon.

"Hey," I rubbed at the back of my neck awkwardly. I could see them clearly from my cot. My stomach growled loudly, and my cheeks heated. I couldn't remember eating the night before, after the tuna and banana at dusk. Wordlessly, Acanthus made a fluid motion to open the refrigerator and pull out some grapes, rescued from my cooler. I blinked, slid out of the cot, and took several steps towards the kitchen as I reached for the bag. "Thanks," I said as they settled back against the counter.

"Don't mention it. Shifts take calories. I bet you're starving," they quipped, before their teeth sank back into the blood bag.

I averted my eyes, leaning down and re-opening the fridge, focusing on the contents instead of their feeding. I grabbed my first and most potent love — coffee — from the cold. The crystalline pitcher was nearly empty. I'd have to brew more. I heard the unceremonious *slurp* of air bubbles in a straw, like someone sucking the last few drops from a soda. I assumed that they were done with their snack and flinched at the noise. Acanthus spoke, ignoring my discomfort. "How much of last night do you remember?"

I paused, standing with the pitcher in my hand. Thinking about it, I admitted, "Not much, but enough bits and pieces to have a rough idea. How did yesterday go?"

"You weren't aggressive, if that's what you're asking," Acanthus replied dryly. "Your shifts seem to be happening easier, but I couldn't get answers from you when you shifted back. I'm guessing you still can't remember when you're a Wolf?"

I shook my head, my disappointment hanging between us heavily in the air. Glancing their way, my frown deepened as they sank their teeth into another blood bag. *Where did they even pull that from? The counter?*

"I still am not fully sure if I can believe I'm changing the way that you say," I said thoughtfully. "I can remember bits and pieces of last night, but I'm not sure what is hallucination and what is reality."

They glared at me. I busied my hands with the coffee, pouring myself a cup before continuing. "Don't worry. You've made it impossible not to believe you. Where did you even get those?"

They blinked at me, thrown off by the subject change as I brought the cup of cold brew to my lips. Acanthus quickly drained the bag before they once again released their fangs from the silicon with a little *pop.* "Delivery," they replied matter-of-factly.

I snorted, my coffee flying through my nostrils and burning my nose and throat as I began to cough. They stared at me, a subtle lift to their eyebrows and a smile playing on their lips as I tried to compose myself. Do you know how much it hurts to literally shoot coffee through your nose? I choked and sputtered through the pain as I exclaimed, "Delivery?! It's not a pizza, Acanthus!"

They tossed the empty blood bags into the sink. "I am in connection with several Witches who have blood supplies, Cypress. It might make you laugh, but it's not a joke."

I huffed, rolling my eyes. An easy comfort had started to fall into our dynamic. I think I'd already started thinking of us as friends, especially with how much they were doing for me. "How does that even work? I've only seen random vampire movies and stuff like that. Wouldn't blood bags make you sick? Or is that only, like, vampire media?"

"One of the unfortunate constants in any Vampire myth is drinking blood. And that is one thing that the humans have gotten right. At least, for the type of Vampire that I am. There are different types of Vampires that can feed on different things. When I drink, I drink small sips from consenting partners, and my appetite is small. I can survive just fine off of animals or blood bags like this, though you can think of that as the equivalent of a fast food diet; filling, but lacking the nutrients I need. Eventually, I will need to feed from a human, but this will get me by."

Without thinking it through, I blurted, "Feed from a human? You're not gonna like, eat me in my sleep, are you?"

I thought of how my skin crawled when they ate from the bags. I wasn't sure why, but it was uncomfortable. I guess it was weird to see someone sink their teeth into a silicon bag full of blood. But, the idea made sense; a portable ration, stable and independent of a food source. Huh. The vampire equivalent of MRE's, I guess. At least, the way Acanthus spoke about it felt slightly more tactical than a fry shack or something. I wondered idly if Acanthus had ever been in the military.

Acanthus once again cocked an eyebrow, tension making their posture straighten as their eyes narrowed. I'd learned that this was one of their tells; they were starting to lose patience with me. "You're a Werewolf, Cypress. I can't feed from you, but that's beside the point. You are a guest, and non-consenting. I wouldn't harm you. Is that really what you think of me?"

I didn't mean to offend them. Ghosts of my old friends hung at the back of my mind, and my shoulders ached with the tension that flooded them. "No," I averted my eyes, cheeks burning as my face fell.

They didn't need to know that watching them drink from the bags made my stomach roll and twist, my insides knot, and bile sting at the back of my throat. It wasn't their fault; they had to eat. Trying to keep the tone humorous and light, I said, "I didn't expect to see you slurping from a silicon bag when I woke up this evening. Though, it was a pleasant surprise to see that you don't have the problem literally every movie Vampire has. The blood wasn't all over your face."

The offense spread through their beautiful hazel eyes, the color blazing. Their gaze fell to the floor, arms crossing and shoulders hiking up to their ears as the corners of their mouth turned down and their head lowered. Their eyes hooded to half-mast, and guilt gnawed at me. Maybe it was a little mean of me to say, based on their reaction. I didn't know why. Acanthus spoke, their voice gentle despite the display of emotion. "Why do you do that?"

"Are we not friends?"

Acanthus paused. The silence lasted for a touch too long, before they sucked in a breath, answering in a sigh. "Last I checked, friends aren't catty to one another."

They had no way of knowing, but that singular sentence may have well been a bullet. "Oh..." Did I really come off as catty? "Hey, I'm sorry. I didn't mean to be a jerk. I was just messing around, we can talk. I do have questions for you..."

They stared, pity in their gaze. I fidgeted, but the tension left and I sagged with relief when they nodded. "Very well. Let's sit down and continue our conversation, but we can do it in between training. Agreed?"

"Yes," I breathed, "Sounds great."

With that, I donned the emerald cloak that they had let me borrow, and we began. I remembered a lot of this second night, this time. Between shifts, Acanthus spoke about the rich history that brought them here, and a little about the Wolves they contacted. They mostly stuck to the more recent past — from the 1800s or so. There was a lot, particularly about their relationship to the local Wolf packs of the area. They kept their own personal history out of the picture. From what I understood, they'd had an 'irredeemable altercation', whatever that meant, with Nekane.

All of this detail is stuff I can recall through that strange dulled-glass effect on my memory. They had a treaty, but hadn't had good luck with the packs in recent years, so they were sticking their neck out for me. Thinking about that too hard gave me a sense of dread. I didn't want to cause trouble, but I couldn't help but wonder what it meant to be connected with a pack. I'd never had a healthy family connection, and the way I handled my friendships was easily an arms' length style. I couldn't imagine the pack mentality, or what it would feel like to move as a unit. Thinking about it made my heart race and my stomach twist.

When I said as much to Acanthus, they hesitated. "I cannot give you particulars, I'm afraid," their eyes were full of regret. "From what I know, the pack Alphas keep houses for those members in the pack who do not have them, but you're allowed to move freely within your territory. I wish I could tell you more."

I didn't like leaving it there, but I really didn't have a leg to stand on. They'd ask me questions as a wolf, and I would close my eyes and picture the feel of standing on my own two feet, and my voice running through my throat. It did the trick and I changed back to human with a gasp and an ache in my bones to answer them. Who was the president? What year was it? What's my name? How many fingers were they holding up? What color was something? What did they just tell me about Wolves?

The more I could remember these things through a shift, the more confident Acanthus had become. The end of this second day left me dead on my feet, and I don't remember when we stopped for the night.

By the third day, I was so tired, the shifting process started to lag. It was getting harder and harder to call forth my Wolf. We'd been training for at least two hours by the time it hit eleven thirty, and I was wholly disconnected from my body. I could feel myself, unsteady and shaking on my feet. Acanthus' eyes lingered on me, and when they didn't ask me a question, I tilted my head, staring back at them. They smiled, but it didn't quite reach their eyes. "I think you've had enough, Cypress. You should eat something and take the rest of the night off."

I shifted back, panting. "But, I've been doing so well! I don't want to take off now, not when I'm starting to remember my shifts…"

"I know," they said, and reached to pat my shoulder. I whimpered, my bones singing in the hateful buzz of pain. "But, Cypress, don't you think you'd remember more, if you gave yourself a day to rest? It's not a race, young Pup. If you fuel yourself, you'll tackle it with a fresher mind, tomorrow."

I frowned at them. "I can take it, Acanthus."

"I know, Cypress."

I took that as a confirmation to keep going and I closed my eyes to call forward my Wolf. The shift was slow, and my energy seemed to entirely dry up when I was finally on all fours. I panted, falling on my side with a low groan. Acanthus gasped and then shook their head, falling to their knees beside me as a jar of something rocketed through the air and into their outstretched hand. I closed my eyes, the muscle and meat around my bones tender, as if they had splintered and the shards were worming their way to the surface. "Cypress, I'm serious, stop it. You're going to make yourself ill," Acanthus chided me.

I huffed in response. The last thing that I remember was a cool, comforting tingling, as their cold hands started to work a salve into my skin. It must have been at least midnight when I fainted.

I was startled awake hours later. The low light left a gloom hanging heavily in the room. There was a singular candle burning off to the right, and it was difficult to wait for my eyes to adjust. I was laying on my camping cot, with blankets thrown over me. Acanthus was sitting at the desk, their face illuminated by candlelight. I groaned, and my head flopped back to my pillow.

I heard them chuckle in their reserved way, and they flipped their hair out of their eyes as I slowly turned my head to look at them. "Shit," I muttered, my voice thick and slow with exhaustion, "I'm sorry, Acanthus."

"Language, Cypress. But, whatever for?"

What was I apologizing for? Averting my gaze, I mumbled into my arm, embarrassed. "You shouldn't have to keep taking care of me."

There was silence, but I felt them looking at me. I raised my eyes to theirs, and witnessed a plethora of emotions cross their face. It was hard to describe; a war between happiness, sadness, pity, anger, frustration, hurt, and regrets flitted across their features. It seemed like compassion and warmth won out as their face settled into something soft, open, and kind. The reaction confused me, and I leaned up on an elbow, wincing at the aches in my bones. "What?"

"I don't mind," their whispery voice glided like cool water across my senses. Something made me want to move closer to them, but I stubbornly stayed in my cot. "But," they continued, "I am more curious as to why you think I would care."

Their focus left me vulnerable. It was like my skin was cracking apart, and they had broken a façade I didn't realize I was wearing. I hated the exposed feeling that came with it. I hadn't readily accepted the existence of monsters or the things my senses told me were there and true. My first gut reaction to this person in front of me was to question and mock, and even now I was having difficulty with all of our conversation. *Am I a bad person? I might be a bad person.*

I thought about the crisis of both worldview and consciousness I'd had over the last several days. They had, in one devastating sentence, shut down my entire perception of how friendships worked. I thought of Junior, who kept me around only to punch at my weak spots; of Kassidy and Kennedy, who largely wanted to treat me like eye candy or a visible protector when they were compromised; of Frankie and Vic, who laughed off Junior's cruel jokes and tried to keep everything focused on alcohol and girls. I didn't even know much of anything about Acanthus; I hadn't asked much. I hadn't cared enough to.

My throat was tight, a lump constricting my airway and making it hard to breathe. I hated how thin and watery my breaths sounded, and I stared at the floor, turning over each and every decision I'd made in the last few months. I'd gone back to my mother's only to get away from the city. I'd completely ghosted Joanna, after stringing her along for months. Regret stung the insides of my stomach and chest, and I chewed on my lip, clearing my throat. Sheepishly, I rubbed at the back of my neck. I was getting really well acquainted with the scratches in the oak floorboards. "Well…"

I trailed off, my voice getting a bit quieter. Clearing my throat again, I took a deep breath and then let it out in a short sigh. "You've been doing a lot to help me. You could probably be doing better things with your time."

Acanthus wasn't having anything to do with my bullshit. Anger flashed in their eyes. I was about to ask if I had offended them, but they spoke before I could. "Better things? This may come as quite a surprise to you Cypress, but…" They paused. "I do not mind sharing my time with you. Don't waste your time worrying about it."

I was surprised. Genuinely. Something about that made my heart warm, but it confused me. They had been so curt and matter-of-fact since

Lemon Balm

I came here. Their words replayed in my mind — *I don't much care for company.* "I almost thought you couldn't wait to get rid of me."

They laughed, a rich full laugh that warmed me. "Young Pup, you are funny. While having my solitude and space will be refreshing, I cannot argue that these past few days have been genuinely enjoyable."

Young Pup. I turned the words over in my mind. It didn't offend me; their tone was warm as they said it, but it was strange to have someone that looked younger than me address me like I was a kid. The thoughts faded quickly enough. As I held the cloak firmly shut and slid out of the cot, that serene calm flooded over me again. It was nice to feel wanted, and the creeping tendrils of self-hatred were beaten back a little bit. I liked the thought of genuinely moving from stranger to tenuous friendship with Acanthus. Maybe there was a way to reconsider leaving. Or at least, if the packs didn't work out, maybe they'd let me crash here, if I asked again.

I stretched my sore arms, and groaned at the stiff tension in them. I was achey, tired, and extremely hungry. My stomach growled in anticipation, and I looked down at it, poking at the fat of my gut. Leaning over, I grabbed some clothes and quickly pulled them on beneath the cloak before abandoning it on the cot. Then, I crossed the room to the fridge in the kitchen. Looking inside, there was half a pitcher of cold brew coffee left from this morning, but my breakfast must've finished off the food. I closed the fridge door, and contemplated. I hadn't kept a ton of food in my little cooler, after all. It was my original plan to go shopping the day after I had arrived, but obviously my fanged friend complicated things.

Tilting my head to look out of the window, the streaks of pink and purple were coming into the sky. It was nearly dawn. I could drive to the city and get food, or I could just tough it out until morning. If I went now, then there would be less risk of people seeing me. But, the thought sent anxiety clawing at my rib cage. I'd spent the last two years relying on grocery deliveries and takeout. I looked towards the main room, thinking of Acanthus and their careful confidence. Maybe I'd just ask them to come along.

They walked into the kitchen, and I felt their presence before I saw them out of the corner of my eye. They were so quiet. "Acanthus," I said conversationally, "I need to go into town."

How much money did I have on hand? I hadn't budgeted since I closed on the church, and I think my phone bill had auto-paid in between. I didn't like how disconnected I'd become. "Ah, a Pup finds their voice," they grinned at me, and a blush crept across my face. "We can't have you going hungry."

Something about their face made my thoughts stop abruptly, as if time slowed. My focus was entirely on them; my hands and feet tingled,

80

a strange swirling sensation in my brain. Why did I find it so hard to think around them? I heard them laugh, and it snapped me out of the strange spell. Was this some sort of trance their powers caused? Was it an obsession? I didn't think it was a romantic or obsessive thing, but I had no idea. Acanthus spoke, their voice playful. "What's going through your head?"

I snorted, embarrassed by my distraction. "Nothing," I replied, smoothing my freshly donned flannel over my stomach. "Do you want to come with me?"

The change of subject was easier to handle than the strange hyper-focus I'd fallen into. It made me nervous to look at them. *I must just be hungrier than I thought.* I wasn't sure what their answer would be, as they had made it pretty obvious that they didn't like going into the city, but I figured that it couldn't hurt to ask.

Acanthus

The cold pit of fear opened in my core before I realized what it was. When Cypress said he had to go into town, he meant Peekskill, but I immediately thought of Manhattan. My trips to the city were always carefully planned, but this was something dropped into my lap. My heart began its familiar hummingbird pattern that started up every time I thought of leaving my little sanctuary. I didn't want to leave Cypress alone to navigate by themself, but I never got used to today's society. It was full of noise; terrible, terrible noise. There were bright lights and technology everywhere; moving billboards and chaos from people shackled to their four inch battery-operated prisons.

Everyone was agitated, and only had an end destination in mind, never enjoying their journey. Empathy had all but died. People cared more for the devices in their hand than the people around them, and there was a horrid lack of spaces to breathe. My little church was only about an hour from New York City. I could already hear the cacophony of sounds in my mind — horns blaring, shouts in the night, music drifting from open windows and the clink of silverware from restaurants, a crying woman on the corner of a block, barking dogs... the overwhelming rush of it all became thick and claustrophobic, a fog that left me spinning.

And, within the terrible hurricane of sights and sounds were all of the smells. The homeless vagabond in the alley, the college student sitting in the dusty corner of a 24 hour cafe, the drunkard stumbling home from the bar; all of them smelled sweet and delicious to me. My stomach churned painfully even at the thought of new blood. When was the last time I had fed from an actual human? I was famished, a victim of my own self-starvation. "I cannot," the words left my lips and I gasped as if I were drowning, the air fighting to make its way into my lungs. "I, I—" I closed my eyes, disconnected from myself as I tried to stop careening. I couldn't think, and it was such a simple request. *Pathetic.*

Lemon Balm

Cypress had been working so hard and was just starting to find their footing. They deserved the company, and yet I could not provide. The overwhelming scent of strong coffee and campfire smoke enveloped me. It accompanied reassuring heat as Cypress came close. He pulled both of my hands up and away from myself, his touch a gentle pressure. It was the calming sensation of a hug without being one. Light swirls of copper and iron began to invade the edges of that smell. A shock of shame that I had been hooking my nails into my elbows. The cold blood had started to pool in the wedges.

"Hey," Cypress' soothing baritone broke the heavy silence, gentle and warm. "It's cool, Acanthus. You don't have to come if you don't want to."

I opened my eyes, tilting my head and meeting their gaze. His shaggy brunette hair caught the flicker of the candlelight, and I marveled at the fact that they had the start of a beard growing. *How long has it been? Three days?* Time was so fleeting. Taking a breath, I carefully followed the pattern of the yellow flannel on their broad chest with my eyes. "I, well…" I trailed off, nibbling at my lip. " You shouldn't need to venture out alone."

Cypress leaned back and cocked an eyebrow, staring at me. "Dude, I was alone for two years, and I *lived* in Brooklyn. I can handle a single night out in the city. I promise, it'll be fine."

I sighed, my body sagging. My heart hurt. Their warm hands around mine grounded me, and kept me from floating away. It meant something profound to me — even though I had been teaching them the ways of supernatural life, I knew they still didn't like to touch me. My skin was too smooth. Like marble, or glass, ending in those matte black claws that promised danger. Both have the strength of steel.

This was a fact that I could not ignore. There were other subtle appearances that made us look slightly more unsettling than the standard human. An 'uncanny valley' effect, people call it. Our eyes glowed, and refracted light like cats' eyes in the dark. Our hair and skin were picture-perfect; we were like walking paintings. Ever since the modern era, these appearance issues have become both harder and easier to hide. Leaning into an all black, modern Gothic style allowed me to blend in more than if I did not. Still, if I am not careful, these are dead giveaways, and that is extremely dangerous for me. My anxiety was palpable; thick and terrible, filling the empty spaces in my being with toxic, jittery sludge. I hadn't gone into society without a solid plan since 1912.

Hunters like to think that Vampires are the most dangerous creatures known to man. Where I can understand the vulnerability of being a prey animal, even the cruelest of Vampires are not known to engage. We get a bad reputation. Hunters were less prevalent than in previous eras, but they still proved a significant risk. They had new technology to find us and hurt us — drones, infrared, night vision, UV lamps that harnessed the very rays of the sun. I needed to be mentally sharp and physically unassuming if I accompanied Cypress to the city.

I pulled my hands away, sighing. "I know you don't need a chaperon."

I cleared my throat and walked towards the big window in the main room, looking out to the lightening sky. Searching the stars, I looked for an adequate reason to say no. "I have been living off of blood bags. I haven't found a donor in too long, and I would likely cause a scene."

The words weren't a lie, but they lacked the depth of my emotion. I would have to approach my normal channels again soon for a proper donor. That was one of the perks of my station as founder of the Night Garden; many of the Witches knew of my unfortunately irregular eating habits, and would bring me supplies, or keep willing donors on speed-dial for me. I'd wanted to take care of it when I sent off the letter, but there wasn't much anyone could do if no volunteers were available. Before Cypress showed up, I must have gone at least a month without feeding from a donor, maybe more.

Cypress brightened. "I could probably bring blood back? I'm sure it's not hard to find."

I sputtered, choking on air. "Are you hearing yourself? Don't be daft. What, will you walk into a bar and pick someone up to lure them to their doom? A hospital to steal away a terminal patient? You can't just bring me back some blood, it's not takeout."

They held their hands up, as if pushing my words away from them. "You don't need to insult me. You told me you got delivery."

It was a stark reminder that Cypress knew nothing of the World of Shadows. This Pup was going to get himself killed. Pushing down my irritation, I made the decision for us both. "I apologize for the offense. There's a gas station down the road that can give you something to eat now. I will come with you tonight, considering I need to run my own errands, but… "

I trailed off, hesitating in an uncomfortable silence that stretched too long before I found the courage to break it, "If we're going to town, promise not to leave me alone. I do not trust myself."

The statement was vulnerable of me to admit, and I chastised myself internally at how attached I had already gotten to this goofy, fun-loving Pup. They would be leaving me in my isolation in a few days. But, their friendship had reminded me what it was like to not be alone, and I found myself more comfortable in their presence than I did in my solitude recently. It was a strange, alien feeling.

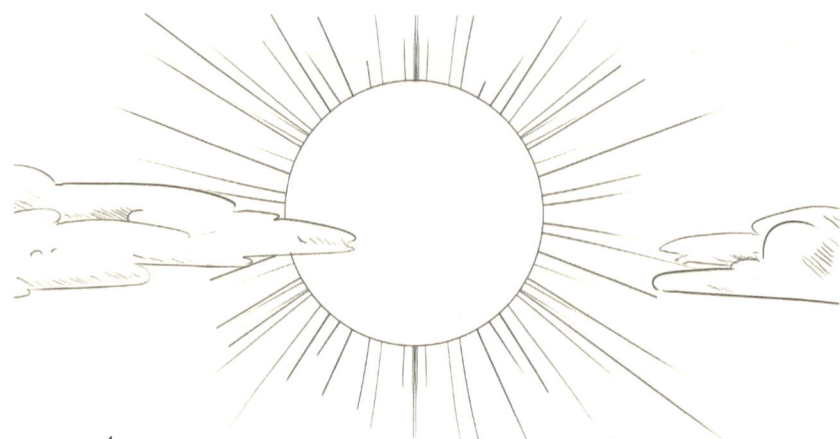

That Time We Flew To The City

Cypress

The next night, Acanthus and I were piled into my car, driving down the gravel road towards the highway. Normally, I wouldn't laugh at car anxiety, or anxiety in general, but you should've seen this centuries old Vampire sitting in the front seat of my Golf. They were rod straight, jumping at any noise that seemed slightly off. I put a reassuring hand on their shoulder, glancing towards them. "Eyes on the road." They bit out.

I laughed, looking back at the road. "You're a million years old, and you're worried about me hitting a deer?"

"I am *not* one million years old," Acanthus' eyes narrowed into slits in my periphery. "You need to slow down, you are driving way too fast."

The frustration was building steadily, and a headache started to pulse at the back of my skull. "Acanthus, I'm literally going 35."

"Too. Fast."

I sighed and pulled over onto the gravel shoulder, shifting the car into park. We'd only been driving for about two minutes. "Okay. Okay. What's your solution? I would've just gone into Peekskill if you didn't have your errands. At this point, this is going to take hours, and I'm starving."

Acanthus pursed their lips. "I could always fly."

"Fly?" I stared at them, perplexed. They had proven their vampirism to me by levitating, but I guess I didn't think of the fact that they could probably do it further in the air and for longer distances.

"Yes. And you can run."

"Acanthus," I flopped my head back against the headrest. "The thought of shifting again makes me want to unalive myself."

"..Unali — CYPRESS." Their voice was full of dismay.

"Yes, Acanthus?"

I heard their voice in my mind as their anger burned into me, and I flinched, surprised by the sudden emotion. ***Do not act coy with your life, Cypress Borne.***

Ducking my head, I whimpered. "It was just a joke. How can I hear and feel you in my mind?"

"It is not a funny joke," Acanthus bit out, and I couldn't help feeling like a child who's been thoroughly chastised.

"You're right. I'm sorry."

I returned my hand to the steering wheel, and stared out the windshield. "If you can fly, why not go to the city yourself, and I can drive into town?"

The fact that they ignored my first question irritated me. Weren't they supposed to be helping me? We sat in tense silence for a while, their eyes boring into my cheek. Try as I might to just ignore their existence, I couldn't. I looked back at them, waiting for them to make their point.

"You are important, Cypress. You deserve to be here as much as any other being, and I hope you come to see that."

My face warmed, and I looked away again. I had expected to be chided, not reassured. Suddenly I felt silly for being so ornery. "It was just a joke," I muttered again.

The silence stretched for a beat too long. Acanthus' whispery voice sliced through the tension. "Cypress. You are very hungry."

My traitor of a stomach growled, twisting painfully. That wasn't fair. A smirk crept over Acanthus' face, and my fingers twitched. *Shut up, just shut up.*

I avoided their gaze by looking down at the steering wheel, and they sighed. "To answer your question, I'm projecting my thoughts. It's an ability that I have. Though, you shouldn't be able to pick up on it as separate from your own. It's odd, but we can figure that out later. We can move faster than this car if we use a different method of travel. Nothing

85

will be open in Peekskill at this time of night. We can make it to the city and back before the sun rises, easily."

I looked at them with worry. "Do you hear yourself? Carrying groceries like that sounds awful. What's wrong with my car?"

Though Acanthus had proven the last few days that they can handle indirect sunlight, the thought of them being outside in the daylight made me anxious. I guess I couldn't shake the myths Hollywood had fed me. But, as I looked at this fragile being, I realized something. The thought of them being in danger left my heart speeding and my stomach knotted. I needed to keep them from harm. "You don't fight fair."

Acanthus smiled, their eyes wide and innocent. It was an effective ruse. "I have to keep on my toes around you, young Pup."

My resolve crumbled. If they thought it was a good idea, I might as well trust them. Grumbling, I turned the car back on, and drove off of the road and into the grass. After a very bumpy three point turn, I was headed back to the church. I parked in the driveway, and got out of the car. The door slammed on the other side as Acanthus slid to their feet in a fluid motion, and I stared at the scratched blue paint on the roof. Acanthus rounded the hood, and stood in front of me. "Thank you for turning around. Do you trust me?"

"Enough to come back here. I don't know if I trust you enough to fly me to the city. And I'm still not sure why I can't just go into Peekskill." It wasn't like I didn't like the guy, but three days was really quick. I wasn't sure if I'd trust them up in the air. "But, I guess we're at an impasse in that case."

Acanthus didn't seem perturbed by that. They inhaled softly, collecting themself as they tried again. "You will be fine. Besides, if you want to go to Peekskill, be my guest. But, nothing will be open."

They waved their hand towards the road, as if telling me to look. I saw their point; we'd been driving on gravel, much like the driveway of the church. The trees loomed on either side, butted up to the narrow road and leaning in. The night gave an inky blackness to our surroundings, and the anxious feeling of eyes watching from just beyond your vision made it impossible to relax here. It was too narrow for a car to pass the opposite direction, and not a single streetlight pierced the darkness. It was creepy how deserted it was. "Come to think of it, I don't think we even passed another property," I hugged myself, cold and hyper aware of the woods.

"Correct," Acanthus' voice was pleased, their arms crossed and fingers lightly curled around their elbows. "Several miles of this road aren't even marked. I own forty of these acres, remember; enough to keep an entire village's length of space away from the noise."

I didn't answer right away, leaning into the car to grab my keys and shoving them into my pocket. Acanthus clapped, delighted. "At last, they see reason! Are you afraid of heights?"

"No, why?"

Acanthus uncrossed their arms, holding one of their hands out. I hesitated, then took theirs in mine. *Fuck it.*

They pulled me close and stood on my feet, wrapping their free arm around my waist. A strange buzzing began to emanate from them, and they were weightless on my shoes. The stance felt like something akin to a waltz, if they hadn't been standing on my feet. "Close your eyes," they instructed, and I did. Wind began to whip around us, tugging at my clothes and hair. "Alright," they spoke near my ear a moment later. "Open them."

When I did, we were above the line of trees, the city lights bright and beautiful in the distance. Taken by surprise, I scrambled to get a better hold on them and roared, "Holy fucking shit!"

"Such language," Acanthus laughed, swooping us closer to the treeline.

"Fuck! Stop that!"

My heart pounded in my ears. I'd bruise them if they were human; my knuckles white with my grip. Adrenaline raced through me, and my throat clicked with a sudden dryness as I shifted my gaze to the sky. At least looking up didn't tell me how high we were. *How could anyone who can do this be afraid of a car?!*

Acanthus laughed joyfully, and lifted us up, so we weren't at risk of losing limbs by smacking into a tree. "I wouldn't let anything happen," Acanthus murmured, their iron-strong grip around my waist.

I could hear Acanthus fine over the roaring wind, but that didn't mean I liked the words. "I didn't say anything," I sulked.

"You didn't have to," they shot back, a playful lilt in their tone.

The air rushed around us, warm and sweet with the late spring flowers. The stars were brighter without the trees to interrupt them, and the kiss of the air was lovely where my skin was exposed. If I had been more prepared, I might even have enjoyed the situation I was in. I closed my eyes, my stomach lurching and head spinning with the height and rushing wind, but still safe in Acanthus' arms.

We fell into silence as they sped us to the city, and the longer the silence stretched and I stayed in their hold, the more my terror morphed into something more wondrous. I found myself smiling with the thrill, resisting the urge to cry out a healthy *woo!* into the night. Somehow, as the noise and the brightness of the city drew closer, I had the impossible thought that things would be okay.

Acanthus

The trip into New York City had, admittedly, rattled me worse than I'd have liked. The flight was quick enough; I landed us in a dark section of Crotona Park in the Bronx, outside of where wandering eyes could see. All in all, the full flight had only taken about ten minutes, instead of the car's projected hour and fifteen. Abandoning the car had allowed me to travel straight, instead of taking the roads away from the city and in a giant U-shape back. Even the darkness of the park was overrun with the sounds of police sirens and barking dogs, and the sky burnt an ugly brownish orange, angry with light pollution and smog. At least here you could still hear the waltzes of the crickets. The scent of iron and sweat hinted at people within the park, but they were on an opposite end, several blocks away.

I stepped off of Cypress' feet and regarded their face as I smoothed out my rumpled black sweater and slacks. My jacket, being leather, was immaculate. The Wolf looked a bit pale in the moonlight. "Are you alright?"

They held up a hand and wobbled it shakily side-to-side. A spark of concern went through me. "I'm fine," they finally said aloud. "Just getting over the fact that we just *flew*."

I relaxed, but I wondered if they had heard my thoughts or if they had read my worry on my face. It concerned me that Cypress could hear my thoughts so easily, but it would have been irresponsible of me to show that concern to the Pup. I'd been alone for a century, my powers enhancing all the while, and I had no way of knowing if I was projecting to the area or not. Perhaps it was our blossoming friendship, or their intense need for connection. Or, perhaps, my own. All the same, I would have to be more closed off. There were Wolves and other Vampires that would gladly take my head, if they could find it. Now was not the time to focus on semantics. "Where to, first?"

The Wolf's stomach rumbled in response, and both of their hands flew to their gut. Their entire body was wind-blown; their wild brown curls permanently swept away from their face in a comical fashion. My lips quirked into a closed smile, amusement lacing into my words. "To a diner, then, I'll take it."

Cypress laughed, rubbing their stomach as they blushed. A shy note bounced in their tone as they asked, "Is that alright? I know you're worried about interactions with people."

I nodded, ignoring the uncomfortable thrum of hummingbird wings threatening to invade my chest again. "The diner is safe for me. I know the lessees, and I know what to expect there."

It was well into the throes of night, and things were far quieter than the busy-ness of the day. So much of my life was held together by careful control and planning. Managing myself in places that I wasn't used to made my intestines twist and boil with anxiety. And, the only place that I was used to in my daily life at this point was my church. This meant that every step in this city was on a landmine and I was walking on borrowed paths.

Thankfully, there was a diner on the Night Garden paths that was a preternatural haven. A lesser Wolf pack sympathetic to the cause owned it, and their Alpha, Austin, leased it to Witches of the area. Nekane hated me for reasons buried in my past; reasons I was not proud to recall. Considering her station in the World of Shadows, the other Packs of the area bowed to her and extended her dislike. Where I generally had bad blood with most of the local packs, they knew I (among other "carefully monitored" Vampires in the area) needed to blend in as much as they did.

The Witch that leased the diner was fond of me, and I returned the sentiment — a dashing young man that appeared to be in his 30s. He'd helped me save over three hundred Witches since he started running this outpost in the 1850's, and he didn't plan to stop anytime soon. However, he had some trauma surrounding Wolves, and was far less willing to open his door to them. It would be an issue, but I'd be able to smooth it over.

Cypress had been quiet as I thought, and their confused voice pulled me from my head. "You were terrified of coming to the city, but you know people?"

My eyes darted to theirs. "I may be comfortable being alone, but I have certain needs. I do not typically come to the city without intense planning. It is very easy for me to become overwhelmed here. I have contacts who would be happy to oblige…" I paused, thinking of the least offensive word to use. "My tastes, as it were, but we can handle that later."

They relaxed into their typical slouch. "So… where's this diner?"

My best hopes failed me. Even at the late hour, people dotted the neat sidewalks. I turned and led Cypress through a series of back alleys and side roads. Even in this less dense part of the city the buildings towered over us, the skittering of rats and their accompanying heartbeats thundering in my ears. It set my stomach alight, gnawing at my insides and creating an uneasy, restless edge in my mind. My mouth had too much saliva, and it set a curious, tingling want in my tongue. The alleyways were a matter of safety for me, if only to avoid the proximity to others. Cypress followed me dutifully, but I could smell their perspiration. The coffee and bonfire smoke scents that clung to Cypress mixed with the sweat and fear as it lingered in the air around me. Despite this, Cypress walked with their head high and shoulders lax.

Lemon Balm

To their credit, we were in a rougher part of the city, but we were two supernaturals with strength that a crook could only imagine. I chuckled to myself. How like them to not be aware of their own power. Another thought, however, was plaguing me as we walked in silence — *How am I picking up on their thoughts without actively trying to read them?*

We turned left at the end of an alley somewhere onto Marcy Place. Dirty yellow light flooded our vision as we found ourselves in a deserted concrete expanse of pavement. The halogens were blinding, and I paused for a moment, holding up my hand against the onslaught in order to give my eyes time to adjust. The smells of freshly fried bacon and maple syrup overtook the far less pleasant smells of garbage and refuse in the alley. The floral undertone of lavender punctuated the scent, making it meld into a sickly-sweet mash.

The small parking lot was empty, except for one beat up gray sedan with the rear bumper crumpled in like paper. It was hanging by a ratchet strap, barely attached to the car. The small, unassuming diner stood at the far end of the lot. The blue and purple neon illuminated the corrugated red roof and cast rich color that cut through the sickly yellow pallor of the halogens. The building was butted up against another massive, five-story building behind it.

No one would know by looking at it, but the buildings were connected; the bottom floor of the office building connected to the "staff hallway" of the diner. There were beds and rooms for the Night Garden's use in that hallway, and that whole building was full of Witches that kept connected to our various paths. I should know; I commissioned the building and had it built. It had fallen under Wolf control when I lost my small chunk of territory in the city during our last war. Austin kept our secrets from Nekane. He also offered protection, but his radius only covered a small portion of the city. Still, whatever allies we had were worth keeping.

The neons on the diner roof cast an ethereal glow that bounced their message proudly off of the asphalt to the bereft spirits of the night. "Magic Manor. Open 24/7! Fresh coffee! 24 hour breakfast!"

So many heartbeats reverberated off of the concrete monoliths of the city, and the scent of sweat caused my inner beast to scream for the hunt, but the sight of the Diner was a promise for relief. I smiled, the anxiety that kept my chest tight slowly starting to fade away. My voice was light as we walked from the end of the parking lot towards the retro, chrome covered doors. "I do hope pancakes are palatable, Cypress. They also have fantastic bacon."

I heard the whimper and another loud agreement from their stomach before I turned to look at them, their nose high in the air like a dog sniffing. The hunger shone in their eyes, and they bounded ahead of me in excitement. Suddenly, they stopped mid-stride, as if hitting a wall. "Acanthus?"

"What is it, Pup?"

"What smells like lav — ..."

They turned to look at me and trailed off, their eyes wide and dazed.

Cypress

The city outing had been going fine. My anxiety about running into someone was unfounded, and the air surrounding this place smelled absolutely magical. When I turned to Acanthus to ask why that was, a wall of cotton smothered me as that trance-like daze from our first meeting set in. They were standing under the only white light in the entire parking lot. The harsh fluorescents reflected back at me from their eyes, and the surrounding halogens gave Acanthus' thin frame a golden highlight. I was struck by the sight of them, and all thought left me.

Acanthus suddenly looked extremely uncomfortable, their arms hugging around their waist as they returned my stare. Uncertain, quiet, and lilting, their voice hung like a ghost suspended in the empty parking lot. "Cypress?"

I blinked and shook my head, trying to clear it. "It's nothing. Let's eat."

Turning, I pushed the doors open, and walked in without waiting for another word. I jumped as the greeting bell on the door chimed. *What's gotten into me?*

Acanthus had lowered their head, hiding in their hair. Their eyes were wide and darted back and forth quickly, their shoulders tense and their arms still around their waist. They paused by the window to look at their distorted reflection. I couldn't be sure, but I wondered if they were trying to see something there because of the way I'd reacted to them in the parking lot. I'd never seen them in such a harsh light. Candle light, daylight, and even lamp light, warm and low and inviting, sure. But in the halogens of the city, they struck me as the Vampire you're warned about in movies. Beautiful, yet menacing. Striking, yet cruel. They were equally vicious and vibrant, their harsh beauty promising ruin and rain. I shuddered, forcing myself to push the thoughts aside as I shifted my focus to the small diner.

It was a beautiful place; looking like it was plucked straight from the 1950's. Chromed, red stools lined a black counter speckled with gray flecks, running parallel to the windows. To the right, red and chrome booths lined the side wall and disappeared from view. There was a big, open window behind the counter for the kitchen staff to look through, and a heavy oak door to the left of it. The bright popping of bacon on a griddle came from the kitchen, muffled by a fan. A man stood behind it to the right of a lift in the counter, sorting silverware into napkins.

I didn't think it mattered much where we sat, so I slid into a stool. The booths were vacant, and there was a silence hanging heavily in the air. I'd never seen a place in New York City so entirely empty before, and the strangeness of it set me on edge. The falsely bright tone of some forgotten radio station couldn't seem to fill the emptiness. The man behind the counter eyed me warily for a moment before turning his gaze towards Acanthus. His green eyes blazed from his olive skin, his sharp features carefully neutral as wisps from his braided bun escaped and fell in front of him. "A new pet Acanthus? I didn't know you were still in the habit of owning dogs."

My hair stood up on the back of my neck, and a growl threatened to rip from my throat. *What the fuck does he mean by that, 'owning dogs?'*

Acanthus calling me a pup was warm and playful, but this 'pet' business was meant to be demeaning. The soft, gentle pressure of Acanthus' hand on my back forced the tension back, and I settled down. As I did, I thought about the impulse, confused by my own behavior. I've never felt the urge to growl at someone before. This man meant no harm. "They are no pet," Acanthus replied, aloof. "Just a displaced Pup I'm trying to help."

"I see," The man said dully as he watched Acanthus remove their hand from my back. "Well, you know the rules about new Pups. Austin prefers to be informed. You weren't supposed to bring him here. Not until a pack has accepted him. Do you take responsibility?"

My gut twisted as Acanthus responded, "I do."

"Keep your leash short then, Lord Acanthus."

He smiled, but the gesture was more an aggressive bearing of teeth than it was a kind offer of peace. I felt like a problem, and I had no idea how to fix that. I hated being looked at this way. His voice was warm enough when he asked, "What can I get for you?" But, I could tell it was the forced customer service charm that came with his position.

"Pancakes... French toast if you have it?" The waver in my voice betrayed me as I slouched. I hated the sound of it. What had I ever done to anyone? It wasn't like I wanted to be attacked by some mangy monster outside of my apartment. I hadn't seen a menu yet, but I imagined they had your basic breakfast necessities. "A side of bacon, and scrambled eggs please. And your finest pot of bottomless coffee."

Acanthus pressed two gold coins onto the counter. What the hell was that about? Gold coins? What are we, in the wizarding world? Maybe I should know better than to question stuff like that. I'd have to ask

Acanthus about it later. It was whiplash; going from confident outside, to completely lost and unprepared within. I had expected something like a run-of-the-mill American diner, not a hostile waiter and a complete change in personality from Acanthus.

Speaking of, Acanthus was far less waif-ish in this establishment, their whispery softness replaced by someone with a clear, commanding voice, and a confident stance. Were they putting on an act for this Witch? Was this a Witch? I had no idea how to even tell. "House special for me please, Arturous."

"Of course," Arturous replied. "We'll feed the Pup first. I'll make arrangements for you, Acanthus."

I watched the man — Arturous — walk back to the kitchen and grumbled, "The Pup has a name, you know."

Acanthus let out a laugh. I always felt ten feet tall when they smiled; Acanthus had a serious facade about them that was a challenge to break. They slid into the stool beside me, their shoulders relaxed and their hair falling prettily around their face. "No need to worry about such things, Cypress. Arturous is a gruff man, but he means no harm. Though, if you are bothered, I can make sure he is more friendly; he knows better than to be so caustic towards my guests."

"He talked about me as if I'm not here. Did I come across as mean?" Maybe there was something in the way I spoke.

"No. There are…" Acanthus trailed off. They chewed on their lip, the silence dragging on long enough to be uncomfortable. They broke it with a gentle lilt. "There are deep inset biases about Werewolves. It's not you. It's your kind."

"That's not very reassuring," I grumbled. *Great. Can't wait to meet my Pack.*

Acanthus had told me a little bit about Wolves, but I had no idea about the standard nature of the Packs, or what I was in for. Maybe that was something we'd talked about during the training, but I couldn't remember. The sudden influx of questions left my mind whirring, my heart speeding to an uncomfortably hard rhythm against my sternum. My back pricked with goosebumps. I gritted my teeth and tried to beat back the sudden overwhelm. *How could I know to ask what I didn't know?*

Acanthus' voice was still light. "Cypress, you'll truly have to learn to control your thoughts, as once you are part of a pack, they'll be able to hear everything."

Something about the way that they said it made me snap. I couldn't believe that they had neglected to tell me this sooner. Did becoming a Supernatural mean that you gave up all privacy? Grimacing, I stood up, and walked towards one of the large windows. "What? And can you? Have my thoughts been my own? Or have you been *listening*?"

I was disconnected from it, but I heard the dangerous edge in my voice, and hot rage pulsed through my veins. "Have you been changing things, too? Fucking with my memories, my reactions?! Is that even *POSSIBLE*?"

I whirled on them, shaking so hard my vision went blurry as I roared. Arturous' head lifted into view from the small kitchen window, watching us intently. "Cypress. Calm down," Acanthus spoke, all lightness gone from their voice as they straightened, staring at me.

"Don't tell me what to do," I lowered my voice, the shaking rage still dripping from each syllable.

"I have not been listening to anything. I would not invade your privacy so, but sometimes you project something towards me. It is hard to explain, but please. Do not jump to conclusions. This is not the place nor time."

If my patience was snapped before, it was nonexistent now. *I'm so sorry my emotions are inconvenient to you.* I couldn't care about anything they were telling me, let alone worry about propriety right now. "Project? What the fuck ever."

My claws began to lengthen, and I clenched my fist. I was too far gone to stop the shift, my anger taking over. *Honestly? Who cares who sees. No one's here. Fucking let them.*

Acanthus was on their feet in front of me faster than I could track, and everything seemed to dim around me in their presence, the ambiance of the diner fading in the distance. "SIT. DOWN. CYPRESS," they commanded, the volume loud enough to make my ears ring.

All the fight left me as I crumpled to the floor, cross legged. I stared up at Acanthus, waiting for their next command. They were lovely, with their eyes glowing green and their body outlined in gold, just like in the parking lot. I wanted them to talk again. I didn't have to wait long. All of the rage was entirely gone, and I couldn't remember what had made me so angry in the first place.

"There is a time and a place. I told you I'd explain. I would not leave you in the dark if it was important," the edges of their tone were icy, but their face was kind. They reached out, putting their hand on my shoulder, and I was floating outside of my body again, strangely disconnected. They dropped down to my level, squatting on the balls of their feet. "You must learn to trust me."

"Yes, Acanthus," My voice wasn't my own, and if it was, I'd never heard it. I felt the claws slowly recede, the fur retracting into my skin. I kept trying in vain to remember what I was angry about to begin with. What could I possibly be angry about with Acanthus here?

Acanthus' eyes softened, and they suddenly looked exhausted. "If you are feeling better, I'd quite like you to stop pouting, and eat your food. We don't need to cause a scene where humans can see, whether they're here or not. And I will warn you only once, dearest Cypress. Do not make me warn you again."

The punctuated sentence was crystal clear. I was causing issues for them, and it would result in consequences. I blinked slowly a few times as the haziness and floating feeling faded from my mind. As clarity returned, I asked, "What... what was that?"

Acanthus stood from their crouch. They were no longer looking at me, sliding into the bar stool with a labored sigh. Their eyes shut and their head lowered as they rubbed at their temples. I slowly stood, glancing at the kitchen window. The Witch was no longer visible. Acanthus' voice was rough, and I was reminded of a parent dealing with a toddler. "Cypress, I am hungry, and grow tired. Eat, and I will explain later."

I sat at the counter again. Apparently the Witch— Arturous, was it? I felt bad not remembering his name— had brought out plates for me during the strange altercation between Acanthus and I, but if he lingered or felt any type of way about it, I couldn't know. I looked around for him, and spotted him staring at me from the other end of the counter. When our gaze connected, he quickly lowered his head, pretending to clean a spot.

There was so much food; French toast glistening with maple syrup, crispy bacon with just the right bit of char, sourdough toast that glistened with the fat of melted butter. My stomach gurgled in anticipation. I guess I had ordered a mountain. I tried to offer some to Acanthus, but they smiled thinly and shook their head. With a shrug, I dug in. It was delicious, and I shoved it into my mouth with gusto. Acanthus was quiet beside me, but I didn't mind the silence. As I was finishing the last bits of my French toast, I heard the door's welcome-bell chime, and glanced towards the sound.

From the corner of my eye, I could see a pretty woman, my age, probably about 5'4" in height. She had long raven-black hair that flowed to the middle of her back. She smiled at me, and I gave a small wave with my fingers towards her. Arturous abandoned his post across the diner. He came out and greeted the woman, kissing her on both cheeks. *Why does she get the red carpet treatment?*

The man held the break in the counter open for her. He gave Acanthus a pointed look that said, *Follow me*, before walking into the back with the woman. I looked questioningly at Acanthus, and my chewing slowed as I realized what Arturous was suggesting. It was like I'd been doused with ice water, horrified as they moved to head towards the break in the counter.

"She's, uh, very young." I didn't know how to phrase the question without sounding accusatory.

Acanthus needed to eat too. They spoke, a tiredness lacing through their words. "Even without your internal monologue screaming that I'm a monster, I know what you're thinking, and it isn't like that. I haven't killed anyone by feeding in many, many years."

My brows knit. Was that what I made them think? Maybe I had thought it under the harsh light in the parking lot, but they had shown me absolutely nothing but kindness no matter how I acted. "I don't think you're a monster."

"Please, excuse my rudeness. Finish your food. I will return in a moment."

"Wait." My stomach clenched, all this food threatening to make a reappearance. Why was I so anxious for that lady? I wasn't sure where this instinct to stop Acanthus was coming from, but they seemed to know exactly where my thoughts were.

"Cypress," they soothed, "It is in your nature to fear me, and try to stop me from drinking. I cannot allow you to come with me, however I do think you seeing it would help. Maybe someday. As you currently stand, your Wolf instincts will most definitely take over, and I am unable to help you if I'm feeding."

I gripped the counter, terrified they'd leave me behind. I didn't trust myself to be alone here, especially not when Acanthus had to use whatever persuasive power they had to stop me from shifting. A part of me realized that their closeness was making my heart pound, my skin crawling as my neck tingled with the thought of their fangs. This was ridiculous. They weren't any closer to me than they typically got, and they've always been what they are. They weren't treating me any differently than usual. Was I scared of them? Was this dread? I couldn't tell. "You made me promise I wouldn't leave you alone," I blurted.

Acanthus paused, blinking. "I promise you, this is a normal, and healthy reaction for your kind, Cypress. Now please..."

They began to walk towards the break in the counter again, and panic gripped me even harder. My muscles were like rubber bands stretched to their limit, tense and taut. I lunged for their hand. "Please, Acanthus. If it's too much I'll — I'll leave. I'll get out of there. Something."

They squeezed their eyes shut, shoulders hiking up to their ears. The silence stretched far too long, before they finally looked at me, their shoulders dropping with a long-suffering sigh. Before they could say anything, I whispered, "Please."

"Fine." Their voice was tight. "But, I have conditions. And they are not nice conditions. Nor do I like inflicting this on your kind—"

"Anything," I squeezed their hand gently.

The look they gave me reminded me of a wounded deer. Some deep pain interlaced their intense stare, the hazel flashing as their eyebrows furrowed, sorrow hidden behind the anger. "Don't say that before you know what the condition is."

"Anything," I repeated.

Acanthus' gaze slipped to the floor. When they brought it back to mine, their eyes begged me to listen. "While I'm feeding, you are to remain shackled in silver. I cannot risk you attacking me, otherwise I may harm the donor, and harm you for that matter."

"Shackled?" Now that they mentioned it, one of those foggy training sessions popped back into my mind. They told me silver would make me drop like a lead weight. I guess shackles would do their job and keep me in place.

"Arturous will hold them. This is my condition, take it or leave it. However, I grow weary, Cypress. I must feed, or I will not be pleasant in the coming days." They pulled their hand from mine, and walked to the back room.

Of course I had to agree, curiosity and fear burning through me.

That Time The Pup Tasted Silver

Acanthus

Every moment Cypress held me back from my waiting donor, my insides twisted and my skin prickled. Ice ran through my veins, slow and sluggish, and a steady pounding was beginning in my temples. Waves of nausea, sharp yet subtle, accompanied each twist of my insides, and my mouth watered with need and anticipation. Every ticking moment left me agitated, exhausted, and impulsive. I had gone too long without feeding properly, and the effects were eating into me; the heartbeats of little critters fought for dominance with the creaks and groans of the surrounding pipes. It was like starving, without being starved.

I was trying my best to be patient. By the end of our conversation I walked faster through the opening of the counter than Cypress could follow. The standard accoutrements of a mid-century diner fell away into a hallway anachronistic to the outer-facing environment. The sweet scent of blood oozed from workers and refugees, hidden behind the solid oak doors. I wasn't certain how many people were housed here tonight. The sounds became a constant chatter in my ears, a cacophony I couldn't block over the incessant thought of *eat, you need to eat*. Cypress' musk stuck in my nose, making my instincts roar within to bare my fangs in his direction. Now that I had the promise of fresh blood, it was all I could think about.

I used all of my remaining fortitude to maintain my outer facade of calmness. *I am in control.*

I rounded the corner into the open doorway of a sparsely furnished room. The raven-haired beauty was sitting in a comfortable chaise lounge that was placed in the far left corner, her hair already pulled over one shoulder and neck enticingly bared. I froze. She had her soft jaw tilted to one side, and I could already feel my fangs lengthening in anticipation. Gone were the scuffed and stained wooden floors and bland, dusty white walls. My eyes were locked on the rise and fall of the pulse in her jugular, my focus only broken by the feeling of Cypress' broad body crashing into me.

I stumbled forward, glaring at him over my shoulder. They looked down, nervous and meek. I could almost see them in their wolf form, their ears folding back apologetically. "Christ, I'm sorry."

"Acanthus," Arturous cut in before I could reply. I whipped to look at him, his green eyes sharp as he stood to the right of the woman's seat.

All it took was one look from me to get him to back down. "I couldn't very well keep my leash short if they were in the diner. You know what to do, Arturous. I apologize, but please hurry."

"Right away, my Lord," the gentleman replied.

He moved with the grace of a dancer to a small dingy cabinet at the back of the room. The paint was flecked away in places, dark wood peeking out from beneath the damage. The raven haired beauty shifted her blue eyes to mine and smiled invitingly. My stomach rumbled, pained and yearning. I could already tell that I would not be able to sate myself with her, and it was taking all of my remaining willpower to not descend upon her.

The musical tingle of chains came from within the cabinet and, when Arturous turned around with them, I stepped towards him. "Let me take those, if you will."

The Witch obliged my request without his usual snark. Taking the light silver chains, which were more like connected charm bracelets than shackles, I turned to look at Cypress once more. "Come."

Cypress came forward, arms outstretched. A pang ran through my chest. *I will not become my maker.*

Gently, I took their hands in mine. "I apologize for what I'm about to do."

I know I had already said it, but I needed to repeat. The scents were driving me mad. The heartbeats of everyone in the room were asynchronous; one calm, one quick, and one a terrible thunder of panic. Veins seemed highlighted in each face and limb within lunging distance, and saliva pooled in my mouth. I should know better than to let it get this bad. *Patience. Only a moment more.*

I knew how monstrous I was in my hunger. I didn't want any of them to fear me. I wound the chains across Cypress' wrists and held their arms as they immediately fell forward, their limbs dropping straight down. Slowly, I guided them to the floor, my loose hair falling into my face. They whimpered as their shoulders strained against the thin silver chain, and I knelt in front of them, watching their wide steel and storm eyes flicker. "I know, Cypress, I know. It doesn't seem possible that such a delicate chain can take down a strong, healthy person like you."

Cypress nodded, though the movement was sluggish and slow. I continued, my tone soothing. "As I've told you, silver is a weakness to Wolves, do you understand? It won't harm you, but it'll stop you from interrupting. I know it's heavy and unpleasant."

They nodded, slumping closer to the floor to lessen the weight. The moment I knew that they were alright, I turned and made my way to the raven haired woman, my fingers shaking in anticipation, my need for her blood sharp on my tongue. "Are you alright, my dear?"

My patience was worth every slowdown in this process. I won't be a monster. She smiled my way, speaking in a soft, raspy voice, "Never better."

"Excellent," I responded softly. She reminded me of Nocturne, a previous Witch companion who was very dear to me, and my yearning for her increased. I slipped behind her chaise lounge and leaned down to her height. She tilted back towards my touch. Gently, I pressed my hand against her shoulder and leaned in. My lengthened fangs sank into her jugular, pulling my first sip.

Cypress

Hearing them talk to another being so sweetly was torture. My temples pounded and I gritted my teeth. I wanted to lunge at them to break them apart in my jealousy, but it gave way to panic as Acanthus bit the woman's neck, their auburn hair cascading over her chest. It was pushed prettily to one side to stay out of their way. Stuck on the floor, all I could do was watch. She moaned quietly at the contact, but otherwise said nothing. Acanthus' stance changed; they became both possessive and protective of the woman and held her closer as time went on.

I had visions of tackling Acanthus; of making this stop. My skin rippled. My muscles corded and tensed as I fought the weight of the silver, but I couldn't find my Wolf to shift. My heart hammered in my chest in a terribly heavy rhythm, and a lump formed in my throat that made it hard to breathe. My breaths came shallow and fast, and I couldn't gulp down enough air no matter how hard I tried. I was fearful of their feeding, though I couldn't make sense of why. *Please, please, get away from her,* my mind screamed.

The logical, detached part of my mind argued and told me I was overreacting. My shaking fingers hooked into claws against the scarred floor, but I couldn't move against the immense weight. They obviously weren't hurting her. She was a willing volunteer, maybe even eager. So really, what was so bad? What was this instinct that screamed from the depths of my soul to stop them? I knew we'd come here for them to eat. I had an idea of what I'd witness, regardless of their hesitation. A growl of frustration escaped past the lump. *Cypress, you're being ridiculous. Breathe. Count to eight and hold.*

I called on every self-soothing technique I learned in therapy. I didn't want to interrupt Acanthus, but every muscle in my body was screaming for me to do something. Anything. Acanthus withdrew, and the woman fell backward against their chest, a serene smile on her face. They caught her, carefully holding her steady. "Thank you, my Lord," she murmured dreamily.

Arturous went to them, a warmed blanket in hand for the woman. I'd forgotten he was even there. "Come along now. The fine Lord doesn't have all night," his words were tender. He wrapped the pretty lady in the blanket and took her in his arms, carrying her to another room and out of sight.

Acanthus slowly turned. They walked past me to close the door, and scanned the room. "Just a precaution, for when I release you," their voice was back to a smooth, ethereal quiet. They came closer to me, and I flinched away. My breaths were short huffs through my nose as the electricity of fear rose once more in my chest.

I let out the most menacing growl I could muster, the weight of the chains pulling all of my focus. My lungs were bruised. Acanthus stopped, putting their hands up in a gentle defensive motion. "Cypress,"Acanthus trailed off, their eyes bright and wide. Their lips turned downwards as their tone slid into something more plaintive and hurt. "It's me."

I couldn't stop my reactions; everything I'd learned in counseling was gone from my mind, and all my coping mechanisms were nowhere to be found. That weird detached logical side of me wondered if this was how a caged animal felt. They crept towards me, and my panic rose. I tried to thrash out of the bonds, but my shoulders barely wiggled. *Get away, get away!*

Their teeth hadn't yet returned to normal, and there was a drop of blood at the corner of their mouth. With all the effort I'd put in, I managed a sitting position, tucking my knees against my chest, and making myself smaller. The problem was now, I was cornered. Acanthus paused their approach, closing their eyes to compose themself. I watched this person turn into a statue.

The constant growling slowed as curiosity took over. *What are they doing? Why are they just standing there?*

I shook my head, opening my mouth to scent the air like a cat. Roses, oud, and sandalwood invaded my nostrils, and I closed my mouth, not sure if I was reassured by the familiar scents. Acanthus wiped their face. Their fangs slowly retracted, and they looked slightly less like a Vampire. My heart began to calm, until they took a silent step towards me. It hammered in my ears all over again.

"Cypress, it must be me who undoes your chains. Please, allow me to do so."

They knelt in front of me, putting their hands out for mine. With all the effort I had left in me, I roared, and pulled my hands to my chest. I couldn't manage to speak past snarls and whimpers. I was nothing more than an unkempt beast, reverting back to before I could talk. Acanthus once again became a statue, their hands paused in mid-reach towards mine. They waited for my whimpering to slow before speaking, their voice so soft my ears strained to hear it. "I am not here to hurt you, young Pup. Think back. Have I hurt you at all these past few days?"

I thought, and I thought hard through the exhaustion, and the alarm bells blaring in my head. Whatever this strange instinct to cower came from, it wasn't me. I stared at the Vampire's kind face, and counted each of the pores in their cheeks to soothe myself. Slowly, my muscles began to release, and my back ached with the effort of keeping my body so taut.

"No," I whimpered, the word taking a gargantuan amount of effort to sneak past my lips. Whether it was from the weight dragging me to the floor, or fighting this instinct, I couldn't tell.

"I think you can trust me, then."

"No?" I said again, unsure why. *This is Acanthus. This is my friend. They've never hurt me.* They didn't even hurt that woman. I kept repeating logic to myself, but it wasn't working. Something about witnessing them feed had awakened a beast deep beneath my logical self, far below in the core of my being. Something feral in me wanted to run. I had come to fear Acanthus.

Acanthus

Any emotion that had been stunted by my hunger had come back in full force. Their terror wrung at my heart, and the pain permeated through my blood, my fingers tingling. I yearned to comfort them, and I once again found myself in the role of the elder that I was. I had to put my emotions aside; Cypress needed me. I moved with slow, calculated movements, and gently pressed my fingers into their shaggy hair, praying my intentions were clear. He snarled, snapping to bite but unable to reach where my hand was. I didn't react, instead moving my hand to stroke their hair. The loud, frantic snarls slowed. Minutes passed. I waited.

I glanced towards the door, counting back the time we'd been in this room. Arturous would be settling the woman in the recovery room across the hall. Cypress fell silent, and my attention shifted back to them. Their muscles were still taut and shaking, eyes bright and lip trembling as they pulled in a deep breath. His eyes shifted back and forth, watching mine as he slowly mouthed the numbers, counting seconds before he exhaled.

I didn't move until the shake started to lessen in Cypress' shoulders. Every motion I made was slow and deliberate, done in such a way that they could watch where I was going at all times. My right hand dropped to their cheek, continuing my gentle stroking. They let out another growl, but this one was weaker and tapered into a whimper. They hesitated, before their head dropped and they nuzzled their nose into my palm. That was a good sign. "Are you calm enough to trust me?"

Cypress still didn't use their words, but nodded, looking down at the chains.

"Good. I'm going to release you now, Pup. "

I shifted my right hand to undo the clasp of the silver cuffs, always keeping the other visible as I fumbled with the clasp. It came apart with a little click, and I gently and carefully pulled them away from their wrists. They shot away from me and I slid back, giving them the space to avoid me as they needed. Using my powers, I floated the chain away and whisked it back into the cabinet, the doors closing and locking in a single fluid motion behind the silver chains.

Cypress

The second the chains left my skin, I was hit with this rush of energy. I hadn't shifted by my own choice, but this was the first time I could remember the action of doing it. The burning of the shift was short, and I barely felt myself change before I was on all fours, standing on top of my shredded clothes. I looked up at Acanthus, who had their back to me. Now that I could call forward my Wolf, that strange instinct to snarl and fight against Acanthus was gone. I was still cautious, because I couldn't quite shake the intense feeling that came with the instinct, but at least my brain was logical, again. I knew Acanthus wouldn't hurt me.

The scent of oud, rose petals, and sandalwood still clung to Acanthus' clothes, tinged with the coppery notes of fresh blood, and undertones of oak moss. I watched them for what felt like a long time, before they turned around, fidgeting with their fingers. It seemed like another eternity passed before they moved again, and I found myself amazed at their ability to be so still. They hesitantly walked towards me, hands raised in a soothing gesture.

I let my tongue loll out the side of my mouth and pranced over to them, running around them with my legs lifting high in a march on each step. Acanthus let out a bright, hearty laugh as they sagged, the tension in the room broken. "Truly, truly amazing, Cypress," they said. I was delighted by their praise, not to mention the relief in their voice at my antics. "Any pack will be lucky to have such a talented young Wolf amongst them."

I was confused by the words. What had I done to be considered talented? As far as I knew, all I'd done since we came to the Magic Manor was cause issues. That train of thought died as Arturous pulled open the door with a loud *whoosh*, holding a bundle of clothes. He looked at me with disdain, before averting his gaze back to Acanthus. "I'm happy you are unharmed, my Lord. I expected—" he gestured back to me as he handed the bundle to them, "— to happen. Though, the fact he hasn't torn you to shreds is remarkable. I could feel the fear from the other room."

Before I realized it, I'd prowled forward, hackles raised, and snarling with dislike at this man. *Why does he hate me so much?*

"Cypress," the Vampire's voice was clipped, and I paused. My gaze snapped up to Acanthus', and that was all that needed to be said. I lowered my head and relaxed my body, forcing the guard hairs to lay flat again. I walked over to Acanthus and nudged them with my nose. At full height, I stood about chest level with them. They patiently petted me, and accepted the clothes from Arturous.

"What a well behaved pet. Perhaps you found a keeper," the Witch drawled.

"You'd do well not to insult them, Arturous," Acanthus replied, glaring reproachfully. "They're on the Garden paths. Soon they'll be with a Pack, and getting more powerful everyday. They might remember this."

Arturous narrowed his eyes, his shoulders squaring and his eyebrows in a deep furrow. "This is a place of peace, but not by choice. You'd do well to remember that, Acanthus. It wasn't so long ago that you were ready for war against the Wolves."

"I'm aware, and I am still prepared. This Pup has done nothing, and I hope they find a suitable pack. One more docile than those that frequently visit you. They were left to figure this out on their own. They know nothing of our history. You'd do well to remember that none of us choose our lot in life."

I looked up at Acanthus, then back at Arturous. Clearly, there was something between the two; more than I could pick up on from the conversation. I didn't know what happened to the Witch, but it made me uneasy to think about it for too long. Also, what did they mean by the Garden paths? Completely lost, I waited to see what Acanthus would do next.

The Witch's eyes still burned, but they softened when Acanthus placed their hand on my head. I leaned into their touch, their scent calming me. Acanthus broke the tense silence with a disarming grace. "As always Arturous, I thank you and your family for your services. I'm sorry I went around the rules, bringing a Pack-less Pup around. By the time you see us next, Cypress will be accounted for." Acanthus shook his hand.

"Of course, Lord Acanthus. Be safe."

"We will be off, then," Acanthus leaned his head to the left, a silent command to start walking.

They pointed at my wallet and keys, summoning them to the top of the clothes pile before opening the door for me. I wasn't quite sure what our plan was, at least for going into the city. Considering I was fully aware of myself, I figured I could stay a wolf. Maybe I would just be their pet for the next few hours. Acanthus is eccentric enough, from the outside looking in; maybe they'd pull off owning a wolf hybrid dog.

"Right, not left, Cypress," they instructed, and followed me down the hallway. They pointed at a door that was open. It was at the end of the hallway on the right side. We closed the distance to the room, and I walked in, swiping at the wall with my nose to find a light switch. After two attempts, the yellow light flickered to life. There was a bed and a bookcase in here; I was starting to get the impression that this place did way more than serve bacon and blood. The door shut behind me, and I turned to see the pile of clothes in a heap on the floor. I shifted and quickly pulled on the loaners. It was a gray hoodie and some unassuming black sweatpants. Christ, these clothes were huge; I swam in them. They were at least a size too big for me, but I wasn't complaining. Clothes are clothes.

Acanthus pushed off of the dingy white wall as I slipped out of the room and left the door open behind me. Here," they said, holding a few bills towards me. Benjamin Franklin's stoic face smiled grimly from the bill, and the money made my insides twist. I swallowed, uncomfortable. Acanthus flicked their wrist, insistent. "Take this," they said, doubling down.

I flushed, frowning at the cash. "For?"

"I'd like not to have a repeat of what transpired in there. While we are waiting on the Packs to respond, you should get all the food and necessities you may need."

I swallowed and stuck my hands into the pockets of the sweatpants to avoid grabbing the cash. "Of course, but why don't you hang on to it?"

They thrust the cash towards me again, their voice smooth. "I need to separate from you for a moment. I have another associate to visit, and I am still hungry. I'd rather not have you wanting to tear me limb from limb again. Not to mention, Cypress, I can't wait another half an hour for a different donor after you pulled that power play."

They had a point, but I wasn't about to tell them that I'd been more scared than aggressive. My reactions still confused me, and I wanted to sort my own head out before I talked about it. I couldn't tell how I'd react, but I made a promise. "I can't let you wander off."

Acanthus took a breath as their eyes flashed. "I can handle myself, Cypress. I've had a small meal."

I shook my head. I didn't want to be alone, and they had given me the perfect excuse to be stubborn about it. "You said not to leave you during our trip to the city. We are still in the Bronx, last I checked."

I waited a beat, watching their perfect face fight between frustration and delight. With a sigh, they pocketed the bills. "Onward, then. We'll head to the superstore first, if you're coming along to my next stop."

That Time I Broke Down in the Cereal Aisle

Acanthus

With each step towards the grocery market, my good mood faded and my anxiety slowly returned. Cypress kept glancing my direction, and I was careful not to meet their eyes. Instead, I reached into the pocket of my tailored leather jacket and pulled out a small pair of cats' eye vanity sunglasses, tinted a deep purple. I slipped them up onto the bridge of my nose before I reached back to pull my hair into a loose tail. Rather than search for a band, I knotted my hair high on my head and pulled a bobby pin from the same place, pinning the knot tight.

So long as I hid my eyes, I could pass easily in human spaces. My skin was a little too pale in fluorescent lights; Cypress' reaction at the Manor was proof enough of that. Having just fed left me rosy enough to pass for a pale human. The modern Gothic appearance that I had fostered in recent years— tonight, it was the vanity glasses, my jacket, tight black jeans with a worn acid-wash pattern and rips at the knees, and a black and gray textured turtleneck that read, "Now I Lay Me Down To Sleep" — gave me armor. The glares I would get in social situations would only come at the derision of miscreant children. I was lucky that I was 21 when I was turned; it made falling into fashions easy, and people rarely questioned attractive young people of any gender (short of the bigoted "What are you" I had hurled in my direction from time to time).

Grocery marts were one of the only places that I rarely blended in. They were a special type of hell, crafted to perfectly push on my insecurities. Did I 'pass'? Was I 'human' enough?

It was maddening, thinking of going into the cold, dead place. I almost wondered if I'd have been better off shopping with Cypress first. At least then I would have an excuse for this anxiety. The heartbeats of the animals and creatures had faded to their appropriate levels, and I was no longer subconsciously scanning for veins. But, there would be so many people in close proximity, in the most awful, noise-expanding acoustic nightmare of a building. The smells would swirl together in a distracting soup, different flavors of blood pulling me this way and that.

I needed more to eat; preferably from two or three different donors so that I could be sated until the young Pup left me. My heart panged at that thought, which confused me for a moment. *To Hell with it*, I thought, *you're just hungry, Acanthus.*

The buildings weren't quite so tall in this area of the city, a detail that I always appreciated. It was far more manageable than Manhattan was. Neat brick apartments lined the streets here. It reminded me of Chicago more than the impossibly tall concrete towers of Manhattan. "Hey, Acanthus?"

Cypress' voice was timid as it cut through the silence, and I nearly jumped at the interruption. "What is it, Pup?"

"What can I expect when I join a Pack? How will I know if I'm accepted or not?"

That was an interesting question. I wasn't certain how to respond to it. "Where is this coming from, Cypress? Do you think you won't fit in?"

Their silence was telling. I shifted my gaze to look at them from my periphery. Their head hung, and they left their hands in the hoodie pocket. When they didn't answer, I sighed. "It's like the opening of a lock on an elaborate door, or so I'm told. You'd feel it. But, I don't think you have anything to worry about. You're charming, and you'll fit right in."

Cypress blushed at that. "Thanks... I hope you're right."

We lapsed into silence for the rest of the walk. The grocery store was on Nelson Avenue, at least twenty minutes away from the Magic Manor. When we were a minute or two out I began to rub my hands together to both heat them and bring a healthy blush into my fingers. I couldn't be too careful. I stopped right before we turned into the harsh light of the parking lot. I had to be honest about my aversion to going inside. "I'll have you know, I do not do well in markets."

Cypress' eyes were concerned as they held my gaze. "You don't have to come in with me. Unless... Is there any way we could skip it?"

"No, Pup. You need food..."

At that, Cypress reached and grabbed my hand. They were becoming more bold, and getting over their aversion to touching my skin. Cypress' voice was eager, their eyes bright. "You've been with me so much these past few days. I will be right there with you. I promise."

I blinked at them, before relaxing, unable to stop the small smile from lifting the corners of my lips. "Very well. Onward, then."

We reached the store, and walked together into the veritable hellscape of cold cases and bargain tables. An hour later, that blanket of comfort and security had firmly fallen into a horrid feedback loop of anxiety and despair. *This was Hell. Absolute, entire, blistering, seventh level hell.* Everything was loud, and each beep in the cold fluorescent lights sent shocks of irritation down my spine. Cypress had already taken their sweet time in the clothing section, picking up several clearance sweatshirts, plain t-shirts, lounge pants, and two pairs of jeans.

People were shouting across aisles and throwing things into carts. Fifteen precious minutes were spent arguing in the soap aisle. They wanted the disgusting chemical smell of this brand known to be featured in the boys' locker rooms of middle schools across the country. Cypress had shoved one in my face. Before they even asked me what I had thought of the scent, I wheeled away from him, hacking and gagging.

I insisted they smell it themself and, when they did, they shut it and quickly shelved it with a suppressed gag of their own. I had no idea why they cared what I thought; once we heard back from Nekane, we'd have to part ways. I couldn't keep them as a friend, because even if they were sent off to an ancillary pack, it'd be risky for both of us. I also hadn't told them the particulars of the Night Garden, because I didn't want Nekane to press him about it. By letting them close, I was setting myself up for failure. *Leave me behind to turn to dust, right where I belong.*

My thoughts skewed negatively in places like this. I was standing at the end of an aisle, tapping my nails on my forearm. Someone who walked by smelled delectable; I whipped around to see where the scent was emanating from. A young man, probably in his mid twenties, stopped at the end cap an aisle over from me. He was dark-skinned, with proud, strong features; a fade haircut that was cropped close to the scalp, utterly relaxed in loose jeans and a baggy black sweater. He regarded the various types of cereal stocked under a sign that screamed a sale in bright red letters, picking one up to read the ingredients. *Dear Gods, his scent...*

I wasn't sated enough to control the signs of my blood lust, despite my best efforts to look human. The man ignored me, though my eyes traced the spider pattern of veins in his arms. I covered my mouth, hiding how my fangs lengthened. Cypress was further down the aisle, oblivious to my plight as he debated over one sugary death pellet cereal or another. The blood in my stomach churned. Amazing, how much my appetite could remain despite feeding once tonight. I wanted so badly to run. I caught the scent of newborn blood an aisle over, and a small groan left my lips before I could stop it. Imagine dangling a thick, juicy steak in front of a starving human. ***"Get me out of here, for all that is holy..."***

I should have been a bit less acquiescent when it came to going into this den of evil. I should have given them the slip; I knew I could secret away faster than they could see. Were we not in one of my least favorite places on this accursed earth, then I wouldn't be in such a horrid way. I wasn't about to start a moral panic by eating a baby at four A.M. in a supermarket. I needed to get out of here. ***"Cypress, please, hurry..."*** The broadcasted thoughts just kept coming.

Cypress

"Cypress, please hurry..." The thought slammed into my mind, ringing in my ears as if they'd yelled across the aisle to me. I threw the S'mores cereal I was debating in my basket, and forced myself to walk calmly and humanly. (Weird concept, right?)

"Hey," I grabbed their hand, looking down at them. "We're almost done... We just need to..." I trailed off, seeing the way they hid their fangs. A flash of first jealousy, then fear flickered through me. I thought back to the intimate, loving way Acanthus held the woman at the diner. *I could be a donor for you...*

The thought made my stomach twist and cheeks heat in a deep blush. My heart sped in my chest, and nausea leapt up to my throat as I considered that. Jealousy was something I'd have to work through later. Fear needed to be handled now. "Come with me, Acanthus. We'll get out of here."

They let out a small hiss of an exhale, their hand clamping tighter over their mouth. Their voice came into my head again, loud and insistent. ***"You smell delectable. Don't come too close to me, Cypress."***

Without another word I pulled them towards the front of the store, breezing past an exhausted woman in pajamas. She was regarding the diapers in the next aisle, oblivious to our new quest for the doors. We passed by a myriad of cashiers, and I settled on a self check. I knew I could scan quicker with two hands, but I didn't want to let go of Acanthus. I pulled them in front of me, and rested my chin on the top of their head, scanning items around them. It wasn't the most efficient way, but maybe I'd stand a chance at stopping them, if they went on a blood hungry rampage.

They let out a tiny, wanton sound, and my skin prickled and buzzed. I cleared my throat and swallowed, scanning faster. Not wanting to deal with the hassle of change, I pulled out my card, and waited for the transaction to approve. Acanthus whimpered and pushed away from me.

They fled the supermarket as I grabbed the grocery bags. I hustled out of the building shortly behind them.

As soon as we were outside, they whirled on me, gasping, "You moronic Pup! I could've killed you!"

I flinched, but didn't take it to heart. Maybe I was missing something here, but they had seemed perfectly in control, despite the length of their fangs. "I was trying to help. I'd rather have been bit if you needed it. It's whatever, Acanthus."

"Whatever? WHATEVER? DO YOU EVEN KNOW WHAT COULD HAPPEN IF I BIT YOU?!"

They were yelling at me now. I looked around nervously, making sure no one was watching. I couldn't see anyone in the sea of cars, thankfully. Still, being screamed at in a parking lot at four in the morning was not what I'd consider a good time. I let out an uneasy whine.

"I... Of course you don't..." They trailed off, eyes widening and head shaking as they backed a few steps away. They looked down at their hands, trembling in front of them as their shoulders drooped and the shock ebbed into something more pained. Taking my chance, I spoke softly, but firmly. "I didn't know what else to do. You were panicked. I would've been okay if you'd have just told me how uncomfortable you were. It wasn't until you were already screaming that I knew."

There was a sullen silence between us. When Acanthus finally broke it, they mumbled, "I wasn't screaming."

I bit back my anger and kept my tone neutral as I replied. "Regardless."

Acanthus was gilded in the light of the halogens, and this was absolutely ridiculous. The tension had built up so ridiculously high that I couldn't take it anymore; I started laughing. As I laughed, the tension immediately broke, like the snapping of a rubber band. And then, I couldn't stop. I laughed and laughed until my stomach and sides hurt. Anytime I'd look up and see Acanthus' concerned face, it'd start all over. Acanthus' tone was dark as they huffed, crossing their arms. "You have utterly lost your mind."

"Acanthus I—" I let the words drip out in short spurts between laughter. "I can't... I- it's.... Too fucking funny."

They turned their back on me, sniffing as if they smelled something unpleasant. "If you're quite finished, I'd like to move on."

I moved to follow them, not wanting to part on a bad note. In the muddy yellow lights, they were beautiful. Their expression was stony and unamused. I grinned at them as I stood in their path. "Tell me where to go. Though, I don't understand why we couldn't just wait for another donor at the diner."

"Would you really want to sit in chains while I had another meal, Cypress? I didn't want to wait another half an hour, and we'd caused a scene. Sometimes I worry for your sanity."

They walked around me and started moving to their next destination. How was it that someone six inches shorter than me was so goddamn fast? "My sanity? Acanthus, the fucking world is insane. For all I know, I could be hooked up to a respirator and dreaming all of this. Maybe I died two years ago, and you're just a fever dream."

He turned and glared. "I am not amused by you, or that thought, any more than I was the last time you brought it up."

"Aww, Acanthus. You don't want to be the man of my dreams?"

They flushed and quickly continued down the road. "I need a drink."

I deflated. Without a word, I followed. I guess I wasn't very funny after all.

That Time At The Spirits Three

Acanthus

I was dead silent for most of the walk to my next nearest haven, passing the huddled brick buildings with no real focus on them. This hour of pre-dawn is the only time within the city that stays mostly silent; too early for first shift workers, too late for night dwellers, and certainly not a safe time for proper society. We stuck to the streets instead of alleyways. I would have to be quick in the club; by the time we were done, the sun would be high and proud in the sky, and I hadn't taken my parasol or a cloak with me.

The second haven, The Spirits Three, was a Gothic and alternative lifestyle nightclub that stayed open until seven in the morning; on its surface a safe space for leather and synthwave. But, its true purpose was a stopping point on The Night Garden paths. Like the Magic Manor, The Spirits Three had a standard, conventionally accepted façade in its main room— a large dance floor and beautiful mahogany bar with Gothic and Baroque design elements, flickering LED candle lights surrounding the drink area— but the back was a series of rooms for people to sleep in and stay, should they need.

The Spirits Three was owned by Esmeralda Garrison, a beautiful Witch I'd helped escape a Wolf pack after being banished. She stayed in one of my hideouts for decades before she returned to the City and bought the bar, vowing to help with my cause. She'd proven to be one of my biggest confidants and a great asset to the Night Garden. As I thought of Esmeralda, I calmed from the near disaster in the market. She'd definitely have donors available for me. Most of the hatred I had for myself in these situations had crept back to the shadows. We came to a long, empty alley, and I stopped, turning on my heel to finally address Cypress. "I owe you an apology."

Cypress looked at me, confused. "You don't need to say anything. I was being a jerk."

I shook my head emphatically. I had turned my worry into a weapon against them, when they had simply done what I asked. But, regardless, I needed to address it later. I stepped away from them, and they reached for me, grabbing my wrist. "I don't want to let you go alone, Acanthus. I have a bad feeling about it."

I pulled my wrist from their grasp, turning to face them. "You're going to have to, Cypress. Wait here, please. I will be back soon. Wolves are not allowed in this establishment."

Cypress started to protest, and my patience snapped. "Did you not see me in the superstore? Let me be alone for fifteen minutes to half an hour so that I may sate myself. Don't move. I'll be fine."

They looked down to their shoes. "Yes, Acanthus," Cypress mumbled.

My heart panged and I reached up, taking their shoulder. "Look. I apologize. My hunger sharpens my claws, as it were. This is a very heavily supernatural part of the city, and I'd rather not be caught here during the day by a pack of rogue Wolves."

Cypress nodded again. Their eyes had widened at the mention of supernaturals. "I regularly used to bus over here for meet-ups with friends when I lived in Brooklyn... Some live on this side of town. I didn't realize…"

I glanced up to the brightening sky and licked my lips. "Just, sit tight? Don't move. If you don't attract attention, you should be fine. I won't be longer than I need to be."

They nodded again, and I swiftly left them in the alley. "Be careful and stay put," I reiterated, shouting over my shoulder as I sprinted across the street. I had to be mindful of the time.

The club stood out amongst the other businesses lining the street, three and four story brick buildings with overhangs of every color. The Spirits Three was painted black, neon red and purple signs tracing the building. Its sign was written in cursive, with the silhouette of a bubbling cauldron behind it. It reflected dully in the black tint of the windows and the crescent moon-shaped glass in the black metal doors.

Esmeralda had made certain to drive the Witch theme home. She insisted that it was a beacon for anyone lost; hiding in plain sight. I didn't doubt her intuition. I also knew it was a beacon shining into Austin's eyes, though she'd never admit it. Esmeralda detested Wolves, and was right on the border of Austin's territory as a free Witch. The way she styled The Spirits Three had to do with shouting at the surrounding Wolf packs, *I'm here, I'm free, and you can fuck right off.* It certainly seemed within her repertoire, foul language and all. I simply utilized her services, and made sure she had contacts with other members of the Night Garden paths.

The music was audible before I even made it across the street, and the glass of the doors rattled slightly with the vibrations from the sound. This noise, however, was comforting; unlike the city or the supermarket, the dark wave music had the promise of bodies in black velvet crushing together in feverish dance, and the pulsing of blood from people overjoyed to offer themselves to me.

Inside, the music pumped through every speaker. Purple and black damask walls with black sconces peppered the short hallway that led to a large room. This was the main room of the bar. Black tufted couches lining the outskirts of the dance floor to the back and right of the room. Sad humans with pasty makeup dotted the scenery like living statues. I sighed, adjusting the glasses before regarding the bar to the left. This is probably one of the only places in New York where my appearance wouldn't cause humans to turn their heads. Esmeralda was behind the bar.

Walking up to the shiny black counter, I gave my most charming smile. "Esmeralda!"

Es' eyes lit up, and she leaned on the counter and tilted her head towards me. Her deep voice resonated softly from behind her full, black painted lips and sapphire snakebite studs. "Acanthus. Been a while since I've seen that smug smile."

I nodded. "I've been a little too in my head, as of late, my dear. Is it too early or late for a Power of Three? I'd also like to talk to you about some roses."

Roses were code for Vampires; I'd heard there was a Nosferatu in the area from another Night Garden agent. I'd thought Nosferatu were extinct in the states; I wanted to extend my protection and friendship. Esmeralda met me with a derisive smile. She pushed her dark purple fringe from her icy blue eyes. "In your head. Aren't we all? I can foster a Power of Three, but you'll need to accept me as the third. We can talk about the Garden in the back. Do you have the coin?"

"As if you have to ask." My voice was smooth as silk as I dropped six golden coins onto the counter with a satisfying clink. The coins were a currency the Witches and those few benevolent Vampires had agreed upon long ago, to give Witches agency that the Wolves couldn't control. To anyone watching, it may have looked like the chocolate coins that are offered around Halloween, but it held real value to the World of Shadows.

It especially held weight for those embroiled in the Night Garden; coin gave us the agency to have untrackable currency, which was invaluable in the modern age. I tossed my auburn hair flirtatiously, my smile widening. "Always a pleasure to pull from you, my dear."

She scoffed, and yet a blush tinged her cheeks beneath her white foundation. Her Adam's apple bobbed with a pleased little swallow. "Hey, Ben!"

I turned to see a young man dressed all in black with gray vanity glasses similar to mine perched on his nose. She smiled, holding up her right hand and hooking her finger to beckon him. He glided across the dance floor, standing politely next to me and nodding towards her. "Esmeralda."

"Hey, darling, can you take over the bar? I have a Power of Three."

"Of course, my friend. Enjoy."

She turned on her heel, making sure to put a bit of swing into her hips as she walked around the bar. Ben rounded the mahogany counter, rolling up his black sleeves. I watched her, waiting patiently for her instruction. "Red room," she called over her shoulder. "I'll meet you in five. Jonathon should already be back there, and I should be able to get Belle as well. I'll make sure she's alone."

"You're a doll, Es." I blew her a kiss before heading towards the dance floor. Walking past it, I slipped into a narrow hallway that offered a series of ebony doors. The last door on the left was the red room. I entered, licking my lips with anticipation. This was going to be a feast. I felt like a glutton, but at least I had the guarantee that I'd be sated for Cypress' acceptance into Nekane's pack. I only hoped Cypress wouldn't get bored in the next half an hour.

Cypress

Acanthus had been gone for all of five minutes when boredom started kicking in. I had found a small alcove within the alley to sit and wait for them, unsure of how long it would be. The crumbling brick was a light sandy color on one building, and the other was a deep red, a fire escape ladder dangling a few feet from the ground. The green of the dumpsters beneath stood out starkly, and it smelled, but at least I could sit my bags down. The music was clearly audible from across the street, and frankly, I was a little glad they commanded me not to follow. What a headache.

Trying to tune it out, I sat and listened to the bustle of the early morning city. What time even was it? 5am? It had to be decently close to dawn. The taxis going by, the people on the street, yelling and rushing from place to place. I almost missed it here in the endless chaos. Almost.

As the sun rose, the sounds grew in frequency and volume; not waking up, but rising in a crescendo. The city never sleeps, after all.

The whooshing of cars past my little resting spot was calming, and as I sat on the concrete, the brick was cool against my back. I could've fallen asleep sitting like that. That is, I could have, until I heard a woman wail about a block away. I tried to stay where I was, thinking someone was just being rowdy and drunk at the bar. I almost had convinced myself of that, but another distressed cry echoed over the constant flow of traffic, "Fuck, Kennedy! Somebody, PLEASE! Help me!"

Before I knew it, I was running. The voice sounded familiar, which set me even further on edge. Bags be damned— if they got stolen, they got stolen. I wouldn't be able to live with myself if I left that scream unheard. I made it to a new street, and stopped short. A few punks with heavy silver chains at their throats surrounded a woman, pressed against a wall. "Hey!" I yelled, trying to get their attention.

All three turned to look at me, and the woman started to cry with relief. "Cypress?!"

Kassidy stood shaking in high heels, hugging her arms as she stood over a bundle of clothes... Wait. There was a shock of blonde hair beneath her. Kennedy was knocked out, and the coppery-iron smell of blood stuck in my nostrils and stoked my rage . "The fuck, guys? I'm sure you have better things to do than pick on a couple of lovely ladies going about their day."

 I casually tilted my head to the side, showing Kas the way she could run to safety.

"What's it to you, tough guy," a gruff voice growled to my left. Something deep below my logic told me that these weren't ordinary men. Kennedy whimpered as Kassidy knelt, whispering to her sister as she helped her up. Kennedy was unsteady, swaying as the Wolves advanced on me. "You think you're tough?"

I gritted my teeth, preparing myself to take them on. So long as I could be a distraction long enough for the girls to get away, I'd brave a fight. I was tall and strong; not much of a seasoned fighter, but I could take them. And, I wasn't about to let them get away with hurting Kas and Kennedy. I sized them up as Kas and Kennedy took their chance to run. *Just, sit tight, and don't draw attention,* echoed in my mind as I lowered myself into a guarded stance. Acanthus was going to be pissed.

"You made a mistake getting involved!" That voice made me pause; another I knew. One of the guys towards the back of the group stepped forward, and my blood turned to ice as I recognized his face. That voice was familiar because I'd been hearing it since freshman year of high school. Junior, my best friend before the bite. The same Junior who couldn't stand me once I came out as non-binary; the one who abandoned me, and openly hated me. "Junior?!"

The bastard smirked at me, malice in his eyes. "Cypress."

Growls of angry beasts began to fill the air, and Junior stepped forward. "Saving another couple of whores? Think that'll mean you can save your mom, buddy?"

"Oh, you fucker," I snarled. Some things never changed. One of the Wolves lurched forward, springing into his Wolf form. Junior let out a dark laugh. The others seemed prime to attack at any moment. They could tell, because I could tell. The lot of us were Wolves, and the odds weren't looking in my favor.

Teeth and claws sprang forth as the Wolves shifted. This wasn't good. They had to be experienced. Maybe I couldn't take on three experienced Wolves cornering me in an alley. Thinking quickly, I rushed forward and jumped over the shortest one, reaching down and vaulting over them with my hand on the Wolf's back. I stumbled forward with the momentum as I landed on the sidewalk. These Wolves were big; bigger than any dog, and certainly bigger than any standard wolf I could remember seeing in a zoo. I knew I was big, too, but I figured I was the weird outlier. It was intimidating to see Wolves that big.

As soon as I hit the ground, I was running. There were three Wolves chasing me down now, much faster on all fours than me on two legs. Screams and frantic shouting came from either side of the street, people scrambling to get out of our way. "Did wolves escape from the zoo?!"

"What's going on?"

"Oh, fuck!"

One of the Wolves behind me leapt, and I ducked. He soared over my head, crashing into a newspaper stand and sending papers flying. The second barreled into my legs, and I went down as the Wolf clamped onto my ankle.

I screamed and flipped over onto my back, taking the Wolf with me. I tried not to shut down, kicking until he let go. He lunged again, and this time I managed to land both feet squarely in his chest, and sent him sailing into the busy traffic. The Wolf landed with a yelp. He didn't get up again. Drivers swerved and blared on their horns. The newspaper stand Wolf howled, struggling to its feet and limping towards the road to check on his friend.

At the same time the third and biggest of the Wolves roared, charging. It was Junior, and it was personal. "Fuck," I shouted. So much for the loaner clothes. I met him as a Wolf myself, the torn shreds of my sweatshirt falling like confetti. Where Junior was big, I was bigger. I snarled, trying to get a hold on his neck.

Our claws scrambled on the concrete sidewalk, unable to find purchase. We barreled into one woman, as another screamed and fell against the nearby building to avoid us. "Someone call animal control!" A man shouted.

I could only imagine what the four of us looked like, fighting in the streets of New York City. It was crowded at the best of times. How did I not know the World of Shadows existed before now? *Acanthus is going to be so, SO pissed at me.*

The thought was quickly ripped away as Junior's teeth tore into my shoulder. I yelped, pushing him off. We both landed squarely on all fours, circling each other, wondering what the next best attack was. He leaped first, almost jumping over me. I lunged upward, sinking my teeth into soft underbelly. The Wolf howled with rage as he landed. We charged again, meeting in the middle.

We crashed together into a tumble of limbs and slashing claws. Junior twisted, landing a bite on my neck. We tumbled. I lost sense of where we were, and the two of us ended up crashing through the front doors of a building. The familiar bass-heavy music throbbed in time with the wounds on my shoulder.

"Oh shit," was the last thought I had before the other Wolf barreled into my side, sending me sliding across the shiny black floors.

Acanthus

"Oh, for fuck's sake."

The words projected from me without my consent. Cypress' dread-filled thought ripped through my consciousness along with the sound of the doors crashing open, muffled by the room's soundproofing. Jonathan and Belle were asleep already in each other's arms upon the black queen-sized bed across the room. I was standing beside the leather couch, and I paused my smoothing of the weighted blanket across Esmeralda's fragile chest. "Mm?" She questioned, hooded eyes trained on mine.

I was thankful for the sound-proofed room insulating us from the cacophony in the main establishment; she wouldn't be able to hear with her human hearing. I kept my voice calm as I replied. "It's nothing, darling. I need to depart now, and save your bar. Don't worry about paying me security detail, just rest your pretty head. Thank you for the meal."

She blinked, confusion spreading across her features. But, she wouldn't follow. The bar had been at less than a quarter of its capacity when she accepted my Power of Three, and was technically closed at this point. Ben would have cleared the bar, but some Supernaturals were probably still lingering; she kept her doors open to those less fortunate in the World of Shadows. Esmeralda herself would be recovering from the blood loss for the next hour. I, however, could feel pain that was not my own. This caused a fluttering in my chest; I'd never experienced such a sensation before. As soon as I slipped through the door of the red room, I sprang into action and sprinted down the hall.

The front of The Spirits Three was not a pretty sight. Wolves circled each other, one of them heavily bleeding from multiple wounds. I could tell it was Cypress by the white and gray-tipped fur, and rage bubbled within, dark and dangerous. *"Not my fault,"* echoed through my head in a desperate plea. There was guilt attached to the thought, and my rage burned even hotter. In a movement so fast that time slowed near to a standstill, I bounded into the room and between the Wolves. Without breaking stride, I pulled my arm back and speared my sharp nails squarely into the under jaw of the large Wolf circling Cypress.

A loud yelp, followed by a whimper sounded through the bar. Any humans who had been milling about had long since cleared the area. I bared my fangs at the Wolf I had speared. "You break a century old peace treaty over a petty squabble?! I should rip your head clean from your neck, you mange-ridden fool!"

Whimpers and snarls met my rage as my voice reverberated off of the walls. I dragged the giant gray wolf across the black tile and towards the damaged double doors. The sunlight was bright in the early daybreak, and it glittered as it streamed into the bar. I could smell other Wolves, and the palpable fear of the remaining beings around the premises. *They want to test my rage? Well, here it is.*

I lifted the heavy Wolf high into the air. My fingers speared deeper and into their upper palate, their whines becoming more desperate. I grimaced as their hot blood fell in rivulets down my wrist. "Hear me, Pack! I will find which one you are! This is the one and ONLY warning you will receive. If I find even the smell of wet dog in my domains, I will hunt you down and slaughter you like the pests you are. Consider this—"

I pulled my arm back, and then, leaping forward with a loud grunt, I threw the Wolf out of the bar and across the street, hearing it thud as it skidded to a harsh landing. "— your warning."

With that, I whirled around and walked back into the bar, shoulders tight and fists clenched. Cypress was pressed against a wall, their ears flat as they whimpered softly. I shook my head, kneeling down and looking at them. "I leave you for twenty minutes and you break a peace treaty. Go. I'll meet you where I left you in a moment."

I needed to clean up this mess first. Cypress hesitated. I pointed towards the doors. "Go. I'm not angry."

They shifted back, a desperate edge to their voice. "I'm sorry, some friends were in trouble. I can help—"

My patience was like broken glass. I spoke firmly, staring down the naked man. "You've done enough."

Their face fell. I sighed. "I'll meet you in the alley, Cypress. Five minutes. I need to do damage control before the cleanup crews come, and you're naked and bleeding."

Cypress' face twisted. If they were still a Wolf, their tail would be tucked between their legs. They moved to cover themself, a blush of shame filling their cheeks. I shrugged my jacket off to hand it to them, and they reached to hold it in front of them as they mumbled, "... Yes, Acanthus."

Cypress fidgeted with the leather. They quickly shifted back into their Wolf, moving to grab the jacket with their teeth. They whimpered around the collar, dejected, and walked away as quickly as they could manage. I sighed, closing my eyes and putting my powers to work. I couldn't worry about their feelings right now; realistically, I only had a very small window of time to comfort the few remaining humans in the area that had just watched me launch a human-sized Wolf across the street. I had no idea how many were left, or how public the altercation was before it reached the doors of the bar. I could feel a migraine forming behind my eyes as I thought of dealing with some Wolf pack's grizzled detectives.

It also would complicate matters if Austin showed up here, of all places. Esmeralda would have words for me, I'm certain. *Cypress, you confound me with your foolishness... I should've known better than to leave you alone*, I thought as I twisted pieces of the bar's door back into place.

That Time The Red Tape Fell Apart

Cypress

I shifted as soon as I hit the alleyway, and threw on some clothes. I didn't move as I waited for Acanthus. The dirty pavement was cold and slick in the early morning, and I sat cross-legged as Acanthus' words echoed through my mind. *Wet dog. Pest.*

The insults stabbed through my heart with each repeat. What made me any different than the Wolves that I'd fought? They didn't choose their fates, either. What made me other than a wet dog, or a pest? I would have started walking back to the church if it wouldn't have confirmed Acanthus' words. I'd done nothing but caused problems since I arrived. Leaving would have reinforced their thoughts. So, I stayed right where they said to, with my head back against the rough, uneven surface of the brick. The coolness was soothing against my irritated skin.

The only movements I made were to look for my wallet and keys, which had thankfully been left untouched by the pile of ripped clothing near the mouth of the alley. The sickly sweet smell of garbage clung to the dumpsters, and my bags were undisturbed where I'd left them. As I waited, I found myself thinking about Kassidy and Kennedy. *I really hope they're alright...*

The fact that they'd gotten away was a small comfort, but my self esteem was sludge on the concrete. Kennedy had been unconscious when I stepped in. I found myself wishing that I'd had my cell phone. It was currently a brick in my glove box, which was useless to me now. I wanted to check in on the twins. Did they see the Wolves shift? Did they see *me* shift? If all of this stuff was secret, then how were humans so oblivious? What even happened? Junior was a dick, but I never would've pegged him as a heinous creep.

I didn't have any answers, and I'd have walked to their apartment if it weren't for Acanthus' instructions. I'm sure the blood on my clothes would stress them out even more. *Kennedy better be okay. I should have ripped Junior apart.*

My emotions stabbed through my chest like a thorn. The wounds I'd suffered were all singing a hateful melody in unison. The one on my shoulder was already bleeding through the new shirt. Acanthus' jacket was draped over my chest to hide the blood stain. The lingering smell of roses, sandalwood, and oud both upset and calmed me. *What a fucking mess.*

I closed my eyes as the sound of sirens echoed somewhere nearby. Underneath the wail, footsteps entered the mouth of the alley, shoes scraping against the uneven ground. I flinched and looked up to see Acanthus glowering at me. *Wet dog. Pest.* They made no move to hide their anger. I shrank further into my shell. "Let's go home," they hissed at me.

Before I could stop myself, I bit out, "Why?"

Wet dog. I knew the words weren't directed at me, though that didn't make it sting any less. *Pest.* I was exactly the same as those Wolves. The look Acanthus shot my direction was full of hurt, coloring the rage with confusion. "What do you mean, *why?* Cypress, you're bleeding, I just attacked a Wolf in *broad daylight* and broke a peace treaty, and the sun is out. I may have put a nearly extinct Vampire in danger. The Spirits Three is going to be crawling with cleanup crews and I'm going to have to explain that to Esmeralda when she's coherent. It's been a very long night and I'm well past done with this city."

Their hazel eyes were glowing brightly behind the vanity glasses, which did nothing to hide them. They had purple smudges beneath the fire, and I winced. ***"I'm a fucking problem to be solved is all. That's all I've been since we've met."***

Their shoulders slouched at my thought, and they leaned against the wall. "A problem...? Cypress, I don't know what happened, but this wasn't your fault. I know you wouldn't have started something if you could help it."

I didn't answer, snorting as I looked away from them and down the alley. When they spoke, their voice lost the angry bite. "I didn't mean what I said as an attack on you. It was wrong of me to lump Wolves into general derogatory characteristics. You must understand, that display in the bar was politics. I'm one of the only established Vampires in this area, I need to show that I'm not weak."

Lemon Balm

I gulped, my throat tight. I wasn't really sure what this emotion was. Anxiety? Sadness? Hurt? Maybe it was a combination of the three. "Yeah. Okay," was all I could manage in response.

Acanthus wasn't convinced. They knelt in front of me and gently placed one of their freezing hands on my shoulder. Or, it typically would have been freezing, but now they felt almost alive with warmth. The change was startling, and I glanced down at their arm. Their right hand was the clean one; their left was dripping with gore. I didn't know how to justify the image it caused. I was being comforted by a terrifying person that just kebab'ed a Wolf in front of me like they were nothing. Their gentle voice made the difference more intense. "Are you all right? I don't like that I've put darkness in your mind."

I mustered up the best fake smile I could manage. "I'm fine, Acanthus."

The wind sent the gray plastic of the bags beside us rustling, and I glanced towards them. *How are we even going to get those back?*

Acanthus frowned and leaned back on their heels, standing. I leaned forward as they reached for their coat and plucked it off of me. They slid it over their shoulder, and if they weren't coated in gore, they'd look almost debonair. I stood in front of them, and they stepped forward, wrapping their arms around my waist. The sirens were starting to echo closer. Acanthus placed their feet on top of mine, and rose into the air. The bags trailed behind us as I clung to Acanthus' neck, and did my best not to get blood on them.

"Acanthus, I—"

Acanthus' voice was nearly imperceptible over the wind. "Not now, Pup. It can wait until we are on the ground again."

It was a quiet ten minutes as we flew back, landing on the small concrete porch in front of the heavy oak doors. I pulled my keys from my pocket and unlocked them, pushing it open and turning to grab the floating bags from the air. Wind *whooshed* past me. Acanthus was already inside, stepping out of the line of the sunlight. I grimaced, looking up at the sky. *Does the sun affect them, or not?* I wondered for the millionth time. It'd be great if they didn't send me mixed messages about it. I gathered the bags in my arms and brought them in in one go, ignoring the pain in my shoulder.

One of my duffels were still open from the morning, and I promptly start to shove my new clothes into it. Acanthus' hair was a sparrow's nest as they tried to look graceful. It was an impossible task; their patience snapped and they used their hands to comb through it. By the time they were no longer distracted, I had already started to fold up the cot. "What are you doing," their voice was a touch shrill.

"Getting out of your hair."

"Don't be ridiculous."

They grabbed the cot, wrenching it from me as if the metal frame was made of paper. I winced, my shoulder stinging with the sudden movement. "You're still bleeding, and we haven't heard back from Nekane yet. The events from last night have vastly changed the stakes, and leaving can put you in danger. Now take off your shirt, and let me look at those bites."

I gritted my teeth, my body going rigid. "What, so I have to stay now? Acanthus, I don't need your help."

"Cypress. Don't. Let me look at your wounds."

I growled in frustration. "I said *no*. I don't need your fucking *help*. I don't want any part of these Wolves, and I think it'd be best if I left."

They were in my face then, floating to put us at an even height. "Is that truly what you think? I've stuck my neck out for you. Not to mention, Cypress, you have nowhere else to go."

I'd worked so hard to manage when I hit these rages. All of my coping mechanisms were out the window; I couldn't put the anger aside. I shoved him away from me, snarling. "I don't care! I'm getting out of your hair, I need to stop being a problem."

We stared each other down as they floated back, fire in those intense eyes. The tension between us was thick and awful. I shook, clenching my fists. They slowly lowered to the floor, their voice deadpan as they touched down. "Are you done?"

"Are you?"

"I'm not the injured one refusing aid," Acanthus' voice could have frozen a pit of lava. They reached for their hair, but then paused and stared at their gore-flecked hand. Lowering them, they began to pace around the small space. If I had been in a different mindset, I might have been amused at the pale divots in the wooden floorboards beneath their feet. They were surefire signs of Acanthus' typical pacing pattern through the years. Instead, I sulked.

"You're not the one who went out and got injured," I mumbled.

They paced more rapidly, starting to become blurry. As they stopped, they exploded. "You are impossible! Completely fucking impossible. We broke a treaty tonight, Pup, and where you didn't know about it, it's a problem! There is very well a bounty on my head because of tonight, and at least a few hundred mortals being manipulated into forgetting the day. I am trying so hard to be a valid resource for you, even though I damn well know I'm not good at it! I am not willing to also be responsible for your wounds getting infected! Let me help you, damn it! You're going to wind up getting yourself killed and I don't know if I can —"

They stopped yelling, and the silence that followed was horrible and deafening. Tears pricked the corners of their eyes. All of my self-pity died. They lowered their gaze to the floor and traces of blood streaked their pale skin as they turned away from me. "Forget it."

I was stunned by the sentence that had been left unsaid. Maybe the way I was acting *was* reckless. Nothing I could say was able to fix this. I barely knew anything about them, not to mention the politics involved. Their unspoken pain hung between us as heavily as the dropped sentence. My voice cracked. "You swore at me today. Exactly three times. Not that… I'm counting or anything. The little bit that I know about you, I don't really think that's a good sign."

I brought my hand to the back of my head, embarrassed. The silence stretched as I tried to find the words for what I wanted to say. My body slowly calmed in the silence, and when I finally broke it, my voice was low. "Look. I appreciate it. Really, I do Acanthus. It just... I didn't ask for this, and you didn't ask for this. I'm in way over my head. I…"

I trailed off, emotion finally breaking free. My own eyes blurred, and I surprised us both when I pulled them to my chest, hugging them tightly. "Thank you."

Acanthus

I sullenly pressed my cheek against their chest, refusing to return the hug at first. The smells of copper and iron wafted around us, mingling from my tears and their wounds. When I relented, I let out a tired little noise as I finally wrapped my arms around his waist. I'm not certain how long we stayed like that, but I was the one to break the silence. I had taken the time to compose myself and find what words could explain the whirling thoughts in my mind.

"Look, I know that this is horrible, messy, and confusing. A good deal of what you've been experiencing is terrifying, even. I may not know what it's like to be a Wolf, but I know what it's like to change against your will. I know what it is like to not know your own nature or limits. I know what it is like to be truly, utterly alone. And, I know what it is to be helpless, and feel like you're perpetuating the problem."

I paused, taking a shaky breath and lifting my head from their chest. My tears had stopped their flow. The dried blood crackled on my cheeks, and I must have looked like quite the sight. Though, so many of my limits had been broken and boundaries crossed over the last twenty four hours, that I couldn't bother to care how I looked. "You will make mistakes. You will stumble into situations that hurt you, without knowing

126

what you did wrong. You will cause problems. It is one of those things where you are like a newborn babe and that makes me, effectively, an ill-equipped adoptive elder. I cannot pretend that I know exactly how you work, but anything that I am saying is truly because I want what is best for you to thrive; ironically, I may have ruined our chances at that this morning."

Tears threatened to spill once more. I shook my head, closing my eyes to compose myself. A wave of self-hatred and regret washed over me. I could have handled the Wolf attack better. *There goes over one hundred years of peace, with a single thrust of my hand.*

With my impulsive display of power, the city could now be on the brink of a war. What would maybe twenty Vampires do against fourteen Wolf packs and countless indentured Witches? The Vampires don't keep in touch; I may even be a solo target. The thought sucked all of the air out of me and left me cold, and a headache was forming at the base of my skull. These all were problems to address later; I could only do what I could with the matter at hand. I turned my attention back to Cypress, staring at the dark splotch on his shirt. "So, please, Pup. Let me tend to those wounds, before they get infected. It is what I can do."

My mind was already racing again, trying to remember which fresh herbs I had gathered before our trip to the city and which ones I would have to go out and gather from my garden. I had already been in the sun so much today, and I was taking a chance with illness with every minute more. The impending summer made the nights shorter. There was not a cloud in the sky, and the rays were intense today. At least now my cloaks were accessible and at hand.

Cypress

Acanthus' emotion was honest and raw, and I was definitely not prepared for it. I didn't know what to do to comfort them, and I found myself second guessing every move. I couldn't stand the thought of being poked and prodded right now. I was too busy blaming myself for starting a war I didn't even know was a threat. I hoped Kassidy and Kennedy weren't too traumatized. I thought about my phone, uncharged and thrown into the glove box of the Golf. I looked at Acanthus, and then outside. The sun was blazing down, and I could feel the warmth from here. We hadn't drawn the curtains closed yet.

"Acanthus, I really appreciate that, but I'm exhausted. You are exhausted. And I know. I know you said the sun doesn't affect you, but your mad dash inside tells me otherwise."

Acanthus opened his mouth to interrupt, but I kept going. "Let's wait until sundown. Sunset even. Then I will let you care for me. But right now, you need to worry about you. I'll help you pick the herbs you need, or, I'll sit on my hands, and drink any tinctures you brew without complaint. But I don't want your help if it's hurting you."

I moved away from them to place the cot back flat in its spot. I wasn't leaving, and I wanted to make that clear. I put on my best imploring face, and added eyelash flutters for effect. "Please?"

Acanthus thought, looking back outside. Their shoulders drooped as they shifted their gaze back to me, their lips turning into a small, serious frown. "Very well. I'm willing to compromise. But, before you rest, I demand you take a shower. Who knows what diseases those mutts had."

"Mange, fleas…. Maybe scurvy." *Who knows what Junior had gotten himself into…*

Acanthus' eyes widened, and then they laughed, shaking their head. "Go shower, Pup. I grow tired."

"Yes, Acanthus."

"Good morning." They floated up the stairs to the loft.

"Sleep well," I called after them. I thought of my phone in the glove box again, glanced at the blankets beside my cot, and sighed. Maybe I would check in with Kassidy and Kennedy after I showered. I jogged out to the car, rescuing my phone and charger, and plugged it in on the kitchen counter before I went to clean myself up.

᛫ 🌙))◡))○◡᠎◡ ☾ ᛫

When I woke up, the sun was setting. I listened. There was no other sound within the church, not even breathing. Acanthus wasn't there. I stretched my hands above my head, and then sat up, blinking the sleep from my eyes. I was sore, and my wounds were still stinging, even after washing them. It was strange; since the dog bite — *Wolf* bite — pain was something apart from myself, not nearly as relevant. I was aware of it, but it wasn't the same as if I were human. I wasn't sure my wounds needed to be tended to either. The bleeding had stopped, and the skin had already healed over from what I could tell, but a deal is a deal.

There were still lingering pangs of guilt from my actions this morning, too. Thankfully, Kassidy told me that she and Kennedy were okay. She thanked me for helping, and said she missed me. If I had stayed put, like I was told, then they would have been hurt. I hoped Acanthus was able to fix things at the bar. The entire situation had no win; I didn't blame myself, anymore, but I was worried about what this meant for Acanthus and the World of Shadows.

Come to think of it, I wondered what happened to all of the humans and onlookers during that chaos. It had been about dawn, but that meant

128

nothing. The city was always bustling with traffic. Maybe I'd ask Acanthus if that was World of Shadows shenaniganry. I had no way of knowing, otherwise. One thing was for sure, I definitely wasn't looking forward to joining a Pack, now.

That Time I Mixed Tinctures

Acanthus

By the time the sun was fully beneath the horizon, we were both out in the garden. Cypress' soft breathing beside me melded with the sounds of crickets and critters in the forest. The soothing chill of the night breeze was tranquil. I hadn't slept long; though, I was content. I'd been in the garden for a while, and my skin was caked with mud and grime. It matched a strange dirtiness that clung to me since coming home from the bar. No matter how many times I washed my hands, I could still feel the gore clinging to me.

My cloak sat squarely on my shoulders; this one was a deep royal purple with gold filament and edging. The deep hood fell into my eyes. I pushed it off, careful when lifting it over my braided bun. It was messy, but it kept the annoying tumble out of my face while I worked. My bare knees poked through the rips in the jeans. The coolness of the earth grounded me. The state of affairs was stressful, and the earth quieted the worry. The simplicity of mud and wind allowed me to feel alive. The herbs sat neatly in a basket to my left.

Peppermint would stave off infection and leave behind a gentle, soothing tingle. Chamomile would promote the skin to heal without scarring. Echinacea flowers would stave off infection and soothe the swelling of Cypress' wounds. Lemon balm would kick their immune system into high gear, and lavender wouldn't add much other than a calming effect, but I felt the need to gather some. I had some dried eucalyptus that I could add as well. If I crushed my fresh herbs in with it,

I could make a powerful muscle soother. I thought Cypress would appreciate that most of all.

I leaned back, gazing at the sky. The first subtle stars began to poke out from behind the oncoming clouds. It would rain tonight. We needed it. Taking in a deep breath, I held it in my lungs. The silence of the twilight was calming, coupled with the scents that I relished in the garden— mint, thyme, rosemary, basil, and lavender. There were undertones of petrichor from far off, confirming the oncoming rain. It mixed with the scents Cypress always carried— heavy campfire smoke, whiskey, pine and maple. The subtle smells that come with the beginning of summer; grass, mud, and the sweetness of rushing water. I wanted to hold onto this feeling; I wish I could bottle this peace.

I didn't want to go inside yet. In a way, this pause within my little garden was a respite. With as powerful as I am, none of my magic could help. Try as I may, I cannot stop time. But, being away from the busy screaming of automobiles and commerce at least allowed me to think. I could try to strategize, and make a plan for when the Wolves inevitably came for me. I wasn't even sure if Cypress would be able to go to Nekane's pack now.

The Wolves Cypress had attacked weren't Austin's Pack. If they were, then I would have recognized the big oaf circling Cypress in The Spirits Three. In that area of the city, it had to have been some of Nekane's. She may rip the letter up before she even read the contents, if my name was mentioned by the injured.

Alas, like all good things, the solace had to come to an end. Going inside, even if it were to treat the inflamed wounds of my companion, would be like admitting that time was in flow again. It would be admitting that I could not stay here forever. Questions picked at my mind. I turned my head to finally look at Cypress. Their eyes were focused on a cloud of lightning bugs that hovered in the nearby grass. The question left my lips before I fully thought it through. "What even happened?"

Cypress blinked, their eyes darting to mine. "Two of my friends... Kassidy and Kennedy. They were girls that I used to be close to, and they were in the adjacent alley. Kennedy was hurt. I heard Kas scream and ran in to help... I had no idea they were being attacked by Wolves until I already confronted them."

I paused. How very noble of them. I guess I hadn't considered the fact that Cypress used to live in the city, and would know people in the areas we were in. I had jumped to conclusions — They were a Pup, and had already pushed back on my instructions at the Magic Manor. I thought they started the trouble. Maybe they'd broken a law without knowing. Maybe they'd attracted attention, somehow. It was unfair of me to blame them, especially without details first, though I was terrified of the consequences from this morning. I'd have done the same, in his circumstances.

We had received a letter from Nekane during the day agreeing to meet. It had clearly been penned before she was aware of the events that morning. While Cypress was still asleep, I read the soulless words over and over — *Meet at the Strawberry Fields, noon, May 14th.*

I vastly preferred Cypress' company over being alone. If we went along with the agreed upon drop, then it could turn south for me, for Cypress, or for both of us. Their calm presence beside me was an anchor dragging me down. I thought about the absence of their smile and snarky jokes, and a rock formed in my throat. Nekane would not attack in a public park during the day. I could use this to my advantage to explain the situation and guarantee Cypress' safety. Maybe after the handover, I would leave New York for a while. I had a friend in Pennsylvania that I could visit, and she would want to know about the altercation at The Spirits Three.

The Night Garden would likely need to mobilize rescue missions if the war started up again. My stomach twisted. Time marched on, whether I acknowledged it or not. However, I still couldn't force myself to stand. The clouds were starting to roll in quicker, and the smell of rain grew stronger. It wouldn't be long now. "Acanthus," Cypress said from beside me, " I think it's gonna rain."

Out of the corner of my eye, I saw them crinkle their nose. I smiled. "Go inside, Pup. I'll follow in a moment. Put the kettle on, and I will get to your wounds."

They rose without complaint, and I waited to hear the door of the church shut before I stood, rising myself up in a slow flight to the roof. Once I touched down on the crumbling clay tile, I sat cross legged behind the small bell tower that no longer had a bell. Using my telekinesis, I gently guided the basket down the opening of the bell tower, and pictured them landing on the counter beside the stove. Water would only ruin the herbs that I had just picked, and gathering them in the rain would both shock the plants and make the medicines less potent. I had no intentions to go inside just yet. The poultices wouldn't take long to make, and I thought the rain would cleanse me of the dirty feeling on my skin.

I pulled my cloak from my shoulders and whisked it down the bell tower as well, leaving me in my torn jeans and old t-shirt. The faded lettering of *The Cure* was barely visible on the black fabric, and the threadbare shirt did nothing to stave off the chill. I looked down at my hands, realizing that there were remnants of dried blood stuck in the creases of my fingers from spearing the Werewolf earlier, coupled with dirt from the herbs. *How filthy*. How hadn't I noticed?

The first drops of rain began to fall, staining the terracotta around me. Each drop revealed my white skin to shine out from behind the layer of filth on my arms. I was cold. I was alone. I was content…. *But, am I?*

I couldn't be sure that these things were true anymore. Perhaps I could tell Cypress to stay now that the treaty had technically been broken. Perhaps that would be safer. But, keeping them isolated from their own kind felt just as wrong as being alone, myself. I could see no easy answers, and so I tried to stuff the emotions down.

Cypress

I got the water started after lighting the pilot light on the old stove. *I really should've replaced this.*

It was funny; I didn't think I'd be here past the end of the week, though as far as I knew, we hadn't heard back from the Wolves yet. If this old thing suits Acanthus, so be it. It's not like they used it much, anyway. I turned the flame on very low. Acanthus still hadn't come back inside.

I glanced out of the window, but I didn't see them. Where were they? Were they isolating? I wasn't sure, but that was my best guess; Acanthus seemed like the type to isolate when they had a lot on their mind. Had it really only been a few days with them? I felt like I'd known them for a lifetime. There was a small part of me that worried about how they'd be when I was gone, but the thought made me grit my teeth. I didn't like thinking about them on their own. Plus, every time I thought about the Wolf packs, my heart jumped to my throat and pounded like I was running a mile.

Four days, maybe five, tops, Cypress. You've already made their life infinitely more complicated. What are you giving back to them? Don't get too attached, too quickly.

The soft patter of rain began on the roof. Peeking through the window again, I couldn't see them in the garden. *Where are they?*

Grimacing, I threw on a hoodie and put the hood up, stomping into the steady rain. I hated getting wet, and there was always the chance of it turning into a thunderstorm. I glared up at the sky. *You better keep that lightning strapped away, Zeus,* I thought. I didn't want to deal with the panic that came with the weather while I was worried for my friend.

The first place I checked was the garden; the only sign of them was the small piles of dirt that had been pushed aside during their gathering. No Acanthus. Turning around, I scanned the line of the trees behind the church. No Acanthus. Rounding the building, I made it back to the front, staring at the gravel driveway with a frown. *Well, what the heck?*

Lemon Balm

I paused, trying to sniff at the air and scent. Acanthus had described what it was during one of our training sessions, but they couldn't exactly teach me how. I did what I could to try and imitate it, but it was significantly harder to trace their scent in the rain, so I stopped trying. They'd come back when they were ready I'm sure. Puddles had formed in the divots of the driveway. I glanced up at the sky, hesitating. I could go back inside and wait for Acanthus, but there didn't seem to be any threat of storms. What the hell? I was already soaked to the skin. What did jumping in some puddles hurt?

Rain puddles were fun as a human, but what would it be like running through them as a Wolf? I absolutely could be wild and free out here, no longer hiding when the familiar buzz and burn of shifting started in my skin. I peeled off my hoodie, and my shirt. Glancing around, I dropped my shorts on top of the bundle too. I was a Wolf before they hit the ground. It was incredible; I felt every drop of rain on the roughness of my fur. They rolled off of me, and I shook them from my pelt. I pranced towards the puddle, my tongue lolling from my mouth. *Man, I was missing out all this time!*

Staring at the puddle, I leaned down, front paws flat and nose nearly to the ground. I wanted to make the biggest splash possible; how big of a jump would I need to take? I wiggled, calibrating my stance, before I leapt and — splash! Water shot up around me, and I yipped excitedly as I pranced through the falling rain and puddle water. *This is fucking GREAT!*

I turned, wanting to run through the puddle again, but a noise to the left distracted me. It was a squirrel. It ran up a pine tree on the edge of the forest, chattering the whole way up. Curiously I prowled closer. *How easy would it be for me to pluck this creature from the tree?*

The thought made me pause in mid-step. *What a beastly thought.*

My stomach twisted, and I lowered my head. My mouth had too much saliva, and I recoiled, stepping away from the squirrel. I hated my baser instincts and their shouts of *kill, kill, kill*. I was glad that I could control them, now, thanks to Acanthus' teaching. It was a much better use of my time to watch the squirrel for a while. They're really quite intelligent creatures.

I caught Acanthus' scent, both diminished by and mingling with the falling water. I looked up, and my eyes met theirs. They were perched on top of the clay roof tiles like a bird, too far for me to see their expression clearly. I tilted my head in question, and they waved. My tongue lolled out of my mouth, and I ran back to my puddle again. It wasn't as fun with an audience. I looked towards the roof one more time before shaking off and lopping back to the church. Rain is so much better as a Wolf. Though, I could already imagine Acanthus screeching about mud in the house.

Acanthus

I sat comfortably under the steady patter of the rain, relishing in the cleansing coolness of it. Bringing my hand up, I felt around before my fingers found the bobby pins in my hair. I pulled them one by one, letting my bun free and shook the braid out of its tangles. It wouldn't do to let my hair knot. The splashing and happy panting of a Wolf caught my attention and I smiled as I looked down. Cypress' play was adorable; it soothed me to see their joy.

They did not know the depth of the chaos they had started. As he bounded back towards the church, I jumped off the roof, slowing my descent and landing gracefully by Cypress' clothes. He stood by the door, tail thumping against the stone. I picked up the abandoned fabric before heading to the doors. As I made my way inside, I held it open for the happy Pup. "Do not shake in here, Cypress," I warned as I saw the telltale tilt to their head.

They whined in response, their ears cocked. I chuckled. "Oh, stop it."

A towel flew from the bathroom into my waiting hand. The fluffy maroon fabric was warm from dangling over the floor vent. I knelt down, looping it around them and gently toweling them off. I was careful to not press too hard to the injuries I knew they had, though I did brush over one or two that I had not been aware of. They'd healed over, but judging from Cypress' reactions, they were still tender. "Apologies, Pup. I'm not trying to harm."

Werewolves had regenerative powers that put human healing to shame. Cypress' healing was faster than most Wolves I'd had the pleasure of dealing with, and that was both a blessing and a curse. I could only hope that the cuts and scratches hadn't closed over with an infection brewing. I couldn't smell disease when they were near; they were safe, for now. The kettle screamed from the kitchen, and Cypress shifted easily back, pulling the towel from my hands and winding it around their waist. "You're fine, Acanthus."

The ease in their shift made me beam with pride, my chest light. I turned around to give them privacy. Holding my hand out, I summoned another towel. I wound it around my sopping hair as I made my way to the kitchen. Cypress stepped towards their bags, and I heard them rifling through them. The progress they had made in their shifting was beautiful to see. They'd make a fine member of a pack. *I hope I'll be able to see them once they're with Nekane... If they're going with Nekane...* I sighed. *Four days, Acanthus, you silly old fool. You're getting too attached, too quickly. But, if Nekane doesn't take him, you can always ask him to stay.*

A trail of rainwater marked my path on the ruined floors. I wound the towel around my hair and piled it on my head before getting to work, ignoring the uncomfortable way my wet clothes clung to my skin. It wasn't long before I had the teas, tinctures, and poultices mixed and put together. There was a lovely blend of smells coming from the various medicines, and I looked over the items, pleased with my work. Placing them on a small wooden serving tray, I carried them to the living room and placed them on the sofa next to Cypress, who was shirtless and twisting their t-shirt in their hands. They wrinkled their nose, giving a little sneeze, but otherwise stayed still, waiting for me to instruct them. I looked at the wound on their shoulder, assessing that as the worst one. Sitting beside them, I touched their arm.

The wound was largely on their back, and I wouldn't be able to help them while also sitting here. "Come here, Pup. Either lay on the couch, or on the floor."

Cypress

I hesitated, because the sofa was cramped and small and I am a very large person, but I didn't want to seem petulant. So, I leaned over when they asked and laid across the threadbare couch. I couldn't say I was exactly comfortable— I was a bit twisted up, and the cushions were flat, dense slabs, but I made it a goal not to complain. The partially healed wound stretched and pulled painfully. My back was screaming at me, and I was tense. "Cypress, relax. You're safe with me."

"It's not you I'm worried about," I grumbled. It may go without saying, but I didn't like pain. The thought of it scared me more than the actual feeling of it most times. I felt them prod the edges of the wound on my back and nearly leapt into the air, but I managed to stay put, whimpering. I think the tension in my back made it far more tender than the bite did.

Their voice was soft and whispery. They leaned closer to where they had prodded. "Let me get my bearings, Cypress, it will just be a moment longer. I'm seeing where to start. They... They did a number on you. This bite is incredibly deep, like they held on and shook. It's almost like it was personal."

"That's because it was personal."

Acanthus sighed, their cool fingers resting just outside of the irritated, freshly knit-together skin. "We should've looked at this sooner."

"No," I tensed again. "You needed rest."

I felt them poke somewhere different on my back. "ACANTHUS," the growl crept to my voice, and I gripped the cushion underneath me, flexing my hands to keep the lengthening claws at bay.

"Hush. I am not harming you," Acanthus chided. A cool liquid flowed over my back; it stung at first, and I clenched my teeth. Then it became tingly, and soothing. I couldn't help the sigh of relief that fell from my mouth. My body relaxed, the tension sliding off of me. I didn't realize how much pain I was in until I just wasn't.

"That's it."

I couldn't find it in me to respond, so I just laid my head on the sofa and sighed contentedly. "Hmm?"

I drifted as they continued to work on my back. They were putting some sort of paste on my wound. I couldn't see their hands, but I could hear them working with a pestle and mortar; grinding this, adding a pinch of that. *Just how long have they been making potions and stuff for? They seem so calm, it's like it's effortless...*

I tried to memorize the small crease between their eyebrows. For some reason their concentration was funny, so I smiled. "Acanthus."

They turned their head. "Cypress?"

You're wonderful. "Thank you." And my eyes closed, and I was dead to the world.

Acanthus

I had continued to work on Cypress' wounds long after they had fallen asleep, making sure each one had a healthy amount of soothing ointment and healing salves. They had been far more injured than I had initially realized. I found myself pitying the youth. Using my powers to set up my normal blend of rose, oud, and sandalwood candles, I set them alight. Cypress dreamed beside me. I could tell by the way they began to twitch and growl that it wasn't a happy one.

They had just been through so many traumatic things in a very short amount of time. Even though I knew it had been our agreement, the thought of them leaving made my chest ache. I would miss this silly little Wolf, but they owed me nothing, like it or not.

May 14th was a week after the fiasco in the city. That week passed far too quickly. I'd read the letter to Cypress, and we agreed on the meeting time. Esmeralda was rightfully upset about her bar and the politics involved with the treaty breach. I promised her a meeting once Cypress was properly with Nekane. The remaining time leading up to this hand-off had gone smoothly. We trained through the week, and I taught them all I knew about Pack life, which admittedly was not very much. I also taught them about some of our history, some ways to forage in the forest, and how to sense if someone was reading them too closely.

My stomach was constantly coiled, and I was jumpy throughout the entire week. I kept expecting a knock on my door, but it never came. The broken treaty was being ignored, and I couldn't understand why. I didn't want to bother Cypress with my worries; they would be embroiled in enough of their own. *Please, let her treat him right. Maybe I will go to Pennsylvania and speak to Azalea.*

The anxiety was all-consuming. I tried not to think about the rendezvous in Central Park. We would be leaving in mere hours in order to set Cypress up with their new pack. As far as I could tell, they would be going with Nekane after all. A hole had already begun to form in my heart.

Two weeks is such a small amount of time within an eight hundred year span. I had known the pain of lost friendships and companions before, and I would know it again. Yet, for it to cut so deeply was something I had not prepared for. Maybe I was more affected by my own carefully crafted solitude than I cared to acknowledge.

And this is where I found myself— hands shaking, making a coffee pour over and ignoring the lump in my throat as stubbornly as I could. My entire being was screaming. Tell them not to go. Ask them to stay with you.

I shook my head, banishing all thoughts to keep it calm and empty. I couldn't be off of my guard when we met with the Wolves. Why do I feel this way?

"Coffee's ready," I called as naturally as I could. When my hands were no longer occupied by the pot, I began to braid my hair. "Are you?"

Cypress

I popped my head into the kitchen. It was the second time that day I'd awoken in a cold sweat, gnashing teeth lingering from my nightmares. I didn't say anything about the dread eating me alive, and Acanthus didn't comment on it. We were playing a careful game of feigned indifference. "Did you say coffee?"

Acanthus laughed. "I could tell you an entire story, but if I said coffee first, you wouldn't hear another word."

I smiled at them, walking to grab the cup. "My life blood."

They rolled their eyes and sighed heavily, "That is not nearly as funny as you think it is, Cypress."

"I think I'm funny,'" I grumbled as I took a sip. Acanthus frowned.

"What?"

They shrugged, their eyes not quite meeting mine. "I'm proud of you. You don't seem nervous at all."

"Me? Nervous? That's funny."

Acanthus couldn't know that I was literally trembling at the thought of leaving this cozy, safe sanctuary, and living with a pack of Wolves sounded as appealing as. Uh. Well, living with a pack of Wolves. "I've," I hesitated, trailing off. Not telling them about how I felt seemed like a lie. I didn't want to lie to Acanthus. "I've been having nightmares. Today's was particularly scary."

Acanthus leaned forward, their hazel eyes flashing and sharp. "What about?"

I scowled at the coffee cup, swiftly losing interest in it. "I don't know, honestly. I think it's the attack, or even the fight at the club, but it's…" Pausing, I searched for the words. It was hard to describe. "It's very cloudy. Flashes of fangs here, claws slashing there… it doesn't make a whole lot of sense to me."

Acanthus' face fell. "Ah, so you are nervous. There is no need to be. You are doing fantastic."

Their confidence didn't soothe me at all. The question that had been on the tip of my tongue for the past week was burning me. I had been too proud to ask, but seeing Junior again outside of the club had rattled me. I blurted it out before I could change my mind. "What if my Pack mates are like those Wolves in the city?"

"Not all packs are quite so cutthroat. Nekane's pack is the one who will take you in. Hers is one of the larger ones, and more bound by duty. They're largely docile."

"Okay." If the pack was more docile and bound by duty, then maybe it wouldn't be like the thugs in the alley. I might even still be able to spend some time with Acanthus. "I can live with that."

I wanted so badly to stay. Who needed a Pack? I did everything on my own for two years after the dog bite. Acanthus had literally put his neck on the line for me, and I needed to hold up my end of the deal. *Join the Wolves, sell Acanthus back their church, profit. Now, in three easy steps!*

I rolled my eyes and took another swig of the coffee. I was already too jittery from nerves, so I promptly set the mug down. I gave Acanthus my award winning smile. My heart was hammering against my sternum, trying to burst out of my chest. There was a sting in every beat at the thought that I'd be living somewhere else tonight. "I'm ready."

That Time I Waved Goodbye

Acanthus

Neither of us were happy that it was the middle of daylight. Both of us were quiet on the flight to Central Park, and the silence stretched longer still as we stood there. Cypress left his car at the church, saying something about parking being impossible in Brooklyn. I made some half-hearted joke about them coming back for it. My cloak was wrapped tightly around me and the parasol was hidden beneath. This cloak was a simple black one, made for travel, and beneath it I wore my leather jacket. It covered lightweight but opaque black clothing that concealed most of my skin. My hair was hidden beneath the deep hood, the hem resting just below my chin.

Cypress wore a pack on his back, where we had put together their worldly possessions. Their wallet held a card to an account with twenty thousand dollars, proof of the sale to return the church deed to my name, and some small satchels of salves and herbs in case they were to get injured again. I had also included a small care package of jerky and some shelf-stable foods for the adventure ahead of them, and one of my candles for good fortune. Not that I had alerted them to such actions.

The Wolf pack trusted me about as much as I trusted them. Where this pack wasn't violent towards me, there was some animosity there from the past. A Pup had attacked me early on in their settlement here. In those days, any enemy certainly wouldn't have lived to tell the tale. That Pup was no different. (I did not live to be as old as I am by being naive and trusting our enemies.)

141

Lemon Balm

Nekane also had an inkling of my ties to the Night Garden, though she certainly didn't know what we did or what it was called. All she knew was that her Witches kept disappearing, and I was likely the cause. The daytime meeting was to keep me weaker during the exchange, as well as discourage anyone from shifting. It was a tactical disadvantage for both parties, and that made it an advantage in showing our good will.

Cypress cleared his throat. "Promise me you'll take care of the car? I'll visit when I need to use it."

The promise of a visit soothed me. Their loss was already looming; the proverbial hole in my chest had expanded throughout my body and it left me cold and numb throughout my being. The tips of my fingers and toes were tingling. We stood in the Strawberry Fields section of Central Park atop the "Imagine" dais in the path. I stood safely beneath my parasol, facing the fork in the road. It was a Sunday; people were walking through the park, talking and laughing. No one seemed to pay us any mind. Cypress stood beside me, and I soaked in the details of their broad chest, their shaggy hair, and their kind gray eyes. *Just another helped soul on the Garden paths, Acanthus. You've done well.*

I glanced over my shoulder. The Wolves would be there soon. A few people sat in the grass, enjoying the cloudless late spring day. I turned, watching for any signs of the other supernaturals in our midst, but there were none on the branching paths, either. I didn't want to share any emotion in front of the Wolves, but I turned and pulled Cypress into an embrace, surprising us both. "Do not forget me, Pup. Promise me that."

I would have to try and keep in touch, somehow. They returned the embrace, and I could feel their chest rise. "Like I could. I promise".

I wrinkled my nose, pulling out of their arms and glancing around as I smelled the deep, dusky odor of the other Wolves approaching. I disliked the strength of it; there were a lot of them. "They're coming."

Cypress' face twisted into a grimace, and they nodded as they forced their shoulders to relax. Shifting to stand taller, I shut down my emotion and stepped off of the dias towards the branching path, pulling the hood up a bit so that I could see better. The group of ten or so walked in a tight formation down the path to the left. They followed the trajectory of a woman. She was clad in an open jean jacket with a plain black shirt beneath and black, high-waisted pants.

The leader of the pack, Nekane. She was a small woman of about 5'1" with a scar across one of her amber eyes, white and stark against her skin. Her thick black hair was pulled into a sleek ponytail, and her angular features were sharp and cold. "Acanthus!" She shouted, no love in her voice. "You're still breathing."

I snorted, giving her a disarming smile. The way she treated me always made me feel monstrous, but I wouldn't give her the satisfaction of seeing it. "Come now, Nekane. We've had a treaty for a long time, no need for theatrics. How are you?"

"You put three of my own into a hospital. I'm not here to deal with you. Step aside, bloodsucker."

She stepped in front of me, nearly toe to toe, and went up on point to seem taller. She had been the dam to the pup that I had killed, and while we were diplomatic with one another, she would never regard me with warmth. Not that I expected or deserved it. I hoped that she would treat Cypress as her own.

"Manners, Nekane. It was not my fault. Perhaps ask your Pups about the twins in the alley," I said softly, but I did as she asked and stepped aside.

She ignored me. But, her demeanor changed entirely when she stepped in front of Cypress. She was softer, more amicable. Her face split into a closed smile, her full lips soft and her expression as kind as it could be after such a tense exchange. I watched carefully, my senses on high alert. The pack stood behind me in a half circle, just far enough away to be out of reach. Nekane and Cypress stood on the dias in front of us, the single path leading behind. A small part of me was screaming to call this off, that it wasn't too late, but I stood still, stubborn. This wasn't about me.

Cypress

I looked down at this impossibly small Wolf, but knew better than to say anything. She was obviously quite formidable to have become Alpha. I cringed at the way she talked to Acanthus, but I wasn't sure defending him would win me any favors. "What, are you mute?"

She looked at me, and I glanced at Acanthus before meeting her gaze and answering. "No Ma'am. My name's Cypress, as I'm sure you're aware."

I tensed as she assessed me. Her gaze lingered on my broad shoulders, and my skin crawled. "You have some training to do, but there's nothing a strong regimen can't fix."

I tilted my head, but again held my tongue, questions swirling around and bumping into each other. Something about her told me that I wouldn't be able to ask her questions as freely as I could Acanthus. I thought I'd feel something, like a door opening, or lock being clicked into place. Acanthus had even explained it like the unlocking of an elaborate door; maybe that was something they didn't know as much about. I didn't feel anything, and there was no authority from this woman.

There was a loud static blasting from somewhere, and it wasn't any external source. The noise was awful in my head. I wanted to talk to Acanthus, but it felt improper in this situation. The other Wolves she had brought were barely disguising their dislike for Acanthus. Many seemed eager to jump at them. At any moment, if Nekane said, I guarantee they'd shred him to pieces. My guts twisted, and I subtly angled myself closer to the Vampire. *Is this because of the treaty breach that Acanthus has been worried about?*

She narrowed her eyes. "Well?"

I bowed my head. I hadn't realized she was waiting for an answer. "Yes Ma'am."

"I did the best I could with them," Acanthus said to Nekane. "They've gotten good at controlling their shifts, and they've made wonderful progress since starting their training."

"For the last time, leech, I'm not talking to you," Nekane sneered, her voice cold. "Your kind should know better. You can't raise a Wolf."

The word kind was spat like a poison. I tried not to react to the words, but she was irritating me, and Acanthus' subtle wince didn't help. Nekane looked at me again and pulled a necklace with a charm on it from her pocket. It was silver; the small wolf's head glinted in the early afternoon light. My eyes went wide at the strength that the small female must possess. Even the dainty chains that Acanthus had put on me when he fed were ridiculously hard to fight against. How could she just carry a silver charm in her pocket?

"Your training starts now."

Her voice was flat. I glanced at Acanthus. One hand awkwardly jutted out from their cloak to hold the parasol. They didn't move, aside from the smallest shake of their head. I stepped forward, and leaned down for her to reach around my neck. The chain fell into place. The charm landed at the base of my throat, and I nearly hit the ground before catching myself. I impulsively snarled, and the Wolves around smirked with delight at my clumsy form.

Acanthus was at my side, helping me up, and I waved them off. "Let me," I growled.

"Very, very good." Nekane's pride shone through her words. "For being Pack-less, you are quite strong. We usually issue charms at birth. This one was my son's," she kept her voice neutral and soothing, but glared at Acanthus when she said 'son'. I wondered if that was where the bad blood came from. "You will eventually get used to it, and learn to fight past it. For now, wear it always."

I grimaced, but bit back a retort and nodded. I was already near panting with effort to stand up straight.Her voice went dangerously and sickly sweet, a venomous edge just beneath the surface. "What was that? I didn't quite hear you."

"Yes, Ma'am," I bit out.

"Good Pup."

Turning to face Acanthus, she addressed them directly. "Acanthus, I'd say it's a pleasure, but you know it's not. We will need to meet again with the other leaders, in order to talk about your aggression."

She walked past them, dismissing them without waiting for an answer. As Nekane walked back up the left branching path, the Wolves fell into rank behind her. I glanced at Acanthus and caught their sad expression.

They put a reassuring hand on my shoulder. "You'll be alright. Good luck, Pup."

"Don't, Acanthus, the silver," I muttered softly.

Acanthus pulled their hand away as if I shocked them. "Apologies, Cypress."

Unable to find the strength to answer, I took their hand and squeezed it. A silent farewell. Then I walked away from the only person in the world who'd ever understood me, into the wild unknown of this venture.

That Time I Dissociated In A Diner

Acanthus

The way they squeezed my hand before they left had my heart throbbing in the worst way, the ache deep and permeating through my bones. The cottony mental detachment was a blanket, smothering the fire of my emotions. Between Cypress walking off without looking back and the reminders that war was looming, the day had me despondent. I leaned into the feeling and tried to convince myself that the tingle in my fingers was nothing more than my sun sensitivity. Something told me that letting them walk away was a catastrophic idea; I steadfastly ignored it. Everything the World of Shadows was built on claimed that he needed his kind to surround him, and my hands were tied by the treaty.

This was solidified for me as Nekane patted his shoulder, leading him further and further away. Cypress hadn't once looked back, their eyes carefully trained ahead of them. I didn't want to watch them leave, but forced myself to keep watching until I could no longer separate their silhouette from the other Wolves'. I was alone once more on the Imagine dais.

They hadn't looked back. Why hadn't they looked back? Was I so easy to throw away? *Call them back*, my mind screamed at me. *Tell them you've made a mistake.*

But, what would that solve? They clearly didn't feel the same. My heart was a pulpy mess; they'd completely crushed me. They would be fine. I would be fine. What truly was I to Cypress? A person they knew for two weeks, and I was only in their life because I refused to leave the

146

building they rightfully owned. I was a blip; barely worth noting. They would be totally fine without me. *How soothing it must be to be in a Pack. Guaranteed to have a community and connection... Connection. I need a connection. It's time to go to the Manor to regain my bearings.*

My eyes stung in the brightness of midday, and my breath caught as I turned violently on my heel. I *would* be fine. What was one more lost companion? I could endure, just as I always had. Two weeks were a veritable drop in the ocean of time that I had lived. On that note; what was one more war? I would endure. I could lead. I had so much to do, to warn the Night Garden of the oncoming battles. Nekane's words were a threat; if she got the Big Five together, it was likely going to be to call for my execution.

Lowering the hood of my cloak, I twirled the parasol to distract my hands. I would be *fine*. There wasn't a cloud in the sky, in stark contrast to my mood. The sun was a danger, but the parasol kept me safe. My hood was claustrophobic and I was finding it harder to breathe. One of the positives of the goth fashion is that my attire blended in. Perhaps I didn't blend in with society at large, but at least no one would question my humanity. I closed my eyes, thinking of which direction I would have to travel. The city felt like a prison, and I was surrounded by chaos. *Acanthus, you fool, go to your community. You have one. This is not abandonment. Think.*

I pulled my violet vanity sunglasses out of my jacket pocket and placed them carefully on my face. *Don't waste any more time lingering on past losses.*

I quickly strolled away from the dais, and with a burst of irritation, I thought, *Fuck it*, and walked at my full speed towards Magic Manor. The power was a boon, allowing me to breeze past the bustling humans like a gust of wind. What would have taken a human over two hours to travel was thirty seconds for me. Stopping at the outskirts of the lot, I watched a car pull into the last available space. *Of course it's busy.* I stared at the polished chrome doors and nearly turned on my heel to head to the Spirits Three. *You're already here, and the sun is going to make you ill.*

Sun exposure was a curious illness. When I was an infant in this World of Shadows, it melted my skin instantly away from the bone. Now, at nearly eight hundred years old, it was slow; a tingling, at first. Then, after a full day in the sun, a persistent stinging that felt like needles, over and over. Then, my faculties begin to suffer; movement is slow, sluggish, and dazed, and there is a persistent burn. My skin starts to feel raw and new, like a freshly popped blister. I've never cared to push it past that. And now, as I stood here in front of the Magic Manor, I was swiftly approaching the 'needling' stage.

I took a sharp breath and closed the distance between me and the doors. Crowds may be damnedable things, but stepping into the busy diner was much more preferable to sun poisoning. And the diner was indeed vibrant, bustling with life. In different circumstances, I'd have been delighted to see it. The overwhelming clatter of silverware against plates and chatter between humans drowned out the staccato pops of bacon frying. Some droning country song whined through the speakers. The savory, sickly-sweet smell of the fat burning off of sausage and bacon mixed with the syrupy tang of maple and eggs.

It created an olfactory nightmare, and it mashed into the overwhelming stew of various chemical smells that humans doused themselves with nowadays. How interesting it was; all to hide both the washed and unwashed smells of their bodies. The vile stench of sweat and coffee breath punctuated it all. My stomach flipped as I stood, paralyzed, and fought the nausea that threatened to overtake me. Everything was too bright, and the movement in the diner left me reeling. Red, chrome, and the colors of flesh blended together.

Three Witches were behind the counter, one being Arturous. It took him one look before he rushed to open the break in the counter, pulling me through. "Come along, my Lord," he murmured, his hand resting on my upper back. His voice was uncharacteristically gentle. "The dining room is no place for you during the day."

They were quite busy, but the nice thing about Arturous is that he always made time for me. He whisked me back through the hallway of heavy oak doors. We stepped into the last door on the left, furthest from the noise of the diner. There was a rushed but emphatic exchange in front of the room; the shorter man assuring me that I would not be bothered and imploring me to rest before leaving me to my own devices. I cannot remember the specifics of what was said. Strange, isn't it? A vampire's memory is photographic.

Unlike the plain room that was meant for feeding, this one was more comfortable, if sparsely furnished. A single wooden bed with beige sheets and a sad, flattened pillow stood against the wall opposite from the door. No windows broke the smooth expanse of cream colored paint. A tall maroon wing-back chair next to a short round table, sitting kitty-cornered beside the bed. A small, stocked bookcase with a few neutral choices comfortably nestled near the chair. Nothing else graced the room except for a massive brown rug and the incandescent bulbs, hidden behind a frosted glass dome. The yellow glow left the stained walls nauseous and sickly.

Good. At least that matched how I felt. Cowardly. Ill. Unworthy of genuine connection. I should have intervened the moment Nekane pulled that silver chain from her pocket. I could still see the glint off of the small charm, and the strain in Cypress' body as they fought to remain upright. I'd harmed them in my inaction. What was I thinking, going to her? I should've said to hell with it and told my ally Coryn instead. Now that I'd given myself some time to process the event, my stomach flopped and lurched, bile stinging at the back of my throat. *Stop it, Acanthus, they're fine. They wanted this, remember?*

My own voice roared in my head loud enough that I winced. I stepped towards the bookcase, staring blankly at the colored spines. I needed to pull myself together. I needed to prepare for the oncoming war. Why did I let Nekane get so far under my skin? Perhaps this was the extent of my misery before Cypress had literally crashed into my life, and I'd just forgotten the feeling. Perhaps I was being dramatic over a comfort ripped away too soon. Perhaps I was overwhelmed at the thought of continuing forward to fight, when I was one of the last of my kind in New York. *I am so tired.*

My thoughts kept bouncing between the broken treaty and Cypress. I wondered if they had bonded with the new Pack yet. It was none of my business, and yet, the remains of my heart wrung and throbbed with each thought of him. I closed my eyes, gritting my teeth as my fangs lengthened behind my lips. I didn't want to think of painful things. I wished I had gone home, because then at least I could have the comforting scents of my candles. But, I had not, and at this point I was crashing and burning, too tired to care or to find the energy to fly.

Slowly, deliberately, I laid down on the floor, opening my eyes again to look at the grungy ceiling. Past traumas played in my mind as I spiraled, loss after loss in a haunted carousel within my mind. *François. Nocturne. Lucien. Alexander. Corbin. Desdemona. Tempest.*

I didn't deserve comfort; the rug was even too much for me, but I wasn't about to move around the little refuge just because of my self-loathing. *I should have stayed in the sun long enough to crumble to dust. Coward.*

My heart ached and my dissociation deepened. The numbness soothed my chest and kept me floating away from my anguish. *Come on, Acanthus, pull it together. You need to rely on your military prowess and kick this weak notion to the side.*

Parting my lips, I bit down hard on my wrist and gasped around the sensation of my fangs piercing my own skin. The copper of my blood soothed me, but the undercurrent of dirt reminded me that this was no sustenance. Still, the flavor grounded me enough to where I could shut out the warring voices within. By the time my fangs retracted, my skin would already be healed. It was a matter of punishment and penance.

The muffled chaos of the diner faded into the buzzing of the overhead light, and I drifted into a much needed void. Rest would soothe the pain; rest would return my logic and let me rise above this. *Let me sleep.*

If only the world would have left me in peace within the darkness. But no, my mind decided to attack me in my slumber, with painful memories thinly disguised as dreams. It started with darkness, as it always does. I think it may be time, dear Reader, to continue the tale of my turning — as that was precisely the memory my mind decided to conjure.

I had been attacked by a vampire in my newly erected church, and been pronounced dead in a puddle on the floor of the inner sanctum. In reality, the vampire attacker had deliberately left me for dead, letting the humans lay me to rest in my finest habits and bury me in the deepest depths of the crypt. He left me there alone, and alone I stayed for sixty years. I never did find out what his true intentions were; or why he left me there for so long.

When dreams are attached to memories, you pick up on the things that otherwise would be missing from a dream. Deep earth and fresh decay stank within those confines, and even with my night vision I could see next to nothing. There wasn't much to see, in any case. Cold blue stones wept the groundwater from the outer walls and muffled cries from the inner ones. The ancient crypt, at odds to the newly built church above it, was adjacent to the chambers in which Inquisitors would interrogate heretics. There was never enough food for me, and I survived almost solely off of rats, weakened and ill.

In the memory-turned-dream, I was backed against the wall of the crypt after breaking out of my stone coffin. My body doubled over, retching and disoriented, wracked with pain. The taste of copper ghosts on my tongue, and there was a blur of white skin. Everything was so chaotic. Those times were full of strife; hungry, my body cold and tender as if every inch of me was bruised. The small hairs across my arms and legs stood on end. Every brush of my waist length locks across my skin was like the cut of a knife. My lips and gums ached. Those memories are days upon days of unending agony, my anxiety a noose, twisting like thorny vines and suffocating me.

My reality for sixty years — confusion, coldness, darkness, hunger. The dream replayed things I had to do to survive. My meals became blood lapped from the stone that flowed in rivers from the iron gates upon the floor. I hid behind large slabs from the loud boots of Cardinals and pallbearers bringing prisoners and corpses alike to the basements. It took me a matter of days to learn that the beating hearts of rats meant food, and my instincts made my fangs grow. I knew nothing of what I was, or why I was in constant darkness.

I'd thought I was a demon. Breaking the bar across the crypt door never occurred to me. It would have been an easy feat with my preternatural strength. And yet, because of who I'd been in earthly life, I was convinced that I was in purgatory, and something had dragged me to the deepest depths of Hell.

Blackness, decay, sickness, death. The sound of rat bones clinking together with my dirty body's movements. My torn habits loosely hanging from my emaciated frame. Footsteps I didn't recognize, soft and lithe as a cat, echoing off of the stones of the hallway. The malnourishment left me nearly blind in the dank chambers. Signs of life left my heart thrumming in chaotic waves. After sixty years of agony, I'd been near feral. Darkness permeated everything.

I had long forgotten what it was to see in the light of a flame, so when a torch entered my little prison, I cried out and hid from the light in fear. My knees did nothing to protect my chest from the hummingbird rhythm of my heart, and the cruel laughter that echoed off the walls left my ears aching. I pressed my palms to them, shutting my eyes. I could barely understand the words spoken to me; the sounds a confusing, chilled cacophony that sent me spiraling further into panic. "Oh, little bat. So lost and weak. Do you not know your nature?"

I knew the ghosts of words. Confused, I tried to remember what they meant. Chancing a look, I tried to speak, but all that came out was a rasp. The language died behind my parched and leaden tongue. The cruel laughter echoed again in waves, and a freezing hand pulled me up before I could react. I screamed. The dream devolved into a confusing flurry of gnashing claws and teeth. An exhaustion mingled with my own, but it was distinctly separate from me. Claws would slash through the darkness from time to time, and I was weighed down with something impossibly heavy, tasting iron and salt on my tongue.

And then, I awoke, gasping and bathed in sweat. The grungy yellow walls, the ugly beige and brown furnishings. The room that I had fallen asleep in greeted my sore eyes. My scream had been aloud, and the light echo still reverberated off of the walls, but I was safe. I was eight hundred years away from those horrible nightmares, and I was alone. Curling into the smallest ball that I could, I pressed my back against the cold sheet rock wall as a dry sob left me. I dropped my damp forehead to my knees.

There would be no more sleeping today. Or, was it night? I couldn't tell. Much like my prison in my youth, passage of time meant nothing today. Perhaps I never really left those dank stone walls. The vampire that had found me back then was one that delighted in being a devil. He had chosen his fate, unlike me. He had been extremely cruel to me in ways that I never again care to repeat, and dreaming of our first meeting always made my stomach turn. It was his twisted games that truly stole my faith.

Suddenly, the room felt too small. Maple, apple-wood smoked bacon, eggs, and fried goods permeated my nostrils. The sweet was punctuated with the acrid smell of old blood somewhere near. I tilted to the side, gagging as my stomach flopped. The air was stagnant and the furniture was closing in on me.

My heart rattled against my brittle ribs, vying for freedom; I needed fresh air. Instead of getting up quite yet, I threaded my fingers through my hair and tugged, the pain bringing me back to myself. I bit my tongue and squeezed my eyes shut, still as a statue in that fetal position. Holding my breath, I forced my heart to stop pounding, and let out a long, slow exhale. *I'm in control. I have nothing to fear. I'm in a safe place.*

I echoed the words to myself in a long-practiced mantra. *I am in control.* Inhale. *I have nothing to fear.* Hold. *I am in a safe place.* Exhale. Rinse and repeat. After several minutes, my chest ached, but the terrible asynchronous rhythm had slowed. Unwinding my hands from my hair, I slowly stood and made my way to the door. Perhaps one day I would be above all these past transgressions. Pulling my cloak hood up and over my head, I stared at the wood grain for a long time. *Put on a face, Acanthus, meet your people. Arturous undoubtedly has questions.*

I finally pulled my shaking fingers up the expanse of the door and pushed it open. The diner was silent. I opened the heavy oak to the hallway, and walked with solid calm to the front of the establishment. My emotional mask was firmly in place. As I opened the door to the area behind the counter, the darkness of night blacked out the windows across from me. I breathed a sigh of relief, stepping to the break in the counter. Crossing through, I leaned on the proper side of the Formica, muttering, "House special, please."

I hadn't even bothered to look at who was working. The voice that answered from my left shocked me and my eyes shot up to see a familiar purple fringe falling into icy blue eyes. "Not even a hello? That's cold, even for you, Acanthus."

I'd forgotten that there was a chance she would be here. "Es? What are you —"

Esmeralda smiled at me, her dark purple lipstick staining her two front teeth. "You've been in the safe room for a day and a half, sweetheart. It's my Sunday shift."

I swallowed. Oh. I hadn't realized I slept for so long. How long was I dreaming?

I tried to ignore the pity in her eyes as she spoke. "You're not looking so hot. Sit down, I'll get you set up."

I winced at the words, but slid on to one of the chromed stools and placed my forehead against the coolness of the counter.

When I was adequately sated, I found myself sitting in the empty diner at two o'clock in the morning with Esmeralda and Arturous. Arturous had shown up shortly after the volunteer donor, his eyes red-rimmed and bleary. I'd caught them up on the events of the past week, and Es was standing against the wall, her arms crossed as she listened. Arturous was taking notes on a legal pad, shorthanded in code. We'd been speaking in the Night Garden code just in case any of the path travelers in the back overheard.

"The purple dogwoods are in the royal grove," I muttered, not looking at either of them. The scratches and chaotic gray splatter in the black Formica were far more interesting. "Perhaps the Garden paths will be well-traveled by the end of the year."

The Witches glanced at each other in my periphery. "I knew the root rot would show in only a matter of time," Esmeralda sighed. "The Spirits Three is repaired and ready for a new season."

"As is the Manor," Arturous added. "But tell me, Acanthus, what are you planning to do?"

"Also," Es quickly cut in before I could reply," Does this mean danger for the black roses as well?"

'Purple dogwoods' was code for the Big Five, and 'the royal grove' was talking about a meeting. If Nekane summoned the others, then she was asking for judgment on me, and perhaps vampires at large. She was asking permission to start a battle. The 'root rot' was a euphemism for the skirmish at the bar; sometimes we spoke of root rot for battles and points of conflict. The 'black roses' was referring to the Nosferatu I'd learned about. "For the black roses, I'm honestly unsure. I never got a chance to look over the bush. But, as far as my plans go, I was debating whether or not to visit the Yellow Rose. However, the knowledge of the royal grove changes things. I fear it would be irresponsible to leave my little church."

"You can't be thinking of meeting with them, are you? That's a death sentence."

Es' voice had an edge to it, and she tensed. Arturous nodded. "If you stay, you stay with gardeners."

"Please, my friends, I can handle my own, you know this. I will utilize the Garden, should I need, but for now, my best course of action is to stay connected with you and to stay here. I will reach out to the Yellow Rose and let her know of the current state of the flowers."

Arturous swallowed, then gave a curt nod. Es pursed her lips, her arms tightening around her waist. She cleared her throat. "Well, we're with you. Travel the paths with grace, Acanthus, and keep eyes on your own back."

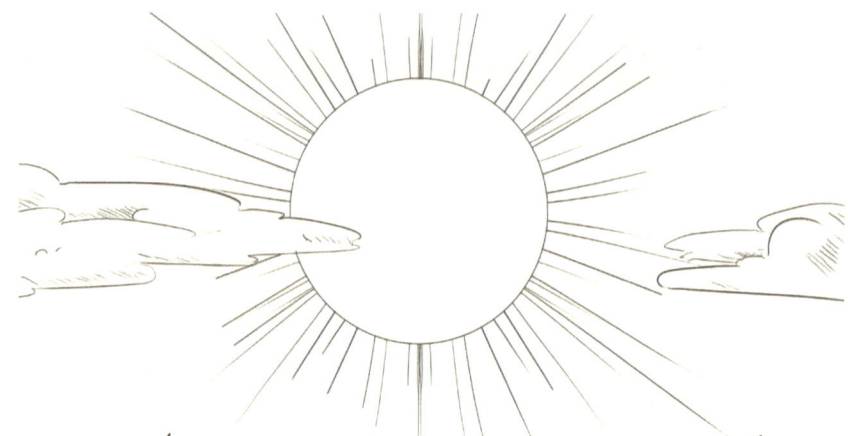

That Time I Stayed With A Wolf Pack

Cypress

By the time Acanthus had awoken in the Magic Manor, it had been two days. Two days. It was not what you would call a good time. Nekane's compound was somewhere in the suburbs north of the city. We were in the sprawling expanse of towns blurring into each other along the train rail of the Metro North between Yonkers and Croton-Harmon. The "compound" was really a glorified apartment building with a fenced-in basketball court away from the sight of the road. The court was surrounded by a small number of trees. It must have cost a fortune, having land in that area.

It amazed me how much of the World of Shadows hid in plain sight. My room was one off of a long connected hallway that felt more like a dorm than separate living spaces. None of the rooms had lockable doors, and people flitted in and out of each other's spaces. It was a huge invasion of privacy. I didn't want anyone opening my door like that.

I'd gone into this trying to be positive. I'd cracked a few jokes as we walked away from Central Park, but no one really responded or laughed. I tried the same once we got to the compound, but the most I got were a few weak smiles or people brushing me off. It'd been nothing but disappointments since.

This damn silver charm made my muscles ache like a mule carrying packs for eternity. The moment that I walked away from Acanthus, all I could hear in my head was static. Not a thought, not even a word. If this was what the "Pack Bond" was like, no thank you. It was no wonder

154

these people were such assholes all the time. I was angry just trying to adapt. With the static came a near constant pulsing headache throughout the base of my skull.

The constant auditory torture was exhausting, and I wasn't sure how long it'd take to adjust to this so-called "Pack Bond," but I'd think two days would have been enough. I really tried to push through and make a connection, but it didn't seem like anyone was interested. Training was awful, too. The first day was chock full of scheduled time sparring with the other Wolves. Partner after partner, we went to a head. It seemed like the others weren't kept up to task nearly as harshly as I was. I spent most of the later sessions wobbling on my feet and wishing more than anything to just sit down and drown out my surroundings. The second day was shifting and running drills, going back and forth between forms and weaving through traffic cones set up in a track on the court.

When it wasn't physical, it was mental. I'd spent hours on the second day, learning what it meant to "have the spirit of a Wolf." To me, it felt like indoctrination bullshit. Apparently, a Wolf spirit is both a part of you and separate. It couldn't just overtake you, but if you were injured, you might lose yourself to your instincts. In rare instances, if a Wolf has a strong spirit and something happens to harm them, they can transfer their sentience to a new person. Those Wolves can carry abilities from the previous person that they otherwise didn't have. The more experienced Wolf teaching the new recruits told us that dealing with our weaknesses made us stronger, and that was why silver was important. They said that vampires were our mortal enemies, and if we weren't careful, then they would tempt us to demise.

That hadn't been nearly my experience, but when I tried to push back, I was promptly scolded and ignored for the rest of the class, everyone else glaring and whispering behind my back. So far, I hadn't learned anything that Acanthus couldn't teach me; at least, nothing that didn't just sound like anti-vampire propaganda. Were Vampires really so bad? Were Wolves really so terrified of everyone else? The Witches I'd met seemed to have the opposite opinion, and I couldn't imagine hating people based on something they couldn't control.

The pack was already so tight knit and closely wound without me. It was like they could read each other's minds, doing things without having to be asked. I wondered if it was just a symptom of being so new to the Pack, or if my head was really that messed up from being pack-less for so long. Acanthus and I had started to do that before I left them. I didn't feel like I remotely belonged to this group of aggressive strangers, and as I lay in my bed at the end of that day I thought, *Acanthus… I miss you more than anything.*

Lemon Balm

As my time there went on, I kept trying to ignore the urge to run back to Acanthus and beg them to let me stay with them. I was fighting against the tears that were constantly threatening to make an appearance. Crying wouldn't bode well for me. While Nekane was friendly enough, she was very tough when it came to being a "Lone Wolf", whatever that meant. It seems like outdated wolf science had a choke-hold on the supernatural packs. I wonder if I should go howl at the moon on the edge of a cliff or something.

I couldn't help but wonder if I was being punished for not even knowing the pack existed in the first place. It seemed like every time I made a misstep, she would get frustrated and blame my "Lone" status. She never explained what that was supposed to mean. I didn't understand, and I was afraid to ask. That woman was intimidating.

The classes wore on. Spar after spar, obstacle course after obstacle course, lesson after lesson. We were on a cycle; spar day, lesson day, obstacle course day. Rinse and repeat. It seemed senseless; whenever I asked why we were training, the instructors would say some variation of, "We need to prepare for war."

I didn't know what we were fighting for, or why. No one would answer me. A lot of the sit-down lessons seemed to focus on vampires and their weak spots; there was very little about the Wolves, and how they came to be this syndicate. I get the idea of, "know thine enemy," but this was excessive.

There were four factions of vampires; Anesh, Alphosine, Chiara, and Nosferatu. The Chiara and Nosferatu were believed to be extinct in the area, and they seemed to spend the most time on the Anesh. According to the instructors, the Anesh were the most dangerous, because they had magic powers and were unpredictable. A drawing that looked suspiciously like Acanthus was on the screen of the power point for that lesson. I stopped asking questions after the third class. Most I learned from those was how to track the Vampires.

Protecting your mind seemed to be a big worry, and the Wolves would drill privacy exercises on obstacle course days. *Picture yourself closing a door and locking it, to shield your mind. Picture your mental space in bars.* I felt silly every time I did it. I couldn't tell if it was working.

There were very few Wolves in the encampment that stayed there all the time like I did. One was Amberlynn, who was nearly mute and seemed terrified any time I went up to talk to her. I didn't try after a few times. A short, stout, skittish girl seemed to disappear whenever I came into the room; I didn't even know her name. Theodore was nice enough, he was quiet, but he laughed at my jokes. Junior was also here; he'd come back from the hospital shortly after my arrival, and we ignored each other. His face was twisted into a permanent scowl, and one of his eyes were blinded and milky white.

I stuck to my room between training sessions. Thankfully, because no one knew me well enough, no one would wander in without knocking. I thought I'd get some peace when I slept, but it was always the same. Fragmented dreams haunted my sleep, just flashes of imagery here and there. Sometimes they'd be quite pleasant— Acanthus' hands as they brewed tea, their eyes as they read a book, or wrote long paragraphs in a journal.

My nightmares, in contrast, were fearsome flashes of a dark crypt, or this figure that I could only describe as a horror. He would crawl closer to me in the dark, eyes glowing a bright green, and I'd awaken in a cold sweat before he said anything. Those dreams affected me worse than any vague flashes of teeth and claws could.

Whenever the loneliness began to smother me, I often thought of Acanthus tending to my wounds that night after the city. Their presence in my mind was as soothing as their salves, helping to lessen the ache of my muscles with the long hours of training and the sting of failure. No matter how hard I tried, I couldn't make a connection here, or do what Nekane asked me to. The static was unrelenting, and I ran drill after drill, while she scolded me for 'not accepting the Pack'. I was here, wasn't I? I wasn't about to lean down and kiss her boots.

There were also odd times where I was dissociating. I could see myself sitting on my camping cot in the corner of what we'd deemed the living room, or sprawled out as a Wolf. It ached whenever I pictured it; I still thought of the church as home. Acanthus wasn't there in those brief moments, and I wondered if I was fantasizing about what it would be like if I'd never met them to begin with. And, when I had those thoughts, my chest became a pulsing, infected void of pain.

The days all melded into each other. I didn't bother really talking to anyone else after a while. No one seemed to want to approach me, either. I'd lost track of how long I'd been lost in the endless slog of training and fighting exhaustion from the silver around my neck. You wouldn't think that a few cutesy little paw-shaped charms would be exhausting. The necklace probably weighed less than a pound even with all the charms, but it felt like a crushing weight to me.

Every nerve ending was on fire all of the time from the strain. I'd loved training as a human, but the Wolf training was senseless. It was like I was at boot camp. The other Wolves would bite and snap during spars, and I still got the sense that I was cut off from some type of communication that they had. Maybe I was just a broken wolf. Nekane must've known I was struggling, because she started to talk to me more.

I distinctly remember one time, where she knocked on the door in three quick, sharp raps, pulling me from my book. I looked up with a gasp, a knot forming in between my shoulder blades. "Come in."

"Hey," she said as she poked her head in. "You good for a talk, Cypress?"

I blinked, before holding my hand out towards a chair in a silent welcome. She stepped into the room, swinging the door closed behind her. She took the invitation and lowered into the chair, keeping her legs spread and her elbows on her knees, confident and relaxed. "Talk to me, kid. I hear that you're struggling in the Pack."

It was interesting; once Acanthus wasn't in her sight, she was actually kind of warm towards me, in a New York 'don't fuck with me' kind of way. It reminded me of Tasha, and I smiled at the memory of my former neighbor. "I appreciate that, Alpha," I replied. I rubbed the back of my neck, flushing and looking off to the side. "I guess I just don't really fit in with anyone."

"Have you tried to talk to them?"

I shrugged. "A little bit. No one really seems to connect. Plus, I'm tired all the time, between the sparring , the silver, and the classes. I don't think I'm used to it here yet. I feel like I'm cut off."

She leaned back, watching me for a moment. Her eyes were narrowed and sharp, and her irises darted back and forth as she thought. "Well," she said. "I'll see what I can do to make it a bit easier for you."

I smiled at her. "Thanks, Alpha."

"Don't thank me yet," she muttered as she stood. "Start getting out of your room and talk to your pack mates, alright? It ain't healthy to be alone all the time."

She stood and slipped out of the room without waiting for an answer. I didn't think she'd cared, but the drills became less frequent. The added free time was a blessing; I was able to take more and more time away from the camp. Nekane's encampment was right on the bank of the Hudson, and I'd sit by the wide river in my free time, whenever I could escape this hell. I started taking the chain off in little increments when I was able to get away, and I felt so much lighter and freer. I'm going to leave, I remember thinking to myself. *This is not for me. I gotta find a way out of this.*

I was confident at this point that Nekane had nothing to teach me that Acanthus didn't cover. I was getting tired of shoving their toxic territory structure down my throat. Maybe they realized that this method wouldn't work on me. *The beatings will continue until morale improves,* I thought, then snorted. The wind rustled my hair, and with the missing weight of the chain, I felt a little bit more like myself.

For whatever stupid reason, I was miserable but I didn't leave. I kept pushing my emotions aside and looking for the positives. Maybe it was because Nekane took the time to visit me and hear me out. Say what you want about this pack life, she made sure we were all fed, clothed, and healthy. I may not be having the best time, but all of my basic needs were met. I guess I kept asking myself, where would I even go? My mother's house wasn't an option, not again. And, I wasn't sure if I was welcome at Acanthus' church, even if it felt like home. After all, I'd only been with them for two weeks, and I didn't want to assume. I couldn't fall back on the ownership of the deed, and it wasn't as if the vampire had a cell phone where I could ask.

I was always at the compound. I had the feeling I specifically wasn't allowed to leave, but many of the Wolves would come and go to human jobs. I wanted to try and apply somewhere, just to break the monotony. One day I asked Nekane. "Hey, am I allowed to go anywhere?"

She raised an eyebrow, cocking her hip to the side. "Of course you are," she replied. "With an escort."

"But, why? No one else has an escort, and they come and go all the time."

Nekane frowned, and narrowed her eyes in her particular way. She didn't like being questioned, and maybe I was pushing my luck by doing so. "You haven't shed your Lone Wolf, Cypress. They are a part of the Might of the East. You have not committed to the Pack bond yet, and I don't need you crawling back to your leech. Besides, where would you want to go?"

I cringed at the slur, and my mind drifted back to Acanthus. "Yes, Alpha. Sorry, I was thinking of getting a job."

She laughed at that. "All your needs are met. What could you possibly want a job for?"

I didn't answer, instead bowing my head at her before I left. I was alone in a crowded complex that behaved like family. In that analogy, I guess I was the black sheep. My days all blurred together in an endless cycle of trying to prove myself and failing. I was losing my ability to laugh it off. Junior was also here; I still hadn't gotten over sharing a space with him, and he'd been nothing but cold to me since I arrived. He was a lot quieter and more reserved than when we considered ourselves friends. Besides, too much had happened between us; we'd never be warm towards each other again.

At first, I'd been overjoyed to see a familiar face, but also by then I realized that everything I feared about joining this pack was true. They moved in tandem, and all they cared about was the Pack. I couldn't understand it; granted, I hadn't exactly reached out to anyone, but no one else had tried to welcome me in, either. They all seemed to communicate with glances and unspoken words, and I was surrounded by silent, private conversations. I resolved myself to really try, and threw myself into connections.

Every sparring match, sprint, and obstacle course, I made a point to make small talk with my sparring partners. Amberlynn was my sparring partner the most, and talking to her was like talking to a brick wall. The last time I tried left me feeling obnoxious and rude. "Hey, Amber, how's it going?"

No answer. I tried again. "So, how long have you been here?"

She'd been standing in a boxing stance, careful and guarded, but lessened it as she stared at me, cocking her head. Her eyebrows were furrowed, as if she'd said something and was frustrated that I hadn't answered. "Oooookay…"

She let out a silent little exhale, then rolled her eyes, tightening up her spar. "No talking, then. Got it."

I mirrored her stance and we got to work. After the sparring session, I ran into Thomas in the mess hall. "Hey, dude. How was your day?"

Thomas shrugged. "Fine, I guess."

Not much of a conversation starter. I let out a little laugh, cheerier than I felt. "Well that's good! Mine was a slog. I dunno why they have me training so much."

He gave me a look, then turned on his heel and walked towards a table. I dropped my smile, and stared after him. I didn't exactly take that as an invite. Sighing, I grabbed my food and walked to the edges of the room, sitting alone on one of the benches.

One day towards the end of June, there was a ceremony to commemorate the pack members who'd gotten stronger. It was a simple thing; Nekane summoned me, Amberlynn, and Junior to the front of the combined mess hall. "Your strength honors us all," she told us when we'd gathered. "Hand me your necklaces."

We held the chains out in front of us, and she added charms to each of us, one by one. Two more charms were added to my necklace, where the others only got one. I couldn't help but notice that I had double the charms of everyone else. *When does it end? I'm so tired.*

I was grateful I was able to remain upright. After a few hours of wearing them, the weight was almost bearable. It seemed I was getting stronger faster than expected. Then came sparring practice with these new charms and I was floored again, the breath whooshing out of me as my back hit the ground. I laid there, eyes closed, and contemplated. *I don't know if I can do this anymore.*

"You're done for the day, Cypress," Nekane ordered, and I opened my eyes to see her reaching a hand towards me, disappointment thinly veiled in her expression. I took the offered hand, suppressing a groan as I moved. I wondered idly what Acanthus would think, then I dropped it. I knew them for two weeks. Why were they even on my mind? Maybe I had to start letting them go. My heart twisted at the thought.

I walked towards the sidelines, and Junior bumped my shoulder as I walked past. "Be easier if you just talked to us," he muttered, tapping his temple. Maybe he was trying to help me, but it would be nice if literally anyone in this encampment spoke plainly.

I had no idea what he meant, so I ignored him and sank into one of the benches on the side of the basketball court. I was putting in all this work to feel like it was possible I wouldn't even survive. My mind wandered back to Acanthus. They were a complete stranger, but I still thought of them as my friend. *I wonder how they're doing. I hope they're alright.*

I was so tired.

July came with its sweltering heat and lengthy days. I had survived nearly two months with this pack. The hole in my chest grew with every passing day, and I thought of Acanthus constantly, even as things started to get slightly better.

I now had eight of the little silver paw charms on my necklace, along with the wolf's head. I could shift and run effortlessly with it around my neck. The sparring and drills were still grueling, but my body adjusted easily. They were like intense cardio sessions. I found the smallest amounts of joy within the darkness if I looked at it that way; whispers of memories from my human days in the garish yellow gym. I kept pushing, and pushing, losing myself in the burn of my muscles with every spar. I craved the satisfaction of losing myself to that strain. And then, one day I managed to floor Junior.

Junior was a great deal stronger than me, and though I had come out on top at The Witches Three, he'd bested me every time since. His fighting style was aggressive, but he always fought fair, to his credit. I think I snapped during the spar that day. I lost myself to the rage that had been building over the last month and a half. I had to be pulled off of him, because I just kept punching.

"Cypress! Enough!" I heard a different Wolf yell, and I didn't even bother to check who it was. Arms wrapped around my chest, and hauled me off of Junior, who was still shielding his face and neck from my blows. I didn't see him again after that.

Nekane had brought me up into a different wing of the compound and locked me into one of the empty rooms for the day. Huh, locks. Imagine that. It was a boring little room; bare, stained oak floors, with a solitary black bench and a tattered green blanket. There was nothing on the white walls, unless you counted the cobwebs. A single window with cracked panes looked out to a boring brick wall across the alleyway. The solitude left me with nothing but my thoughts, and the static. Static was just constant in my mind. It ebbed and flowed like a river, and I caught glimpses of the church in the clearer moments. Flashes of the garden, or the rain outside of the kitchen window.

I'd been separated in mid-morning, and Nekane approached me late that afternoon. This time, I couldn't deny that I was once again the problem. I leaned my head back against the wall while sitting on the bench and closed my eyes. Existence was exhausting. I was more alone than ever. It'd be better for me if I just accepted that my head is a wreck, because I would never fit in with the rest of the pack.

"Cypress," Nekane knelt beside me. "You're too much of a Lone Wolf. I can't have you injuring your Pack mates on a whim like this. If we can't get you to talk to us, then you'll need to start wearing a silver band around your wrist at all times."

"What do you mean, talk to us? I've been trying so hard to relate to anyone here."

She shrugged. Her voice was cold and distant; any warmth she had used to show me was completely gone. I guess I failed as a pack member. "You've been shutting us out from the start. It's like you don't even want to be here."

I didn't answer, and she huffed, standing straight in front of me. "I heard you lost control today. For the safety of the Pack and yourself, you'll continue to wear this."

She held the bracelet out for me to see. It was a thick band, covered in carvings of the moon stages, filigree filling out the spaces between the spheres. It was a gaudy thing. My necklace was already a massive weight; that thing had to weigh at least a pound on its own. I didn't see how I'd be able to move with it, without feeling like I was being perpetually crushed. I tried to keep the apprehension from my voice as I asked, "What's it for?"

"It marks you as one of us."

No one else wore one of those, and I knew it. I was too tired to argue, resigned to a deep apathy. What was the point of pushing forward? I didn't say anything other than, "yes, ma'am."

Nekane crossed her arms. "No snarky quips? No questions, no explanations for your behavior?"

I shrugged. "Will you answer me if I have any? I lost my temper. I'm sorry."

"What kind of Alpha would I be, if I didn't hear your questions?"

I looked off to one of the dingy white walls. I couldn't answer that, and she knew it. I had zero knowledge of Wolves outside of this place. She held me in her gaze for a long time, her mouth a grim, thin line. When she relented, she walked to the door and held it open. "You may leave and do as you please around the camp," she said to me, and I gave her another apathetic "Yes, ma'am."

I stood and rushed away from her as fast as I could. There wasn't a reason to do a whole lot of talking those days. It was way easier to run away from this reality, and so I jogged to the very end of the camp. I found myself curled, arms hugging my knees as I rested my forehead against them on the muddy, forested river bank. The mossy boulder beneath me was soothing. A short while later, a commotion interrupted my pity party; I rose my head from my knees.

A rowdy band of Wolves were coming around the river bend. I sniffed the air, trying to see if I recognized anyone. Imagine my surprise when the pungent scent of unwashed humans wafted into my nostrils. My first instinct was to dart into the bushes to hide, but I was already hidden. I couldn't see anything from my vantage point, but I perked my ears, straining to hear the conversation. This wasn't good, whatever this was.

"The other leaders are taking too long to respond, and I am tired of waiting," Nekane's strong voice cut over the bubbling current of the river. "It's high time something is done about him. He's made it clear that he's a threat to the pack, and we've waited long enough."

My stomach dropped. *Me? A threat?*

"Nekane, you've had a treaty with him for over a century."

No, not me. I leaned closer, dialing in my focus to try to hear better. Nekane's voice was a growl as she responded to the person that dared to question her. "He's never shown this," she paused, thinking of a word. "This brute force before. Look at Junior's face! Brandon didn't come home!"

I chewed my lip. *Could be me*, but probably not me. I'd beaten Junior's face to a bloody pulp that morning, but I hadn't had a treaty with *anyone* for a century. Then it hit me; Junior's face had been marred in the fight, very publicly, by Acanthus. Even if the Witches involved in the cleanup crews had pulled some magic bullshit for the humans to forget, Nekane would obviously know of Acanthus' threats. My insides turned to ice and I leaned forward, listening more intently. "I guess that's true," a male voice finally responded. I didn't recognize that one. "He never was the nicest in treaty talks. Always brandishing those nails."

Nails? Can anyone else extend their nails like Acanthus can?

Nekane's voice went dark as she spoke again, her point made. "That bastard bat wasn't even this aggressive when he murdered Mikael. The warning issued in the city extends to all of us. As the leader of the Eastern territory I would be morally bankrupt to continue leaving him to his own devices. Something needs to be done. Let the ancillary packs know that the Might of the East is on the move."

The order froze my blood. *Acanthus.*

There was no one else they could possibly be talking about. I couldn't be sure, but that certainly sounded like a declaration of war. I hopped off of the rock that I was sitting on and peered through the leaves of the bushes. They were nearby. Nekane's back was to me, and three men stood with her. All of them were in casual clothing; black denim jeans and inconspicuous t-shirts, mostly. They seemed like run-of-the-mill bikers; no one I'd be able to pick out definitively from the crowd.

One of them was wearing a black denim vest with cut-off sleeves, long chestnut hair pulled back into a tight bun. A gun dangled from his hip, glinting in the sunlight. *Guns? What the hell?*

Another man was leaning against a nearby tree; I could only see the bend of his leg behind Nekane, but a giant navy pack sat in front of him. The silver net on top of the pack was glinting in the sunlight. The third was wearing a set of black sunglasses, his stringy black hair hanging in his face. A scraggly, unkempt goatee hid his upper lip as he stood with his hands in his pockets. He had a few leather belts hanging askew off of his hips, various pointy things hanging from them. These humans carried a huge amount of equipment. I couldn't tell what all of it was from here, but the one with the vest had a giant box that they were leaning against. It was a massive speaker shape; it looked like it may be a work light. My stomach somersaulted at the implications.

The man with the belts turned to look at Nekane, and some of the pointy things hanging off of him clanked together with a dull thud. "When do we strike?"

Those are stakes, I thought, horrified. Stakes and giant lights made their plan to attack crystal clear. My skin started to buzz, and adrenaline surged through me. *Are these Hunters? No way...*

My chest panged as my heart sped. *Fuck, fuck, FUCK.*

The Might of the East was Nekane's pack. If she was mobilizing, that sounded like a *lot* of Wolves. And when I attacked Junior at The Spirits Three two months ago, my ignorant ass had landed the perfect reason in her lap to go after my friend. Red tape must have made Nekane move slow in her response. Or, maybe the delay had to do with training me. Either way, I wasn't about to stand by and let her attack them. *I have to warn them. I have to get them out of there. I have to* - Snap.

Shit. I hadn't been watching the ground as I tried to back away. I had forgotten to account for the heaviness the new band added to my steps. Nekane's piercing gaze found me immediately. We locked eyes, and she gave a simple command. "Kill his *pet*, too."

Shit, I thought as my stomach opened into a yawning pit of dread. I ran through my options as I scrambled out of the bush. *Think, Cypress, think!*

Running past the encampment would leave me in the densely populated streets, surrounded by Nekane's allies. I didn't know what way to go, and so I took off in the opposite direction, tearing the chain from my neck as I attempted to shift. *Odd.* I felt lighter, and freer without the necklace, but I couldn't find my Wolf. I couldn't tear the band off of my wrist. That was something I'd have to handle later, if I could just get away from this place.

The Hunters overwhelmed me with their silver nets. As I looked up, I saw Nekane's cruel smile. The sound of scrambling paws and growls filled the air and I could only think one thing, praying that the vampire could hear me despite the distance and the silver.

Run, Acanthus. Please.

I was in a concrete box of a room for hours, covered in bites and cuts criss-crossing my arms and legs from the razor sharp pieces of the nets. They'd left me tangled in it, and I couldn't find it in me to fight. My eyes were closed, and I didn't bother to open them when someone slipped into the room. The net began to lift, and a sharp whisper echoed off the walls. "Get up, you silly creature. Have you given up already?"

My eyes flew open. I didn't recognize the person talking, but they smelled like lavender and vanilla. Her hair hung in her face. *A Witch?*

She definitely wasn't a Wolf. I'd never seen Witches in the encampment, but I knew Nekane kept them in her service. Their different spells and uses were talked about in the lessons, more like weapons than people. If she was one of Nekane's Witches, I didn't understand why she would go through the trouble of rescuing me. She threw the net to the side and offered her hand, and I took it, struggling up to my feet. "Cypress, you don't have much time. Perk up, get out of here."

I furrowed my brow, tilting my head. "You're letting me go?"

She huffed, glancing towards the door. "Yes! Don't let the Vampire forget us. There are still Witches caught in the snare. Go, go!"

I didn't hesitate, taking off into a full run out of the room.

That Time I Got Sun Poisoning

Acanthus

In the months Cypress was suffering through the encampment's cruelty, I went back to my old normality. I hadn't been involved with running the Night Garden dealings since the nineteen-aughts — that was the job of my closest confidant, Azalea Barclay, at the Yellow Rose Bed and Breakfast in Pennsylvania. It was easier to withdraw from my friends than it was to explain my mental state. I prepared the best that I could, but I stopped taking good care of myself. A random Traveler or two showed up on my door, only to move on a day or two later. I stopped meeting with Arturous and Esmeralda as the days passed and the threat became less urgent. Nekane's pack hadn't moved.

Maybe I had overblown the issues regarding the treaty. I began to question how strategic I could actually be, and I thought of Cypress, Es, Arturous, and Azalea all the while. My mind wandered to Cypress the most. Time became irrelevant, and I drifted in between the fragments of lucidity and madness, refusing to leave the confines of the church grounds.

But, helping Cypress had awakened a part of me that longed to help others, no matter how deep I buried it down. *Maybe I should go to the Yellow Rose, or at least speak to Azalea,* I thought on one of my more lucid days. I promptly shut it down. I was not fit to be a part of this world of quiet resistance, if I could not even figure out this treaty business.

Candles burned on every surface of my little crumbling church always. I worked in the gardens and gathered things from the

167

surrounding forest, regardless of the time of day or night, and my skin was buzzing with the uncomfortable feeling of having gotten too much sun. I wasn't sick yet, but I was very close. I hadn't been taking care of myself, and the effects of low food and insomnia-driven exhaustion were starting to take their toll on my body. I would have to go into the city again soon, and I had honestly been trying to avoid it ever since the incident at the Manor.

Time passed as anachronistically as it always had, but I knew that it had been at least a few weeks, if not over a month. I'd avoided the stressful trip with my blood bag rations and deliveries, but I needed a donor soon. The uncomfortable summer heat and short nights had settled firmly in, though it hardly mattered to me. I may as well have been a ghost haunting the forest, lost in kaleidoscopic colors and drifting in and out of starvation. I only bothered to address my hunger when I was dangerously close to losing control and falling into a frenzy. Esmeralda stopped by once or twice, and Arturous a handful of times, but I didn't speak to them long. Each visit ended with them leaving me more blood bags.

In one moment of lucidity, I was soaking in the claw-foot tub in the bathroom, the cold of the water soothing my burned skin. My hair formed a thick curtain, the ends drifting listlessly in the water. As much as it soothed me, I had been in the bath for too long and my body was starting to wrinkle and prune. With slow and delicate movements, I rose, dripping as I pulled the plug from the drain in a singular motion.

My body ached. My skin was too sensitive for clothes quite yet, and the rivulets coming from my hair made it scream. The pain was exquisite, and it kept me grounded. Leaning over, I twisted my hair to wring it before wrapping it into a deep red towel. At least that would keep it off of my back and shoulders.

The myriad of candles were probably well past the point of a fire hazard, but the flickering soothed me. It reminded me of simpler times, ages past. I moved past them, through the living space and into the kitchen. Opening the fridge, I stared at the shelf only to see a single blood bag left. I sighed, chapped lips cracking as they parted. When was the last time I drank? A few days? It was fuzzy.

I pulled the last bag from the fridge and drained it, tossing it into a trash can as I walked past. *To hell with the stairs*, I thought as I rose into the air. I ascended to the loft, touching down with a soft *thump* in front of my old wooden armoire. I dug through the right-hand shelves, looking for loose, soft clothing to give my skin a rest. Soon enough, I had settled on something suitable; black lounge pants that swayed in big swooshes when I walked, loose around my burned calves. They accompanied a tank top depicting a white graphic of a female Death from a popular comic. It took longer than I'd like to admit to get the pieces on.

By the time I had gotten dressed, the sun was high in the sky. I hadn't looked at my clock in days, but I assumed it was close to noon. I had no desire to sleep. The return to the nightmares of decades long past was worse than the stinging of my burnt skin. So, I descended down the stairs and flopped on top of one of the couches. My thoughts naturally drifted to Cypress, as they often did. I'd sent letters, and tried to reach out mentally, but neither option seemed to yield results. They truly had left me behind. *I wonder how he's doing, if he's happy...*

A loud clamor happened near the door, and every muscle in me tensed as I groaned aloud, "Dear Lord, please don't let me find someone else needing aid. I can't even help myself, right now."

As I suspected, no answer came; speaking to the Lord never did yield results. A thump hit the doors, and then the heavy oak splintered as they crashed open. I gasped and flew to my feet as my eyes adjusted to the beams of sunlight pouring in. I brought up my hands and extended my nails, preparing myself for battle. *This is it*, I thought. *They've come for you, and you've made yourself an easy target by being impatient for this moment.*

The hulking figure panted as the sunlight silhouetted them. The smell of copper mixed with campfire smoke and whiskey before I realized, my entire body reacting to the shock as if I'd been doused in ice water. "Cypress?"

I was on my feet immediately, staring at him as he panted. "Acanthus, we need to go. Now."

Cypress

They weren't moving. Acanthus was staring at me like they'd seen a ghost come back from the grave. "Jesus fuck. Acanthus, NOW," I snarled, and grabbed a bag that was shoved beside the parasol planter. We didn't have time for this. I started grabbing robes and shawls at random. Anything within reach. The sound of engines were echoing through the forest. *Fuck.* I couldn't wait for Acanthus to come to reason.

"I see your language has only gotten worse, hanging out with those mongrels." Their voice was small and far away. This wasn't good. I didn't have much time. They were still frozen in place, eyes wide and wavering. "I can't believe it."

"Acanthus, I'm serious. Please," the urgency in my voice made it sharp, and I winced. Grabbing their hand, I nearly dropped it immediately. Their skin was freezing; on top of that, it was extremely rough, cracked and bleeding, chapped to a dangerous degree. I was suddenly hyper aware of the dirt and blood covering my own hands, and

I prayed I couldn't get them sick with the filth. "You've been in the sun, haven't you?"

"A bit more than usual," they admitted in that strange far-away voice, "but that's fine."

Engines cut outside. Clearly they had been lying about how much the sun had affected them, and I was about to yell at them. But, then I heard it. The clunk of equipment, and the high pitched whine of it powering on. *Fuck.*

The Hunters had been carrying those weird speaker boxes filled with lights. I didn't know what the whine was, but it couldn't be good. Acanthus' brows furrowed as they shot an annoyed glance towards the broken doors. "What is —"

"ACANTHUS, GET DOWN," I cried out as I pulled them to my chest, dropping to the floor. It was the only thing I could think of to protect their body from the lights as they started blasted into the windows and doors.

It was blinding. Shouting and the loud pops of people shooting things at the building melded together, adding to the chaos. The shattering of windows mixed into the cacophony, and Acanthus' startled cry from beneath me made my insides twist. "Fuck," I growled.

Acanthus' heart was pounding. I could feel it in their closeness, a frantic chaotic beat as their breaths hitched, quick and shallow. I hovered over them in a push-up, protecting them from the light as they stared at me, blood outlining their eyes in unshed tears. "Acanthus, it's Hunters, what do I do?!"

I searched their face, looking for answers that weren't there. I wasn't fast enough; I'd taken too long getting here. It was a miracle that I had gotten here in the first place. My warning wasn't enough. The Hunters had a perimeter set up already. My own heart was thundering in my ears. "Fuck, fuck, fuck, *fuck*."

I needed to get us out of there. "Acanthus, I need you to trust me, do you trust me?"

My voice shook, but I needed to be brave. I waited for a small nod before I continued. "I need to move. Where are my car keys?"

The sharpness of urgency and understanding replaced the fog in their beautiful hazel eyes. "My desk," they replied, their voice hoarse. "Drawers."

That would have to be good enough; I nodded. *Think, Cypress, think, you need to be the rock right now.* How was I supposed to protect Acanthus from artificial sun lamps like this? I couldn't exactly expect a parasol to fix this. *Fuck, what do I do?!*

I looked around the room, my shoulders twitching as someone yelled outside. I didn't catch what was said. *Come on, come on....*

My eyes landed on a blanket hanging off the couch. That was the answer. "Wrap yourself in as many things as you can. I need you to do this, please."

They were still dazed, but nodded again. "Alright. First, move with me. We're gonna get behind the couch."

"On your count, then, Cypress."

"Okay. One... two... three!"

I started to army crawl. The electric hum of the equipment outside pulsed in time with the buzzing from Acanthus' powers. They used them to slide along the floor beneath me. Shouting and the clomping of boots echoed off of the walls and through the broken oak door. "We need to hurry," I muttered as I sped up. Acanthus kept in time, and as soon as we got to the couch I pulled the blanket down and over them. "Just stay put, and I'll be back, I need to get my keys."

 I leapt to my feet, bolting across the living room towards their desk. Why did it have to be next to the door? Fabrics began to fly into the air and towards the Vampire. *Nearly there, Cypress, come on!*

The Hunters threw something inside. I thought it was a smoke bomb, a blackened substance hissing through the air. I was a little too close for just slightly too long as the weapon released its terrible powder. *Oh, fuck!*

It was silver dust. I'd been lighter without the chain on my neck, but this weight was something different and more sinister. Pain blossomed in my lungs, coupled with some static that crackled through my mind. It was difficult to think, and that gravity pulled at me and slowed my trajectory. Acanthus was already reacting too slow, like a sloth stuck in molasses; I couldn't afford added slow downs. *Move, Cypress, move!*

I coughed, the powder clinging to my throat and clouding into my mouth and eyes. It was like drowning. I kicked the silver bomb thing back out the door and finished my mad dash for the desk. The good thing was, if they had Wolves with them, they'd be slowed by this much silver, too. I had no idea if there were any Wolves; I couldn't smell shit.

Work, brain, God damn it!

I paused and stared at the drawers, willing my brain to push through the fog. I knew it. I knew all of it, despite the changes that had happened since I had left. Stuff had been moved, and it had been cleaned, but I knew every detail as if I'd put the items in place. I'd seen the keys in one of those flashes at Nekane's camp.

Electric shock paralyzed me, and shouts from outside faded. They were in the right drawer beneath an old journal with random papers added in. Somewhere I would never have put them myself. Right where Acanthus left them. Right where they were in those brief flashes of memory. Those weren't memories at all. The knowledge hit me square in the chest; my skin prickling and thoughts skidding to a halt. "My pack…"

I blinked slowly. I'd bonded with Acanthus. No wonder I hadn't felt a connection at Nekane's. A bullet narrowly missed my head, and it brought me back to the present. I dropped to the floor, breaths heaving. I felt like I couldn't get any air into my lungs. *Not the time, Cypress, there's enemies! Get moving!*

I reached for the drawer and blindly grabbed the keys. I could let myself be dazed when we weren't threatened with certain doom. Through some small miracle, I got back to my feet and ran back across the living room, stuffing the keys into my pocket. Acanthus was up, albeit wobbly under what seemed to be one thousand cloaks, towels, and blankets. "Grab on," they spoke with confidence.

I hesitated. "I don't think—"

"I'm going in, I can't see them from here and I'm pretty sure I missed my shot," I heard from outside.

Acanthus grabbed me by the waist, and we flew up, over the loft and out of the bell tower. I didn't know how anyone could see at all as we rocketed into the sky. The brunt of the lights were focused on the front of the church. We were lucky to be out of the main beams, but the peripheral light still made things impossibly bright. And with the true sun blaring down from the summer sky, I knew we were in trouble. "Hey, Pup?" Acanthus spoke dreamily.

"Yeah?" Oh no. That tone of voice only hinted towards bad things.

"I'm passing out," they replied, and my eyes darted to their face just in time to see theirs roll back.

"Jesus fuck, Acanthus!"

And then I felt the downward pull of gravity. *Fuck, fuck, fuck! Not good.*

I grabbed Acanthus and pulled them to my chest in midair, rotating so I landed first. My back crashed into the roof. Acanthus landed on my chest as the terracotta shattered beneath me. We started to slide down the intense slope as I lay paralyzed beneath the Vampire, dazed and breathless. Everything was so bright, and I couldn't breathe.

My hip and shoulder were hot and sticky, like the wounds from Nekane's encampment reopened. We were now coated in a fine layer of dirt and silver dust. My body was on fire as I skidded to a halt right at the edge of the roof. Hunters were shouting below, and I laughed humorlessly. *So this is where it all ends, huh? Silver riddled, sun fried werewolf pancake. Delicious.*

"How do we get up there," someone shouted.

Another voice answered gruffly. "I dunno, I can't get a good shot from here. Someone angle the lights!"

"The leech can't have survived this!"

I gritted my teeth, closing my eyes. Think, Cypress. Come on.

The Hunters have to climb through the bell tower to get up here. There had to be at least a dozen of them. They were focused on the front of the building with their equipment and weapons set up. There were no ladders. I had maybe a minute or two. Acanthus was still on top of me, motionless. *Please, please be covered enough.*

As the lights were angled towards us, Acanthus' hands and parts of their exposed face started to crackle and smoke. I had to keep checking that they didn't turn to ash on my chest. "Okay, we're just getting out of here," I said to no one in particular. It was hard to think over the thundering of my heart and the weird drowning feeling. I shifted to try and shield Acanthus from the lights. I fumbled with my pocket. *Please, please be okay, Acanthus.*

If I shifted any more, I'd be in the gutter and probably pole-vaulting to the ground. I looked over the edge of the roof, praying to whatever listened that the touchy remote start would work. A loud crack echoed through the air as something smacked the wall of the bell tower. "Come on, come on," I muttered, clicking the remote start button.

The first Hunter peeked over the half-wall of the tower, scowling as he rose into view. My headlights flickered, and my car came to life. There was no one near the car; it'd been parked at the side of the church, and they had all moved towards the house. They were like sharks, smelling blood in the water. The Hunter on the roof with us had raised his hand, brandishing a canteen and a cross. This was my one and only chance for some John Wick shit.

I pulled Acanthus into a more solid hold, right as the Hunter dumped his holy canteen on us. I didn't *think* it affected Acanthus, but they had lied about the sun. We were both drenched, and I made the leap to my car, landing near it and rolling. The impact shot through my knees and elbows with each roll, but I couldn't let the pain stop me. I staggered to my feet, panting. "Please don't burst into flame, please don't burst into flame," I pleaded to the unconscious vampire in my arms.

Their skin sizzled in reply, burning off the water. My knees were stinging, along with my hip and shoulder. Blood soaked my torn shirt.

Lemon Balm

Shouts came from inside the church, and the Hunters started pouring back out of the building. I opened the door, and threw Acanthus in the back seat, before hopping into the driver's seat. The first of the Hunters made it to their vehicles, and the thrum of an ATV engine roared to life behind us. *This is a win, there's no way any of those vehicles could keep up to an actual car. Time to floor it, Golf! Do me proud!*

I shoved it into drive with my pedal to the floor, not caring who or what I hit. My Golf crashed forward, sliding on the gravel with how fast I sped out of there. It was over in a matter of minutes; The gravel road was a straight shot, and by the time we hit the open highway a minute later, I didn't see any of them in the rear-view mirror. I sighed at the bundle of blankets in the back seat. "That was a hell of a way to come back home.".

Talking to them gave me a comfort that I hadn't felt in over two months. It was all that I could do to drive, and drive, and drive. I'd rather be sitting with my friend on our couch, catching up and putting all of this behind us. I guess, at least we were getting out of this mess. *Welcome to war, Cypress,* I thought bitterly.

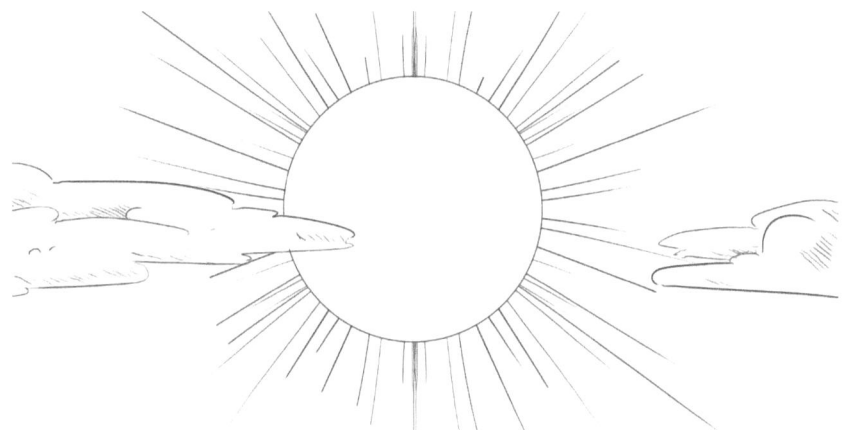

That Time It Was Us Against The World

Cypress

I'd driven for about six hours, and the dashboard's glowing display suggested that we were approaching 8pm. It was still light out. I'd only stopped once to take a piss and fill the gas tank, and only after making damn sure I wasn't being followed. I grabbed a few survival materials — a first aid kit, some shelf-stable food for me to eat, a muscle relaxant, some tea bags, and the finest cup of coffee that the gas station had to offer. I made sure to move as quickly as possible, scurrying out of the bright fluorescents and back to the car. I'm pretty sure we were a state or two over, though, I'd lost track. The silver in my lungs and wounds burned, and my eyes were beginning to sting with the effort of staying awake. The bangle around my wrist was like a brick dangling from my arm as I drove. As much as I wanted to keep running, my wounds weren't healing and I was exhausted. The adrenaline had long since worn off.

I pulled into the first motel I saw with a vacancy, and checked in. The man behind the desk blinked at me, but didn't comment on my ragged appearance. I kept my face stony, and he smiled as he handed me my key. "Enjoy your stay!"

I'm pretty sure I grumbled some platitude back to the man before wandering back to my car. *Enjoy your stay.*

The place was one of those cockroach-infested depression huts that you don't want to touch the sheets in. You know the ones; they dot the edges of towns, where the people down on their luck gather. The ones with grungy stains on every wood-paneled surface and condoms in the vending machines. As much as I didn't like the motel's feel, I needed sleep. With the last bits of my energy, I prepared the room for my injured friend.

Acanthus hadn't so much as moved during the entire drive, stock still and mummified in their fabric prison. I tried to ignore how anxious that made me and focused on arranging one of the beds with pillows. If they tossed and turned, they might injure themself worse; I wanted a barrier to stop them from moving. I didn't bother to turn on either of the desk lamps. The ugly brown panel gleamed in dirty yellow light pouring in from the parking lot. It was already soul-sucking. *I picked the best place to promote healing*, I thought sarcastically.

I glanced towards the air conditioner beneath the window. It was one of those huge units that spanned the whole wall underneath the glass. *Acanthus said cold is good for them, right? Or did I get that from the lessons?*

The thing didn't look very promising. I walked over and turned the flimsy plastic knob, and the machine roared to life. It was cheap, huge, and obnoxious; clearly broken in some way with how loud it rattled. I sighed. The curtains weren't blackout curtains, but I drew them shut anyway and made sure that the blinds were shuttered. If it wound up being too bright, then I could always try to throw a blanket over the windows or something. I could worry about what amenities the room had later.

Heading back to the car, I grabbed the vampire burrito. The sun was finally set. They dangled over my shoulder, stock still as I carried them in. Anyone seeing this would have thought I had a body draped over me. I glanced from each neighboring window as I walked. "You better wake up in the morning, you fucker," I muttered at the cloak pile.

Their coverings were damp, and I didn't want to think about what that meant as I brought them inside and laid them down. There were two beds, covered in some ugly patterned comforters that I couldn't quite see in the low light. I set Acanthus on the one I prepared, furthest from the windows. *The more cautious, the better.*

I was too tired to strip. Besides, I still had to un-burrito Acanthus. I made sure the door was locked, as well as the deadbolt. Then, I thought better of it and grabbed the press-wood and plastic chair from the corner to wedge under the door knob. Was I doing this whole fugitive thing right? I had no idea. *We're so fucked.*

I turned my attention back to Acanthus, and walked over to the side of the bed. As I started to pull at the fabrics, I made sure to be as careful as possible. Each item seemed to be more and more soaked with blood. I stared at the pieces, laying them across the bed. The stains looked black in the darkness. I reached towards the lamp, clicking it on and illuminating the little brown room. The added yellow light deepened the dread in my gut.

Blood was everywhere. The Vampire had clearly been bleeding. "Oh, what the fuck..."

I didn't want to move Acanthus to toss the stuff aside. Maybe the cloaks and towels were functioning like a bandage. I didn't want to fully uncover them if that was the case. I couldn't tell the extent of the damage, but it didn't look like their wounds were healing.

I didn't want to think anymore. I hadn't been able to breathe right since I inhaled that silver smoke, and a deep cough rattled through my chest. My stomach flipped, and I reached with trembling fingers to move the last thin linen away from their face. It might as well have been a burial shroud, and my skin prickled if I let that thought linger for too long.

They were covered in black, flaking scabs. I could barely make out their skin, or even if there was any left. I winced, staring at their cracked and partially charred body for a long time. They've got to stay covered, I thought as I replaced the layers. I was distant and numb, shock slowing my movement. Please be okay, I thought over and over. Please, please be okay.

This was hell. I had no idea what to do. I flopped onto my stomach next to Acanthus and slung an arm protectively over them. As I shut my eyes, I tried to ignore how the tacky wood-panel walls felt like they were closing in on us.

Acanthus

Darkness. Confusion. Hunger. I'd think I was having one of my recurring nightmares, if not for the blistering pain. Every bump and word vibrated through my own personal void, muffled and strained as if it came through sheet rock. With the extra exposure that the UV lamps provided, on top of the summer sun, I was severely ill. If I had been at full health when the Hunters had attacked, things would be vastly different.

On some level, I think I knew that the Hunters would come for me. Nekane and I had always been on the knife's edge of battle. Where her Wolves broke the peace, it was I who publicly declared a threat at The Spirits Three. I should have known that the stasis after that treaty breach was only due to her gathering her resources.

In fact, my actions probably left a ripple, causing Hunters to go after every vampire in the Tri-State area. I was truly an idiot to let myself stay half-alive while in danger of such a vicious attack. I could have been somewhere with Cypress, both of us healthy and laughing at death, if I had just mobilized in time. Instead, here I was, stuck in a crypt of my own making.

Now that I was in this perilous position between life and death, I realized how stupid I was to throw everything away. But, that was just a testament to how tenuous of a hold I had on life. And, this strange coma was plagued with nightmares. Faded, chaotic, overtly violent images of snarling maws. I couldn't tell if the Wolves were searching, or if I was picking up on Cypress' dreams. We had to be dubiously safe. Even if the Hunters followed us, Nekane's core pack wouldn't. She was far too important of a figurehead, and couldn't move so freely.

I tried to search for a spiritual tether to my body. I swam through the inky blackness, and as I surfaced into my conscious mind, I could feel fire everywhere. I knew it wasn't literal fire, but my nerve endings disagreed. With the amount of light I had endured, my skin went from merely chapped to outright blistered and cracked. Perhaps some of it was gone entirely. I managed to twitch my fingers before the cottony disconnect deepened and I lost my body again. It was my mind protecting me from the pain. *This isn't good.*

The strange nothingness held me in a vice grip. I reached for that pain, and as I managed to surface, I felt my teeth grit, hissing. Every sense flattened with the constant searing sensation. The bitter, earthen taste of my own blood clung to my leaden tongue. The tingling throughout my skin was like a million bugs; crawling, stinging, and biting across every tangible surface of my being. I managed a small, shuddering gasp, and tried to focus on what else I could sense.

The dim sound of labored breathing was beside me. Maybe Cypress was awake. If that was the case, this frail, brittle bridge of awareness would be my only chance to connect. There was no way I could open my eyes. ***"Help. Pup. Help."***

I projected the thought towards Cypress, though static screamed in my ears. I could only hope they could still hear me. The bed shifted. *A bed? Where are we? Are we on the run?*

A whimper broke through the static. "I don't know what to do!"

My hold on reality slipped and I floated in the thick, staticky nothing. I gritted my teeth again, at war with my own body. *No, no, no! Fuck!*

My lengthening fangs pierced my lip and the sharp pain cut through the numbness, the smell of my blood mixing with Cypress'. Mine splashed against my teeth, the wound not healing due to my other injuries. Fresh blood from a donor would help, but I could hardly feed from someone when I couldn't move.

"Silver?" If they had endured silver dust, I knew that they were in pain and likely struggling to heal their own wounds.

"Oh, fuck you," Cypress growled, their anger and fear rippling in waves. Their voice dissolved into a series of reedy coughs. When they finished, they said thinly, "You, Acanthus, how do I help you?"

My grip on consciousness was slipping again. I didn't answer immediately, floating in that liminal space of void and cotton. I don't know how long I was silent, but I felt strong hands touch my shoulder. The pain was excruciating, and though I had hardly gasped aloud, a scream ripped through my mind. The sound echoed in waves off of my own skull. They flinched away. I could see only one way for them to help me. *"Shower. You. Then dig. Bury me."*

I hoped he understood because the pain and exhaustion overtook me after those words left my mind. The pain was too great to stand. Darkness reclaimed me, and I was disconnected from my body once more.

Cypress

According to the calendars in the lobby, two days had passed. *July 12th.* I was starving, battered, and unsure. I thought of the cellphone, sitting dead in my glove compartment. I hadn't kept it charged regularly for years; still, sometimes I missed having a portable assistant in my pocket. The looks I got made my skin crawl; people shrank away from me, and one mother held her little boy close, staring at me with a threat and a promise as she hid his eyes. I always hated when people acted scared of me.

My shirt was shredded beyond repair, so I ditched it. My shorts were thankfully intact. I had wrapped my wounds the best I could with the first aid kit. There'd been no time to grab any of Acanthus' remedies. *I should've gotten to them faster…*

The fact that I was able to warn them at all was a miracle in itself. I was groggy and slow, but I'd gotten Acanthus and I out of the decimated church. I hadn't exactly been able to assess the damage at the time, but I knew that the doors were busted in and many of the windows were smashed. Who knew how much silver powder coated everything inside. My heart panged; no matter what happened, we wouldn't be able to go back there. It felt like we'd been robbed of something.

I was thankful that the front desk hadn't disturbed us while I drifted in and out of consciousness, but in the back of my mind I worried about the charges racking up on my credit card. *How fucking ridiculous…*

I guess when you're in crazy situations, your brain just kind of latches onto what's normal or easy to control. It couldn't be helped. I was starving, and my chest was heavy. I hadn't felt like this since I had bronchitis in high school. *Is this what covid feels like? Oh, fuck, do I have covid?* The panic spiked through me, but I immediately shot myself down. *No Cypress, you idiot. It's probably your injuries. If anything, it's probably pneumonia.*

The thought made my stomach twist with unease. It's not like I could move with Acanthus still partially mummified in twenty cloaks, towels, and blankets on the bed. At least I could deal with my hunger by snacking. I took my chances on a trip to the vending machine when something changed. The static in my head grew less intense until it quieted completely. I froze with a dollar clasped in my outstretched hand, leaning forward and holding my breath. The vending machine full of empty calories disappeared from my radar. I couldn't explain it, but it felt like someone was trying to speak to me. *Acanthus?*

It was like surfacing after a deep dive underwater. I rushed back to the room and threw the door open, my quest for a candy bar forgotten. My heart was soaring, breaths quick and light as I prayed to whatever deity or spirits listened. *Please, please, please...*

Acanthus lay deathly still on the bed, where I left them wrapped in blankets. The curtains were drawn tightly shut. I stared with bated breath for what felt like a lifetime, but they didn't move. My shoulders sagged and my chest ached. Had I just gas-lit myself into thinking there was a change? ***"Help. Pup. Help."***

It came into my mind so, so quietly, I thought I'd imagined it. My heart stopped its free-fall, and began a cautious climb back to its normal seat in my chest. I closed the door behind me, stepping forward. "Acanthus?"

Silence. A rock formed in my throat, and I backed away from Acanthus' bed, stumbling onto the one behind me. I reached up and ran my hands through my hair, before tugging at it. "Dammit Acanthus, I don't know what to do!"

The static grew for a minute, and then faded as their voice strained in our minds, panic and desperation lacing each word. ***"No, no, no! Fuck!"***

My blood ran cold, fingers shaking as I slowly lowered my hands from my head. Where was the calm I had during the attack? I needed that steadiness. I stood, walking over and sitting beside their motionless body. The movement jostled them, and they grimaced, their fangs long over their bottom lip. "Acanthus, I need you to tell me what to do to help you. Let me help you. Please."

"Silver?"

"Oh, fuck you. Yes, it was fucking everywhere," I spat, but then I took a breath. Anger was useless. "YOU, Acanthus, how do I help YOU?"

"Shower. You. Then dig. Bury me."

"Bury you? You're not dead!"

My indignation fell on deaf ears. The static was back, and there was a decided absence where the ghost of Acanthus lingered. I sighed out my frustration, tilting my head back and looking up at the popcorn ceiling. "Fuck."

I'd already showered a few times since I'd awoken, but no matter what I did, silver stuck in the wounds. My shoulder was a hot and bloody mess. My hip was constantly aching with a persistent black bruise expanding out from a deep bite. My arms and legs were shredded from the silver nets. I kept them covered and clean, but they weren't important right now. Right now I had Acanthus to deal with. *Bury them? Bury them where?!*

I'd draw far too much suspicion doing it in broad daylight. "Fuck me," I sighed out a rattly breath and got up from the bed, taking the least flashy cloak I could find, and tying it around my chest in the semblance of a shirt. I had to go to the store. I guess I needed a shovel.

Questioning looks followed me around the soulless big box store, but no one was brave enough to confront the ragged hulking beast I'd become. I grabbed a few shirts. The search for a shovel had turned up empty, but at least I could morph my hands into claws. *Wait, can I still do that? I couldn't call my wolf forward at Nekane's.*

I guess I would figure that out later. I grabbed a sad excuse for a garden trowel that was in the clearance section, just in case. Even if I had to use my human hands, I'd be able to do it. All the training, coupled with the intense weight of the silver, had turned me into the biggest I'd ever been in my life. *That's right, avoid the monster in the toga and ripped shorts.*

Thinking about Nekane set me on a spiral. The time at her encampment proved to me just how little I knew about the World of Shadows. I think it was because of this that I also stopped at the library in town to catch up on some Vampire lore. The poor woman at the counter looked me up and down several times, and asked if I needed medical assistance. Eventually my calm demeanor broke. "I have a severe case of leprosy. I'd appreciate it if you stopped staring."

Lemon Balm

She nodded politely, showed me to the section I was looking for, and scurried off. I didn't have a library card, so I made some copies of the relevant book pages and walked out with a stack of paper a mile high. At least I had something to occupy myself with. I was exhausted, and the coughing was getting worse. Maybe I should've told her I had consumption instead, like a poor Victorian child.

Upon returning to the motel, I carried the items inside, the purples and pinks of the sunset reflecting off of the windows. When I got the door opened, I paused, staring around the room. The groceries dangled uselessly from my hands as I processed the sight. Acanthus' cloaks and towels were everywhere; two were draped across the yellow lamp between the beds, three had fallen haphazardly onto the television and knocked it askew. Several lay in a crumpled pile on the thread-bare brown carpet. I blinked and slipped the door shut behind me, glancing at Acanthus. They still hadn't moved.

Their powers must have lashed out subconsciously and threw them away. I sighed, dropping the bags on the ugly wooden TV stand. Christ, if I spent enough time in this room, I'd probably start seeing in sepia tone. After picking up the cloaks and towels, I dropped them in a pile on the back of the uncomfortably straight chair. Satisfied, I stocked the mini fridge with bottles of ice coffee, protein shakes, lettuce, and a pound of turkey. Food successfully stocked, I peeked outside through the break in the curtains. I didn't think anyone would notice if I went out past the treeline behind the motel. *I never thought about preparing for a burial.*

Sighing, I slid my gaze towards Acanthus. *We're a sorry sight.*

My eyes lingered on them for a long while, soaking in the details of their face and committing them to memory. Something made me want to protect them; I never wanted to see them like this again. It almost looked like their skin was rubbed away. I was worried about touching them. They looked so fragile like this; my heart wanted to shatter. *How did things get so hard?*

And, they had gotten hard. I wasn't sure how far I should spiral down the paranoia rabbit hole. Could the Hunters track us? I'd been using my credit card, and they knew my name. Could they tap into police power? Did they use trackers and stuff like that? Maybe I should check my car for AirTags or something. Watching Acanthus' motionless face, I wished they would wake up. I needed their knowledge, but I also just missed their voice.

I lightly dabbed their lip with a wet cloth, cleaning the blood, before wrapping a light scarf I'd bought around their face. I'd never buried anyone before. How does one breathe? I hoped the scarf would at least keep them comfortable. On top of that, I didn't want dirt getting in their mouth. With Acanthus truly looking like a well tended corpse, I gently lifted them bridal-style, and checked outside again to make sure there were no nosy humans milling about. Seeing none, I left the room and made a mad dash for the trees. *I wish I had Acanthus' super speed.*

I stayed still just past the tree line, breaths heaving between coughs. I was not fit to run right now, and I wondered how much that little burst of exertion would cost me. I'd always been a healthy guy; I wasn't used to feeling so sick. When the coughing subsided, I straightened up, adjusted Acanthus in my arms, and began to walk further into the trees.

They were young, scraggly things, heading into a thicker forest further down the path. Someone had tied a used condom and tossed it up onto a branch just above my eye level. I screwed my face up in disgust at the sight. Cigarette butts and beer cans littered the ground before the trees got thick, but as I followed the path deeper, the litter slowly began to disappear. A short way past the thickening of the trees, there was a clearing. *Perfect, this has got to be shaded during the day.*

With the sun just beginning to set, it was already near dark in the clearing. Maybe it'd help Acanthus heal. "My friend, you are getting a shallow grave," I muttered, gently setting them on the ground.

I just want to point out, I think I did a pretty damn good job. Especially since I was using a garden trowel. I dug deep enough to have Acanthus completely buried, and undisturbed, but not deep enough that I couldn't dive in and rescue them if I thought something was wrong. I laid out a blanket, and stretched out beside the newly dug grave site.

There was no way I was going to leave Acanthus out here alone. I sighed, knowing it was going to be a long boring night. I headed back to the room just long enough to make some food and grab the scans from the library. *Maybe I could find some insight into this odd ritual*, I thought as I walked back to the clearing.

That Time I Was Buried Alive

Acanthus

The next time that I had any semblance of awareness, the cool earth was packed tightly against my skin. I had no idea how much time had passed. The sharp, intense pain had dulled to a soft, barely-noticeable stinging. Considering my pain levels, I'd wager that it had been a full day; perhaps, a day and a half. I didn't feel nearly as ill; still weak and achy, but alive. For the first time since Cypress had left, the damnedable static I heard had faded, and I was grounded in my body.

I smelled the cool, chemical-laden mud through — was that a scarf? Yes, the smell of cashmere mixing with the earth around me. Slowly, I began to fit the pieces together. Cypress had wrapped my mouth so that I didn't inhale the dirt. My heart swelled, and my fingers tingled with the sudden lightness. *He listened. How sweet of them, to think of my comfort.*

I couldn't tell what this very large emotion was. It projected from me without any words attached. Gingerly, I bent the joints of my fingers, and they complained with the stiffness. Every movement was slowed and labored, as if I was under sandbags, but at least I could move. The dirt didn't help with the weight. The next thing I tested was wiggling my toes. This was harder; my lower body felt like it was made of stone. My upper body may be slow, but my lower was completely unresponsive.

"Is it…" I trailed off, trying to find words. *"Qu'est-ce que la nuit en l'Anglais…Moon?"*

184

Still struggling, I sent a picture as a thought in Cypress' direction; endless swirling stars, galaxies, and deep colors dancing together. Then, I wondered if they saw the night as I did. My face was hot and tingling with shame. I hated when I couldn't communicate effectively. It had been a wonder that I was able to speak at all in my previous state, in a language that was not my native tongue. It didn't matter how long I went in America; my thoughts would always be in French. In these moments of near death, my brain would behave as if I were freshly turned; still in Toulouse. I wouldn't chastise myself now; at least, not for my language.

Their thought came back, already being petulant. *"Well, it's night, yeah."*

I let that one slide. He had every single right to be angry with me. I still was marveling at the fact that Cypress had come to warn me at all. They had saved me. With great effort, I projected my powers around me, the dirt lifting up in small chunks until I was exposed. I gritted my teeth as the dirt lifted. The strain left me unable to move, and so I let the earth neatly fall to one side. Once I dropped my telekinesis, I tested my arms. *"Merci, mon Dieu,"* I thought as I found myself able to move again.

I pulled the scarf down before clawing my way out of the shallow hole, my legs stubbornly refusing to work. *"I'm not God, Acanthus, sorry to say,"* Cypress' mirth was strong in their tone. I could see, but a strange hazy fog had taken most of my sight. There was a dull gray cast to everything; blurred and soft.

Lunging for the hulking silhouette beside my burial plot, I wrapped my arms tightly around them. I ignored the stinging in my skin, pain blistering through me at each contact point, and pressed my forehead against their collar bone. I'd knocked a pile of paper out of their hands, and they fluttered around us with the whispered promise of knowledge. They whimpered, and strong hands pushed me away with some force, causing me to fall back and skid across the cool grass and partially back into the grave. *"Ouch."*

"Fuck, I'm sorry — don't do that, Acanthus!"

"Language."

I still couldn't find my voice. The grave, though shallow, had helped speed up my healing process. Dirt and earth had that effect on vampires — I never found out exactly why. My best guess was it was due to the dark and cold, and Vampires thrived in the coolness. *"I am fine, but cannot speak yet. Sorry, young one. Thank you."*

Cypress didn't answer. Or if they did, I missed it. I was far too focused on the effort of sitting up. I couldn't quite manage it, leaning up on my elbows but unable to make my core muscles contract. My frustration ebbed into our link. I was completely open and vulnerable right now, unable to keep anything to myself. Their voice was quiet as they spoke aloud, soft and concerned. "Do you need help? I read somewhere that I'm not supposed to help, but…"

They trailed off, chewing at their bottom lip. I blinked at them, rattled, and slowly shook my head. ***"I do need help. Where did you read that?"***

The thought was followed by an intrusive one, breaking through. *Weak and pitiful, Acanthus.*

The specter of a cruel, laughing Vampire flashed behind my eyes. I fell back into the cool grass, full of anguish. *How did I put myself in this position? I had promised myself to never let it get to this point ever again.*

Flopping back, my eyes threatened to start spilling; I was seconds away from full hysterics. Cypress' voice once again cut through, and I found myself grateful that he was speaking aloud. I had spent enough time in my own head. "I found it from a couple of different sources. "

My throat felt like I had swallowed broken glass. *How long had it been since I fed?*

Cypress must have moved to help me out of the grave. The blur of their silhouette was above me, and I felt those strong hands come underneath my shoulders. What little control I had made me tense everything that would, shocked at the contact. A scream immediately rang through my head, more flashes of both current pains and past transgressions behind my eyes. *Shut up, you stupid creature,* I forced myself to relax. *This is Cypress. They are safe.*

I was in their arms, my head once again on their chest, the soft rise and fall beneath my cheek hypnotizing me. The repetitive rhythm had my shoulders slumping as the tension eased away. "I'm exhausted," Cypress murmured, their voice a strained rasp.

Silver. I would have to help them with that. "Me too, Pup."

"We should go back," Cypress muttered, but they made no move to stand.

"Do you need a moment?"

"Yeah, I think I do."

They lay back in the grass. The motion disoriented me, but I settled soon enough. They had fallen asleep in the grass not long after that, and I was not about to wake them up. They had been running non stop while I… *While I what, exactly?*

What had I done, other than sulk? This was ridiculous. I was an elder being. I had lived nearly a millennia. What on earth had I been thinking, leaving myself so open to attack? I should never have brought Cypress to the exchange and carried through with it. They had nearly died for me, and they were suffering now. It wouldn't surprise me if the entire Eastern territory was mobilized and looking for us. *I handled this entire situation so badly...*

Though I was exhausted, I didn't need the rest. Every slight shift of the warm summer breeze made me want to crawl back down into the earth. My stomach flipped with both hunger and pain, but there was nothing that I could do about it. I watched over Cypress throughout the night, my vision slowly coming back to me as my strength returned. The reflection of silver embedded in his wounds shined an eerie silver cast in the dull glow of the moon.

They slept peacefully beneath me. I didn't dare move through most of the night for fear of waking them, but at the first inkling of light creeping into my vision, I gently prodded with my mind. **"Pup. The sun."**

They jolted awake mid-snore, and slurped as if they'd been drooling. "Nn?"

"The sun, Cypress."

They processed my words then, and gently wrapped their arms around me before hopping up. I gritted my teeth at the raw burn of my nerve endings. "Don't strain yourself," Cypress grumbled, but there was an exhausted edge to their voice still.

Cypress

"Speak for yourself," Acanthus replied to my grumble. I carried them across the parking lot.

"You fuck," I huffed back, but I was happy that they were talking.

"If I wasn't so tired, I'd wash your mouth with soap."

Even their mental voice seemed to have a strange rasp to it, like they were straining to speak. I grinned down at them, but it faded when I saw their face. Their eyes had a dulled, blank cast to them, as if they were looking past me instead of at me. "Acanthus, can you see right now?"

The joking tone died. They swallowed, then shook their head. They were completely blind. A jolt shot through my heart. I ignored it, leaving the panic buried way below where Acanthus wouldn't be able to feel it. *Is that permanent? I hope it's not permanent.*

I needed to be strong for both of us, right now. *Right, they threatened to wash my mouth out with soap.*

"I want to see you try to wash out my mouth."

They stayed quiet, and I didn't know what to do with that. I threw a bad joke out there, an idle threat with a dramatic flair. "I swear to God, if you ever make me dig another hole again, I will bring you back to life, and end you myself."

"That bad, huh?"

Their voice was lighter than I had expected, and I was grateful for the carefully crafted levity between us. "I had to use my hands, and a shitty garden trowel."

They laughed, their frail body shaking silently with jerky movements and it faded to a small, closed-mouth smile. *"Well, your efforts are appreciated. I could have healed without it, but it would have taken a month, instead of a day."*

"Try two days," I said nonchalantly. I opened the door to our room and set them down in the chair after tossing the dirty laundry to the floor. Assessing the sheets of the bed they'd been laying in, I frowned. It was covered in blood, but they were also covered in dirt. I wasn't about to put them on the clean bed either. "Hmm."

I'm sure Acanthus could hear my thoughts, but I was too tired to try and guard against it. I knew eventually we'd have to talk about that. *Did they know all along, and just not tell me? No, I had suspicions even at the diner...*

The flashes of memory just confirmed it. It wasn't the time or place for this conversation. We both were a wreck. I had so many questions that were burning in my head, but they were dead and forgotten when I turned back to look at my friend a bit closer. I'd forgotten how awful they looked when I unwrapped them. "Acanthus, you're caked in blood."

"I nearly died. My skin barely exists."

The ugly yellow lighting of the table lamps did them no favors. I chewed on the inside of my lip, contemplating what to do or say. They must have been in agony. Their thoughts were starting to feel like they were coming through an old tin-can radio, thin and full of static. My gut twisted at that, my heart rattling against my rib cage. They were exhausted, just from making their way inside, and I hated the nature of their tone; vulnerable, fragile, and ready to shatter, like porcelain or glass. It scared me.

"I mummified you. I can only imagine how it looked to the humans staying here," I said, deadpan. *Great deflection, Cypress.*

Acanthus' mental voice went squeaky. *"YOU DID NOT BURY ME IN FRONT OF HUMANS."*

I laughed, and it turned into a cough. I rubbed my chest and swallowed, ignoring the burning raw feeling of my throat. "No. I'd probably be sitting in jail right now, Acanthus."

"Fair point."

It was quiet for long enough that I thought they had fallen asleep in the chair. Their mind buzzed with pain, and it mingled with my own constant aches, both separate and a part of me. The silence made me antsy. "How can I help?" I blurted, hoping that if I woke them, it wasn't upsetting.

Their voice was frayed and thin. *"You and I both need rest."*

A heat flooded into my face, and a vein pulsed in my temple. *Oh, come the fuck on.* They needed to care more for themself. "Acanthus, I'M thirsty."

"You don't say," they drawled.

I scowled. *Stop pushing me away, dammit.* "You're such a pest. I'm saying I can feel your hunger from here. Neither of us can go anywhere looking the way we do. You look like Carrie on prom night, and I…" I trailed off.

Acanthus' eyes slid to me, looking far more bright than they had before. It was a relief to see the sharp humor in that hazel fire. A smile played on their lips. *"Look like you've been mauled?"*

I rolled my eyes. "Well, I was, in fact, mauled. Are you strong enough to bathe? Will it hurt you? I just…" I trailed off, but my brain couldn't stop before my lips could. *"Really want to sleep."*

The thought slipped through our link, and I cringed. The last thing Acanthus needed was a snarky attitude. I'd been nothing but snarky the entire time they'd been awake, because my own pain was making me bristle. *"Rest, please. It can wait."*

When I woke up, my body was still aching, and I had the distinct sensation that I was covered in a thin level of grime. *Gross.*

I felt like I hadn't slept a wink. I was stiff and sore, and I'd said that line more than I care to admit during this time. It was starting to scare me. Maybe I should go to the hospital, I thought. I hadn't thought about it before this, but I was pretty sure the bites were starting to get infected. The thought of explaining all of the silver embedded in my skin made me want to run away screaming.

I glanced around the room, and relaxed when my eyes rested on the little alcove where the mini fridge was plugged in. Acanthus was there, holding an ugly brown travel cup full of tea, and appearing relatively human again. Their skin was darker and covered in freckles that I'd never seen on them before, but they were no longer caked in mud and blood. I blinked, wondering if I was dreaming, because Acanthus looked unruffled. Or, maybe I was misreading them.

Naturally, I went back to my white male-coded antics of making light of things and ignoring the problems staring us in the face. "Acanthus," I whispered as if I was sharing a dirty secret. "That tea? it's store bought."

"Hmm? I wasn't aware." What should've been a bold confident statement came out as a whisper. Their voice was still shot, but I could sense the sarcasm. They held up the box of cheap, generic black tea. "This is the best you could get?"

They winced, a hand flying to their throat and rubbing.

"I wasn't even sure you were going to get to enjoy this awful tea with me," I snapped, taking the cup from them as I shifted to a seated position on the bed. I guess I was angrier about it than I initially thought. *Deflection, failed.* I took a sip, then coughed. My throat felt like I'd been gargling razor blades.

"That's my own fault," Acanthus thought.

I blinked at the tea, and looked up at them. As easily as we had fallen into it, something bothered me about all of this. I was hesitant to ask. "Why can I hear you in my head? You can talk to me without talking... We started before I left, but you never answered why."

Acanthus faltered, wincing again as the tea shook in their hand and splashed across their knuckles. It was still steaming from the travel cup in delicate little wisps, and it was still full. Their voice was quiet and unsure as they asked, *"Is this a, 'needs to be answered now' thing?"*

"No," I replied, shrugging. "Not now. But eventually."

"We'll talk. For now, I have some questions."

I crossed my legs and hunched forward, cupping the thin paper travel cup and sipping at my own tea. "Shoot, I'll answer what I can."

"What happened, Cypress? Why did you come back?"

The words may as well have punched me. I straightened up, then winced as my wounds pulled. How could I put the last two months or so into words? I swallowed, looking down at the garish brown and sap green comforter before I shrugged. "I guess Nekane got tired of me. I attacked a Wolf during training because I'd had enough of the constant insults and goading, and got put in solitary. When I was let out, I went to the river to think, and I overheard her talking to Hunters."

Acanthus' eyes narrowed and they leaned forward at the word. I took a sip of tea to stall, before speaking again. "They caught me in a silver net, because I couldn't shift. I was shackled for hours, but some Witches helped me. I don't know who they are or where they came from, but I imagine they were some of Nekane's. One let me go, and then a few others pointed me towards a safer exit. They made sure to say, 'Don't let the Vampire forget us'..."

Acanthus' lips parted, and they took in a sharp breath as I trailed off. "Just who are you, Acanthus? Why do the Witches kiss the ground you walk on? Why does Nekane and her Pack hate you so much? So much of the learning side of being in that pack talked about how dangerous Vampires are. Are you really so violent? I don't think I've once seen you be aggressive, outside of The Spirits Three."

Acanthus shook their head, wrapping their arms around their waist. *"It is a tale I'd rather tell when I have my voice,"* they thought, their eyes darting to the ugly paneled walls. *"It's a long one. Does that suffice?"*

It was frustrating, but it was a fair request. "Fine, I won't push. But I think I deserve an explanation."

They nodded emphatically. *"You have my word. But, I want to see how bad the damage is. You've been in pain long enough."*

"I really don't think you want to do that," I replied, my stomach pooling with dread. I swallowed another sip of tea, and set the cup down on the table. "Are you okay? I felt your hunger. I don't, uh," I trailed off, chewing on my lip. *Fuck it. Just be brave and speak your mind,* I thought. "I don't know where to go for that. We're a few states over. The local maps and news stations say Pennsylvania."

Acanthus had fixed me with a deadpan stare. They tapped their long black fingernails against their cup, their voice flat. *"You're rambling and distracting."*

"My life's goal achieved," I grinned at them. "You've no further use for me."

Making light of the situation was the only thing that I could do to keep myself from spiraling deeper into a panic. I put my hands behind my head and leaned back against the wall, sticking my tongue out, playing dead, the bed creaking with my movements. "Bleagh."

The band on my wrist glinted in the light from the lamp, and caught my eye. I put my hand in front of me and glared at it. I didn't want anything that marked me as part of Nekane's pack. There were little inscriptions on it; besides that, it was pristine. No matter what I did, I couldn't get it to budge. The moon phases taunted me. Oh well. Maybe we could stop somewhere and have a jeweler look at it.

Lemon Balm

Bored of the band already, I smiled up at Acanthus, but their murderous glare made me pause. They were giving the band a look that promised certain death and a cursed first born. "What?"

"A shift lock," Acanthus thought my way, their tone a venomous hiss. *"Interesting choice."*

"In human, please, Shadow Lord."

Their reaction to the band had my stomach flip-flopping, and I glanced back to the offending metal bangle.

"Have you..." They paused. Acanthus' face was pensive as they stepped forward, sitting on the corner of the bed and setting their tea to the side. The tone in their thoughts was far gentler than a moment ago. *"Have you been able to shift with that on your wrist?"*

"I haven't felt the urge to try—" the words dissolved into a coughing fit. The force was harder than usual this time, so I covered my mouth to be polite. When I pulled my hand away, it was speckled with blood. *That's not.... Good.*

That Time I Pulled Silver From Flesh

Acanthus

I stared at the blood glistening on Cypress' fingers, unblinking. The silver was tearing them apart from the inside. The fresh copper and iron smell in the air made my senses sharpen and my mouth water. *Oh, dear Gods, he smells delicious…*

I'd speared werewolves through countless times, and never had I smelled a blood so delectably rich. The thought thankfully didn't make its way through our link, but I jolted away from them as if I'd been shocked. I covered my mouth as my fangs lengthened. *My lip curled and my stomach lurched. Pull yourself together, Acanthus,* I thought. A more rational side of myself was screaming, *Werewolves are poisonous. You're just hungry.*

Closing my eyes, I steeled myself with a long, slow inhale. The deep coppery smell lingered in my nostrils, and I tried to partition the different smells, ignoring my hunger. I wouldn't be surprised if some of the open wounds had been infected. Panic rose in my chest and a sharp, commanding edge leached into my thoughts. *"Enough distraction. If I don't do something soon you're going to have worse issues. Let me see your wounds."*

My throat hurt too much to talk, so projecting was easier. But, I was gaining strength. I nearly felt normal, the equivalent of a human with a bad case of the flu. Cypress' eyes were wary. They licked their lips before sighing, their gaze sliding down to the comforter. Their voice had a lost, defeated edge, and their breaths were thin and rattling. "Acanthus, are you stable enough to? That is all I need to know. Don't lie to me."

The 'don't lie to me' sent a spike of irritation through me and I clenched my jaw, but I understood that it wasn't necessarily about me. It had been a two months, and clearly, Nekane's camp wasn't a positive experience. That thought quickly killed my irritation, the guilt gnawing at my rib cage. I kept my thoughts gentle. *"I can't answer that before I see at least the outer wounds. But yes, I am stable. Just hungry."*

Cypress tensed. "It's not pretty. I did the best I could. I kept them clean at least," he said, gulping down the last of the tea before carelessly putting the mug aside. They reached up and pulled their shirt off in a fluid motion.

He wasn't exaggerating. Thin cuts, swollen and inflamed, crisscrossed their chest in a netting pattern. Deep gashes were taken out of their arms, and a significant chunk out of their left shoulder. Their arms were more torn flesh and infection than intact flesh. They stood, tipping their head back. Their eyes bored holes into the popcorn ceiling as they dropped their pants and underclothes in a fell swoop, their face burning with shame. His fingers twitched at his sides. More lacerations and defined bites and claw marks went up the expanse of their legs. Their lower calves matched their arms. A huge bruise that had mostly faded to yellow emanated out from deep black puncture wounds of a particularly nasty bite on their hip. Everything glinted in the iridescent light of the table lamp, the silver throwing out a sickly cast of yellow.

I gasped, my ragged throat throbbing at the rude influx of air. My eyes stung, threatening tears. I could feel the skin tightening, but I knew they wouldn't come. Cypress looked at me, anxious. "Please don't cry, I've been managing fine."

I shook my head in disbelief. Clenching my teeth, I balled my fists at my sides, seeing red on his behalf. Nekane was supposed to protect the young Wolf, not leave them covered in silver and half-dead. *"How? How did you even go about and care for me in your state?"*

They shrugged, crossing their arms to finally cover himself. "I just did. I'm huge, no one stopped me."

"You look like roadkill, Cypress," my watery voice sounded like it'd break at any moment.

I hated that my reaction was causing them discomfort; they were shifting their weight from one foot to the other, as if they were mentally trying to run from my gaze. "I know. I kinda told the librarian I had leprosy."

I reached out, hovering by the bite on their hip. They yelped and jolted away from me, and I couldn't help but wince. I hadn't even touched them. *"Pup, I have to get this silver out of you. Start the bath. You're going to want to be in water."*

Cypress tilted their head and scrunched their brow. "Why a bath?"

It was a miracle they were still standing. *"The water will loosen your skin and make it easier to extract the silver. It will be less painful, overall. The silver will also stay in one place, instead of coating the room."*

I was carefully trying to keep the anger off of my face, but hatred had sharpened into a cold blade within. Nekane had truly outdone herself. She was strict, but I'd never heard of her actively harming another Wolf to this extent. I wanted to wring her neck for this trespass. A pang of regret and pity ran through my chest once again, but I squashed it deep down. Now was not the time to regret my actions; we both needed to heal and prepare to move. *"You are far stronger than you know."*

Even in the most intense cases, I'd never seen a Wolf take such significant damage and still be able to go on as normal. Cypress chewed on his lip, but he didn't question me as he walked towards the bathroom and disappeared around the corner. When I heard the water kick on, I began to search. Maybe there was a chance Cypress had taken any of my ointments or salves. I didn't see any, but I did find some menthol lying on the table, sold as a muscle relaxant. I sighed. *It's chemical, but putting it in the water would at least tingle and numb their wounds. It will have to do.*

Dubiously confident with my muscle relaxant in hand, I slipped into the bathroom to see Cypress idly kicking their feet in the stream of water, carefully holding their arms above the waterline. It was one of those standard modern tubs, safe for children and low to the ground, an ugly beige that both mixed and clashed with the drab dark brown tile. I walked over, kneeling and pressing one of my cool hands to their forehead. They were radiating heat, nearly enough to irritate my not-quite-healed skin. They groaned in response as they leaned into my touch, murmuring, "You're nice and cool."

I nodded. *"You're hot."*

Cypress shot their eyebrows up and gave me a mischievous smirk. "Am I? Tell me more!"

I rolled my eyes, though a small close-lipped smile made its way onto my face. *"This is not going to be fun, Pup."*

Cypress whined like a wounded puppy, lifting their gaze to mine. "Should I go to, like, a hospital or something?"

"No, we can't know which hospitals Nekane has her fingers in... She's one of the Big Five, her influence spans the entire east coast, all the way West to Michigan, and south to Kentucky. She is definitely

looking for us. Once I get the silver out, I can help with the infection if it lingers. Are you ready?"

As I spoke, I tipped the muscle relaxant into the water, and then switched my hands to keep them cool. They sighed softly, then tipped their head with a small but decisive nod. Leaving my right hand against their forehead, I pressed one of the least injured spots on their chest with my left fingers, and gently began to probe at the silver in their lungs with my powers. Even as my sight dimmed, I worried for him; the next several hours would likely break him.

Cypress

I began to cough. And I mean really cough. The specks of blood spattering the surface of the water were nothing compared to the amount of silvery droplets also being spewed. These were the kind of coughs that probably broke ribs.

Acanthus let up a little when I coughed out a ball of silver the size of a quarter. It fell into the water with a heavy plop, droplets splashing them in the face. Their expression went from blank to a scrunched up scowl of disgust. I sent the thought his way, and I'd be grinning at them if I wasn't currently fighting to catch my breath. *"Come on. You know you're dying to say something about it."*

I didn't want to think about how damaged my lungs probably were from all of that metal sitting in them. I think Acanthus was beginning to understand that my humor didn't come from a place of flippancy. *"I thought hairballs were for cats."*

I may not have been able to laugh, but at least the massage on my lungs had stopped. For now at least. I took what felt like my first full breath in days. My throat was raw and ragged, so talking was out of the question for me, too. *"Thank you."*

Acanthus was quiet, their eyes slightly brighter than they'd been a moment ago. *"Don't thank me yet,"* they finally replied, their voice going darker, *"this is not going to be pleasant at all."*

"So you keep saying."

They let out a huff of air, their shoulders raising as they snapped. *"Cypress, I'm trying to prepare you. I don't think you understand. You are literally ground hamburger, and I am amazed you can even hold a coherent conversation."*

"I can't. You haven't talked to me once since you woke up."

I stuck my tongue out at them, and they snorted. At least I was still able to get them to laugh. *"Stop it, Pup. I am going to start on your arms*

196

now," they said. I gulped, my stomach twisting. Their voice was softer when they continued the thought. *"I know it seems like a bad idea, but you should put your arms in the water."*

I nodded wearily and sunk my arms under the water. This is gonna sting like a motherfucker.

I gritted my teeth, curling in on myself as nausea swung in my stomach. I searched for a joke to make, but every brain cell was focused on the fire in my arms. Acanthus gently put their hands on my left arm, the least damaged of the two, and my skin erupted into a searing pain that raced all the way up to my shoulder. I made a sound that was horrible, even to my own ears.

I snapped my mouth shut and clenched my jaw again, closing my eyes and furrowing my brow. I was painfully aware of how their fingers trembled against my skin. *"It needs to be done,"* I thought at them sulkily.

Their shoulders sagged, and I winced as their fingers twitched. They licked their lips and sighed. *"I know... But I don't delight in hurting you."*

Acanthus moved their hand up my arm, and their eyes dimmed again as they started using their telekinetic abilities like a magnet. It burned; every nerve ending alight with the stinging of silver granules exiting my skin. My stomach flipped and I swayed, gritting my teeth as I fought myself to stay still, woozy and fighting the pain. It was a marvel to see how much silver actually came out of my arm. It was like I was dunked in a vat of silver paint and left to dry.

"I scrubbed these in the shower..." I trailed off, frowning through the burning and pulsing of my arm. It was hard to make a coherent sentence through this pain. *"Why didn't the silver come out?"*

Acanthus' forehead was scrunched in concentration and covered in a light sheen of pink sweat, their beautiful eyes dull and blank. I knew I shouldn't be distracting them. I knew it was taking a great deal of effort on their part to do this. They answered me anyway, small crackles of static in their thoughts.

"As you know, a Werewolf begins healing rapidly. You were already in the process of healing when the Hunters arrived," Acanthus paused, and my stomach lurched. I desperately held onto their voice as they continued, ignoring the burn of bile at the back of my throat. *"The silver found its way into your wounds, and essentially melded with your healing skin. The healing process stopped, and the irritation began. You couldn't have known this would happen, and you were in survival mode. I'm just shocked you've made it as long as you have, Cypress. Please, never do this again."*

I met their eyes, and blinked at them. *"Never do this again?"* I couldn't believe what I was hearing. They couldn't be serious. *"What choice did I have? Let them come and kill you? Keep my nose out of it entirely? I needed to get to you. They stood in my way."*

"I would have been fine," they thought, a cold tinge seeping into it. I glared at them now, but said nothing. *"I am almost a millennia old. I know how to handle myself with Hunters. If anything, I'd have gladly gotten caught if it meant saving you from this. Though, judging from the shift lock..."*

As they trailed off, I couldn't help but ask, *"Is a shift lock so bad? All it does is stop me from shifting, right? Is it so bad to feel somewhat human again?"*

And there it was, wasn't it? I had moved to Acanthus' church as a last-ditch effort to return to the mundanity of life, or to fade away as the obscure monster that I had become. I think at the time, I was grieving the loss of my humanity.

Acanthus froze in place, their powers pausing and eyes brightening. I cringed, and couldn't meet their gaze. In the short time we had been together, I had come to know that Acanthus had a sore spot for humanity. They both yearned for it and felt completely disconnected from it. *"I'm sorry,"* I said. *"I know you haven't felt human in a very long time, and that's cruel for me to say to you."*

They went back to working on my arm, their eyes dimming again, and our thoughts were quiet. The silence was punctuated with the staccato thunk of pellets dropping into the tub, and my own labored breathing between gasps as they exited my skin. *Say something. Anything. Please.*

I didn't think in their direction, and I wasn't sure if they heard it or not. When they finally spoke, their voice was laced with a cold, dark venom. *"I am so angry with myself for not understanding this would happen. I just wanted to leave you with resources. I am outraged; she played me entirely like a fool. Perhaps if I'd waited longer, you'd have come to kill me yourself at her command."*

The fury rolled off of them in waves. *"Acanthus, that never would've happened. They..."* I trailed off, trying to put my thoughts into words. It was hard to figure out exactly how to say what was on my mind. *"They tried to break whatever connection we have, and it didn't work."*

Admitting that made a surge of emotion flow through me. I wasn't sure if it was from the pain, or the last months weighing heavily on me, but the dam broke and a river of tears flowed down my cheeks. I let memories of the pack dance freely between us, showing fight after fight, injury after injury, and each and every numb moment to Acanthus. I was in so much pain, and here we were cutting our hearts out for one another.

I was the one who broke the quiet in our minds as the visuals faded. Acanthus' fingertips were shaking against my skin as they diligently worked, their eyes red and raw even as they stared blankly ahead. *"I still saw you, Acanthus. And I thought you were okay. I saw you enjoying the rain by the window. I saw you making tea, and journaling, and living life like I hadn't existed. I was delighted by the fact that you were okay. When I came back to you, I didn't expect to find you in the state that I did."*

Acanthus froze again, their hand on my shoulder now. *"You saw me?"*

Their voice was quiet and vulnerable, as if they couldn't quite believe that such a thing could be real. I needed them to know that I thought about them constantly in the time I was away. *"Little flashes, here and there. It was the only time my head was clear. The rest of the time I heard static. I wondered if that was the pack bond trying to take place in my head, and thought I was just defective. I realize that's not the case now. The static is gone when I'm with you."*

Acanthus took a shaky breath, their fingers trembling harder as their head dipped low. I saw the start of tears in their eyes, but they didn't spill over. *"Acanthus."*

I gave them a grin, and then realized they couldn't see it. *"When I've recovered enough, where do we go from here? You need to eat."*

Acanthus hesitated. *"Even after all this, you still worry for me."*

"You are my pack now, Acanthus. I go, where you go."

Shock and wonder filled their eyes, then an ocean of sadness that faded slowly into an awed acceptance. *"Oh..."* Even the thought felt watery and thin, as if they were close to sobs. *"Is that all?"*

Acanthus' hands left my shoulder and they covered their face. They flopped over onto their hip, crying into both of their slick palms. At first I worried I'd said something wrong, but the barrage of emotions that came flooding through told me otherwise. I grabbed one of their hands, and pulled them to me, awkwardly hugging them over the wall of the bathtub. "Hey, it's okay," I whispered.

"It definitely will be," they rasped. They switched back into our heads, their voice stronger internally. *"I'm so sorry for everything, Cypress."*

Acanthus

After my embarrassing display of emotion, we stayed in that embrace. The wetness soaked into my shirt and my skin itched and stung in protest. I didn't even notice the discomfort until I had gone back to the silver extraction. It was long and arduous. They did their best with keeping quiet, but pained grunts and whimpers filled the ugly brown bathroom. Cypress bit their tongue to keep the sounds from growing to screams. Around the time that I reached his hip, he lost consciousness. I understood; after all, I had just pulled myself from a coma for the same problem. Sometimes your mind just needs a break.

Moving someone six inches taller than you and twice your size in muscle mass is awkward for anyone. Add the facts that they're slippery, damp, naked, and unable to aid you, and said moving process becomes nearly impossible. It was moments like this that I was well and truly grateful that I was not human. My powers helped me hold him up as I gently toweled him down.

Already, the skin where the silver had been extracted looked less irritated and had started to heal. There was a lot of it; the stained, cream-colored tub may as well have been crusted with the stuff by the time I was done. It circled the drain in great big clumps. I couldn't imagine anyone moving around with that much metal embedded in their skin. Using what I could of my powers, I condensed the offending metal into a pellet the size of an orange. It had to be at least half a pound. I put it in one of the bedside table drawers for safe keeping.

I didn't have a single other scrap of silver on me. After Cypress had left, I hadn't cared to grab it out of the hiding places around my little church. Every time I met with Arturous and Es, it was at my home, but if I had gone back into the city, the silver would have been a tactic to keep myself safe. I had no time to grab any in the chaos of the Hunter attack. Besides, now that Cypress had gotten a taste of how harshly it could bite, I highly doubted they'd be comfortable with knowing I kept it. I could use the chunk of silver as a weapon in a pinch; the motel didn't feel safe, and I didn't want to take any more chances. We'd been here for too long.

Between my powers and my weakness, I was blinded once again. My veins were screaming as I burned off the blood I did not possess. I wasn't hungry, but I needed sustenance. The healing process had taken a lot from my body, and it would take me a while to bounce back from the sun damage. At least I no longer looked like a walking wound. It took so much effort to float Cypress towards a bed. I ignored the sensations and felt around for objects in my path. After what felt like an eternity, Cypress was heavily bandaged and sleeping peacefully in the clean bed. The process had taken much of my strength.

Once that was done, I found myself nursing a severe headache in the darkness of pre-dawn. Now that I wasn't focusing my powers, my sight had returned, but there was an icy hollowness in my chest. I sat in silence as my thoughts to the earlier conversation. I was Cypress' pack. I was his pack. Me.

How did they know? How was that even possible? I didn't answer their question earlier about our mental conversations, because I didn't know the answer. This was unprecedented, and entirely new to me. Wolves were only supposed to be able to bond with Wolves. As far as I knew, Pack bonds couldn't happen between different species. Originally, I had thought it was my own telepathic abilities amplifying our friendship. But, now I wasn't certain. When they came back and the static disappeared, I knew it was something magical, but I hadn't thought of a Pack bond.

Perhaps they were right. The thought was so alien, but the warmth from the sentiment was like an embrace. I was a Vampire. I shouldn't be able to bond with Cypress. We were friends, sure; but, Witches, Vampires, and Werewolves all resided within their own separations. Witches used to marry into Wolf packs for coven protection or territory purposes, and anyone could fall in love, be friends with, or find a family member in anyone else, but bonds weren't like normal relationships. They were strengthened by a magical element; ancient, unknown, and intrinsic to the supernatural power.

On top of that, Vampires aren't the most extroverted creatures. Any companion I had in the past either left me in bad graces or died in a horrible way. The only exception was Corbin, who'd opted to leave America before the wars between factions began. *Corbin...*

Thinking of my old friend, I smiled; perhaps he would have something in his library that would enlighten me. I would have to reach out to him when we were in a safer place. At this point, I missed him, but I couldn't say I blamed him for leaving. Vampires are solitary creatures for a reason. We are bombastic, we feel too much, and we are entirely too strong for our own good. Vampires are prisoners of our own minds. I had been alone for so long, I wasn't sure how to handle the thought of someone actually caring for me. *I must be defective. I'm worthy of connection; just let yourself be, Acanthus.*

For *me* to be Cypress' Pack? I couldn't wrap my head around it. Cypress must also be a defective Wolf, to bond with a Vampire. They were not normal for a Wolf — I found them agreeable, for one thing. Images of my first "companion" — François, my sire — flashed through my head, as they always did, and my headache worsened. Out of all my past, he was the oldest and the most frequent haunt. He'd plague me until the day I was laid to rest. Gritting my teeth, I stamped the thoughts down. *Just let me have silence, please.*

My own inner voice sounded more desperate than angry, and I hated the thought. Could I not have one night to be happy? "'Canthus."

A sleepy mumble came from the bed, hoarse and raw, dropping the A in my name as if it took too much effort to add the syllable. My gaze snapped up, stomach tensing and breath hitching in my throat. *"Yes, Pup? Are you alright?"*

Cypress huffed, raising a heavy arm and pumping their fingers in a childish grabbing motion. "C'mere."

I laughed; though, no sound came from my wrecked throat. Silently, I slid from the chair, gliding to the bed and slipping in beside them. The weight and warmth of their embrace quieted my thoughts and soothed my pain. *Fine, then; let us be defective.*

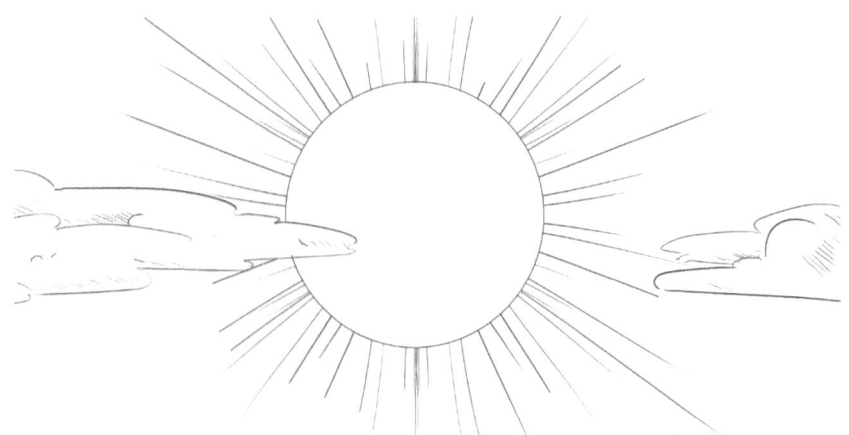

That Time Acanthus Taught Me History

Cypress

Acanthus curled up next to me with no hesitation, and I smiled. I waited until I felt their breathing stop to close my eyes and drift off again. I don't know what caused them to stop breathing, but I had come to know it as a sign that they were really asleep.

Thankfully, the next few days were uneventful. Acanthus was adamant that we stay in the room. Whether they suggested it or not, we didn't have much of a choice. Most of the time was spent with one or both of us sleeping, and a mountain of take-out boxes, courtesy of me, began to grow on the spare bed. Acanthus and I took turns having nightmares. My body was still sore and aching, but it was slowly healing. When my wounds had transitioned from angry red infections to tender pink scars, Acanthus declared that I was recovered enough to travel. I suggested we check out of the motel.

This was largely for Acanthus' mental health. They were paranoid, checking out of the windows and worriedly thinking about whether or not we'd been tracked. "I know you didn't have another option," they said. They had gained their voice back, but it sounded like a raw and open wound. "But there's a good chance that they're combing the entire Tri-State area for us right now. We may be in Pennsylvania, but that doesn't leave us much time. They are likely searching for our names in card records, and you used your card."

I didn't want to think about that. Every time we started talking about Nekane and her pack, I'd see flashes of silver nets and UV lights behind my eyes. I'd found Acanthus staring at the Golf from the window multiple times, muttering something about the broken treaty with Nekane. Towards the end of our last night there, I finally plucked up the courage to ask, "Hey, so... What does this broken treaty mean?"

Acanthus whipped their head around, their eyebrows raised. "That's right, you have no idea!'

"That much is obvious, Acanthus," I grumbled. "Nekane's instructors only said that Vampires should be eradicated from her territory, whatever that meant. Any time I asked questions, I was told we needed to prepare for war. She sprinkled in some bullshit about using Witches as weapons and pack communication being gold... I don't know shit about the history of this, or why they think you're so dangerous, other than you're an Anesh."

Acanthus swallowed, their eyes darting back to the window. I sighed. "I already checked the car for trackers and airtags. I don't think they followed us. Don't you think they'd have ambushed us by now?"

"You're right." Their shoulders sagged, and they finally closed the curtain and shifted their full attention to me. Licking their lips, they cleared their throat and grimaced. "Wolves and Vampires have been fighting for a long time. We're talking centuries. Nekane and I have been at war on and off since the seventeen-thirties."

I let out a low whistle, sitting down on the bed. "That's a long-ass time. What could you possibly fight about for that long? Can't you both just agree to disagree?"

They scoffed, their eyes taking on an offended cast. "This isn't just letting bygones be bygones, Cypress. Maybe one day I will sit down to tell you the minutiae of politics through the last three hundred years, but it will have to wait until after I've eaten something."

I dropped it, but I cringed each time their gaze shifted back towards the windows. *I poked a centuries old rot spot, and started this war again...*

We moved to a fancier, more classy hotel. The lobby was a gaudy mess of marble and Baroque-inspired decor; mahogany wood a third of the way up the walls, meeting a deep coppery green. The walls were tall, embellished with rectangle trims. They went to scalloped crown mouldings and an ornate ceiling with a plaster coin around a massive crystal chandelier.

This time, Acanthus took care of checking in, smoothly giving an alias for both of us. They were Benedict Le Fanu, and I was Victor Healseng. *Are those references to something? Healseng, like Helsing?*

They used a card, but it definitely had their alias name on it. I kept my face neutral as we were at the ornate mahogany check in desk, but once we were safely in the elevator, I gaped at them. "That was straight-up spy shit."

Acanthus suppressed a smile. "Language, Pup."

I didn't answer, but I stared at them as the creaking mechanisms slowly pulled the mirrored and gold car to the fourth floor. *Who exactly are you, Acanthus?*

We'd fallen asleep shortly after getting into the room. As soon as they were awake, Acanthus made a phone call, using the hotel phone to reach their Pennsylvania connections. Turns out, they had safe havens here as well. When I met them, I assumed that they were a hermit in the woods, squatting at my new home. I was starting to get a bit more of a picture.

"Azalea, darling, so great to speak to you! Are there any vacancies at the Yellow Rose? ... You know better to call me that, Azalea, if you keep it up I will have to start calling you my Queen... Yes, yes, always business. Might I inquire about the recipe of your fertilizer?... Yes, bone ash... There is a problem with the roses, yes. I have a dogwood that needs some perking up, as well. Poor thing has silver scale... Gargoyles at the gates, yes."

The conversation over the phone made zero sense to me. I couldn't make heads or tails of it, and so I drifted in my own thoughts as Acanthus did their thing. I rubbed at my arms absently, my nerve endings singing as I went over the fresh, itchy scars. It just sounded like Acanthus was having a really intense conversation about roses and garden paths. *Maybe they'll have us stop to pick up fertilizer.*

"The stones are in a spiral.... Perhaps? .... Very well. I will gather up the clippings and add some clay into the soil."

When they hung up, they quietly nodded. *"We're in the clear to move around midnight. From what I can gather, we're about two hours away from a safe house, and if we leave by 10pm we can get some help."*

I blinked at them. *"You got all that from talking about gargoyles and gravel?"*

They laughed, but didn't answer. *"Oh, laugh it up,"* I grumbled. *"You're not getting off that easy. I thought you were a shut-in, aside from the few Witches you know. How do you have contacts to call, let alone a code to speak in?"*

I should have been surprised that they let me listen to the code at all; I didn't know it at the time, but it was a sign of extreme trust. They chewed on their bottom lip, distracting themself by reaching for their hair and starting to braid it. The silence stretched. Then they took a soft breath, their eyes meeting mine. The hazel burned with an intense fire. They touched their throat as their voice came out in a rasp, grimaced, and then decided to speak in our link.

"The World of Shadows has been rife with war for centuries. In the sixteen hundreds, I began a covert operation with my friend Corbin. It's purpose was to help Witches, Vampires, and even a Wolf or two to get out of less than ideal situations. Supernaturals had long been hiding in the World of Shadows, and humans were largely unaware of our existence. The main mortals who knew of us were a small collective of Hunters and Black Market merchants. I originally started the organization to help people flee from Hunters. As time went on and word spread, Wolves and Witches alike fled oppressive, abusive Alphas and covens, but then things began to change."

"When the Wolves learned how to shift at will, it caused a power imbalance. One of the more prominent Alphas, a Warlord named Bleddyn, led the charge. The Warlords were aggressive Alphas that were constantly squabbling with other Packs and Vampires. Bleddyn was the one who began to speak to other packs. Together, they formed cohesive units that worked together. He started the Big Five, the Wolf power structure that exists today. This allowed the smaller Packs to share territory under a larger leading pack. The Leading Pack both directs the smaller Packs, and speaks to the Alphas as if they are partners. The smaller, ancillary packs help the entire territory have access to food, building materials, and other such necessities together."

Acanthus paused, looking down at their hands. *"We were all hiding from humans because of the superstitions involved. We had to be careful about how long we lingered in a single place. This made it hard to keep stories straight and find solid access to supplies we didn't have immediately available. If a Vampire left a victim, it would put the humans on edge. The Warlords blamed Vampires and Hunters for their lack of resources."*

"Because the Wolves can blend in effortlessly with a bunch of humans, they began to settle in villages. They would work to take office, to gain trust with the mortals. It's quite amazing how oblivious humans can be to our presence. The Wolves would make entire villages for their Packs, and none of the mortals would be any wiser."

"They stoked rumors of Vampires amongst the humans, and Hunters increased in volume. Whenever a human went missing, it was blamed on Vampires. Wolf attacks were also blamed on Vampires; one of the rumors was that we could shape-shift into Wolves. So many of the Wolves abused their power. I'm not certain how it came to be that the Hunters are now under Pack employ, but... these things dwindled

the Vampires numbers to near extinction by the early nineteen-aughts. The Warlords won."

I leaned forward, my elbows on my knees as I listened, rapt. They stood, pacing back and forth. I counted each time they turned. One. Two. Three. Four... On the fifth turn, they faced me. *"Just like any war, there were people from all sides who both agreed and disagreed with the leaders in charge. Vampires were decentralized; largely separated from each other, which led to their demise. Some were just as vicious as the Alphas that we fought. Some Vampires fought just to sow chaos. I wanted the fighting to stop and to create a peaceful existence for us all, so I tried to move things a subtly different way. My little path was what I could do to keep people safe from the resulting wreckage."*

Acanthus' mouth quirked into a close-lipped smile, their eyes soft. *"The path was something that symbolized life and growth within the darkness to us. So, we began to develop a code. We call it The Night Garden."*

"Holy shit." I don't know what I expected, but it hadn't been a history lesson. I had leaned forward at one point, my mouth dropping open. *"That's so cool."*

Acanthus flushed, crossing their arms, but they couldn't hide the way they straightened, their chin jutting confidently. *"Yes, well. I cannot abide leaving those in need without aid. I stepped back before I became a recluse when the last war ended. But my dear friends keep the routes alive, keep me up to date on the codes, and maintain safe-houses for me. I have multiple territories throughout the East coast and Midwest, and many are occupied by Witches who have been freed from bad situations. The odd Wolf or two are brought to an ally in the Midwest. Vampires have largely disappeared from America, but I know of one in one of my Pennsylvania strongholds, a few scattered across New York, and a small coven in North Carolina. All in all, we have friends in many places, willing to help. Though, I must admit that I am not used to being on the other side of the garden paths. I don't like inconveniencing people, and I don't like the thought of asking for help."*

I raised an eyebrow, but they averted their gaze. They put so much of themself into helping others. It made me think about how much they did to help connect me to The Might of the East. What exactly did they risk for that to happen? *"So, where does Nekane fit into all of this?"*

Acanthus bristled and busied themself by braiding their hair. *"We have hurt each other in many ways. She's one of the Big Five, and was a member of Bleddyn's Pack before it broke apart. She held no love for me back when I started the Garden, and she has even less for me now. In hindsight, I should have reached out to another Pack where I have allies, but I assumed you would not have wanted to leave the area."*

I winced as shame flooded my core, whispering, *"and what have you done, Cypress? Fart around feeling sorry for yourself? It's all my fault that this war has kicked back into motion. I never should've engaged Junior in that fight."*

I had taken so much for granted, in my ignorance. Acanthus sent a sharp look in my direction, and their irritation swelled in our bond, and their lips pressed tightly together. I must've been projecting towards them, because they scolded me. *"You stop that right now, Pup. I'm not telling you any of this to make you feel bad."*

With that, the conversation died. I was glad that we'd be driving to a safe house later that night. We'd been resting, but Acanthus wasn't healing as fast as they could, and every time they engaged their powers, the strange glassy blindness would dull their eyes. In the silence, Acanthus started to think about birds and they licked their lips, slipping their eyes shut. I latched onto that; a conversation topic! "Birds?"

"A true delicacy. They are sweet, but hard to catch."

I wrinkled my nose. "I imagine they don't have a lot of blood. Sounds like a Capri Sun for a Vampire."

They fixed me with a blank stare. I blinked, asking innocently, "You've never had a Capri Sun?"

"Cypress, I've been out of the popular culture loop for over a century, hardly engaging with modern life. Please, go on. I'm intrigued."

Their voice broke on the word intrigued and they winced, their hand flying up. They'd pushed themself pretty hard to have that conversation on the phone, and though the banter was positive, it clearly hurt them to continue speaking aloud. Their normally whispery voice was barely audible even as a rasp. It was easier to keep the conversation light, so I latched onto the thought of Capri Suns. "It's not much to brag about," I shrugged. Their eyes were sharp with curiosity, so I continued. "A small splash of juice that doesn't even begin to quench thirst. You had to drink like 10 of the things, and they were loaded in sugar and salt."

"Why bother with it then?"

"Birds."

They grinned, massaging their throat, before resting their long, tapered fingers at the base of their neck. *"Fair point."*

We lapsed into silence again, and that made me antsy. I didn't want to go too far into my head. I had so many questions about this Night Garden they mentioned, but I didn't even know where to begin. I blurted the first thing that came to my mind, thinking of the rose window at the first church. "Is your haven here another church?"

Acanthus blinked, surprised and pleased that I had guessed. ***"Where we're heading is a Bed and Breakfast, the Yellow Rose. But, our final destination is a church, of course. Did you expect anything else?"***

I snorted. "How dare I dream of white picket fences."

They chanced speaking aloud again, their fingers resting at the base of their throat. "Do you really?"

I shrugged. If I really wanted white picket fences, I wouldn't have lived in the city, for one. I gave a shy smile. "Nah. Too plain for me, I think. At one point in my life, I could say I was chasing the American dream. Get a good paying job, marriage, maybe kids."

I looked down at the fresh pink scars on my arms and laughed harshly. They were jagged and sunken into divots. *Yeah, right. No one would go for me, now. Too scary for women, too ugly for men, and too male-coded for everyone in-between. I had small chances in the first place, when I thought I was hallucinating. I look like I've done hard time in Sing Sing, now.*

"We'll be stopping by a less religious-leaning establishment beforehand, as I mentioned," Acanthus interrupted my inner monologue, voice far more gentle than the statement needed it to be. "I don't think you'll mind the church, or the Bed and Breakfast. Both are bigger than the last church. You'll have your own space to decorate however you wish, and not be shoved into a corner."

I got up and stretched my arms above my head, groaning. "Sounds like a plan. I think we're ready to go. I know you've been amicable for the short car rides we've had, but will you be okay on this slightly longer one?"

Acanthus scoffed, "I trust you."

"Okay, let's go."

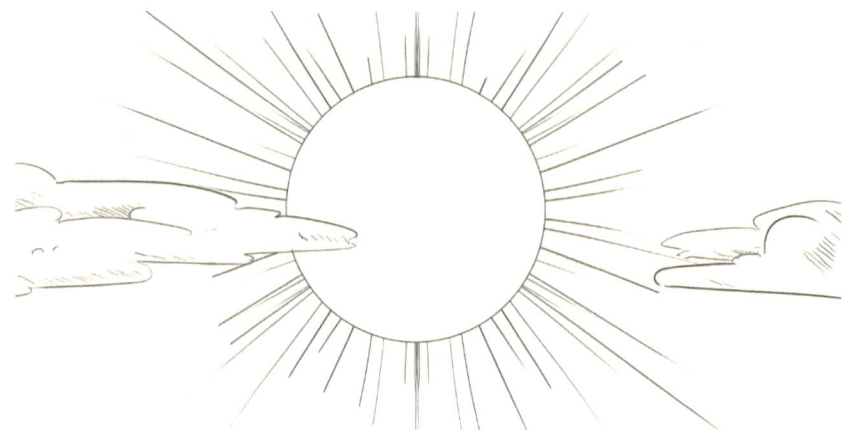

That Time We Met A Witch at a Bed and Breakfast

Cypress

True to their word, Acanthus didn't so much as make a peep once we were in the car. I think their first freakout in the Golf had been less about the machine and more about being trapped in it with very little control. That wasn't their fault, though; they were just trying to keep themself safe. I wasn't going to hold it against them now. True to their timeline, two hours had passed and we were in a quaint little town at the north center of the state, when they said, "Turn here."

I brought the car up a long driveway leading up to a large, mansion-like Queen Anne Victorian building. It was surrounded by maple and pine trees, and the pavement was doused in lights from little solar lamps dotting the driveway. They veered off to the right and the line of lights followed a small cobblestone path to the stairs of the porch. Pennsylvania is heavily wooded, and this property was no different; in a town, but the back of the building was silhouetted by a thick forest.

From what I could see in the harsh light of the headlights, the building was painted in rich maroon and browns, with bright yellow accents carefully painted on the ornate wooden embellishments. A double door sat at an angle off of a spire on the corner of the building, encased with the wraparound porch. The silhouette of potted plants were rimmed with a warm yellow light pouring from big bay windows. Bats and moons were set into the cobblestone path, just like the first church. Is that a signal that this is a Garden house?

I'd have to ask Acanthus more about the Night Garden when they were feeling better. For now, I admired the decorated building. It was like a palace. *I wish I could see more of it in the dark,* I thought as I brought the car to a halt. I stared at the building, stalling in my seat. Butterflies came alive in my chest as I fidgeted. I knew better than to question Acanthus, but there was one thing that bothered me, and continued to bother me. Every person that they had interacted with since I met them was a Witch, and every single one of them had been extremely unhappy that they'd had me tagging along.

I felt like a problem again, and my stomach twisted. *I started a war. This is my fault.* I shut the thought down and asked aloud, "Are these more Witches?"

They paused as they were getting out of the car. I think Acanthus picked up on my discomfort. "Yes."

My face fell into a scowl, but I quickly tried to push it off into something carefully neutral. I knew I should be grateful for the help, but I didn't like the thought of navigating snide comments and sneers. The Magic Manor had been an experience I didn't care to repeat, and I wasn't even allowed in The Spirits Three when Acanthus went there. The last thing that I wanted was to deal with people who looked at me like a villain.

Acanthus spoke again, their voice crackling. "These ones are free Witches. They run their coven on their own accord." They trailed off again, and I could feel their uncertainty as they tacked on, "Is that okay?"

I laughed. It wasn't about me right now. "We need a place to stay, and you're dreaming about birds. Of course it's okay."

Acanthus narrowed their eyes, but gracefully exited the car. There were four others in the lot — two sedans, a van, and an SUV — though they were parked far enough away from the lights that I couldn't make out colors or models. I sighed, sliding out of the seat and into the night. *This is sure to be a fun time...*

Acanthus

Cypress' demeanor had turned on a dime. I knew his moodiness had to come from something, but I was distracted by The Yellow Rose. Several hearts beat within, and I was done dealing with my needs. I had spent most of my fledgling years hungry; the pulling in my veins was now from my hunger just as much as the sun damage. My fangs refused to fully retract, poking out slightly longer and sharper than a typical human's canine. I was impatient, now that the option to eat was near.

Putting on my best pleasant face, I came to the door and knocked. People deserve their privacy, even in a public establishment. After all, Azalea lived here full-time. I'd been thinking about visiting her since Cypress went to Nekane's pack; it would be a relief to see her. She came to the door after a short pause; a beautiful, tall, African-American woman.

Her thick hair was held back in a purple patterned scarf folded into a headband. She was wearing a matching dress. The pattern was multiple different hues of purple, layered in a batik beneath ornate, shimmering silver scroll work. Her curls exploded behind the headband, and her initial worried look brightened as she saw me, her full lips growing into a big smile. "Lord Acanthus! What a pleasure," she beamed.

As she spoke, her honey-brown eyes slid to Cypress, and joy lit up her face. "Oh! The Lord mentioned he had a guest! Hello!"

"Azalea," I said, tilting my head to her in a bow.

Azalea was one of my most trusted confidants, and had been running the Night Garden for me for a long time. The tension from the car was still clinging to me like cobwebs, and I tried to force my shoulders to relax. Something was wrong, but I couldn't tell what. It wasn't Azalea's to fix, and I didn't want her to pick up on my disappointment. I smiled at her, the gesture probably a bit too wide and forced to be genuine. "You are radiant, as always. May we come inside?"

"Certainly," she stepped aside. Cypress straightened up; a grin and a blush took over their face as they were acknowledged with basic human decency. Guilt gnawed at my rib cage. *Arturous was probably not the best person to introduce them to as their first Witch experience, but what else was I to do in that situation?*

I stepped into the cozy Yellow Rose, my eyes adjusting to the caramel and yellow tones of the painted walls. Big cushioned chairs in chocolate upholstery with yellow throw pillows were angled in the main lobby, inviting and bold. The room was warm and cozy; the space equivalent to taking a sip of spiced cocoa. The colors reminded me of sunflowers. Azalea shut the door behind us, leading us into the den. "Come in, make yourselves comfortable."

As we reached the center of the room, she turned on her heel and curtsied. "Azalea Barclay, at your service. And, may I ask, what is your name, my new Wolf friend?"

They stared, stammering. "C-Cypress. Cypress Borne. Nice to meet you, Azalea."

I could imagine their wolf-self wagging their tail. Cypress gave a short bow, and then hopped onto one of the deep brown chairs. Azalea walked around me and placed a hand on my shoulder, gentle and warm.

"My Lord, it's been quite a long time since we've seen you! What can I do for you tonight?"

"You know the particulars already, Azalea. No need to keep up the pretenses in front of Cypress. Although, I am quite famished, I'm afraid," I leaned towards her. "I took some extensive damage from the sun, as well as from UV weapons when the Hunters attacked."

Trained in healing, Azalea's touch always gave me a little bit of life. She could probably feel how drained I was just through the contact. "And as you can see, my dear friend is still healing. They've also been bound without their knowledge or consent. Have you spoken to Arturous?"

She glanced between Cypress and I, the joy of the moment fading. I hoped that I hadn't hurt her feelings by skipping the pleasantries. Azalea's dulcet voice was low and serious. "I have. Aside from my conversation with you earlier, Arturous knows very little. We knew that Nekane was on the move, but… My Lord, they went after you? It's so strange and out of character. To break a treaty that's been standing for over a century…"

"Azalea, my dear. Just Acanthus. But, to answer, it's my fault, I'm afraid." My voice was gentle enough, but a cold edge had crept back into the words. "Cypress is the only reason I stand before you, despite Nekane's best efforts. Technically, I broke the treaty; I made an example out of a Wolf in Nekane's pack that attacked Cypress while I was otherwise indisposed. As you know, any aggression on my part was obviously seen as a breach of the agreement. Once I did that, all bets were off."

Azalea sighed, shaking her head. "The peace couldn't have lasted," she murmured, eyes dulling a bit as she deflated. Her hand then slipped from my shoulder, only for her cheer to come back tenfold and her eyes to light back up. She clapped her hands. "Well! I shall not have guests hungry in my humble little home! Lord Acanthus, will you be needing multiple courses tonight?"

"I should think so, yes," I replied, swallowing as my mouth watered. "I need a push to come back to my former strength."

"Right away, Lord Acanthus," she said, and I gently touched her arm as she turned. She tilted her head.

"Wait a moment, dear. Would you also be able to take a look at Cypress? The shift lock is complex, and I'm unsure of how easily I could remove it. They also had some silver stuck in them for several days, and I am no magical healer. The infection seems to have faded, but I'm not certain if they're in the clear, and I don't trust the hospitals."

Azalea's eyes softened as she stepped over to Cypress. Her powers were strong, and though it was subtle, I could tell that she had already gotten a decent read on Cypress' inner moral compass. She had already decided to heal him. She held her hand out, and he took it, furrowing his brow as he looked up at her. Her shoulders rose to her ears, bristling as she picked up on his pain. She was silent, her eyes glossing over with the intensity of it. Swallowing, she took in a long, shaky inhale, letting it out before she finally spoke. "We will get you both taken care of."

She patted Cypress' hand. "I know long periods away from your Wolf can be draining, and how exhausted you must be from such an experience. You're in good hands. Even better than your friend's."

Cypress' eyes went from happy, to confused, to concerned. "Wait. Not shifting can hurt you?"

"Well," Azalea hummed softly, pulling her hand away. "How to explain…"

She trailed off, tapping her chin. When she finally spoke, it was slow and soft, as if to a child. "Not hurt you. But your soul begins to drift. From what I've seen, fits of rage, losing sense of time, and long periods of depression are common. It also takes far longer to heal, and can cause stiffness in the joints. Your first shift afterward will likely leave you aching worse than anything you've experienced."

Cypress paled. I cleared my throat. "Azalea, my dear, I trust you have some blood bags in the fridge?"

"Oh, certainly! You know where to go, Acanthus. Help yourself."

She hurried away from us and around the front counter, heading towards the landline phone. I smiled at Cypress. "She's not so bad, is she?"

He nodded. "I like her," he said.

I tilted my head towards the room to the left of the counter. "I'm going to grab a snack while she's arranging for donors. You're welcome to relax here, or there's more than enough seating if you'd like to accompany me. I'm certain Azalea will want to take a closer look at your hurts, if you'd allow her. There's also the shift lock."

Cypress groaned and flopped his head back against the chair. "I'll wait here, Acanthus. I want five minutes to not think."

I laughed softly. "Very well. Enjoy your rest."

As Azalea arranged for donors to come, I wandered away from the lobby and waited in the common kitchen. It was cozy, painted yellow like the rest of the bottom floor, with chocolate tiles as a back-splash. Most of the front of the room was taken up by a large banquet-style table, eight chairs on either side. An L-shape of cabinets and counter lined the left back corner of the room, an island in front of them. The sink was set into the island, a persistent drip echoing through the kitchen. I rounded the island and turned off the leaky faucet. Once I was satisfied that it had stopped dripping, I turned to open the stainless steel fridge behind me. She always kept at least a few blood packs on hand for the needy. It was part of her vow to never cause harm, and never let someone go hungry in her domain.

She always gave special attention to Vampires. Despite being a free Witch, Azalea felt as if she owed me her life. I didn't know why so many Witches held so much respect for me. Azalea was the one running the Night Garden since 1903, when I handed over the operation to her. I may have started it, and helped many of the Witches including her away from dangerous situations, but none of that mattered now. It was part of the reason I kept a lot of the Witches at arms' length; I wanted to be treated as an equal, not something above them. I wasn't like the people I rescued them from. *This place is so full of memories...*

I'd sat in this kitchen countless times. The Yellow Rose was the heart of the Night Garden, and it was at the center of every major path. If I sat in silence in this room for too long, I would hear the ghosts of past conversations. I closed my eyes, sinking my teeth into the silicone of a blood bag. I wasn't alone for long, because Cypress came to the doorway, leaning in the jamb.

Cypress

Azalea rounded the counter after she wrapped up on the phone. "Dear Cypress, please let me see the bangle on your wrist again?"

I nodded, lifting my arm and holding it out to her. The band was so heavy. I glared at the filigreed moons with disgust. She traced the curves of the inscription with her eyes, mouthing something silently. I didn't think the carvings said anything, but it must have meant something to her. She frowned, bringing her hands up to cup the silver. "*Aperi hanc portam lupinam,*" she murmured, and her fingertips began to glow with a bright green cast.

I stared at the light, transfixed. No matter how much the World of Shadows showed itself, I didn't think I'd ever get used to it. Magic like this blew my mind. The metal started to heat around my wrist, and she pulled her hands away with a sharp gasp as her fingertips sparked. "Oh, oh my!"

"Azalea, are you alright?!"

She shook her hands, before bringing them up to inspect her fingertips. After a moment, she shifted her gaze to me, giving me a troubled frown. "Fine, dear Cypress. I managed to escape a burn. I didn't expect this to be such a powerful band, I'll admit."

215

I twisted it around my wrist, asking curiously, "What, like you can't break it?"

"No," Azalea's voice was heavy. "I'll need to gather the coven to even have a hope of getting it to budge. Who knew Nekane had some of the most powerful Witches on the East Coast in her employ?"

That didn't bode well. My stomach twisted, and I sank further into the cushions. "Why can't we just get a human jeweler to break it open? It's on a hinge."

Azalea shook her head, a small smile playing on her lips. "Dear Cypress, it would break the physical band, but not the spell. You still wouldn't be able to call forth your Wolf. Without the band, the Witches don't know the counter. We need to be able to read the inscriptions here."

She pointed at the symbols on the top and bottom of the band. That made sense, even if I didn't understand a lick about magic. I sighed. "Well... Thank you for trying. I appreciate it."

"Certainly. I'll let Lord Acanthus know that I'll be gathering the coven. It shouldn't take more than a day or two."

"Oh, please," I stood and respectfully bowed. "Let me. It's something you're all trying to do for me, after all."

"Certainly. If you wouldn't mind, I'd like to use another spell? Healing, not unbinding. Your wounds feel black. I'm worried there's still infection lingering."

I slowly lowered back into the chair. I don't think I'd ever thought of pain as a color. "If you have something that you think will help, sure."

She brought her hands back up and steepled her fingers. They were red and irritated from the spark, and my gut twisted into knots. The green glow reappeared, climbing from her fingertips to about mid-forearm. Leaning down, she reached and touched my wrists. The glow spread to me, tracing up the thorn-like scars with a pleasant, warm pulse. The warmth filled my body, and I was reminded of pulling on laundry fresh from the dryer.

I closed my eyes, my fingers and toes tingling. My heart raced. It was another moment of not realizing how much pain I was in until I just wasn't. The subtle smell of freshly cut grass stuck in my nostrils as the tingling faded, and I opened my eyes. Azalea had backed away, a triumphant look on her face. I brought my arms up in front of me and looked at my scars. They didn't look any different, but every lingering wound on my body felt a million times better. "Thank you, Azalea."

I wanted to cry. I don't think someone has ever done anything so nice for me. I swallowed, and she grinned. "Feel better?"

"Much."

She clapped. "Excellent. I'm happy to have helped. Now, when you go into the kitchen, please also tell Acanthus that their first donor should be here in ten minutes?"

I nodded, and she went to the book shelf in the corner as I took my leave. A minute later, I was standing in the door of the kitchen. I cocked my head, studying Acanthus. Their fangs were sunk deep into the silicone of a blood bag, and they held it with both hands. Their eyes were shut as they slowly slurped. *Like a Capri Sun,* I thought again, and snorted.

I thought that maybe I'd be more perturbed by them feeding from the bag. Maybe it was the shift lock, but I felt nothing. No fear at all. Just a strange curiosity. The lack of emotion surprised me. I wondered if it had something to do with finding out that Acanthus was part of my pack. They never answered me back at the motel about our new connections. *I know they said that our mental speech was a power of theirs, but maybe we can hear each other because of the Pack bond...*

Acanthus pulled their teeth from the blood pouch and dabbed their lips with a napkin, their cheeks a bright pink. That flush that would have been impossible fifteen minutes before. "Cypress, I apologize. I didn't realize you were finished with Azalea."

I looked down at my shift lock and sighed. "She told me she'd reach out to some of her coven and see if they could help. Your donors will be here in ten minutes, but the way."

Did Wolf packs and Witches fight alongside each other? Were the Hunters human or Witch? I had so many questions, and as I stared at the band on my wrist, more just kept stacking up. Nekane... I cringed at the thought of her, and the words kill his pet, too, flashed in my mind.

"Are you okay, Pup?"

Acanthus' whispery tone pulled me from my thoughts, and I was glad to hear that the strain in their speech had disappeared entirely. I looked up, forcing a smile and pushing my worries away. "Excellent, actually. Azalea healed me, and I feel great. Why do you ask?"

They squirmed in their seat. "I'm not sure. Something has felt off since we've arrived. Are you cross with me?"

A strange itch tingled across my brain, and I broke eye contact, staring at the kitchen wall. It was like cold fingers poking around my thoughts. "Don't do that," I snapped.

"Do what?" The innocence in their tone made me grind my teeth.

"I can feel you prying." I realized how aggressive I sounded, and tried to force my shoulders to relax.

Lemon Balm

I really hated the breaches in privacy, but I also had to remember that my friend was an eight hundred-year-old Vampire and likely wasn't thinking about how they were crossing boundaries. "Maybe unintentionally, but it's like we lock eyes, and I'm just your..." I trailed off, the word that'd been eating at me all day weighing on the tip of my tongue like a piece of lead. *Kill his little pet, too.* "Little pet..."

Their eyebrows shot up, and they scoffed incredulously. "That's what has been causing your foul mood?"

My shoulders hiked up to my ears, and I pulled my arms tighter. I didn't appreciate their judgment. "Well..." I didn't have a leg to stand on, or anything to say in response. I gritted my teeth again, irritation making a headache pulse in my forehead. "That's what it looks like, doesn't it?"

They were very still, anger etched into their intense hazel eyes. Their voice was low and cold, a sharp edge to it. It was a warning to choose my next words carefully. "Have I done anything but treat you like an equal?"

My mouth went dry and a spike of adrenaline raced through me. I gritted my teeth, and suddenly they were in front of me. They moved faster than I could track. "Answer the question, Cypress. Have I treated you like a pet?"

My hands were fisted, and I was shaking. I needed to gain control of the anger that was building before I lashed out worse. Taking a deep breath, I held it. *One... Two.... Three...*

I counted to ten before I exhaled. "That's not what I meant."

"What did you mean then?"

I need to go. "Forget it. Enjoy your meal." I turned away.

"Cypress, STOP."

The petulant part of me wanted to ignore it. How dare they try to treat me like a child, after everything we'd been through? Acanthus' voice broke. "You cannot start a conversation and then end it to leave me guessing! I asked, have I ever treated you as lesser, you have yet to respond. I cannot fix something if you leave me on a ledge. You honestly have no idea how — how— infuriating that is!"

I turned back to them, and we glared at each other in stony silence. *Even when we're at each other's throats, they take my breath away.* Taking in their beauty, I did my best to hold their gaze. I looked away first. *God. Why are they so pretty?* I shook my head to clear it, and bit back a sharp retort. *Slow down. Don't be a dick, Cypress.*

"Acanthus. Enjoy your meal." With that, I turned and walked out.

I didn't know where to go after my confrontation with Acanthus, so I put myself in time out in the woods. I'd have gotten in my car and left if I knew where we were. I'd never been outside of the state of New York and I was not in the mood to get lost in a backwoods town. Who knew if there was Hunters nearby, anyway. I thought of my dead phone in the glove compartment. I wish I had charged it; I'd kill to have a distraction right now. Word puzzles, maybe?

If I could stand being in the house, I'd have pulled it out and done just that. I wandered around in the woods until far after dawn, and collected cool things I found in the wet, muddy forest. It was full of pines, hickory, and maple, and the smells intermingled as they hung in the air. I felt at home here. I found a neat rock. Things were good. And then it started to rain.

"God fucking dammit," I muttered as I glared at the droplets. I didn't want to go inside, so I found some cover under a maple tree. A raindrop landed on my forehead and I grimaced up at the offending leaf. I'd been sitting out here in the cold and wet behind the ornate Queen Anne, moody as ever, for an hour. It wasn't anyone's fault that I couldn't get these emotions under wraps, and no one in that house deserved to deal with it. I missed the sun, and at this point, I was pretty fucking tired of the entire minefield of supernatural bullshit I'd fallen into. *I'm tired of feeling like a problem.*

I had accidentally adapted to Acanthus' schedule. Despite the rigorous two months of training with a day-dwelling pack, it had taken me next to no time to get back to being nocturnal. Maybe I should make it a goal to separate myself from the daylight. Leaves crunched under approaching footsteps, and I looked up to see Azalea, carrying a tray of food with the pole of an umbrella tucked between her arm and side. *Well, now I feel even shittier.*

Her dress swayed around her ankles, and she gingerly stepped around rocks and tree roots as she kept the tray level. My self-esteem crumbled in real time. "You didn't have to do that. I would've come in eventually."

Azalea shook her head, her warm voice instantly soothing. "I wanted to, dear Cypress. You need to eat."

I smiled gratefully as she put the food down. "Thank you Azalea. I appreciate it."

She watched me curiously, pulling her skirts in to sit beside me. The stare made me squirm. I wondered if this is what a lab rat felt like when scientists watched them going through a maze. "What?" I barked, and then immediately regretted it. "I'm sorry. I don't understand what's happening to me right now. My mood has been atrocious, and no one needs to deal with it."

"Dearest Cypress, these mood swings happen with pups. I can't begin to imagine how frustrating that must be."

I couldn't answer her. She was being far too kind. I hated my mood swings, and I hated that she had to deal with them. I pulled my knees to my chest, hugging them as I curled in on myself. *Maybe I should just go home.* But, where was home? Where was I going to go when a fifth of the country was looking for us? Going back to the church definitely wasn't an option, and thinking about that left my chest aching. I loved that little building.

My apartment also wasn't mine anymore, and my mother's house? I don't think I could face her after everything that had happened in the last few months. *I don't think I have a home anymore...* But, being with Acanthus felt like home, when I wasn't at his throat. *I'm a stupid, mangy, aimless wet mutt.*

"You know," she said offhandedly, breaking me from my thoughts, "You and Lord Acanthus aren't so different."

I looked up at her, puzzled. "What do you mean?"

She laughed, and dropped her voice to a discreet tone, as if she was telling me a secret. "Lord Acanthus fed last night, and then sulked in his room. No one could enter."

"That sounds like Acanthus," I grumbled. *Stupid pretty Vampire with their stupid magic eyes...*

Her voice was playful as she bumped me with her shoulder. "But here you sit doing the same."

Fine. She has a point. She sighed as she leaned back on the palms of her hands. "I've known Acanthus Sylene for a good, long while. And I know they won't seek you out. Acanthus is good at letting people take the time to process. But, they often get stuck in their head. And it is wonderful to see them with a companion again."

"What do you mean, Azalea? Why did they retreat from the Night Garden? Why didn't they stay with you?"

Azalea's eyes lidded, and she looked down to the forest floor. "There were a string of unfortunate circumstances that led them to that decision, young Wolf. Several betrayals, a fire that took out one of our more well-traveled paths, a devastating loss of a fledgling, and a failed attempt at relocating a Witch. The details are not mine to tell."

She licked her lips and sighed. "By the time they relinquished control to me, they were a husk of themself. The Night Garden is a lot of work to run, and there are many risks involved. They were exhausted by the constant fighting. Everyone needs a break from time to time. But, the way that they retreated…"

A haunted cast came into her eyes. "Well, we were all dreadfully worried for them."

I frowned. With that laundry list of bad luck, I wouldn't exactly want to be in their shoes. I guess a century was a really long time to be alone, but hadn't Acanthus wished for it? They seemed perfectly content when I first met them. I fucked that up for them, too. "I dunno, I feel like I've done nothing but treat them poorly." I looked down at my hands. "I like being around them, but sometimes it feels like we're oil and water."

"I don't suppose you've tried to speak to them about it?"

Of course I hadn't tried to speak to them about it, and thinking about that was entirely impossible. I didn't answer, but she knew she struck a chord. She smiled warmly and stood, turning towards the house. "I'll leave you to your breakfast."

"Thank you Azalea. Truly."

She smoothed her skirts, turning to head back to the house. "Of course, Dearest Cypress."

That Time My Demons Won

Acanthus

This stress was going to be my undoing. I hadn't slept through the day, and I was exhausted as night set in. The interaction with Cypress sent lances through my heart and left me reeling. I didn't understand where it came from; we'd been joking and laughing before getting here. I repeated the night in my mind, picking it apart. Where did I go wrong? I knew logically that we both had a very hard, very stressful week, and that was an understatement. The last few months, let alone several days, were full of fear, pain, and sadness. I had been vulnerable with them more times than I could count, and I couldn't stop the persistent ache in my heart.

There is nothing worse than being in a mental spiral, and being self-aware of that spiral but unable to stop its course. It wasn't Cypress' fault; not necessarily. More so, the entire situation was catching up to me again, much like at the Magic Manor. I didn't want to think about the war, Nekane, or this fight with Cypress. It was easier to be numb than it was to be hurting. And so, I gave in to it; isolating in my temporary room and allowing myself to float in the cottony dissociation. *To Hell with it.*

This room was on the second floor. It was a hexagonal room in the spire, painted cream with chocolate wooden accents. A full sized bed, a chair, a writing desk, and a dresser were the only furniture. The windows had a static cling film that was made to look like a floral stained glass; in the sunlight, it likely danced a rainbow of colors across the mahogany floor. This was one of the bigger rooms in the house. I'm fairly certain

222

Azalea kept this one unused and open for me, whenever I chose to visit. I had the chair pulled away from the desk and angled towards one of the two sets of recessed windows, the glass open and letting in the breeze.

I deliberately kept the link between Cypress and I shut as I stayed in my chambers. I closed my eyes and pictured an ornate garden gate between us in my mind. A thick padlock was shoved between the wrought iron spokes, a key safely in my pocket. It seemed to work. This was how you protect yourself from mental invasions, but I had no idea if it worked with Pack bonds. I distracted myself from my own thoughts with a new journal, left in the room for me by Azalea after our coded conversation over the phone. My surroundings were far calmer than my mind, and the walls would close in on me if I let it.

I moved my hands idly, sketching without any purpose or care as to where I ended the scratchy little doodles. I had a tendency to return to the arts when my mind was restless, and this was no different. Writing, painting, and drawing soothed me; in times like this, the stream of consciousness kept my hands busy and my mind engaged enough to avoid a breakdown. Pictures of Wolves, of rose windows, and of people I knew and cared for both present and past danced from the end of my pen. Lines started before the previous ones had a chance to dry.

This place was as painful as it was soothing. I'd only come back three times since I retired from the Garden, each time at the edge of a kaleidoscopic lucid frenzy. So many memories existed under these pointed gable roofs. It was in this very house that Azalea nursed me back to health from a vicious poisoning attempt. This was also the location of a devastating fire that nearly took out the Night Garden entirely. There had been betrayals, losses, and injuries in this house. And, in a good mindset, the past would stay in the past. But in this accursed spiral, each hurt played on repeat in my mind. The paint colors had changed, and the building was restored, but the memories were just as vivid as if they happened yesterday.

The Pennsylvania stronghold was the center of our Paths. It was the heart of the Night Garden. It became a hub during the heaviest portion of the supernatural wars. Originally, it was a Colonial style box of a house. After the fire in the 1880s, we built the Queen Anne. It was larger than the original floor plan and allowed for far more guests. So many people were flowing in and out of the Yellow Rose. Twenty five years after that, I left it all behind; half mad, fully done with my duties and the war. When I left, I was wished more than anything, for something to come along and kill me.

I didn't want to think about it. Connection was hard. Keeping people close, trusting them, and staying soft and compassionate in this cruel world was hard. I had fought an uphill battle for seven hundred years, and I was done trying. It was easier to be alone than it was to make a connection. Wasn't it? *Christ alive, I'm a mess.*

Lemon Balm

If I was Cypress' Pack, then why did I feel hatred emanating from them? A Pack, as I understood it, had an unbreakable bond that went past any kind of normal human connection. It was pure and true — romantic, familial, platonic. Whichever relationship it was between the members of the Pack, that bond was as unshakeable as a string of fate. I may have been reading too much into their mood; a side effect of centuries spent being harmed under someone else's thumb. Something in me grew cold, and my eyes welled up. *No, God damn it all, I will not cry again over these petty issues.*

But, were they petty? So much happened in the last two months. I lost the home I had kept for over a century, and all of my earthly belongings yet again. My beloved little church lay in ruins in New York, with smashed out windows and a broken-in door. We had left it a husk full of poisons and tainted sorrow. I wanted more than anything to go back. If only I could rewind those months, and return to the nice, easy stasis I was surviving in. I wanted to be surrounded by the endless blur of countless lit candles and the passing of nights. I wanted monotony, peace; I wanted an end.

Instead, I was recovering from having been attacked and injured within an inch of my life, in a Bed and Breakfast where I had lost everything. The Night Garden, as fond of it as I was, was a dying, desperate hope. The Yellow Rose was a burial shroud; these walls held the faces of dead companions and fallen refugees. It was a monument to all of my failures and losses in an unending war. No paint could cover the blood in the structure's bones.

Just how many more people had to die because of me? How many more would I have to lose? Hell, Cypress was slowly being poisoned right now by that damned bangle. We came here to get it off; otherwise, I'd have gone straight to our next location. Bringing him here likely put the Bed and Breakfast under a line of fire, or even direct scrutiny from Nekane if she found out. The bitter betrayal burned my tongue; I never should have trusted her, or sent Cypress there. *Every move I make is the wrong choice.*

I needed to get out of my own head. Perhaps leaving the confines of the room was in order. But, then again, I didn't want to speak to Cypress, either. I'd had enough of thinking about all of this. This was a losing battle, and I didn't want to play this game of chess again. To hell with strategy. I didn't have any resources this time. I didn't want to see the past replaying on my eyelids with the scent of fresh cinnamon bread in the kitchen. Perhaps I would reach out to Corbin and let him prattle on about France until I felt better.

I turned the page of the journal while lost in these thoughts. The stream of consciousness doodling had my hand arching frantically across the paper. I stopped scribbling when the cool sticky pull of ink drying on my hands caught my attention. Horrified by what I had drawn, I dropped the pen and it clattered to the floor, the sound too loud in my ears. The cold hollowness blanketed me as I stared at the page. Blackness, a bright spot in the center, and the illuminated cruel eyes of a hateful man. *François. I left you so long ago, and yet you're still just behind my eyes.*

A knock pulled me from my thoughts and I all but threw the notebook off of my lap and across the floor, every muscle tensed. I couldn't care where it landed, and I glared towards the offending noise. "Go away. Leave me be."

There was a silence, long enough that I thought whoever visited had left, until I heard a timid voice from the other side of the door. "Acanthus?"

That small tone pulled at my heartstrings. Cypress nearly sounded scared. I stood, leaning into the recessed window, closing my eyes and relishing the breeze as I shifted my hair across one shoulder. I didn't want him to see me like this, but perhaps a conversation was in order. My back was to the door. At the very least, speaking with Cypress would be a distraction from my own mind. I needed to do something with my hands, so I started to braid my hair as I called, "Come in."

My voice was careful, neutral, and devoid of too much emotion. I was in control. I was calm, I was safe. The door creaked slowly open as Cypress came into the room, hesitant. I could almost physically feel their dread, heavy and poisonous. Ah, yes. There was the distinct feeling that they hated me, once again. I was a proper fool to think I could have any kind of connection with anyone. *Vampires are disgusting creatures, after all. Parasitic, sadistic, cruel. It's alright. I know how to be alone.*

A slight pressure in my head told me that they were seeing if I'd let them in. With shaky fingers, I undid my hair and started to redo the braid. I still had my back to them, but I could see them in my periphery. They held the distinct posture of a clumsy person surrounded by broken glass and eggshells; head bowed, steps exaggerated and light so that I could see every animated movement.

"Bad night?" The words were light hearted enough, but their concern grated on my nerves like barbed wire.

"Isn't it always with me?" The venom in my voice was as surprising to me as it likely was to them.

"Ouch. Yep. Deserved that one. Got any more for me?"

I whipped to face them, and was dismayed to trace their gaze to the notebook I had thrown. Crossing my arms tightly, I hunched down, fighting the urge to fly into a corner and curl until I was nothing. I slammed the journal shut with my powers, pointedly asking, "Do you have something you wish to speak to me about?"

Cypress

Well, this was going smoothly. I could tell that Acanthus was having a hell of a time, but I couldn't begin to guess why. My stomach twisted. This was my fault. "I'm sorry?"

Acanthus stared at me, their eyes dull and lifeless. They had either shut themself down, or they were numb. Either way, I didn't like it. It was a knife in my heart knowing that I had caused them to spiral. "I was a dick and what I said was entirely out of line. And I'm sorry."

"Shush. For one moment."

I snapped my mouth shut, but the order made my skin bristle. I wasn't about to fight them more, not when we were on such rocky ground. They leaned back against the windowsill, finishing their braid before picking it apart. We stood in the horrible silence across the room from one another, my ears ringing like a gunshot had gone off. I wasn't sure what Acanthus was waiting for, but I was squirming under their gaze. Their eyes scrubbed me raw, and the pain just past the anger in those hazel pools left a yawning cavernous dread in my stomach. I wanted to be able to help, but I didn't know how to bridge the gap..

"Can I hug you?" I tried to push a thought through the bond. To my surprise, it succeeded. Acanthus' bottom lip wobbled, and they nodded. I was across the room before they blinked, pulling them to my chest. *"I'm sorry, Acanthus. I was horrible to you."*

Acanthus' breath hitched as they returned the hug. Their shoulders were tense, and although they had seemed steady enough from across the room, they were shaking like a leaf. *"You are an asshole. I told you not to say anything."*

I grinned. *"I didn't say a word."*

They relaxed against my chest. I let the silence stretch between us for a long time before I felt confident enough to speak. "I'm learning," I murmured. Then I pulled back to look at them. "Did you just call me an asshole, Acanthus?"

They blushed. "Indeed I did. I was just reinforcing what you'd already said."

I laughed and rested my chin on the top of their head. "Can you forgive me?"

Acanthus sighed softly, voice fragile as they spoke. "This isn't just you, Pup. There are a lot of different things on my mind. I appreciate you coming to me to talk. We could save a lot of grief in the future, you know."

I cringed. They were right. "Yeah. I know. How are you feeling?"

"Much better. And you?"

"Yeah, I'm not a small talk kind of guy," I went to pull out of the embrace, but they still held on.

"Please, don't leave me yet." The quiet whisper of a thought surprised me, but my heart broke. I guess I didn't realize how much Acanthus had been affected by the last few months. They always seemed so calm and in control, and I couldn't think of them in any other way. This whole time, I just assumed they were strong, and focused on myself. I wished that they had been more open with me. I need to protect them.

"I'm right here," I murmured, brushing my hand along their back reassuringly. There was still something bothering me, and I decided to try and put my ego aside, jerking my head towards the journal. "I'm curious about your sketch of that dark and gruesome gentleman, over there. Can you tell me?"

Acanthus

My blood ran cold and my face hardened into a mask of pure hatred and disgust. "A festering wound that won't heal," I spat, my voice small and tight.

Before I fully realized what I had been doing, I was out of their arms and across the room again, tense and wary. A small, frightened part of my mind was whispering, *run. Hide. Run. Hide. Runhiderunhide.*

Every muscle stood taut, and I kept finding the exits in the small room. *Window, window, door. Run. Hide. Window. Door.*

My breaths grew shallow and fast. *Window, window, door.*

Another, more rational side of my mind was screaming at me. *I am in CONTROL. I am SAFE. I am SECURE. For Christ's sake, Acanthus, pull it together.*

"Woah," Cypress breathed.

Unable to stay still, my hands found my hair again. I dimly realized that I was against the wall, my heart thundering in my ears as my hands fumbled. Braid. Unbraid. Braid. Unbraid. I measured the time with frantic movements rather than seconds. Closing my eyes, I tried to find my center. I couldn't cut through the racing thoughts, and my lungs were on fire with how fast I was breathing.

I was shivering like a caged animal. My hands were in mid braid when Cypress was beside me again. They had approached slowly, and were kneeling in front of me. When did I wind up on the floor? They gently cupped my hands as they dipped down to catch my eyes, their voice gentle and apologetic. "Hey, hey. Breathe," he stayed arms' length away, his voice soft. "I'm sorry for asking. You don't have to tell me."

A knock on the door interrupted us. I closed my eyes again and willed my heart to slow. "O-One moment!"

I hated the stammer in my voice. Cypress gently stroked his thumbs across my knuckles, taking in a deep breath. He held it, then let it out. And, when he breathed in again, I found myself matching his pace. A few cycles of this left me calmer, and I opened my eyes, letting my shoulders fall as I finished my braid. My cheeks burned with shame as I called, "What is it?"

Azalea's voice was muted by the thick oak of the door as she replied, sounding rather anxious. "So sorry to bother, Lord Acanthus, but have you seen Cypress? The coven is here."

I glanced back to Cypress, who calmly replied, "I'm here."

I swallowed, and he stood, offering his hand to me. I took it as the door tilted open and Azalea's head popped in. As Cypress helped me to my feet, I nodded. "Lead the way, Azalea."

That Other Time I Forced A Werewolf To Shift

Acanthus

The coven was large. Azalea pretty much took in every Witch that had left their own, and so she had a vast network all across the Eastern territory. There were dozens, if not hundreds of Witches in her circle, and many of them helped keep the Night Garden running. Some chose to re-join kinder packs in order to keep an ear to the ground and find information for us. Some stayed free, and helped their own communities.

Eight people waited for us in the cozy little common kitchen, already seated in a series of chairs in a circle where the table had been. Candles had been lit around the room, and the lights were off, giving the usually cozy space a somber, heavy air. An empty seat had been left by the island for a ninth Witch; Azalea. All of the Witches were chattering and murmuring to each other, but they quieted as we entered the room. Perhaps when you're thinking of Witches in a ritual, you're thinking of a gaggle of old crones with warts and donning pointy hats; maybe with a green, smoking cauldron somewhere in the mix. In reality, the people throughout the room were of all genders, sizes, and colors.

They were all donning ceremonial cloaks of various colors, nothing coordinated. Even Azalea wore a cloak, gold and shimmering in the light of the flame over her vibrant green dress. "My Lord," a young man with curly brown hair called from the corner of the room. "It's good to finally see you back with us."

I cringed. "As good as it is to see you, Benji, you know that I have not been involved with the Garden for a century. I'm here as a guest."

He nodded, his eyes darting towards Cypress, who glanced at me. I had composed myself by the time we had reached the kitchen, and on the surface I was the picture of calm and poise, but my emotions were still causing chaos within. *My hysteria can wait,* I thought, irritated. *Getting the shift lock off of Cypress is more important.*

I held my hand towards Cypress and made introductions. "Cypress Borne, meet Benjamin Walker."

Cypress nodded politely, and Ben shook his hand. We went around the circle, Cypress polite and quiet through each introduction. *Benji. Julia. Roderick. Belle. Vera. Celia. Florence. Barbara.* All of them were capable Witches, most of them with wind or water powers. Ben was a Chaos Witch, a Witch with powers that came from light patterns. Chaos Witches could manipulate emotions as well, and this would be important for the spell ahead. Shift locks were a powerful use of a werewolf's weakness, imbued with magic to keep the Wolf's will inaccessible. Of course, we could just break the band open, but that would not break the spell; Cypress would still be unable to shift. Florence was particularly skilled with breaking shift locks, and so I was relieved to see her here.

Azalea would likely be leading the spell. She had sat in her chair by the time we made our rounds, and she smiled warmly at us. "Are you ready?"

My stomach twisted into knots, but I nodded. *I am calm. I am in control.*

She had already explained to both of us what this would look like — Cypress was to sit in the center of the circle with me. I would remain standing while they were seated, tugging at their band with my powers. This unbinding spell would likely pull out the wolf in its strongest form; there were no guarantees Cypress would have any control over their faculties. If they tried to attack, I could mesmer them; making me the only one who was strong enough to prevent harm to anyone. I knew what I had to do.

The Witches created the boundaries of the circle, and Azalea nodded to both of us. "When we begin to chant, Lord Acanthus, I need you to chant along with us. Your powers are important here, as well."

"You know I am no Witch, Azalea."

"You have powers enough, my Lord," her voice was firm. "The chant is this: With the powers of three times three, we unbind thee. *Aperi hanc portam lupinam.*"

I nodded. "*Aperi hanc portam lupinam.* Open this wolf gate."

She smiled warmly. "Precisely. Now, take your places!"

Braid. Unbraid. Braid. Unbraid. My anxiety was already higher than most of the strange energy vibrating in the room. Cypress reached over, grabbing one of my hands and forcing me to stop. They gently led us to the middle and took their place on the final chair. I shot them a small smile, then swallowed. The deep abyssal pit in my stomach gnawed at my ribs, and nausea collected in my throat. If this group of Witches couldn't get this thing off, I shuddered to think of the possibilities. Cypress would lose his mind before the year wound down.

"I trust you, Acanthus." The words reverberated in my head, and my shoulders sagged. I gave his hand a soft, reassuring squeeze before letting it go. They shot me a big, goofy grin. I guess it was time to begin.

Cypress

Acanthus' hand in mine was reassuring when I grabbed it. What if I hurt Acanthus? *Did it have to be them in the middle with me? Couldn't I just pull the damn thing off myself?*

A large part of my mind screamed at me that this was irrational. What were the chances that nothing would happen? The silver bangle would stay stuck, and I'd feel like an idiot in the center of chanting people and burning candles. It had the emotional weight of 'thoughts and prayers'. Questions still swirled in my mind, but I grinned at Acanthus. They were anxious enough as it was. Besides, I had no reason to doubt; Azalea had healed me, and I no longer questioned my senses.

"Oh!" Azalea stood from her seat and reached for a flower wreath that had been sitting on the island. Stopping in front of me, she held it up. "For protection, dear Cypress."

I cocked my head and blinked at her, but bowed at her request. Acanthus cleared their throat. "White roses for purity, chrysanthemums to ward off evil energies, marigolds to protect the inner self, and lavender for healing, strength, and resilience."

I trusted these people, but my gut twisted. How could flowers protect me? This was way too woo-woo for me. I don't know the extent of what I believed anymore, but my inner skeptic was screaming. I rolled my eyes. *Shut up,* I thought. *I literally buried my friend and watched them come back to life for it. Maybe flowers CAN protect me.*

My mind wandered to my old apartment, and I thought of Tasha playing with her amethyst point. What worked? What didn't? *Am I sure I'm not hooked up to a ventilator somewhere in Albany?*

The petals of the crown tickled my forehead, and I looked up at Acanthus from underneath it. They smiled at me. About then was when I let that spiral of thoughts drop, because not believing in this current reality meant losing Acanthus. That thought made my chest ache and my heart contract. I don't want a reality without them.

Instead, I focused on a leaf in front of my nose. Puffing my cheeks, I blew at it, earning a small chuckle from Acanthus. *"Do I look like a pretty princess, Lord Acanthus?"*

They bit back a smile, shaking their head. *"Don't start,"* they scolded, then their thoughts slipped into a more soothing tone. *"It's going to be alright."*

I should be the one telling them that. The timing wasn't great; I knew their calm was just a mask, and I wanted to let them rest. Maybe breaking the shift lock would help. I knew they still blamed themself for my struggle at Nekane's. Azalea took her seat. I was trying so hard to be the strong one, but I was a rubber band, seconds from snapping. I thought about the way Acanthus darted across their room upstairs and frowned. My gut twisted. If they could show me how panicked they were, I guess I could at least share my own uncertainty. *"How can you be sure this is going to work? How can you be sure things will be okay?"*

The thought had plagued me since the Witches arrived. Acanthus' voice was firm and confident. *"I trust you, and I trust Azalea, and these people. We are good, competent company."*

I blinked and swallowed. Somehow, their confidence loosened the knot in my stomach. I wished that I could remember how to feel that sure of myself. *"I'm nervous. You are my pack, Acanthus."*

Acanthus shot me a look that was full of several emotions, but they settled on reassurance, in the end. *"I will be beside you the entire time. Be still, Cypress, I am here."*

Azalea rose from her seat to lead the charge. "Coven, we gather today to unbind our poor friend who has been cruelly separated from their Wolf. With the power of water, fire, air, earth, and spirit, we shall overcome the bind and set our dear Cypress free."

Ben, Florence, Roderick, and Barbara were at the cardinal points. They reached beneath their seats to grab some small cauldron-shaped incense burners beneath, where various spices and plants were prepared. One by one, they picked up a match from within and set fire to the bundles. The smell of smoke and burning herbs — cinnamon, I think, and maybe sage; earthy and fragrant — filled the air and mixed with the scent of the flowers in the crown. Everything became a saccharine haze. The Witches' chanting began, slow and steady, before it grew in speed and intensity. "With the power of three times three, we unbind thee."

My stomach lived in my throat, my tongue heavy, and chills racing down my spine. When the wind started whipping through the room, I focused on Acanthus; the only thing left in this whole situation that offered safety. Lights began to glow from the hands of each Witch; a blur of blue, green, white, and yellow hid their faces. Acanthus' hair was dancing wildly around their head, unrestrained. They had their hands out in front of them, pulling at the silver band with their powers and chanting inaudibly with the Witches. *"Aperi hanc portam lupinam."*

I watched their lips move, entranced. I couldn't look away from them; they were just so ethereal. "The power of three times three, we unbind thee."

Power emanated from them and swirled with the energy from the Witches. A strange, thrumming pulse emanated from them like a heartbeat, sending cold shock-waves through my bones with each tug to the band on my wrist. My breathing fell into time with the pulses, and their eyes flashed a brilliant green, glowing with the rise of magic in the air. The pulsing rose in intensity as the voices rose in volume. "Aperi hanc portam lupinam. With the power of three times three…"

My stomach dropped and I cried out as extreme pressure captured my head in a vice. I rolled my eyes shut with a pained moan and reached over the flower crown, tugging my hair with one hand. My banded wrist was still stretched, extended towards Acanthus. Through the sound of my own blood rushing in my ears, I heard their voice in my mind, *"It's coming loose."*

I cried out again as the pressure worsened. *This is what death feels like, my head is literally going to pop.*

I curled into a ball, trying to protect myself from whatever this was. Then it happened; a loud crack sounded through the room as the bracelet flew apart, silver shards of shrapnel shooting everywhere with musical little *plinks*. The Witches' magic circle had created a barrier, and it protected them from harm. There was a soft cry, followed by the skidding sound of Acanthus being thrown clear across the floor. I opened my eyes as they skidded to a halt in front of Benji, arms thrown over their face. Several of the shrapnel pellets were hovering in front of them in a glittering wall of silver. They leaned back against Benji's legs. The force of the spell breaking was intense.

And me? I was a Wolf. A wild, uncontrolled Wolf. With a flower crown.

Acanthus

The chanting stopped abruptly, leaving the room dead silent as the wind slowly calmed and the glow dissipated. The lack of noise was deafening, the silence leaving everyone in the room on the edge of their seats. I lowered my arms to find the shrapnel from the silver hovering inches in front of my face, held in stasis by my powers. Benji's knees

pressed harshly into my back, and I swallowed as I slowly pushed the shrapnel away from me. I gathered it into a ball and floated it to the side as I leaned forward. It fell with a little clatter.

My hair settled around me, and I murmured an apology to Benji, keeping my eyes on the giant Wolf in front of me. He responded, but I didn't process the words; staring at Cypress and debating whether or not to engage my mesmer. He was the size of a lion and towered before me, the lavender in the crown sticking up in a chaotic pattern. It was still perched on their head, but it was askew. *This is the image people speak about in omens.*

Slowly gathering myself, I rose to my feet and squatted before them with my hands out. Fearlessly, I held their steel gray eyes with my gaze, sans mesmer. Were they to bite me, so be it. I waited for a snarl or a growl, but it never came. Instead, their tail began to happily wag as they tilted their head. All was silent for a moment, then — they *licked* me, leaving a gob of slobber on my cheek. I laughed, astonished, as they clumsily jumped on me, their paws trying to land in my hands. "Cypress! You're not a dog, don't lick me!"

He opened his mouth in a huge smile, panting. I shook my head, then wrapped my arms around their thick neck in a hug. I felt their stance change as they plopped down on their rear, making a soft silly sound that was a strange mix of a whine and a ruff. The whispers of the Witches around us banished the circle, and the smell of the sage, cinnamon, palo santo, and rosemary intensified as the flames were extinguished. I was dizzy with relief.

The scent of campfires and strong coffee mixed with animal musk rolled off of the Wolf in waves, and I buried my face in their ruff. "We did it, Cypress. We did it."

They wriggled and whined, and I pulled away from them. He still had that smile on his face. I could smell the sage, but also… oud? Roses, and … sandalwood? *Odd, I don't think the Witches had any of that in their spell ingredients.*

The subtle scents of a damp forest and decaying riverbed left a sharp accent to the mix. But, the sensation wasn't coming from my own nose. *Strange. Is Cypress projecting what they smell to me?*

Cypress yipped in reply, before going back to their goofy panting. *"Pack!"*

I wasn't certain if the words coming from them were Cypress, or purely their inner Wolf, but I wasn't about to try and separate the two. As far as I know, Wolves are not separate and sentient on their own; they are their human and their human is their wolf. However, their instinct could take over, and the human could lose their control. If the sentient mind loses its grip completely, then sometimes the Wolf will run off and live in the wild.

Azalea's exhausted voice broke my thoughts, and I whipped my head to look at her. "Coven! We are successful. Please, make yourselves comfortable. We should leave the Lords be and allow them their space. Please rest! You've earned it."

The energy and joy within me was intense, and I needed a release. I let out a little tumble of giggles before I called to her, "Azalea! Thank you, my dear! All of you, I owe you a great debt!"

"Nonsense my Lord," Azalea replied with a small curtsy. "We shall take our leave."

As the Witches retreated single-file towards the stairs, Cypress made a mad dash to the door. They knocked over chairs in their haste, scrabbling and falling over their own legs. When they got there, they plopped down on their rear and whined. I laughed, shaking my head, and followed after them. Looking back into the kitchen, I brought my hand in front of me and pointed, using my powers to right the room and replace the table in its proper position. I didn't want to leave it for Azalea. It wasn't long before I met Cypress at the door and we slipped outside. If they could shift back, they didn't want to yet, and that was alright with me.

It had rained during the unbinding spell, and now puddles stood in the mud. I wanted the night sky, and they apparently wanted the puddles. I listened to them frolic as I took in the quarter moon and the swirls of stars. Cypress' presence in my head without the band was palpable.

Which, admittedly, was bad, because my emotional countenance was horrible; I didn't want my mood to drag him to my level.

Though pulling off their shift lock had calmed some of my anxiety, I had a plethora of unkind things in my mind. Pent up emotions from the panic attack started to worm their way out from underneath the initial joy of the successful spell. The ugly monster beneath my skin wasn't done with me yet. And, with the events of the night slowly drawing to a close, my inner voice went back to mocking me once more. I hoped Cypress couldn't hear the intrusive thoughts. *Pure dumb luck, Acanthus.*

You see, I was content. And in my centuries of existence, I had learned that when I was content, everything good was about to be ripped away. I started braiding my hair, watching the swirling of the stars. My stomach flipped in time with the movement of my fingers.

Braid. *You know better than to think that this will last.*

Unbraid. *Nekane is going to attack, and you're completely vulnerable.*

Braid. *It's only a matter of time before the Hunters find us here.*

Unbraid. *This is going to end in flames.*

Cypress

Acanthus hadn't noticed in the moment, but I'd stopped playing in the puddles. I stared at my reflection, my ears twitching and eyes moving back and forth. Their thoughts floated across my face like a news broadcast ticker. Shifting my gaze up, I watched Acanthus from across the yard. They looked so alone. Desolate. *I can't allow that.*

I couldn't pretend to know what it was like to fight for so long. But, I knew that life was better than they thought it was. I couldn't stop the issues of the Hunters or Nekane, but I could remind them that I was here, and we were in this together. I projected thoughts their way, and flashes of memories started to play between us. I thought about the first time seeing them, bits and pieces of our week together before I left for Nekane's pack; all of the happy moments we had since I met them.

I casually laid down next to the puddle, pretending I didn't have a care in the world. As I knew they would, Acanthus left their post on the wraparound porch, a mystified expression on their face. "Cypress, you..." They trailed off, kneeling and petting my fur. "Thank you."

I let us enjoy this peaceful moment for about thirty seconds before the urge came and I licked their cheek again. Acanthus scowled at me as they wiped away the slobber. I let my tongue loll out of my mouth. After all, I was a big, happy pup. It was a dream to turn into an animal and take time away from the stress of humans.

Not to mention, I felt more alive than I had since Nekane placed that first necklace on me. I was moving through the motions like I was half alive for months. Shifting was like taking a full breath of fresh air; vibrant and vital. My thoughts flashed back to when the silver was in my lungs, and I shuddered, hiding it from Acanthus. I was strong and my muscles were buzzing with life now. I wish I could bottle this feeling.

"We should head back inside, Pup," Acanthus sighed.

I whined, but they were resolute. They stood, and I followed them into the Yellow Rose, heading up the stairs. We had our own rooms set up, but I didn't want to be by myself. I also didn't want to leave Acanthus alone. Their panic attack had scared me, and they would probably do better with company. I folded my ears back and whimpered at Acanthus. "What is it, Cypress?"

I sent a conjured image of him laying in bed with a white wolf stuffed animal. Their laughter was musical. "You are not that small."

I whimpered again and tapped back and forth on my front paws. They rolled their eyes and opened the door for me. "Once. And only once."

I gave them a wolfy smile, walked into their room, and hopped on the bed. Getting up onto the mattress was awkward, and walking on it made me unsteady on my feet. I waited for them to get comfortable, and curled up around them, doing my best not to trample them in the process.

That Time The Peace Disappeared

Acanthus

This Pup was entirely impossible. They had been traipsing in puddles and were caked in mud. I made a mental note to wash the sheets for Azalea in the morning. Somehow, by the end of the night, the worst of my thoughts had quieted and I was floating in an easy, comfortable haze, warmth and affection pulsing around me. The unkind inner voice was forgotten, for now.

Cypress' fur was soft, and warm. I kept an arm slung around them, their heat emanating from them and enveloping me. The heat was a security that I hadn't realized I needed, and it left me blinking and struggling to stay awake. The purples and pinks of dawn crept in through the open window and the crack in the curtains., My eyes grew heavier, slipping shut and leaving me in the darkness with my contentment.

For the first time in months, I slept without too much fuss. It was strange, waking up past sunset fully rested and calm. When I awoke, I was laying on Cypress' chest, instead of nestled into their soft, warm fur. My head slowly bobbed with the rise and fall of their breathing. I drifted pleasantly, keeping my eyes shut and smiling as they stirred. It had been so nice to finally have a night of peace, especially after the events of the last several days. The change of pace was all too welcome.

Nekane is probably looking for us as I lay here foolishly drooling on Cypress' chest. We need to talk about the war, and where we're going next. I stubbornly pushed the thoughts away. I wouldn't let them ruin my slow ease into consciousness. ***"Cypress."***

238

"Mm?"

They sounded about as happy as I was. I tapped his chest with a finger. "This isn't fur."

The air around us heated at least five degrees with the intensity of their blush, and my own stomach flipped as their embarrassment eked into our mental connection. They quickly extracted themself from my hold. "Ow," Cypress thought as a whoosh of energy pulsed through the room.

I sat up, stretching with a soft groan as my joints popped, and by the time I opened my eyes, Cypress was a wolf again, wagging their tail. I smiled, reaching to scratch him between the ears. He panted, his eyes lidded and tail increasing in speed. "You are so happy to have your Wolf back, aren't you?"

The small yip in response made me laugh. Something about them in Wolf form was, dare I say, adorable; their goofy personality shone brightly at all times, but the Wolf almost made him a caricature of himself. I slipped out from beneath the covers and glided my way past Cypress towards one of the windows, glancing outside. Then, I knelt down to grab the journal that had been left forgotten on the floor. Looking at it, I flipped to the page I had doodled before the blackness. Face after face of kind and caring people stared at me from the page. I shut the book with a soft thump. *Where there is darkness, it is always important to remember that you are also loved.*

The thought drifted through my mind, not projected but certainly loud amongst the otherwise easy silence of the early evening. I tossed the journal onto the writing desk. The hexagonal cream walls thankfully didn't feel like they were closing in on me tonight. An image of a wolf stuffed animal popped into my mind again and I laughed, tilting my head to look at Cypress. "You are ridiculous, Pup. Absolutely ridiculous."

I said the words with fondness. *Who cares if vulnerability is a weakness? François is dead and buried, I don't need to worry about being gas-lit ever again.*

I walked over to Cypress, squatting beside them and ruffling their fur once more. "Let's get you something to eat? You must be starving."

The whimper that followed confirmed my thoughts, and I tilted my head towards the door. "Go on ahead, Pup. Azalea should be either in the lobby or tending to the kitchen. I heard from a reliable source," my voice slipped into a playful cadence that felt alien to me, but welcome. "She is making a full course breakfast for the Witches to celebrate their success. That spell was a hard one to break."

The intense yearning for meat filled my head, and they licked at their teeth, then whined again. ***"Pleeease bacon."***

I laughed a full throated laugh, and stood as I gestured towards the door. "Go. There should be clothes waiting for you in your room, if you want to shift back. I have some things I must do, and I will join you in a small while."

With a happy little yip, they made a mad dash towards the door and hopped up to paw at the knob. They tried once or twice, then whined when they couldn't open it. Hopping up again, they took the knob in their mouth, twisting their head. It didn't work; they couldn't maneuver the door in wolf form.

My face ached from smiling; I opened it for them telekinetically. They ran back to me, bumping their head into my legs and making me stagger, before scrambling out of the room. I caught myself against the side of the bed. My heart was light with joy, and as the door swung shut, I began to gather the sheets into a pile. After the sheets were thrown into the washer, I decided that it was high time for some self-care.

The bathroom was painted a beautiful sage green, matching the hallway of the second floor. The wainscotting was a deep plum, and the colors left a magical feeling in the little room. Alas, no claw-foot tub; instead, a walk-in shower, simple and befitting a standard modern bathroom, with plum-colored tiles.The mahogany floor paired well with the warm purples and cool greens. The mirror above the marble sink had a matching, ornately-carved frame; something more reminiscent of the Rococo period than modern day.

I found the comfiest of my new clothes to slip into. Soft black lounge pants, coupled with a long sleeved but thin shirt depicting a swarm of bats. Across the front, a terror font all in white exclaimed, 'Creature of the Night'. I was nothing, if not a being with an appreciation for irony. (What does Cypress say? "I am a parody of myself?") Satisfied with my choices, I stepped into the beautiful bathroom and went for a warm shower. *I must thank Azalea for providing us with a new wardrobe.*

When I was finally clean and dressed, I left my long hair down and dripping dampness across my back. I looked at myself in the mirror of the bathroom, for the first time in a very long time. Perpetually twenty one, my skin was marred by thin white scars, criss-crossing in irregular patterns, though in another day or two they would fade to nothing. Freckles dotted my face that would not otherwise be there.

To still have scars... Mon Dieu. I must have come close to Heaven's gates. I slid my gaze down to my hands. The backs had actually taken on a deep tan; a color that nearly passed as human. It made sense to me that they held the worst of the damage; more sun exposure, thanks to the careless gardening I had indulged in, in Cypress' absence. They'd also taken a brunt of the Hunter's UV light when I fell unconscious. The freckles were darker here, and would take longer to fade. *I was far too careless with my life before Cypress returned. I almost wish the scars wouldn't fade; a mark of my idiocy, and the penance needed.*

My mind drifted to Cypress, and how he hid his newly acquired ribbon-esque marks. *Dear Lord, this guilt is going to consume me.*

Dropping my hands with a soft sigh, I looked at myself again. The person I saw did not deserve the hatred that came from within, but then again, maybe that is why I felt disconnected from the reflection. *I will be kinder to you*, I vowed to my dour face. *I will not let myself fall victim to the cruel words of a long-dead man.*

Turning from the mirror, I shut off the light, and walked towards the stairs to find Cypress.

Cypress

I padded back to my temporary room, nudging the door shut before changing back to human. There was a peacefulness in the air, and I sighed, content. This room wasn't as fancy as Acanthus'; a simple four-walled room painted the same cream color with chocolate accents and mahogany moulding. There was a set of windows on the far wall. A long, low dresser with an attached mirror to my left took up most of that wall. The mirror was in a scalloped old-style frame. The full-sized bed was still neatly made to my right. The dresser and the bed's head and foot boards matched. Both had pretty, scalloped engravings along the flat surfaces.

The only time I'd been in here was the day Acanthus locked themself in their room. I had no idea if the dresser was filled when we got here, but Acanthus said I'd have clothes waiting. I walked across the small room, and pulled a drawer open. It was fully stocked with t-shirts in my size. The next drawer had pants and underwear.

I wondered if Azalea sent someone shopping as I was sulking the other day. The clothes were my exact measurements. At that moment, my stomach sang. Showering could wait until later, I'd murder someone for a pancake. Instead, I pulled on a snug fitting t-shirt and a pair of jeans. I could smell maple and bacon being fried in the kitchen, and my mouth watered. But, something was stopping me from making a beeline downstairs. I looked at my arms, frowning. *Maybe she bought some hoodies? Can't hurt to look.*

I opened the bottom drawer, and I was pleasantly surprised to find various flannels. The stereotypes of lesbians and ragged, haggard men with five o'clock shadows ran through my head, and I laughed. I grabbed a checkered blue one, and pulled it on. The mirror very much reflected that stereotype; albeit, younger, and decidedly less tired. My hair was messy and the curls bounced wildly away from my face, and I'd likely need to shave later. Ugh, I'm a disaster. *Maybe I should look for a beanie,*

I thought, then immediately shut it down. *No, Cypress, that's stupid. No one knows you hide your curls with beanies. Think, you just met Azalea.*

The enticing aroma of bacon, eggs, and French toast grew in intensity. It pulled me down the stairs and into the kitchen. Azalea was cooking a huge breakfast; she scooted past me with a tray of food on her way to the table. I brought a hand up, but thought better of reaching towards her. "Anything I can assist with, Azalea?"

"Nonsense, Dear Cypress. All you need to do is sit and enjoy the food," she smiled warmly. "A little bird told me French toast was your favorite."

"A bird, or a bat?"

She laughed. "It is good that Lord Acanthus has you. You brighten them. Now; tea, coffee, or orange juice?"

I brightened them? What was that supposed to mean? I blushed and looked at the spread laid out on the table. "Uhh... Coffee, please."

The coven of Witches were beginning to filter in, though Benji was already sitting at the left corner of the table. Vera nodded politely, giving me a close-lipped smile as she moved past and sat at the far corner of the table across from Benji. Roderick walked in next, dark circles under his gray eyes and salt and pepper hair a tangled mess. "Hey, Cypress, how are you feeling?"

I blinked, pleasantly surprised. I hadn't even thought about it since I woke up. There was a low-grade aching in my arms and shoulders, and my knees were protesting like I'd run a solid marathon, but it wasn't anything worse than a day after an intense workout. "Kinda sore, but not bad. I'm hungry, more than anything."

He nodded, his long hair falling into his face. "That's good to hear. I'm glad you're doing relatively well."

I smiled, my heart lifting. These people were so nice. I was still getting over the fact that they helped at all; I didn't think Witches liked Wolves, no matter how good of a person they were. It was a refreshing correction. I should know better than to lump everyone in with my first experience.

More people slowly moved into the kitchen, one by one, and I sat at one of the open seats close to the center of the table. A tingle tugged in my mind. Pack, it whispered, and I looked towards the door. Soothing calm filled my chest as Acanthus and I locked eyes. "Good evening, everyone," Acanthus' looked from one person to the next, a small smile playing on their lips. "I hope you enjoy your meal. I'll just be here for the conversation."

Some casual greetings came from the people in the room, but I was studying Acanthus. There was still something sad and guarded in their pose; I couldn't place it, but I wanted to distract them from wherever their mind was. Their casual attire reminded me of a college student more than a millennia old Vampire. "Hey. 2002 Hot Topic called. That shirt is out of warranty, unfortunately."

They grimaced. "That's okay. Thanks for chopping the firewood last night, dear generic lumberjack."

I grinned, leaning back in my chair. Benji laughed at the interaction, trying to hide it behind by reaching for his coffee mug. Affection thrummed through the bond like a note hanging in the air. They sat across from me and one seat over to the right, leaving the chair at the center open. Azalea bustled over, placing a mug of coffee in front of me, and a mug of tea beside Acanthus' hand. They nodded to her. "Thank you, my dear."

I tilted my head curiously. I hadn't thought about it at the motel, but now it hit me like a bag of bricks. *They don't eat human food.*

"I enjoy some, tentatively. Mostly drinks, though; too much makes me ill."

I jumped, hearing them reply like I'd asked it aloud. I hadn't been pushing my thoughts towards them, or even making an attempt at communication. My pulse raced, and my stomach twisted. Was this just how it was now? It was as easy as breathing without the silver blocking it. Did they hear every little thought? I didn't want someone to know my mind like that; I thought of stupid stuff all the time.

The last of the Witches filtered in and sat down, and Azalea took her place at the heart of the table. I waited for everyone else to grab food before piling my plate high with French toast and bacon. It was bustling; laughter and conversations between the members of the coven mingled and intertwined. I found myself talking to several of the people around me, and I was struck by how accepted and included I felt.

I'd never had a meal that felt like a family gathering, but this is what I always imagined it was like. It'd always just been me and my mom, and she would stay out partying more often than not. Usually I had to fend for myself with boxed mac and cheese. Nekane's pack had been all silence and schedules. No one really interacted with me; I'd often even found myself sitting alone, while people went to their little circles. The closest to a family meal I'd ever gotten was in college with my group of friends, but even then was more ribbing and less actual acceptance for who I was. I fell quiet after a pleasant conversation with Julia about how her water magic worked. My heart swelled as I looked around the table. *This is... beautiful.*

Acanthus' lilting voice drifted through my mind, interrupting my awe. *"Little bat, huh?"*

I blushed, though I pushed down the embarrassment. *"You heard that?"*

"Of course I did."

Acanthus' calm demeanor did not reflect the amusement emanating from them. Feeling their emotions made it so much easier to understand where they were coming from; they were so reserved that it was sometimes hard to read them. *"I'll have you know,"* I huffed, *"I don't actually think you turn into a bat."*

I thought of a show where the vampire yelled, "Bat," in order to transform, and snorted into my coffee. They smiled. *"I assumed."*

The banter between us was pretty freeing. It felt like the teasing I was used to from my previous groups of friends, but less catty and more wholesome. I hadn't noticed, but the table had started to go quiet. Azalea's eyes had grown sharp, but her smile was bright and excited. "Your bond is truly spectacular. Listen."

My attention snapped to her, my ears strained to hear what she was hearing. Acanthus and I exchanged confused looks. "Your hearts," she said, as if it was the most obvious thing in the world. "They beat as one. Even the shift lock couldn't prevent it. Though, we haven't heard of a Vampire and a Werewolf having such a bond before. It is truly special."

Julia nodded. "You are both incredibly in sync. It's like you compliment one another."

"Twin souls," Benji added.

My confusion deepened. I watched Acanthus. Maybe it was just a coincidence? I didn't know how bonds formed; maybe it was like a duckling and their mother. "You were the first one I saw, when I pulled up to the church as the owner."

Acanthus shook their head. "The first supernatural that you know of. I very much doubt that's the reason." They sat back, frowning as they cupped their mug. "You saw countless people after the bite, before you saw me."

Okay, so maybe that thought was naive. I felt foolish; time to double down. *"Why else?"*

"Silly, silly wolf, you are not a duckling. It can't be from first sight, or else there'd be far more supernaturals that were bound outside of their own species."

I shot them a look. "Please Dear Cypress," Azalea interrupted, "if it is a new form of Bond, then it is a new form of Bond. It may just be that

I haven't seen it, and it is rare. I have contacts who are more knowledgeable than I; I will reach out. The 'why' doesn't matter, only that it exists. Eat more food. We are celebrating our successes, after all."

I jumped before laughing, disarmed, and dug into my plate. The rest of dinner was pleasant, and the time moved quickly, filled with banter and warmth. Azalea pretended to be indignant as Roderick, Benji, and I cleared the table and assisted with the dishes. After protesting three times, she relented and thanked us for the help in the kitchen. As we cleaned, the coven began to filter out one by one. Benji was the last to go, and he gave me a solid handshake after giving me his phone number. "Do keep in touch, Cypress," he said. "I enjoyed talking to you."

"Of course, Ben. Safe travels," I replied, and as I watched him slip out of the door, I decided that it was time to rescue my phone from the glove box.

Hours passed, and around eleven I was restlessly fidgeting in Acanthus' room. We'd only been here for a few days; and it was the hottest point of the year. Even in the middle of July the nights were pleasant here in the mountainous area of Pennsylvania. They said we'd head out at the end of the week, allowing us time to gather ourselves and relax. We could pack on Friday, which gave us three days to take our time, visit with Azalea, and prepare for the journey to their church. It was comfortable here, and I didn't want to leave. "Can't we just stay?"

Acanthus blinked, surprised. "I suppose we could, but we would have to pay close attention to the bulletins and news in the area. I haven't checked anything, and so I don't know what Nekane is doing. This worries me; if we're found here, then the people here, as well as the Night Garden will be in grave danger."

I lowered my gaze to the floor and nodded. Their reasoning was sound. "I don't want to put anyone in danger. How do we know if Nekane followed us from the church?"

Acanthus looked towards the door. "I intend to find that out tonight. I have to speak to Azalea, and perhaps put together some resources. Will you be alright waiting for me while I take care of some business?"

I didn't want to be in the way, so I nodded, and they left me to my anxiety. I found myself wandering the Bed and Breakfast. The house was huge. There was enough room for twenty different sets of guests to stay at a time. There were four floors in all, if you included the attic in the spire. The first floor was that yellow and chocolate theme, and there were only two rooms on that level for guests. Azalea's room was to the right of the kitchen and just behind the counter in the lobby, with a staff placard on the simple wooden door.

The second floor was sage and plum, with pretty little purple flowers painted in a pattern throughout the sage. I wouldn't expect the colors to go together, but they contrasted beautifully. The plum wainscotting went halfway up the walls. There were eight rooms; four on either side of the hallway. Acanthus' room was at the end of the hall in the base of the spire; the ninth room on the floor. The stairwells were painted the same cream color as the rooms.

The third floor was painted a blush pink that made the mahogany trim intensely dark, and there were eight rooms up here. Between the doors, there were portraits lining the walls. The hallway ended in the spire, with a metal spiral staircase that went up to the attic. I didn't go up there; assuming it was storage. The spire surrounding the staircase was a hexagon, and there was a window on each of the outward facing walls. I spent some time looking at the paintings, wondering about the people's pasts. None of them were labeled, but all of them looked important.

Were these people who had connections to Azalea? Were they people who were connected to Acanthus? Maybe the Night Garden? I had no idea. I made a mental note to start asking more questions, but then I thought of the panic attack Acanthus suffered when I asked about their drawing. *Maybe I need to find a better way to ask.*

I wandered down to the main floor, idly pacing the common rooms. Azalea had been sitting in one of the comfortable chairs, knitting. She watched me walk through the lobby for the third time before she finally broke the silence, lowering her needles as she spoke. "Dear Cypress, can I help you with something?"

My anxiety buzzed as I blurted, "Is there anything else that needs to be done?"

She laughed, shaking her head. "There are many chores that need to be done, but you're a guest. You do not need to worry about it."

"You did so much for me," I replied, my voice warm and full of the gratefulness that swelled in my chest. "It's the least I can do, Azalea."

"You aren't the handyman, Cypress."

I was, actually. But, Azalea had no way of knowing that. I had taught myself so many ways to fix things throughout my teenage years. Not to mention, my years as a handyman after the dog bite. That was part of the reason I felt so comfortable buying the church in New York. I could handle anything this old place had to throw at me. Besides, I needed something to do with my hands. "Please. I've been pampered enough. If something needs fixing, I can try."

She didn't push back again, setting her needles aside to lead me to a problem. I started by fixing a loose faucet and some leaky pipes beneath the kitchen sink; next was patching the drywall in a bedroom, and other odd tasks. Eventually, she even had me take a look at the slightly off-kilter front door, in order to stop it from slamming against the jamb on windy days.

Acanthus walked up as I was replacing the last screw on the bottom hinge. They raised an eyebrow. "I was told you were up to no good, but I didn't expect this."

"No good, my Lord?" I tried to pull my best English lilt into my voice, and it failed miserably.

Acanthus groaned, but couldn't hide the smile that played on their lips afterwards. "Please never call me Lord again. You are my friend, not a child or an employee. I've told the Witches the same, but they refuse. Azalea is the most stubborn about it."

"When you have friends like Azalea, why did you choose solitude?"

A jolt of tension ran through Acanthus, and I was disappointed to see them close up so quickly. Every time I thought we were getting closer, they'd shut me out. Their eyes darted away from me, and their arms flew around themself as if they were trying to both comfort and protect themself from the question. ***"It was my choice. Do not pry."***

I frowned. I wouldn't push the very clear boundary, but I wasn't going to let it lie there, either. I thought to myself, Acanthus, how can you think so little of yourself?

With all of the self-deprecation I'd been hearing recently, I needed them to know how much they mattered. "You won't believe me when I say this, but you are worthy of love, respect, and companionship, Acanthus."

They stared, and I wondered if I was overstepping boundaries. Their throat bobbed as they swallowed. Dropping their arms to their sides and lowering their shoulders, they slid their gaze to the floor and stammered, "Finish your project. It's… It is a lovely night for a walk."

I turned back to the door, testing its swing. With the jamb realigned, it shut easily. I turned back to Acanthus, smiling. "Lead the way."

Acanthus

I don't know how Cypress does it. The conversation was overstepping, but it made me blush and second guess all of the truths I had learned about myself. *He's infuriating, or. No. That wasn't the word I meant. Exasperating.*

Lemon Balm

Making my way out into the night air, I took in a long, calming breath. It was cool for the time of year, and a gentle breeze rustled through the trees. The stars shone brightly, and there wasn't a hint of a cloud in the sky. Cypress stepped next to me, their presence protective and warm. Without thinking, I reached for their hand as we slowly walked down the stairs, towards the path into some of the thicker spans of woods. There was an easy silence between us. It was calm enough, but there were small flits of restlessness coming from my right. "Is everything alright, Pup?"

The moon was a sliver of a crescent, painting the trees and earth with an ethereal, silvery, dreamlike hue. They pulled their hand from mine. A moment later, he was a Wolf beside me, their clothes sloppily thrown onto his back. *Well, that's one way to avoid talking to me.*

I focused on the balmy breeze, the warmth in a sharp contrast to the coldness of my skin. I remembered when these woods were devoid of civilization; an endless sea of trees and animals. Now, I could walk down the driveway and take a right, and be at a gas station in five minutes. How quickly things change. Cypress' quiet voice broke into my thoughts. ***"It's nice, tonight."***

I smiled. The crickets were playing their song around us, and fireflies darted in and out of the leaves of the underbrush. We followed the path down a small hill, the croaking of frogs joining the chorus of the night. The soft whispering of a flowing creek came from somewhere nearby, and the scent of wet wood and muddy water wafted in the air. I closed my eyes and took a deep, slow inhale. *How peaceful...*

Cypress bumped my leg, and I reached down to pat his head. The soft hoot of an owl came from somewhere in the distance. We followed the turn of the path across the little creek, and made our way around the large, ambling loop. The clicking of Cypress' nails on the occasional stone added to the music of the night, and I relaxed into the easy silence.

The moment was short-lived as another stronger pull of restlessness came from them. They ran ahead of me back towards the direction of the Yellow Rose, alert and staring down the path. My senses sharpened, and I instinctively hunched down into a guarded stance as I shifted my gaze to scan the trees. Seeing nothing, I closed my eyes and pulsed my powers, scanning the outlines of the things around us. This power was not unlike sonar or echolocation. I could see nothing. There were no bodies in the forest. Cypress whimpered. ***"There's danger."***

I frowned, my mind drifting to Nekane and her cronies. *Please don't tell me we led them here...*

This was a massive stronghold for the Night Garden, and I couldn't bear the thought of Azalea in danger because of us. Once again the gnawing teeth of guilt nipped at the bottom of my heart. *I shouldn't be traveling my own Garden paths.*

Now was not the time for emotion. I cleared my throat, and, seeing nothing in the forest, spoke aloud. "Cypress, please tell me what's going on."

They ran back. *"I honestly don't know,"* they whined. After a moment, Cypress lilted their head to the side. *"I can't explain it. I just… Danger. I feel like there's danger."*

My hair stood on end, my heart quickening. If they felt danger, then there was danger. I had learned from our experience at the first church that their instinct was sound. I suppose my anxiety ran true; the things that we had to talk about were starting to catch up to us. Cypress continued, and I knelt beside them as they whined again. *"It makes my hair stand on end, like there are eyes on me. But, it's deeper, and more intense than paranoia. Like thousands of hostile things are flying from the East, and there are glowing targets on our backs. I'm a fucking mess."*

My heart wrenched, and that ever-present guilt pulled me down. I had caused that insecurity, and that was unacceptable. *How do I always handle things in such damaging ways?*

"Cypress," I murmured gently, "You aren't a mess. You are likely sensing the Hunters and Nekane's Pack. And we have lingered too long. I do not think that they can track us here to Azalea's, but if I had to guess, they are probably at the motel that you first brought us to. We need to leave tonight."

"But…" A flash of Azalea's kind face came into my mind as their voice trailed off, and I nodded. Cypress asked, *"We didn't put her in danger, did we? Will she be okay?"*

Technically, we hadn't. Azalea lived in danger every day, but I wasn't about to say that aloud to Cypress. "I believe we haven't yet, we've been careful. But, if we linger much longer, we put her in danger. And I cannot live with that. It is always hard for me to leave here, but we need to."

Cypress whimpered, and I opened my arms to wrap him into a tight embrace. "I know."

His wet nose nuzzled my shoulder and I tousled the hair on the back of their neck. He pulled back, staring at me. *"Should we go now then? I know you keep worrying about the car being track-able. I could run, and you could fly. We could go."*

"No. Azalea deserves a proper goodbye, and she also deserves a warning. If the Wolves are coming this way, then she needs to prepare. If we aren't bringing the car, we cannot leave it here. Azalea is a powerful Witch, but anyone can be caught unprepared, and I will not endanger her further."

Lemon Balm

I'd wanted to talk to Azalea about potentially helping with the Garden. Perhaps we should stay, and help if Nekane *did* show up. But, then again, Cypress was hardly good in a fight. And, I was the whole problem, wasn't I? If they found no traces of me here, then she would be safe. I cleared my throat, trying to steer the conversation somewhere lighter. "Besides, she went through all that trouble to make sure we had clothes and necessities. I don't want to leave our new things behind."

Anxious flashes of past attacks on Witches played just behind my eyes, and I shuddered, thinking of Hunters dragging my sweet friend to a pyre. I would move heavens and earth to prevent that from happening; if I could do anything to erase any trace of us being here, I would. These were skills I would've possessed a century ago, but with the dawning of technology, I didn't know how to, anymore. She'd be able to help with that, at least.

But, it would have been nice to hold on to the peace we had found here. Our walk in the woods was now sufficiently ruined by reality knocking on our proverbial door. I shrank away from Cypress and stood, holding myself and slouching. The air was now suddenly too warm, or I, too cold. "Well, we should go inside."

Cypress turned and darted back up the path, and I followed not far behind. It took all of five minutes to make it back to the porch. Since we were abandoning the car and Cypress wanted to remain a Wolf, I would take care of packing the items that we had. There wasn't much, but it had been custom to make care bags for Night Garden travelers since its inception, filled with various things that people would need for their journey. Many of the people traveling the paths came with nothing, and Azalea liked to send them off with more than what they came with. The packs were essentials; Cypress and I were just lucky enough to have extra clothes provided.

Cypress really hated the thought of saying goodbye to their Golf. *"This car got me through high school,"* they grumbled, *"It survived my mother. I don't want to leave it."*

They didn't say anything about it, but I think the car was also the last thing they owned that symbolized their human life. But, anywhere it was seen became a giant target. Cypress left me alone to speak to Azalea, opting instead to watch the woods from the backseat of the car.

Saying goodbye to her proved to be just as hard as we had anticipated. I found it hard to launch directly into the conversation, and so I sat across from her in the lobby, watching her knit as I drummed my fingers on the arm of the chair I was in. She finished two rows before she spoke to me. "I know that look, Acanthus, and it generally brings bad news."

I blinked and licked my lips. She always could read me like an open book. "My dear," I paused. "I wanted to speak to you about potentially rejoining the Garden, but I'm afraid my time here has come to an end. Cypress senses danger, and I know when Nekane sees the car in the driveway, it will launch an attack. I cannot put you, or the paths, at risk."

Her warm, inviting face crumpled, mouth in a frown as her eyes went to the floor. "I see."

"I am sorry," I murmured, leaning forward in my chair. "I wished for a few more days, to come up with logistics. I wanted to help with the paths."

She shook her head, setting her needles aside. "It was bound to happen, Lord Acanthus. You had a different end destination, yes?"

She stood, not waiting for an answer as she tilted her head towards the stairs. "Shall I help you pack?"

I nodded, and we made our way up the ornate mahogany stairs. We started in Cypress' room, packing his clothes. Azalea fished a duffel bag out of the bottom drawer, rolling a pair of pants, socks, underpants, and a shirt together into a tighter coil. "What is your plan when you leave?"

I looked down at my hands as I fidgeted with Cypress' pack. There was a hiking backpack each; Cypress' was black with blue trim, and mine was black with red. They'd already been partially filled with the standard self-care items such as brushes, deodorant, and dental care, a salve jar, and a first aid kit in case of any injuries. Cypress had a bottle of water, some jerky, nuts, and seeds in his pack. I had a lunch bag in the fridge waiting for me, filled with four blood bags and an ice pack.

I tilted my head vaguely towards the West. "I'm nervous about leaving the state, because Cypress used his true name at a motel we recovered at. No aliases. It means that Nekane knows we must not be far, and I'm terrified she will track us here. The radio and television have bulletins in the news about Cypress and I. They were looking for us in New York, but now it seems as if they've moved on to the entire Tri-State area. Moving is going to be a challenge."

I must've looked like I had the weight of the world on my shoulders, because she paused in her packing and leaned against the dresser. "It's going to be alright. I do not think you've endangered the Night Garden, me, or yourselves, by coming here. And you are careful enough to travel without getting caught."

I shrugged, unconvinced. The quiet between us lingered, thick and burdensome, for far longer than I would have liked. She went back to packing, and I lifted my fingers, twitching them to beckon the clothes from my room. She rolled outfits into sets, and I floated two from her pile over to me and stuffed them into the top of Cypress' bag. As I switched to my bag, I was the one to break the heavy quiet. "I never once thought I'd have to travel my own garden paths, Azalea."

Lemon Balm

"They are here for any supernatural in need, right? You are supernatural, and you are in need. If it soothes you, you can think of them as my paths, instead of yours."

I paused in my packing, giving her a grateful look. She straightened and smoothed her skirts. This woman was the epitome of strength and grace. She cleared her throat, narrowing her eyes as she crossed her arms. "I will not have you self-destructing under my roof. You entrusted me to bring people to safety centuries ago, and wholeheartedly transferred the responsibility to me when you no longer felt you could manage it. Despite your feelings on the matter, I still look at you the same way I always have."

I swallowed past a lump that had formed. I don't deserve such kindnesses.

She reached for some of the clothes that had been bought for me, and started to roll them together. "I implore you to trust your brilliant strategic mind and intuition. Danger is breathing on our necks every day. Just like every other visit to my home, you have been careful. And, just like I told you at the beginning of the 20th century when you handed me the keys to the Garden gates— you know what you are doing. You know you came here without being tracked, and I trust you to leave no traces."

I looked down at the backpack in front of me, frowning. I had been so sloppy. "How can you be certain, Azalea? I haven't done this since the nineteen-tens. There's so much more to keep track of; cellphones, drones, security cameras, tracers, *digital money... Merde.*"

I closed my eyes, tilting my head back and taking a deep breath before letting it out in a frustrated whoosh. I opened my eyes as she grabbed my hands, her warmth and healing energy consoling me further. I swallowed, not quite able to convince myself to meet her eyes. The shame wracked me, and I felt scrubbed raw on the inside as I said, "I nearly died because I went too far into my own head after two weeks of spending time with another soul. I am not thinking clearly. I have not been thinking clearly for a century, and my judgment should be the last thing that you trust. I don't know anything about this century. When I was doing this, it was traveling without lanterns, through the woods, and covering our scent with heady herbs and — I'm out of my depth. My strategies don't work in the modern age. *Gaslight* was still common, for God's sake."

"I know well how quickly you get attached. But your strategies do work," she doubled down. Her eyes took on a compassionate and pitying cast.

I tried to search for more words, but found that I could not locate them. She broke the silence, her voice careful. I hated how everyone was approaching me like I was made of broken glass. "You have suffered for a long time. And I admit to being privy to that, but... I am not, and cannot be the one who fixes that in you." She looked down at our clasped hands, her smile waning to something sadder. "I do not know how to help. You know my door is always open. My ears are always open, as well. You are not so alone that you cannot come to your friends, Acanthus."

Her shoulders dipped with the weight of her emotion. "There is also Corbin, and our friends overseas. They are there for you, should you need it. But, I implore you," she spoke fervently, her eyes meeting mine once more. "Please do not push me away. We are long-time friends, and I'd be devastated to lose you."

Red tinged my vision as my eyes welled up, emotion choking me. I was frozen. Swallowing, I closed my eyes, trying to compose myself. Azalea's hands slipped out of my hold, and she cleared her throat again. "What we know of your departure from New York — you were attacked by Hunters, which means that Nekane is working with mortals. We know that, despite Cypress using his real name at the motel, you were not tracked to the second hotel you went to, which means that they either hadn't found you yet, or have not had time to search if they have found the motel. These are good things."

I sniffled and opened my eyes as she spoke, pulling my hair over my shoulder and beginning to braid it. She had a point. Talking over the strategy was helping to fade the anxiety fluttering in my chest. "You're right. That means that you should be relatively safe. But, the car is a problem, isn't it? Cars weren't common when I was still involved."

"When you're in a better place and can re-join the paths, I'll have much to teach you, Lord Acanthus," she teased.

I laughed softly. "At least someone around here knows how things work."

"So, yes. The car is a problem. If the motel had any cameras, then they can confirm the make and model. The Hunters that attacked you likely know these things already, and I would not be surprised if they wrote notes before launching their attack. We know of Nekane's ties to the hospitals and police force. This means that they could be combing the traffic camera footage for sightings of your car. If you went on any toll roads or through heavily traversed towns, there can be footage of you."

She crossed her arms, leaning against the dresser. "The police force ties are especially troublesome, because we don't know who is in her pocket, and they have the ability to trace your license plate — ah, tracing, that is when they take the license plate numbers, and run it through their computer. It goes through their files at lightning speed to pick up the file with the owner's information."

"It would be registered under Cypress. So, don't get pulled over?"

She laughed. "Don't get pulled over. Avoid drawing attention, go the speed limit, and avoid commonly-traveled roads. Just like how you used to bring people through the untraveled paths in the woods, but with more bells and whistles."

I chewed on my lip. Maybe we could do this without too much trouble. "And if a hit is announced while we're traveling tonight?"

Azalea went back to rolling outfits at the dresser, and I followed her lead, floating two over to me for my bag. As I stuffed the fabric in, she zipped the duffel up and turned to face me again. "If you stay off of the traveled paths, you should be able to make it to your destination without difficulty."

I nodded. "And you will strengthen your wards?"

"I'll bury new protection charms as soon as you leave," she reassured me. "Your last scattered visit, I gave you a cell phone, do you remember?"

My brows furrowed, and muddy, confused flashes of memory began to bubble to the surface — depression, anger, hunger. Azalea's kind face and healing touch. I finally found my voice. "Vaguely," I admitted with a touch of shame. "I wasn't fully within my mind, in those days."

She nodded. "I remember. And I know you do not always have a solid grasp on time. You left the phone in the drawer, saying you couldn't bear such modern technology."

I blushed, crossing my arms. "Well, you know the moods I can fall into."

She laughed, shaking her head. "There have been attacks on members of the Garden who have been caught, Acanthus. We keep burner phones available here for this very reason. Ah, phones that you pay once a month without a contract. Follow me, I will give you one when we are downstairs."

Azalea spoke with an air of authority, and I grabbed the backpacks. She crossed the room to the door, and I followed her out of the hallway and down the narrow stairs. She bustled across the lobby and behind the counter, digging through a drawer. When she found one, she pressed the phone and its charger into my hands. "Call me and I'll come," she said. The thing was a block of a device, all screen and three buttons on the right hand side. She smiled. "It should have a charge, and my number, as well as some other allies'. They should be programmed in it. If you need help with it, then ask Cypress. I will answer at any time of night or day. Do not be afraid to reach for me. I am your friend."

She had me so fully overwhelmed that I once again lost my words. My body tingled, and I was detached from myself as I slipped the phone into the bag and nodded. She seemed pleased with that. With the packing done, the time came to leave.

"Oh," Azalea gasped, and hurried to the kitchen. She returned and pressed the lunch bag, as well as a canvas tote housing some blood bags into my hands. "Just in case. If you get stuck, this should be more than enough blood for you. The tote has more ice packs and a thermal blanket, so they'll last far longer than the lunch bag."

I smiled and pulled her into a hug. "Thank you, Azalea. For everything."

A vampire guest with dark eyes and a careful bob haircut was watching us from the kitchen doorway. After a lengthy goodbye and promises to return to Azalea when things were safer, Cypress took off into the woods. Azalea had given me another tight hug. "Promise me you'll be safe."

"Of course I sh—"

"No, Acanthus. Promise."

Her voice was firm and sharp, and so unlike her that it made me hesitate. She must have been scared for us, to speak that way. I swallowed, then answered, "yes, I promise."

She gave a wide smile, but something sharp and painful lurked just behind it. "I promise to ward the Yellow Rose thoroughly, as well."

With that, we said one final farewell, and I slid into the car before I could change my mind and stay. I would be able to fly faster than the car could go, and faster than Cypress could run since I could go as the crow flies. Cypress fought me. *"Do you even know how to drive, Acanthus?"*

"I can figure it out," I shrugged.

"No, you cannot just, 'figure it out'! Come on, man, that's ridiculous. Let me drive."

"You didn't even want to shift, Cypress. It makes no sense for us both to drive away from our destination only for me to carry both of our packs and you across the sky."

Cypress huffed through his nose, giving a little growl from the backseat. "Well," I said, aloof. "If it bothers you so much, show me how. You can sit in my head the whole time, and give me directions."

Cypress didn't seem to like the idea, but moved to jump out of the car and push the door shut with his shoulder. *"Fine. But I don't like this."*

That Time We Ditched The Car

Acanthus

I was tired of being stuck in the currents instead of actively a part of our survival. I found myself pushing ninety on the freeway at midnight, in the opposite direction of what would be our new home and back towards the border of New Jersey. I was far more confident behind the wheel once I learned the basic controls. By the time I was out of the little town and on the highway, I'd been able to pilot the machine fine. They were simple, and it wouldn't be hard to carry out the plan we had come up with. *"Jesus, Acanthus, slow down,"* Cypress scolded me.

"The quicker I get this done, the sooner I can get away and meet you at the new church, right? Besides, the night is not infinite. I need to be sure I don't wind up in the same situation as New York."

Cypress didn't answer, but their discomfort, worry, and frustration were heavy in my mind. The plan was to push the Golf as close to New York as I could until it ran out of gas, and abandon it somewhere that seemed like an accident. Cypress didn't like my plan at all, and had all but screamed danger in my direction when I proposed it. But, they had done enough for me at their own expense. This was largely my fight that they had been drawn into. *I have teeth, too.*

The car stalled around the border of Pennsylvania and New Jersey, and I pushed it down a hill and partially into a river. Bags in hand, I checked the perimeter to make sure no one could see me. I'm certain I looked like a pack mule. I took the tote bag and threaded it through the lunch bag handle, then tied it around the duffel bag strap. Then, I took the duffel and threaded it through one of the arm pads on both backpacks. I finally put my arms through the backpacks. It was unwieldy and annoying to carry, but at least nothing would fall as I flew. Satisfied, I rose into the air and flew as fast as my powers could take me.

The flight was far faster than the drive; where the drive took nearly four hours, the flight was only about one. The sky had been lightening at a rapid rate, and when I saw the burgundy shingles of the boxy building I breathed, "Thank the Gods. Just in time."

I touched down on the old wraparound porch just before dawn. The white vinyl siding was starting to glow gold in the rising sun. Cypress was yet to be seen, and I hurried to grab the spare key from beneath the windowsill. Opening the plain white-washed doors, I plopped the bags down on the inside to the left of the door. To the right of the door, there was a small side room that housed the furnace and heater. I deliberated for a moment, before I went in and started both. *These should make the building comfortable by the time Cypress gets here.*

Three things stood between me and rest. The first were the blood bags; I used my powers to float them into the fridge as I worked on the second. Digging through the red and black bag, I emerged triumphant with the cell phone and turned it on for the first time. The screen blazed to life, and I squinted my eyes. *Christ alive, these modern lights…*

The little battery symbol was half-full, and it informed me that there was 46% left. Not bad, for a phone kept in a drawer. I sat on the couch and touched the screen. To my surprise, it reacted, giving me an animation that showed a new slide at the bottom. I swiped my finger up the glass. The screen switched from the lock screen to a lovely wallpaper of a yellow azalea flower. I smiled, reading the text beneath each icon. *Texts. Internet. Contacts.* The contacts opened as I poked the icon, and I scrolled through. Clicking Azalea's name, it opened a card with a phone number and icons. One icon looked like a receiver. That must be to call.

The next icon was one I didn't recognize. It looked like a bubble, with a tail at the bottom. I tilted my head and touched the picture. Another screen opened, with a spot to type. *Fascinating. Like a real-time letter.*

I poked out a message, and clicked the little paper airplane symbol to send it. *Made it to the shed. Any dogwoods?*

After a few moments, an ellipses popped up, animating. I suppose that meant she was typing. *Red and blue,* was the response. I frowned at the screen, my stomach dropping. Police were at her door. Did we linger too long again? Maybe we got caught on the traffic cameras she mentioned. The ellipses popped up again, and I anxiously watched the dots rotate. *No pesticides. Wagon was found this morning. The labels are loud and clear. Zone 6 seems to be safe. Dogwoods are threatening the roses in zone 5.*

No pesticides; they weren't pursuing us tonight. But, they'd found the car, and there was a bulletin out, likely on the radio and news already. The zones were a clear nod to the portions of the Night Garden; we referred to it as if we were speaking about the growing zones, to keep our code on theme. The wolves were still looking for me in New York, New Jersey, and Eastern Pennsylvania. Western Pennsylvania and Ohio still seemed clear, for now.

I should ask her if there were any guards left near her. *No gargoyles in the Yellow Rose's gardens?*

No. Get some rest.

You as well. Thank you.

Satisfied, I lay back on the couch and floated the phone and charger to the wall, plugging it in. Azalea was safe for now, and so were we. My last order of business was to find my Wolf companion. Closing my eyes, I reached out to Cypress.

Cypress

I ran until my legs were tired. I hated cardio as a human and often complained about it. Now, as a wolf, I craved the burn in my legs and the wind through my fur. Pennsylvania is large swaths of protected forests broken up by small towns, so most of the run was through the forest. Based on the images in my head and Acanthus' careful direction, I was about an hour out from the church. I slowed as a lake came into view and paused at the edge to lap up some water. A tingle in my mind led to a small curious whisper. *"Where are you?"*

The familiar voice released the tension in my shoulders. I'd been worried about them the whole run. *"Oh, good. You're safe."*

I sent back images. This beautiful lake, the wonderful wooded area around me, and my face reflected back to me in the water. I could communicate with words, but how could words describe this kind of beauty? A warm understanding flowed between us. One last drink, and I took off running; pushing myself even faster.

I lifted a paw and placed it on the whitewashed door, whining. The door creaked open on its own, and I stepped in, swinging my head as I looked around. There was a large inviting living room area painted a deep plum, with two plush black wing-back chairs, and a matching love seat and couch. The couch was angled with its back to the kitchen, a small table butted up against the back with trinkets and a cup of writing utensils on top of the mahogany polished wood. The room was large enough to house several people comfortably, and I could already see a few cozy spots that I'd easily be able to relax in. A set of stairs led up to the second floor. Acanthus was laying on the couch, a blanket draped across them, and I smiled when I saw them. *"Hey."*

Acanthus' beautiful hazel eyes flipped open. "Hey."

They stretched with a soft hum, then sat up, the door swinging shut. A small part of me wondered how long they'd been sitting there as I went to my over-the-shoulder bag. I pushed my head through the strap and wore the bag as a collar, walking into the tiny room off to the side. It was more of a walk-in closet, cut in beneath the set of stairs (and kind of a useless addition, honestly, if it hadn't been holding the water heater). Pushing the door shut with my nose, dropped the bag and shifted. I reached into it, putting on a hoodie and sweatpants Acanthus had packed for me. Satisfied, I walked back out. "Okay. I'm human again."

"I see that. You know, you should really stop tearing your clothes every time you shift."

I hadn't torn my clothes this time, but I leaned into the banter, grateful for the levity. "I'll let you know as soon as I stop running into situations where I have to tear my clothes."

"Okay, Pup," they huffed, "Don't be petulant."

I didn't answer, and we fell into a short silence as I sat in one of the wing-back chairs. "Should we start with tea? Turning up the heater?"

A smile stretched across their beautiful face. "I think tea is a fine place to start. Take some time to look around while the water is boiling."

I hopped out of the chair with a small groan before heading towards the kitchen, with Acanthus following behind. It was large and had nicer amenities than the last; a gas range and modern appliances that looked to be relatively recent. Acanthus busied themself by putting the kettle on the stove as I looked around. The room started at an indent that the small walk-in room created, open-floor and completely attached to the living room. It had a rectangular island in the middle with four stools at it, two on either long side.

This church was bigger than the last, but not by much. The general lack of dust and debris in the area told me that it was regularly up-kept, but I had no idea by who or how frequently. *Maybe Acanthus has friends who care for their properties? I wonder how this whole Night Garden thing works.*

I tried to put these thoughts into words as I explored. The Night Garden. I still knew almost nothing about it, even after spending a few days at what was supposedly the hub. I knew there were a ton of Witches involved. I knew that Acanthus had started it, and was no longer running it. I knew Azalea ran it now, but I had no idea what that meant or how relevant it was. Nekane had Hunters, but just how many Hunters existed? As far as I could tell, they were human, and most humans had no idea any of this existed.

I wished I could have Azalea as a part of this conversation. She likely knew more than Acanthus, if she was running the Night Garden. How many people were fleeing from their covens or Packs? And, where were all of the vampires? I'd only seen one other vampire, outside of Acanthus. Nekane's camp talked about how dangerous they were, and how they were the enemy, but I just couldn't see it. *Why were they so scared of something that barely existed?*

The building looked nothing like a church; it must have been remodeled extensively. The first floor restroom had a claw-foot tub and a vanity sink with a big mirror cabinet on the wall. I grabbed the bags that Acanthus dropped and climbed the stairs at the side of the kitchen and front of the living room. They led to a bigger loft than the last one, with a room on either side. I didn't pop in to look at the rooms, unsure which would be mine.

There was another large rose window here; the only hint that this building used to be a church. The window looked out to a cobblestone courtyard below. The courtyard was surrounded by patches of overgrown grass. The cobblestone had inlays that looked like bats and moons, leading towards the edge of the forest. *This is the third time I've seen that pattern now. That must be to show that this is part of the Paths.*

Two more chairs sat in front of the window, candles scattered all around. The small bathroom upstairs had a walk-in shower. By the time I found the loft bathroom, the kettle was screaming, and by the time I joined Acanthus in the kitchen, they had the tea fixed in two identical navy mugs. They had the curtains drawn carefully over the windows, and they were leaning against the counter, carefully out of the square of sunlight filtering in. "The stove is so easy to use! I was lost for a moment, I must admit. So many dials. I'm starting to see the merit of upgrading appliances."

I laughed as they grabbed one of the piping hot beverages from the counter and handed it to me. I cupped it in my hands as I slid into one of the island's stools. "Hey, Acanthus, this place is in the middle of nowhere," I said. I hadn't seen a town for a lot of my run. "Was this ever really a church?"

Maybe they were just houses, built in the style of churches. That was confusing, but it made more sense than having a church hours away from any town. Acanthus laughed, their cheeks tinging pink. "Caught, red handed, I suppose. This one was built for the Night Garden. Some are churches that have been refurbished, and some are in areas where the town died around them. The Garden has added hideouts since I stepped away from it, but most of the original routes have churches, or buildings fashioned to look like churches."

"Why is that?"

They paused, chewing on their bottom lip. "Well, I was a priest in a former lifetime. And, I suppose that I've always seen churches as a haven. When you have nowhere else to go, where do you turn?"

That wasn't the way that I thought, but I could understand and appreciate the sentiment. "I guess so."

The heat kicked on, and I blinked. It's hard to tell when you're at ground level, but we must have gone higher into the mountains, towards the peak. It was colder than it should be for this time of year, and definitely colder than it was at Azalea's Bed and Breakfast. But, once the sun was up, I was sure it'd feel more like the end of July. I watched the steam rise from the mug and sighed. Acanthus' whispery voice stole my attention from it as they pushed off of the counter and slid into the stool next to me. "What do you want to talk about, Cypress?" They bumped me with their shoulder in a playful, fluid motion.

My insides twisted. I couldn't ask what I didn't know, but there was so much. So far, all of the knowledge I had about the World of Shadows came from the half-answers Acanthus provided during our week together, and the perspective of Nekane's camp. I was missing pieces, and I didn't care for it. I raised an eyebrow, smirking. "There's a lot less dust in this church."

Acanthus laughed. "I pay people to upkeep my houses when I'm away. Mostly Witches, and all people we have helped. When people use the Paths, they're leaving everything behind and often travel with nothing. It's another way to help, and one of the only things I kept up once I gave Azalea control. I pay for the entire Garden's upkeep."

My friend lived in a crumbling church in the middle of nowhere, and they had enough money to bankroll an entire underground? That was hard for me to believe. They continued, flipping some of their hair out of their face. "Once a week, they clean the empty hideouts. It's never guaranteed that one will be empty, so Azalea keeps track of who is being paid, where. Luckily, this one happened to be unoccupied. Azalea called ahead to Simone and told her that I was on my way."

All of the questions that had popped into my head as I was exploring withered and died, replaced by the thoughts that had been bothering me since I came to rescue Acanthus. I tore my gaze from the mug, looking at them. "Did you…" I trailed off, chewing at my lip. It had been a restful day after the coven removed my shift lock, and I didn't want to break the peace, but I had to know. "Did you know, before handing me off to Nekane?"

Acanthus blinked at me, confused, and I took a deep breath, elaborating a bit clearer. "Did you know that we had a bond?"

The silence was deafening as the last syllable of my question died. Their eyes widened, and their face paled. "Do you think I'd have gone through with it if I did?"

I immediately reached for the hand that wasn't holding a mug. There was so much I didn't know, and they clearly had no trust when it came to finding out my intentions. I tried very hard not to take their distrust personally. The heavy fact between us was that they knew far more about me than I knew about them. And, what I didn't know was clearly negative. "Don't assume I'm asking for nefarious reasons, Acanthus. I don't know what you know, knew, or otherwise."

"Please don't think I'm jumping to conclusions," they said. Their shoulders hiked up to their ears. "I just hate to think that crossed your mind," they continued, their shoulders dropping from anxious to defeated and voice just above a whisper. "No, I had no idea until you said it to me. I missed you terribly, but I had assumed —"

They cut themself off, shaking their head. That took me by surprise. How couldn't they know? I had always thought of them when I was in Nekane's camp. The moment with the keys had proven for me with startling clarity that I wasn't just homesick. Looking down at my own mug, my cheeks flushed. "I was seeing you. The whole time I spent with the pack, I always came back to you in my mind as a safe place. Did you see me at all?"

That Time We Bared
Our Hearts

Acanthus

This is going to be a more difficult conversation than I anticipated. I took a deep breath, but I refused to crawl inside my own head like I usually did when they were direct. I wanted nothing more than to have a companion to speak to for centuries; and here I was, sitting with a Werewolf that absolutely refused to leave my side. I had spent so much time being afraid and letting myself be alone; loss after loss and betrayal after betrayal. Wouldn't it be wonderful if I could connect with another? I needed to let my friends in. I needed to allow *Cypress* in. *No more of this,* I resolved. *New rule, Acanthus: let your friends in. Accept help.*

The conversation with Azalea rattled me more than I'd realized. Most of the Witches were companions, but in such a way that left me feeling awkward and separate from them, like a boss speaking to an employee. Perhaps it was because of their utter refusal to treat me as an equal; I hated that divide more than anything. They'd raze cities if I'd only ask, and I already asked them for so much. I loved them all, but the friendship was weighted in such ways that made me uncomfortable with being myself, especially with the Night Garden being what it was.

None of that matters right now. I had asked for this conversation and Cypress did not deserve my coldness. "I did see you, but it's complicated. Bits, and pieces. Flashes. But..."

Another pause. An ocean of conflicting emotions ran through my head, both memories of the time and current. I'd been so certain in my convictions that they were happy to leave; that they'd never look back.

I'd expected it, even, and it scared me how quickly I had fallen into friendship with this charming, intense person. I swallowed, clearing my throat. "Never anything definitive. And, please, you must know, there are things about my past that make me doubt—"

I cut myself off, closing my eyes. A flash of François' face danced there, smiling cruelly. *Too much, Acanthus.*

"Let's just say I was thinking the wrong things. I mistook what I was seeing as remembering you, and missing you."

I tilted my head to lean it on their shoulder. *I've never been so forward in affection with a friendship. What's gotten into me? Is it that they came back? What is this?*

My thoughts were carefully locked behind my own mental door as an easy silence passed between us. The tension eased from my shoulders at the smells of campfire smoke and whiskey. My eyes slipped shut as I listened to their soft breathing. Cypress' voice broke the silence. "Had I known my leaving would hurt you, I wouldn't have left, Acanthus. I was in hell. But I didn't want to displace you. I felt like an intruder, and I didn't think there was any way you'd let me come back."

I was in hell. The words echoed in my mind, and I stared at our clasped hands. The guilt came back full force, those sharp teeth gnawing at my heart. We really weren't very different. "And I thought you'd be happier without me, among people you could relate to."

Being this direct and vulnerable was so difficult. Deep inhale. Hold. Exhale slowly. I focused on the patterns of my breathing to keep the panic from rising in my chest.

Cypress pulled away, turning to stare at me. "What? People I could relate to, because they're Wolves? Acanthus, we were starting to become friends. I was closer to you than I ever got to any of them, and I spent triple the amount of time there."

"I…" I trailed off as my voice cracked. Clearing my throat, I tried again. Deep breath. Hold. Slow exhale. "I thought I was doing the right thing."

Cypress closed their eyes, and memories of their time with Nekane's pack began to flood my mind as I watched, horrified and helpless to stop it. All of the altercations with Junior and other members of the pack blurred and blended into each other. The agony, the burn and the exhaustion in their muscles, and every tear and cut from teeth and claw. *"No, no, no… Oh, Cypress…"*

The tears were welling up. I braved a look at them, as much sincerity and desperation in my voice as it could hold. Their eyes opened, and I met the steel and storm directly. Now was not the time for deflection. "I need you to know — I never meant you any h-harm, and I am *horrified* by your experiences. I was misguided, I tend to think people want nothing to do with me. I didn't want you to leave by the time you did. But, I spent sixty *years* in the dark, with no idea of what I was —"

I cut myself off. *"Painful,"* I explained, hoping it'd be enough.I swallowed and shook my head. "I thought..."

I looked down at my trembling hands. *What am I trying to say? I suppose we are kindred spirits, in the terms of our fledgling isolation.*

"I thought if I could give you a piece of who you were, that it would help in ways I could not."

I was hyper aware of their hand on mine, and I tensed, pulling it away and holding my mug. I realized I was holding my breath, and let it out with a soft whoosh, and with it, my shoulders sagged. I kept my gaze on the tip of their nose, not quite able to meet their eyes. Cypress' voice was gentle, as if they were soothing a child. "Acanthus. I understand that now. I appreciate you trying to help me along. I imagine that's not what you expected when I walked off with Nekane."

I shook my head, silent. I wasn't trying to pull away, but my voice left me. We were quiet for a while, and I twisted the mug in my hands. "I didn't think she would hurt you. She's always despised me, but she even gave you her son's silver. Nekane's practices are repulsive, but I thought she'd look after you as one of her own. I didn't think that she would treat a new member of her pack so cruelly. As much as she hates me, I wouldn't consider her a monster when I reached out to her. And I thought that I was extending an olive branch, helping you and healing that wound at the same time. We had a treaty, and I had tenuous trust."

Regret twisted my heart, and Cypress smirked, though their eyes didn't quite match the mischief as they shifted the topic. "By the time they came after you, I had eight charms on my necklace, plus the wolf head *and* the shift lock."

"*Eight* charms? *And* the shift lock? Cypress, they were probably terrified of you. That's like running with a thousand pounds strapped to your back. " I laughed, shaking my head. "I should have expected nothing less, though."

A genuinely pleased grin replaced the smugness on their face. It was almost like we were turning it into a game of twenty questions, even if the questions were hard to answer. This playful back and forth was just competitive enough to keep me open. I blurted, "When you came back, what made you risk so much for me?"

Cypress stared at me as if it was obvious. "Because, you're my Pack, Acanthus."

Cypress

Acanthus' hair gleamed in the light filtering through the curtain. They were no longer looking at me. Their bright hazel eyes were turned towards the kitchen wall as I admired the delicate curves of their strong features. Fragile strength… Acanthus is a walking paradox, but somehow they make it work. How do they always have me so awestruck? "I don't know, aside from that. At the time, there was something driving me back to you."

The strange compulsion to be around them freaked me out sometimes, even now. *This is definitely more than what Nekane described the Pack bond to be. I'm still not sure if they bewitched me somehow. Or, maybe it has something to do with their mesmer…*

I was comfortable around them, and I wanted my actions to reflect that. The memory of the first time I touched them flashed behind my eyes; my reaction hurt them, and I never wanted to be the cause of that again. "Even before I knew they wanted to kill you, there was this pit in my stomach. This," I paused, trying to find the word that fit. It was like a numb, hollow void. "This emptiness I felt. And the static? It was loud enough to drive anyone insane. The static isn't so loud when you're around. It only gets bad when you shut me out, like that night we fought at Azalea's."

I swallowed, my cheeks burning in shame. Their spiral that night was my fault, and I still haven't forgiven myself for it. "But now? There's very little I wouldn't do for you, Acanthus. I'd move mountains and stop rivers, if you asked."

I took another sip from my cup. Acanthus was blushing, almost shy as they gently chided me. "You're starting to sound like romantic poetry, Cypress."

I laughed. "I was never one for Keats, or the Brontë's."

Acanthus' eyebrows shot up, a genuine grin spreading across their face. "You are a fan of poetry?"

"Of course. A person should be well rounded to find themselves a *suitable* lady."

Acanthus laughed now, and my confidence soared. I looked down at the scars on my arms, and my stomach flipped. They were a subtle white and slightly recessed in my skin; a jagged asymmetrical pattern, like thorns across my arms. I shifted to roll down the sleeves of my hoodie. "I think romantic poetry is off the table."

Acanthus scoffed. Their brilliant eyes were fixed on me as they spoke defiantly, "Poetry should not be something to indulge in just to find a mate. Besides, anyone skipping over you is missing out on the light of their lives."

Now it was my turn to blush. If I didn't know any better, I'd say this beautiful being was flirting with me. "Why do you say stuff like that?"

They shrugged. "I've no reason to lie."

"You are a mystery to me, Acanthus." I took a deep breath in, trying to slow my pounding heart, and let out a long exhale. We'd gone on a tangent. "So, Nekane is out to kill us," I said, my voice far more confident and aloof than I felt. "She may not be able to follow us, but she has a lot of Hunters. On top of being an outsider, I outsmarted the best and brightest of her pack." I trailed off. "That automatically made me a target. But, why were you?"

Acanthus drew up their shoulders, and they started working at their lip with their teeth. Each word fell from them slowly, a hesitant drip. "Nekane and I have blood on our hands from the past wars. Tensions were high between everyone those days. Humans were aware of us in some capacities back then, mostly as myths and rumors. The World of Shadows had been in hiding since I was a fledgling, but history sometimes takes centuries to forget. Sometime in the late seventeen hundreds, a vampire crawled out of the woodwork and started to attack Witches and Wolves. He was active for fifty years in the states, tugging the strings and starting that war. It was in part to break what I was building, and in part to sow the chaos."

Acanthus sighed, picking at their fingernails. "He was my Sire, and I'd thought he was dead. That relationship is more than I'm currently willing to divulge… But, he traced me to America when the whispers began to spread. Corbin, my co-founder, had established safe-houses in Europe for anyone who needed to flee the country. By the time François faded from the picture, the damage was already done. Many Wolves saw us — Vampires — as a prominent threat, Nekane and Bleddyn included. In 1838, Nekane had established her own ancillary Pack beneath Bleddyn's as a new Alpha. She launched an attack on me, hoping to catch me unaware, and I killed her son. I was," they trailed off and closed their eyes, swallowing again before they finished their thought. Their voice was small and full of shame. "Far less pacifistic, a century ago." I didn't like the air of defeat that surrounded them. "Now you think I'm a monster." They looked a thousand years old. "Speak your mind, Cypress. We are not here to wound each other."

"I'm sorry, Acanthus," Acanthus wasn't callous, nor was he stupid. I was a little hurt, knowing their history. "You killed her son and you thought peace was an option? Why did you think sending me to her was a good idea?"

"I can understand why you might think that. I was cruel, but I wasn't sadistic. I was going to leave Mikael alone, until he killed Theophania —

Tempest. My fledgling. She was exceptionally young to her vampirism, and accidentally crossed into the pack's home territory. Mikael was cruel and vindictive. She suffered. He didn't."

Acanthus scowled at their cup, before sliding out of the stool and pouring it into the sink. I cocked my head, asking as gently as I could, "Was she your mate?"

They gasped and started coughing. I patted their back as they spoke between coughs. "Good lord, Pup," They paused for a moment to compose themself. "No. She most certainly was not. I doubt Tempest would've allowed any attempts of the sort anyway. When I turned her, she became my daughter. She was twenty-six in human years, and very, very, gay. She'd suffer no fools, and in her eyes, all men were fools."

They gave me a side eye, as they slid back into the stool. "I adored her. She was only five years past her turning. Barely enough time to experience being a vampire. Her passing devastated me, and then I decided peace wasn't worth it."

Acanthus was trembling as they spoke. What an awful situation; I couldn't imagine being in their shoes. *A life for a life... It didn't bring her back.*

I reached for their hand, steadying it. "Why did you trust Nekane, then?"

Acanthus shrugged. "She's one of the Big Five, and I thought she'd grown to be past it. I didn't expect warmth, but I didn't expect revenge, either. We had a treaty for over a century, and I'd helped her during those years. We'd spilled enough of each others' blood, and I thought the treaty protected us. I should have called off the entire plan when we broke the terms at the bar."

The situation made a lot more sense, at least. I held their hand between both of mine, gently massaging it. When I felt the trembling slow, I finally broke the fragile silence. "Thank you for telling me."

Acanthus

My chest ached. It was hard to look back; losses felt as fresh as the day they happened, if I lingered too long. But, I would not allow myself to dwell. Not tonight. I owed it to Cypress to be present, here and now. "Of course. I asked for this conversation, and I promised you I would not run away."

Cypress didn't answer. There was nothing malicious between us, and there was a comforting pulse that came from them always, keeping me from floating away within my thoughts. In the back of my mind, I was in a garden, lush and surrounded by thick trees. I could almost smell the heady sweetness of fresh rain lingering in my nostrils. I wanted so badly to escape there. *Christ, how do humans navigate today's communication?*

Even with my irritation, I don't think I could lie and say I preferred my solitude anymore, no matter how much I tried to convince myself. "Acanthus?"

"Mmm?" My mind drifted as I turned my head to look at him. Their eyes were downcast, their brow knitted into another worried frown. My stomach dropped. *How does one comfort someone? I'm useless in this department...*

His voice was small, and he reminded me of a lost child. "What about the Hunters?"

The church had protective wards around it, and we'd been careful to throw them off our trail. Still, we would likely have to lay low for a while. I closed my eyes, thinking about how I would soon be back to my irritable starving state. "Vampire guests are rare. In New York, we were established because it was my home, as well as a few other vampires throughout the state at large. But, most of the Vampires have either fled America, or have been hunted and killed. Here, I won't be able to find donors for at least a few months. Azalea gave me enough supplies for about a month with careful rationing. I will have to hunt and live off of the woods until Nekane's search dies down."

"What? Can you even do that? I know we talked about birds, but..."

I snorted. "I'm surprised Nekane didn't verse you in all of the Vampiric weaknesses while you were at her camp. Yes; I can survive off of animals, but I'll fall into irritation quickly. It will only sustain me for so long before it gets..." I trailed off, flashes of kaleidoscopic memories, lengthened fangs and sharpened nails, cloudy in a mist of blood in my mind. I swallowed, finishing my thought as I banished the images. "Problematic."

If they had seen the flashes of memory, they didn't react. Instead, Cypress frowned. "Well," he replied with stubborn conviction, "I will do anything I can to help prevent you from getting to the point of starving. You have my word, Acanthus."

The next few months would not be pleasant for me. I appreciated the conviction, but it would be risky to stay here. It would also be risky to leave. We were playing a centuries long game of chess, and I'd been in check for a long time. *I need to see what the new bulletin Azalea mentioned says.*

Trying to find a strategy, any way to keep going, was exhausting. What's worse is, I think Nekane knew this. The timing of her Hunters attacking was not random. Cypress' fight with Junior had given her a reason, but she could have attacked at any time after that. I had shown too much of myself at the handover; she knew I cared for Cypress, and perhaps that is why things turned out the way that they did. My softness was a curse. As it stood, Nekane did not yet know of our whereabouts, but she'd easily be able to find us once we made ourselves known in nearby cities.

My loose plan was to wait until we could find a quiet moment to leave Pennsylvania and head to one of the largest safe houses of the Night Garden. We would end our journey at a monastery in Wisconsin, filled with a large coven of Witches that were loyal both to the cause of the operation and to me. Nekane's bulletin would be on the local news and radio. This did two tactical things for her; it kept her ancillary packs aware and put humans on alert. If luck was on her side, mortals would report us if we were seen.

This was a common tactic for the Big Five to root out threats. If we took a chance to leave, we'd be able to go to the next temporary stop in Ohio, but without knowing her radius, I couldn't be sure. We were somewhere outside of Grove City, and heading any further west put us into heavier population density.

Part of the reason I reached out to Nekane in regards to Cypress was that it was written into the code of the World of Shadows to notify the Big Five when lost Wolves were found, and it was within the bounds of my treaty. I would have preferred to reach out to Austin. Alpha of a smaller Pack in the area, but I didn't know how to contact him, thanks to keeping the Night Garden at arms' length. And, if Nekane had found out, it would have annulled the treaty. *A fat lot of good my caution did, in the end...*

Even here, in the Western areas of Pennsylvania, we were still in Nekane's territory. She would not sit idly by in New York if we left any shred of evidence that we were still within her reach. It was a long shot, but if we were to make it to Wisconsin, we'd officially be in the far end of my various land pieces, and within the realm of a different Wolf leader.

The Big Five leader of the Midwest Territory was Coryn Tanner, and a staunch ally to the Night Garden. I would've preferred to reach out to her in regards to Cypress, but that also would have annulled my treaty with Nekane. Coryn had helped move many people out of harm's way, and even over the border to Canada if they needed. She may hesitate to openly join a war, but I knew of a few Vampires lingering in Wisconsin that would likely come to our aid. Getting to the monastery meant having new access to resources.

Nekane was cruel and vindictive, and leaned deeply into the discrimination between species; whereas Coryn has long been the Wolf representative for peace within the World of Shadows. Between the Witches of the monastery, the Vampires in the Midwest, and the potential ally-ship that Coryn could offer, we may wind up with a fighting chance. Nekane couldn't freely roam in another Wolf's territory. She'd already sent the police to Azalea's door. Maybe the Golf was keeping her busy, but I couldn't be certain. She could just as easily be combing through the state, looking for any sign of us.

There was still the matter of my food supply, as well. I'd spent so long in New York, and there were so few Vampires on this end of Pennsylvania, that supply lines were not set up. The Garden would have to find willing donors, and that took time. I also did not want to put the Witches here in danger by asking for help, but I did not want to fall into a starving state. Before, my starving states had been out of negligence and passive suicidal ideation. Now, in an ironic twist, it would be brought on by necessity of survival.

"We will do what we must," I said after finally tearing myself from my head. I pulled my loose hair over my shoulder and began to braid it. "With any luck, we won't stay here long, but we need to wait out any alerts of our presence. If anything falls through, we can move on from this hideout, but we'll have to travel a long way to safety. I have others that we can flee to that are entirely out of Nekane's jurisdiction. Hopefully, if we *do* have to flee," I tried to lighten the mood, "may it be before it comes to silver bombs and UV beams."

"We'll manage, Acanthus. I can deal with your foul moods, as long as I'm aware of them. I'll do my best to help." Cypress paused. "I have a much better understanding of things now than when I first stumbled into your church."

I stood and offered my hand to him, and he took it. Together, we walked to the couch, and I pulled the blanket around us as we sat down. "Yes. I'll deal with my vampiric equivalent of fast food... I'll be hungry hours later."

He tilted his head curiously. "Couldn't you just bite me?"

"I don't know," I paused my braiding. Perhaps I could, but it would be a risk. "I'm not sure. I have conflicting information on it, and I have never bitten a Werewolf, for fear their blood was toxic to me. It probably shouldn't be risked."

"That sucks," he grumbled. "Could've solved the donor problem then and there."

"You'd do that for me?"

"If I could, sure. But I won't be the reason you get food poisoning," he grinned. "I know I'm all that and a side of fries, but I am part animal. Maybe I'd just be fast food too."

The joke took me aback, and I found myself giggling. "Cypress. Come on, now."

Lemon Balm

They waited until my laughter faded before they spoke, more somber than before. "This is a good time to get to the real beast. Boundaries."

had nearly quipped something about the bag of fries comment (What, full of oil and definitely not good for me?), but then they brought up boundaries. I don't think I had ever once been asked in my (near) thousand years of existence, what my boundaries were. *Is this healthy communication?*

Their voice dropped into a more contemplative tone."I know at the other church, I wasn't allowed in the loft, unless expressly invited. Are there any rules you wish I would follow here? I need you to tell me."

"Well," I hummed, before letting the word trail away and die.

Cypress' eyes were reassuring. *"It's okay, I asked."*

I took a soft inhale, pulling my legs closer and making myself smaller. I was extremely aware of their warmth beneath the blanket. My throat was dry, and clicked uncomfortably as I swallowed. "I would ask you to please not come into my space, in this case my room, without express invitation."

My voice was simultaneously too loud and too soft. *Oh, but what if that's too much?* "This isn't because I do not trust you, Cypress. I'm sure you've noticed, when I am dour, everything feels like an attack. It isn't fair to you."

"No uninvited room time," Cypress replied. "What else you got?"

Oh. That was surprisingly easy. Confusion, and perhaps a bit of satisfaction and pleasure radiated through our link; I couldn't stop that from happening. I blushed, looking off to the side. This is so strange.

Reeling, I cleared my throat, stalling. "For the same reason, I must ask you not to touch me when I am actively panicking, unless you have asked first and I've given you clear permission. I have things in my past that leave me liable to lash out when I am touched, and I don't know or trust myself in those moments."

Cypress gave me a look that I could feel more than see. I would not take that without protest. "Don't pity me, Cypress."

"Pity? Never, Acanthus. I'm sad that someone gave you these feelings. I trust you, but I understand. No touching in those moments."

The sharp sting of tears threatened my eyes, and I blinked them away. My voice was thick and syrupy in my throat as I averted my gaze. "Thank you, Pup."

"Anything else you got for me?"

I nodded, taking a quick inhale. Each accepted term bolstered my confidence. "I need this most of all," I murmured, my voice once again both too soft and too loud. "I need you to talk to me. Like this, if I hurt you, as soon as you are comfortable and able. I have worked very hard to not be one to wound, and I can be very cruel without realizing. I never, ever want to harm you. I couldn't bear it…"

A realization dawned on me, and my jaw dropped with a gasp. "I think," I murmured, tingly feedback buzzing through me. "I think that may be why I spiraled at Azalea's."

I knew they had been hurt, and that I had been the cause. It was odd, realizing why my mood had gone the way that it had. "I apologize."

Cypress shook their head emphatically. "Stop it. I know that I was awful, too. It wasn't just you, Acanthus."

Oh. He dumbfounded me more than I could count tonight. I was lost, but in the best way. *This can't be real.*

I couldn't see how they could be so forgiving, or handle this conversation with such grace. My skin erupted into goosebumps, and some frayed rope broke deep within me. I couldn't help myself, I needed to ground myself in reality. I threw my arms around them, hugged them tightly and buried my head in their neck, surrounding myself in their scent. *"Thank you."*

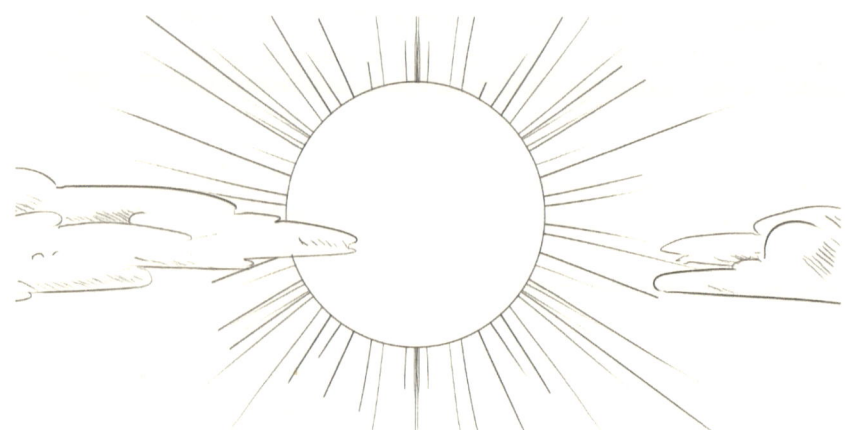

That Time We Shared Nightmares

Cypress

The display of affection and emotion caught me off guard, and I wasn't sure where it had come from. "You're welcome?"

If they picked up on my confusion, they didn't react to it. Instead, they silently asked, *"Tell me your boundaries."*

Something about their reaction told me that they had lost the ability to ask aloud. I shrugged, rubbing their back as I thought about it. I really didn't have many. "I'm a pretty simple guy. I don't have any immediate boundaries. I like my things to stay mine, but I think that was already established with 'ask before entering'." I paused, chewing on my lip. "I have a problem with not being clothed. I was fine before, but ever since the injuries at the motel, I can't stand looking at myself, or others looking at me. I don't like it. I don't care if you are, of course," I backpedaled quickly, flustered. "I just have an issue with myself not being clothed. And I'm sorry if I imposed that on you, without making you aware."

Acanthus' mouth quirked into a small closed smile. Their voice was clear and smooth as they leaned back. "Nudity does not bother me, but I too, am reluctant to be in front of others. I understand, and will be very aware of not looking at you post-shift."

"Thank you Acanthus," I replied. "I appreciate having this conversation." I hugged them a little tighter, before letting go. "I'm hungry. Show me around the place."

"You already showed yourself around the place," they teased.

"I want you to tell me about it," I shrugged as I stood. I wrapped the blanket around their shoulders and held out my hand. They took it and I helped them to their feet.

Acanthus showed me to my room, the one on the left of the rose window. They avoided the colored light beams, wrapped in the blanket. The room was cozy, painted a pretty deep blue with an odd shape. Like a finished attic, the walls on two sides sloped with the slant of the roof. There was a large oak bed, with wispy white lace curtains over a canopy and a comfortable mattress. The bed was pushed to the center of the side wall, and there was a strange outcropping from the far wall, as if the building had been expanded to accommodate for the loft. The second thing I noticed was the amount of blankets in this room — two were folded at the end of the bed, one resting on top of the dresser, and a pile of five or six were in the alcove. I assumed more were piled beneath the bed and in the closet.

I could tell Acanthus was tired; their heavy eyes kept slipping shut. Guilt started to eat at my stomach and I looked towards the bed. It had to be mid-morning, if not, near noon. "I'll be good to go, Acanthus. If you're tired, please don't stay up because of me."

"Thank you, Cypress. Is there anything you need before I —" I grinned at them and they trailed off. "What?"

"You are rambling and distracting," I said, quoting them from earlier.

They muttered dryly, "Point taken. Good morning, Cypress."

"Sleep well, Acanthus."

They turned on their heel, making their way out onto the loft and across to the other room. I wasn't quite ready to sleep yet. Most of my night had been spent running, and I wanted to relax before I passed out. So, I grabbed a book off of the little shelf between the chairs and started reading by the big rose window. The sun was hot through the thick colored panes. I loved it.

The book was *Fairy Tale*, by Stephen King. I wasn't a huge King fan, but I knew his work, so I figured it was a good choice despite the length. I sat in one of the wing-back chairs, cross-legged with the book in my lap. I must have fallen asleep in the loving arms of the sunbeams, because the next thing I knew, I was dreaming.

In my dream, I was in the dark, starving and alone. My heart pounded in my ears, and my eyes pulsed in the low light. Every vein was on fire, and I reached out to claw at the slimy brick in front of me with long, black claws. *A monster, I'd become a monster*, my mind screamed at me. I didn't know how I knew, but I did. Demon was a better word for it. Only, I wasn't alone. There were eyes, gazing at me from across this... *What even is this? Is it a crypt?*

I didn't have much time to question, because with a voice that wasn't my own, I cried out "Lord! Protect me!"

My blood ran cold. I knew the voice well. *Acanthus.*

My eyes snapped open, and the pounding of my heart didn't mix with the gentle warmth of my surroundings. I'd fallen out of the chair, my hip aching from the way I landed. Acanthus' panicked voice cried out, muffled by the wood of the door, and I was on my feet in an instant. *"Acanthus, you're safe, please wake up."*

I didn't have their express permission to enter, so I stood at the door, fighting the urge to throw it open and shake them out of the hell they were living. *"Acanthus. Acanthus, please wake up".*

Acanthus

Raucous, discordant laughter echoed through my ears, nearly drowning out Cypress' words. The nightmare was old, but the terror was the same. It repeated enough for me to know how the script went; almost as comforting as it was horrific. The damp, cold stones scraped against my back as I pressed away from the cruel laughter and intense light. I think this nightmare conflated two situations with my maker, and I didn't care to go back to either one. One was when I'd first met the bastard as a Vampire, and it was blending with the time he imprisoned me.

My breath caught in my throat as a cruel hand jolted out of the darkness and reached for me, and Cypress' voice cut through the horror. Their presence was unusual enough, and threw me off enough to where I was able to find my will to take control through the panic. I woke with a shout, my heart a frantic hummingbird in a cage. It took me a moment before I fully realized where I was, tangled in the covers like a net. *"Non, non, non, s'il te plaît…"*

No matter how much I gasped, I could not find air to fill my lungs. It was still bright outside, the sun pooling into the room through the partially opened curtains. The bed was safely angled out of the dangerous path. When I registered the beam, my heart began to slow. My reason returned, and I soaked in the outlines of my tall dresser and the bookshelf to the right of the bed. *Home, not the crypt,* I reassured myself as I slowly disentangled from the blankets. It was comforting to see the light within reach, despite its promised harm.

I pulled my knees up to my chest, pressing my sweaty forehead into them. The world pitched, and the nausea that stuck in the back of my throat threatened me. I closed my eyes, weakly trying to protect myself from the disorientation and vertigo. *How many times must I torture myself like this?* "Dammit… God *damn* it."

I didn't know how much Cypress had seen, but I knew they had seen it, and the knowledge made me want to disappear. *Weak, pathetic, stupid creature.*

Curled as small as possible, I inhaled through my nose and held it. I didn't want to explain it; *couldn't* explain it. When the air was stale and my lungs felt like bursting, I exhaled, trying to force my tension away. I felt the question emanating before they even had to say anything. "Yes, come in."

The door opened, and I didn't move. I felt the hulking body of my companion sink onto the side of the bed, and I focused on my breathing. Inhale. Hold. Exhale. Inhale. Hold. Exhale. The panic slowly ebbed away with each held breath. Cypress held a hand towards my shoulder, and I felt it hovering, but they didn't touch. "Acanthus?"

I didn't answer right away, my trauma winning at first. I gritted my teeth, angry with myself. *This isn't his fault.*

I invited Cypress into the room, didn't I? There was no reason to be so cold. Despite the fear that kept me curled, I tried to relent, and tipped towards their waiting hand. Permission, granted. They gently rubbed my shoulder as I stared at them with exhausted eyes. "Yes?"

Concern and awkwardness filled his voice as he asked, "Do you… want a hug?"

I nodded, uncurling and moving towards him. Cypress pulled me against their chest and rested their chin on my head. I calmed down to the music of their heartbeat. Their strong arms were a barrier from the horrors of the world, and the tension ebbed from my shoulders. "Your shirt is going to look like a butcher's apron," I muttered despondently.

They laughed. "I don't care, Acanthus."

My heart swelled at the words. They wouldn't let anyone touch me, if it came to that. *I'm so tired,* I thought while drifting off against the steady rise and fall of their chest. Cypress' voice pushed through my daze, soft and uncertain. "Do you want to talk about it?"

I snapped to alert, quiet. Pulling in a deep breath, I held it before sighing it out. Something had shifted in the conversation between us this morning; I guess I trusted him to see the darker parts that I hid. "Do you want the short version or the long one?"

"Whatever you're comfortable with," they replied quietly, loosening their hold as I straightened back up to a sitting position. "I'm here, either way."

I nodded, and images started flowing through our connection with my words. "My Sire," I murmured, before the words caught in my throat. The hummingbird in my chest began fluttering again. Swallowing, I closed my eyes, counting the spaces in between my breaths. I calmed, and tried again.. "My maker was a cruel and unusual Vampire. I had a..."

I faltered again, my fingers flying to my hair. Quietly, I focused on the rhythm of my fingers. Over. Under. Braid. Unbraid. "I had a religious human life that ended in a puddle of blood in front of a gilded effigy of the Lord. I woke up in a crypt adjacent to a torture chamber, in the basement of my church. I didn't know what I was or what had happened. But, I had known that I definitely was considered dead, as I woke up entombed in a raised coffin."

I swallowed past the lump in my throat. "I was dressed in funeral garb, and when I managed to pry the stone top off, I realized I was locked in with the coffins. I was weak, and couldn't bend the steel bars. I didn't know anything of my strength or my powers, only that I was hungry. For sixty years, I knew nothing but darkness and hunger. I lived on rats, and puddles of fresh blood that leaked through grates."

Cypress listened, crestfallen. "Jesus, that's awful," they blurted.

I snorted, nodding against their warm chest. *"Understatement of the year."*

Licking my lips, I continued. "My first interaction in those dark crypts was my Sire finally coming to see what I'd become. And, I'd become a husk of a person, nearly mute and feral, ever starving and believing that I was a demon. I believed that I was cursed to be kept in darkness and starve for eternity. I'd forgotten language and reason. And how he had laughed at me," my throat constricted again, and I closed my eyes, pausing my braiding.

My voice was thin as I forced myself to continue. "I didn't know he was my Sire until far later. That happened in 1327, and François — may he ever rot in hell— kept me with him until 1406. I did unspeakable things to free myself of him, and yet, every time I think he's dead, he seems to return. He completely destroys everything I build with perfect malice. The last time, I set him on fire, but I also know better than to expect the bastard to stay dead.. Perhaps, that explains why he haunts my nightmares."

I found myself unable to continue. So many things flashed through our link. Moments of pain, of confusion, of deep sorrow, of screaming, of red mists and my own flashing claws, of being bitten — and then I shut it down, all within less than a minute. My heart was both a raw, aching wound and a blackened void. Somehow during all of this, I had found my way back into Cypress' arms; a dry, heaving sob falling from my lips. I took a shaky breath, squeezing my eyes shut. *"Sorry... I cannot do this anymore."*

Cypress

I stroked Acanthus' hair, holding them to my chest. The flashes of memory were awful, and the skin at my neck was stinging as if I had been the one being bit in those visions. The thought made me nauseous, my stomach flipping somersaults in my abdomen. *How could someone treat another person like that?*

"I'm not sorry for asking," I whispered, worried I'd break them if I spoke any louder, "but I am sorry you went through that." I don't know when I had added swaying gently into the mix, but it was there. "You're here with me."

So many things about them suddenly made sense. All the intense reactions, the closed off behavior, pushing people away... I had no idea that they were so traumatized. Acanthus' silence was telling, and I decided to move the conversation into our mental space. *"And I hope you feel safe. Thank you for telling me."*

"I do feel safe. No one else knows any of this about me, you're the first I've let in. You've proven to me that I can trust you to see this side of me."

"The only ones I'll tell are me, myself, and I."

Acanthus was nearly completely shut down. I'd had plans to train — after all, if I was the cause of this war, then I should be able to fight in it — but I was afraid to leave them alone. Maybe spending some time together and having something to look forward to would help them relax and go back to sleep.

"Did you want me to stay? I can wait until you're sleeping again. I wanted to work on learning to fight when the sun sets. I don't know if there's a way you can help, but I'd appreciate you being there with me, anyway."

They pulled away from my chest and blinked at me. "I may be able to give you some tips."

I tilted my head at them. "You need to sleep. I can leave if—"

I cut off as they wrapped their arms around me again, and snuggled up, closing their eyes. *"Please, stay."*

The scared, soft voice made my heart shatter. "Always," I promised, and I meant it. I need to protect them, I thought, and not for the first time. I sat with them until their breathing was even and steady again, and then disappeared. Sleep never came for me. I sat, thinking about the revelations of the last hour, let alone the past few weeks. I kept my eyes closed, holding Acanthus close; the world feeling *right.*

Lemon Balm

I was still awake two hours later when Acanthus began to stir. I stilled, not sure if they'd remember I was there or not. They snuggled their cheek against me. "Hmm. You're warm."

I laughed out loud. Acanthus' hair was messy, and they lay against me, making no attempt to move. "Acanthus, you can certainly stay in bed all night if you want. I, however, want to do some training."

That Time Cypress Lost Their Words

Acanthus

It was a lovely night, despite the restless sleep. The wind outside was howling its laments through the forest as it rushed past the walls of the church. I opted for a bath rather than shower; heading to the lower bathroom with a trail of candles floating behind me. They placed themselves across the available flat surfaces in the room. I used my hands to turn on the tap.

The steam began to rise as the claw-foot tub slowly filled, and I undressed. The bathroom was painted the same lovely plum color as the main room of the house. It complimented the white marble tiles. This bathroom was small; the tub took up most of the room, and the toilet was separated from view by a half-wall. The sink was round, sitting beneath a boxy medicine cabinet that had been disguised with an ornate oval frame. The fashion was fairly timeless; meant to mimic a modern design, but the colors were Gothic in nature.

I closed my eyes to search for the buzzing energy within that would light all of the candles simultaneously. The familiar pop in my forehead and the soft, satisfying puff of the burst of fire was barely audible over the rushing water. I couldn't harness fire, per se, but my wind powers could cheat by causing friction. It was a handy little addition to my arsenal, that I assumed came from being telekinetic. Leaving my dirty clothes in a small pile on the floor, I slipped into the tub as the familiar, comforting scents of oud, roses, and sandalwood filled the air.

I was relaxed and clean within 45 minutes, and the tub was draining as I toweled myself down in the dark little room. I left my hair loose, going down my back in dark rivulets of dampness. The flicker of the candlelight was soothing, and the smells in the air kept me calm. I hadn't felt connected to my body at the Yellow Rose; in an effort to fix that, I had opted for less casual clothing tonight. I needed to feel as if my body belonged to me; that it was something I should appreciate and decorate, should I see fit.

I pulled the clothing on before going to the medicine cabinet and peering into the mirror. My reflection stared back at me, and rather than the typical disconnect, there was a spark of recognition in my eyes. *This is me.*

I smiled at my reflection, my empty chest feeling light for once. A long, flowing shirt that had elements resembling bat wings on the sleeves sat with a low scoop around my neck, and tight jeans with black-on-black patterning of old damask hugged my figure. I would typically save clothes like this for places like The Spirits Three, but, tonight, I wanted to feel confident.

Deciding to really lean into the aesthetic I was channeling, I opened the cabinet and grabbed an eyeliner stick from within to ring my eyes, and a tinted burgundy gloss for my lips. Makeup still wrapped in its plastic, left behind as a gift from Simone, the Witch that had cared for the hideout. I stared at the mirror, taking in my reflection with a critical eye. Satisfied with the results, I smoothed my clothes and prepared myself to step out and greet the rest of the night.

A pointed flow of wind blew throughout the room and all of the candles went out at once, leaving it in darkness behind me. I stepped into the inviting warmth of light and strong smells of coffee and sizzling bacon. Reaching out to Cypress, I crossed through the expanse of the living room. ***"Got hungry while you were waiting for me?"***

I twitched my fingers, picturing a mug in the cabinet. "Holy shit," Cypress gasped as the door opened and the mug moved from the shelf to the counter. I laughed. The coffee poured itself into my mug as Cypress sent me an image of a wolf pup stuffed animal sitting next to a pan of smoking bacon and eggs. I returned the image with one of my own, a little black bat flying across the living room.

I leaned against the island and floated the mug my way, and my eyes found Cypress' back. They were humming along to some pop music playing from an outdated machine — an iPod, Cypress later told me — that was plugged into the house's speaker system. Judging from the boy-band style, it was from the early 2000's. I'd never heard it before, but I could definitely see why Cypress liked it. *Someone else must have installed that*, I thought. "Smells good."

They grinned as they flipped the eggs in the pan with an impressive flick of the wrist. "It's almost done. Hey, the coffee's gonna be ice, since you took so long. Shower, my ass. Do you want some e— ..."

They turned around, the sentence dying as they saw me. Their cheeks flushed and their eyes darted up and down, a shy smile dancing on their lips as they drank in my appearance. "Eggs?" I asked. *Did I really look so different?*

They nodded, turning back to the pan. "I made a bunch of scrambled eggs, there's more than enough."

I chewed on my bottom lip, the taste of cherries invading my mouth. "No, thank you. I'll drink one of the blood packs from Azalea's."

They did one of their fancy flips one more time before cutting the heat. Mug in hand, I glided to one of the cabinets and pulled a black ceramic plate out. I floated it over to Cypress, letting it plop down onto the counter with a small clink.

"Thank you," they said, moving to plate their eggs.

"Of course. I know you want to train tonight, so thank you for being patient as I had my bath."

"Oh! It might have taken two hundred years, but if you feel good, then it's cool," they laughed and scratched at the back of their head, blushing.

Cypress

Acanthus was beautiful without makeup, but add a bit of black liner around those eyes and I lost all coherence. I fumbled with my fork, dropping it into my eggs as I tried to keep myself from staring at them. What was my brain doing? *Did I compliment them? They deserve compliments. Crap.*

"You look lovely, Acanthus," I tried not to sound too tongue-tied. "Is there something I missed? Do you celebrate your birthday?"

Acanthus blushed at the compliment, and my grin broadened. *There, you take that blush back.*

"No occasion, just self care. I don't celebrate my birthday. At least, not typically…" They trailed off, opening the fridge. Holding a blood bag in their hands, they twisted and knocked the door closed with their hip. I'd moved the blood rations to be isolated on their own shelves in the door, so it took them a moment to find. "But, it is, technically, coming soon. September 9th. What's today? July… Something?"

Lemon Balm

September 9th, I repeated to myself to remember it. *September 9th.* I liked to remember these things. I didn't care much for my own birthday, but I loved celebrating others. Laughing at their woeful time blindness, I chanced another look at them. "Today's the 20th. We'll do something when your birthday rolls around. Maybe we'll go to a club."

I looked down at my jeans. *Totally not my scene.*

Acanthus leaned against the counter, sipping from their coffee. "I remember how little you wanted to go into The Spirits Three, not that you would've been allowed in. I know you don't feel the most comfortable in a club... You'd put aside your discomfort for me?"

"If you'd enjoy yourself, of course I would."

I finished plating my food as Acanthus slid into a stool at the island. I pulled a bar stool around to sit across from them to eat. "When is yours?" Acanthus asked almost shyly, their fingers playing with the silicon of the bag.

Sufficiently distracted by eggs, I hummed a questioning sound in response. I couldn't exactly make a fool of myself if I was shoving food into my face. They leaned their elbows against the island, kicking their feet as they waited patiently. *They're beautiful.*

I had to fight myself from going slack-jawed as they laughed, and my eyes darted back down to my plate. They had to have a spell on me, or something. "Your birthday, Cypress. When is it?"

I scooped some eggs into my mouth, savoring the perfect fluffy texture. "December 24th. My mom likes to tell the story of how I'm a "Christmas Miracle." The snow was piled ten feet high, and the ambulance couldn't reach her. Dad had already taken off by that point, and no one was around to drive her. Honestly, I think she's dramatic. But here we are, twenty-five years later, and still dramatic."

"Cypress, like an evergreen. Hmm."

"Strong and dependable," I replied, my tone somewhere between sarcastic and bitter.

Acanthus reached across the counter top, and grabbed my hand. Their sincerity made my stomach flop, guilt gnawing at my ribs. "Did I upset you?"

I gave their hand a squeeze. "No. It's not you. My mom and I don't have the greatest relationship. She was a young mother, all alone in the world, so I can't blame her too harshly. But, it was tough for a while." I sighed, setting down my fork. "I'm generally not a guy that likes schedules when I'm in the moment, but when it comes to long-term situations, I like plans. I like control. And I like things going according to the established plan, but thus far, nothing has." My heart ached as I soaked in their beautiful, effeminate features. "Strangely, I'm kinda okay with that."

I pulled the plate back, and tried to force some food down. When the plate was half gone, I hopped up, wrapping it in saran wrap for later. I'd need protein if I was training, and where I hadn't eaten all of the eggs, at least I knew I had something ready-made for when I was tired. Acanthus took the opportunity to sink their fangs into the silicon. Somehow, everything seemed to be so normal, and I loved it for what it was. It was domestic, and alluring, and everything about it felt so fresh and exciting and close. Maybe there *was* room in my world for poetry.

"I will not let you be my sparring partner. I don't want to hurt you."

Acanthus had asked what I wanted to learn shortly before we headed out to the yard, and how they could help. To be clear, I was not in doubt of their abilities as a teacher. They were scowling at me, arms crossed and bat wing fabric draping. Their burgundy lips were pursed. "I am centuries old. I have seen wars. I think I can take care of myself in a spar, Cypress."

"I said no."

The frustration was building as Acanthus stared me down. ***"How do you intend to learn anything?"***

"Get out of my head, Acanthus," I replied, deadpan. I pictured myself slamming a door and locking it. To my surprise, my head went silent. I guess those mental exercises did something, after all.

They narrowed their pretty eyes at me, anger sharpening them. "I am not so fragile that you have to protect me from yourself, Cypress."

This conversation was making me more uncomfortable than I'd like to admit. I was doubting myself; I don't know my own strength. I think it stemmed from training with The Might of the East. I didn't think it was weird when I had double the silver charms of a wolf my age; I thought I was being punished for something. Acanthus' words from the motel echoed in my mind, and I cringed. Eight charms? They must have been terrified of you, Cypress.

I met their lined eyes, looked over their lovely face, and pictured it bleeding. It made my stomach lurch, so I grinned at them. "No."

Acanthus

I rose from the deck of the porch, floating a few feet off of it and crossing my legs. Unblinking, I moved backwards and flew into the forest, watching them grow smaller. "If you won't fight me, Pup, then you best come catch me!"

"Hey!"

I laughed, rising up over the trees and tipping my head back to look up at the sky. Just like the previous church, I owned a lot of the land around this one. As I rose over the trees, I glanced towards the glowing arc of light in the distance to my left, signaling Grove City and the surrounding towns. Kilgore was the closest; it was at least ten miles away, but the light went in a sprawling line to the west and heading north. My gut twisted as I once again thought about the cops at Azalea's. *I should have reached out to her before coming out here tonight... If the police are still sniffing around, then we'll need to contact some help for her...*

I pushed the thought out of my mind and tried to focus on Cypress. Their stubbornness was exhausting, but I would wait until they were ready to work with me. The church, boxy and unassuming, was the only building in view. Its white siding gleamed, a muted cyan in the low light. It was a new moon, and that made it perfect for a night of tracking; Cypress would have a harder time seeing and have to rely on their nose. I twisted around under the stars to look at the expanse of the forest, turning my back on the light.

It wasn't long before the staccato snap of branches breaking sounded beneath me, and then a snarl, followed by a howl. I tensed, my eyes darting below me to find Cypress. My shoulders sank in relief. Laughing, I looked down at the white wolf. "Oh, you want to play now, don't you? Well, I'm quite comfortable up here."

Spreading my arms and legs wide, my shirt fluffed out to look like bat wings as I circled overhead. Cypress let out a howl again, and I flipped in the air to look at them, swooping down to hover just out of reach. They lowered and snarled, warning me against an attack before leaping towards me and falling short. I laughed again, gracefully landing on the top of a nearby maple and holding up my hands in a concession. "Fine, we won't spar. What can I do to help?"

They flopped their tongue out of their mouth, panting. A thank you for dropping the matter, though they still kept our link locked tight. I didn't like feeling disconnected from them when they were in Wolf form, but if they didn't want me in there, I could hardly force them. (Well, I could with my mesmer, but I didn't want to. I had only used the mesmer on them twice, and those were dire circumstances.) I sighed, jumping down from the tree and gracefully gliding down to the forest floor. I leaned down, eye level with them. "You are going to have to get better at wolf-to-human fighting, Cypress, but I'm not going to force you."

Cypress whined, his ears pressing back against his skull. I smiled, reaching and tousling their fur. "Go find a log for your training dummy, Pup. Chop down a tree, if you have to."

By the time the sun was starting to rise, Cypress' glorified tree trunk of a dummy was set up in the rear of the church, constructed from some dead fallen logs. It loomed amongst the little shrub-filled courtyard, pink roses surrounding the wooden fiend. I had carved angry eyes and sharp teeth into its face with my nail to make Cypress laugh. He said he'd have a hard time attacking it now. Somehow, I doubted that.

That Time I Flew Like A Bat Out of Hell

Acanthus

It had been several weeks since we had set up Cypress' training dummy. The cellphone told me that it was August 26th. The nights melded together seamlessly. Cypress would go out to punch his log. I found the training regiment absolutely ridiculous; punching a log was about as useful as eyes without a trace of light. I spent my time alternating between checking the internet for hints about Nekane's plans, messaging Night Garden members for news, and watching their form. I'd given hints and pointers to Cypress as they trained, but there was only so much I could do if they refused to fight me.

The messages from the Night Garden network were not encouraging. Word traveled quickly; Azalea must have told our connections about my mad dash away from New York. Messages were filtering into the little phone from numbers both saved and not. I should have trusted my instincts and checked the bulletins when I'd woken up after the nightmare, and instead I took a long soak and gallivanted around like a bat without a care in the world. Because I took a day to feel normal, I missed our window of opportunity. *Every choice I make is the wrong one.*

Image after image came into my texts of bulletins around neighboring towns, pictures of my face in the news and active warrants in the police network. To the humans, I was being broadcasted as a dangerous individual, armed and violent. There was code interlaced into the bulletins for supernaturals to decipher. It marked me as an Anesh vampire, and a dangerous one at that. *Do not approach this individual.*

They are known to have multiple weapons and are prone to attack. Last seen in Allegheny Springs, PA. Reward being offered for information.

Allegheny Springs was near the Bed and Breakfast; I wasn't sure how or when we were spotted, but it explained the police showing up at Azalea's door. My guts twisted as I read each bulletin. They were coming in from every county of Pennsylvania, and the ones closest to the West of the state were particularly nefarious after the trail from the Golf went cold. Azalea sent me Simone's number — the Witch who had been caring for the property. I promptly messaged her to see if there was anything we could do. *Briar patches in the woods. I need some plant food and fertilizer for a dogwood. Can you send deliveries?*

The response was not ideal. *Red, blue, purple, and lilac dogwood patches are in the Grove and surrounding areas. I can deliver fertilizer, but the briar roses will need a different source for food. No local nurseries for their care.*

I'd known this, but my frustration was beginning to build. The code was simple; police, Nekane, and her Hunters were in Grove City. It'd been five weeks that we were stuck here. I was restless and hungry. We'd been out of blood bags for several days, and Cypress had only been able to go shopping for food once. We were nearly out. The stabbing pangs in my stomach and the pull in my veins were a stark warning that I was getting dangerously close to losing my reason. *Send fertilizer when able. Preferably in the next day or two. Thanks, my dear.*

The next night, Simone sent a single message. *Pots are being watched. Red and blue dogwoods block the path.* I gritted my teeth at the message. Nekane was keeping an eye on the local covens, and Simone would be tracked to the hideout if she chanced coming to us. Our supply lines were cut off completely.

I needed a distraction from my hunger and the stress. Every night, I offered to spar with Cypress. And every night, they stubbornly refused both as a human and as a Wolf. The repeated refusals were maddening; the dummy idea was something straight out of a cartoon, and would do nothing to actually prepare them for war. They needed to work on learning evasion techniques, not punching a static object. *We're sitting ducks and I'm enabling them with a false sense of security.*

Each night that ticked past, my patience waned. Last night, I snapped at them and they sulked most of the night. They stuck by their dummy, punching it until their knuckles bled. If they didn't listen to me soon, we'd wind up stuck at this impasse until we both starved. That, or until Nekane turned up to rip us both apart. I didn't know what sounded worse, at this point. Cypress relied on their Wolf a lot, and instinct alone would not work; they'd never be able to hold themself in a fight against a pack that had been established for centuries. Even if they knew how that pack operated, they were at a stark disadvantage.

Opting to keep my own sanity, I decided not to bring it up tonight. I had no doubt that they had an idea of what they wanted to do because of Nekane's pack training them. They also had a solid foundation, thanks to their hobbies as a human. Still, they were a Lone Wolf in the dark of their own species' customs. From what Cypress had told me, Nekane's training had to do with fighting as a Pack; they worked in tandem. Cypress didn't have anyone watching his back. Well, that was not true. They had me. But, he didn't know how to actually get stronger on his own. I wasn't sure if they knew how to evade and defend in human form, either. *I won't let Cypress get hurt again, I vowed. I'm on guard this time, and I will protect him with my life if I have to.*

We'd hit the window of where it'd be impossible to carry on if one of us wasn't safe to go into town. A new message from Azalea came; they changed the bulletin tonight, upping the stakes. Now, they'd been spreading lies of the "young man" threatening several gas stations and grocery stores with a pistol. One online article had an interview with the Grove City sheriff. *We have reason to believe that the perpetrator might be hiding in the woods. We're starting to map out areas to search with K-9 units. We also believe he may have accomplices, but we've got our best teams on the job.*

Anyone wearing a uniform could not be trusted. If I was to go anywhere near the city, we'd be picked up easily unless I was under heavy disguise. I could dress as a woman, I suppose, but I wasn't certain if I had the clothing to do so in this hideout. We still had some time to strategize, because they were searching to the southwest of Grove City, but there were countless units posted along heavier travel routes. In order to get to Wisconsin, we would have to leave this church unseen and unscathed. *Unfortunately, this bulletin changes the situation. Maybe I should try and talk strategy with Cypress; he might think of something I have not.*

I hadn't told Cypress the details of our circumstances quite yet. I didn't want to scare them. On top of that, the animal hunting hadn't been going as well as I'd hoped; I'd been able to nab two raccoons that were attracted to the trash we'd had yet to burn, and a few squirrels, but nothing big. My Witch friends, as invaluable as they were in situations like this, would be unable to help me under Nekane's watchful eye.

Any move to establish a blood donor or supply line in this situation would be carefully monitored in this area with the bulletin released. Asking for volunteers wasn't just limited to the Garden, and meant alerting supernaturals to the presence of a new Vampire in the area. Any alert of a new Vampire meant alerting them to me, which defeated the logic of everything. And, without being able to go to town meant bringing someone to our hideout, which could very easily turn into a trap. I couldn't risk giving our location. This left animals, or leaving.

Going into town was dangerous at best and suicidal at worst. Like it or not, this check was beginning to feel like checkmate; supply embargoes were exceedingly effective. Thankfully, there seemed to be no mention of Cypress in the bulletins; at least, none that I could see. Some mentioned an accomplice, but there were no descriptors. I was out of ideas, but maybe Cypress would be able to find information in town, when I could not.

I couldn't hide the danger from him anymore. "Cypress, there's a wanted notice out in every county for my arrest, in both human and supernatural circles. I can't go into town."

"What? Since when, what do you mean?"

"I've been in contact with Azalea since we left," I admitted. "I didn't want to worry you, but the Witches are currently compromised. I can't set up my supply lines, for myself or for you. Nekane's less than fifteen miles away. I don't know what to do."

Cypress' face fell, and he chewed on his lip as he thought. "I can stop by one of the Witches' havens in town while I'm shopping," they proposed. "I'll go during the day, to make sure that I blend in more easily."

The haven in Kilgore belonged to Benji from Azalea's coven; if we were able to set up blood supplies, they would be easier to fudge, or harder for Nekane to track, but it was a long shot. Simone mentioned that the havens were being watched. With any luck, they'd be able to help us, even if it was dangerous. "It's worth it to try," I finally said. "The covens in Grove City are currently being watched, but no one has said anything about Kilgore. It's a smaller town, so it's likely to be less guarded. Benji runs the haven there. It's on the corner of Columbus and Fifth, it's called The Apothecary. He may be able to find a way around the police presence. Better than waiting to starve like I am, now. If you can be discreet, you may actually be able to bring back some information, or maybe get Ben to find a blood bag source. It's not perfect, but we could get it to work."

Hope lit up his steel and storm eyes. "Cool, we have a plan! Operation: Cypress rocks."

I smiled, but I couldn't bring myself to laugh. I wished I could be so sure. I had a feeling that something would go wrong, my stomach twisting and tension keeping me straight-backed and jumpy. "Just, keep your wits about you and be careful, alright? They're after me, but that doesn't mean there's no danger for you."

"C'mon, Acanthus. I can handle myself."

"Are you certain? I could always try to disgui—"

"No. I'm not letting you risk that. I'll handle it, okay?"

I nodded, though the twisting in my gut didn't cease. *Stop it, Acanthus. Trust him to do this.*

I made my way to bed in the quickly approaching dawn.

Cypress

As soon as Acanthus went to bed, I got ready to head into Kilgore. The backpack Azalea had given me would be perfect for the trip. I could probably fit most of what I'd buy into it. I could stop at the grocery store in town, and then grab some resistance bands, a reusable water bottle, and maybe even protein powder if I found the right place. I wanted to up my game with training. I knew that the dummy was stupid; hell, I was surprised Acanthus was letting me go along with it. But, I needed to do something. I remembered the teachings from Nekane's camp, and I couldn't spar with Acanthus.

It wasn't only the fact that I didn't want to hurt them. The endless sparring at Nekane's had felt senseless, and the sting of bites and snap of wolf jaws throbbed in my skin when I thought of it for too long. I didn't want to lump anything to do with Acanthus into that. I double-checked that I had my wallet and grabbed the spare key from beneath the windowsill.

Kilgore was the closest town, but it was at least about ten miles away. If I ran at top speed as a wolf, I could get there in about twenty minutes. I made my way to the line of trees, folded my clothes into the backpack, and took off with the straps between my teeth. The bulletins in the news sounded really bad; it bothered me, and I didn't know what to do. Acanthus was starving, and I didn't know the first thing about talking to the Night Garden for supply lines. They did things like a spy novel, and I didn't know anything about the code. Luckily, Benji knew me, but it wasn't like I could rock up, give him a high five, and go, *hey, bro, can you hook me up with some sweet sanguine sustenance?*

I also had no idea how Acanthus was keeping track of things. I was getting tired of being in the dark. We'd been at this church for five weeks; on top of each other constantly. The stress and their descent into starvation was making us snip at each other, and it made it harder for me to feel comfortable with serious talk. I knew I should ask Acanthus more about our current situation, and how the Garden worked. But, I also knew how anxious and jumpy they were recently. We were running out of options.

As I ran, I kept thinking about the bulletins. I wondered why I wasn't mentioned. Acanthus may be eccentric, but the two of us together would be easier to spot. Maybe Nekane thought they'd abandoned me. Or maybe, I wasn't a threat. I don't know which thought was more offensive. When I got to the edge of the tree line, I paused out of sight from the buildings and shifted, taking a little bit to drink some water and give myself a break before I breached the trees and stepped onto the sidewalk.

Shopping went without incident. I was confident that the streets were safe as I rounded the corner next to a park, a few blocks away from Ben's apothecary. It was then that I heard my name from the left. "Cypress Borne?"

I turned to look behind me, confused. No one should know me here; I was born and raised in New York. "Yes?"

A thin man with gaunt cheeks stood there. He was a solid head shorter than me with scraggly blonde hair and ice blue eyes. He didn't look familiar. I furrowed my brow, tilting my head as I asked, "Do I know you?"

The man lifted his hand and lunged. My heart sped and I stepped back, but I wasn't fast enough; searing pain cut through my shoulder as the man pushed a blade out of his sleeve and stabbed me. The sting was deep; silver. I cried out, nearly missing his words. "Nekane will be so pleased when I bring you to her," he smirked. "I hope you're ready to be rid of your little leech."

Thinking fast, I lurched to the side and threw my backpack into a nearby bush, turning around and shifting.

Acanthus

I was asleep for what felt like less than a minute, my slumber a peaceful void for once, when I heard Cypress' distressed scream and bolted upright. *"Acanthus, help! Hunter!"*

"Where, what is it, where are you?" I shot back, pulling on the closest cloak before floating as fast as I could out of the door and into the blinding light of the day. Right now, I didn't care about the sun; I needed to get to the Pup.

"Columbus and First."

I recognized the words as a street corner, and rocketed in that direction. Barreling towards Columbus and First, my head filled with Cypress' emotions; danger accompanying glimpses of blue tinted vision. They showed the face of a man carrying silver chains like a lasso, and my blood became ice. A busy intersection was behind them, and Cypress' eyesight was partially obscured by bushes and what looked like some wooden beams to his left. I hadn't expected there to be a Hunter presence in Kilgore. Police, yes, but Hunters? The bulletins were focused on the southwest. How had they found us so quickly? *"Hang in there, on my way."*

I was there in less than a minute, my hair and cloak whipping in wild arcs out behind me as I sped through the air. Houses dotted the streets on either side, and one corner was a playground with a few maple trees lining the sidewalk. This must have been one of the residential areas of the town. Cars were parked on the street, and people whizzed past, paying the scene in the park no mind. I landed in the park at the corner of Columbus and First, twisting around wildly. *"Where are you?!"*

I heard the snarling before I saw them, and I whirled around to see Cypress beneath a bridge on the playground. There was blood criss-crossing their white fur, silver shining in a thin net around them. My vision went red and I twisted my hand up, raising the offending filth of a Hunter into the air with my powers. He rose with a scream and I bared my fangs, projecting my voice so that it was unbearably loud to his ears. "Your meddle brings your doom, little Hunter."

He covered them, his legs kicking wildly in the air. If people were watching, I didn't care. I couldn't. Slowly, I started to increase the pressure of the air surrounding him. *Crush him slowly, and let him explode. Let Nekane see, I'll crush her, too.*

He flailed as he screamed, shaking his head. "Please, I have a family!"

"How quaint," I snarled coldly. "You should have thought about them before trying to take mine."

Blood began to leak from the Hunter's eyes and nose, and the screams faded to whimpers as I increased the pressure further. *"Acanthus, stop!"*

I paused my onslaught, the Hunter dangling as I whipped around to look at Cypress. They whimpered, struggling with the net. The Hunter slumped in my hold, and I threw him aside carelessly as I retracted my fangs. He skidded across the pavement, his head cracking against the tire of one of the parked cars on the opposite side of the street. He easily had a concussion at the very least, and was unconscious. I ran to Cypress and fell to my knees. Worry and fear emanated from me through our bond, but the anger still ran in undercurrents to the other emotions, even as the red faded from my eyes and the nausea of anxiety set in. *"Come. Let me see you."*

I'd left the Hunter alive, thanks to Cypress' intervention, but there was no question now that Nekane's pack had found us, and we were in extreme danger. I'd probably agonize over how I treated the Hunter later, but for now, my attention was entirely on Cypress.

Cypress

With my ears pressed flat against my head, I tried to shake the net from myself, and it just got tangled around my paws. I sent a hopeless picture of a wolf stuffed animal in handcuffs to Acanthus, though, it really wasn't a time for joking. I couldn't help it. Even through the static the silver caused, the emotions Acanthus was throwing off were intense. Their voice was frantic in my mind as they reached to help disentangle me from the net. *"How did he manage to get the upper hand, Pup?"*

"Took me by surprise."

Acanthus treated the Hunter like a rag doll. The image made my stomach flop and my heart pound, and I was fighting my own instincts to lash out at them. *"I… I was walking to The Apothecary, and suddenly I had a knife in my shoulder,"* I tilted my head, lifting my injured shoulder. *"I shifted to get away, and he caught me in this net."*

Their fingers shook as they felt through my fur, looking over the stab wound. *"I'm fine, Acanthus."*

"For now," they replied. The thought came through as a frustrated growl, followed by a spark of distress. There was a split-second glimpse of me in the tub at that ugly brown motel on the other side of Pennsylvania. I shuddered as they continued. *"But what if you hadn't been? What if they captured you, Cypress? Killed you? Then what was I to do? You're likely going to be added to the bulletins, and now both of us cannot do anything! We have no food, and they have a good idea of where we are now. Nekane will start gathering her forces as soon as she hears this Hunter's report. This is checkmate, Pup."*

They pulled the tangled mess of silver from my paws. This was exhausting. *"It can't be checkmate. We can figure something out. What would you have me do Acanthus? I didn't expect them to jump me while I was walking down the street."*

"You should have! And if you'd let me spar with you, a silver dagger would have been child's play. You need to understand, people don't pull back in war."

I whimpered at the rage that tempered their voice. Pressing my ears back to my head, I tried to look as apologetic as possible. *"I'm sorry!"*

"I am not angry with you. Frustrated, certainly, but not angry. This childish dance of avoiding harm to each other ends here. I need to help you train."

The fight with the Hunter still had me reeling, and I could barely keep a coherent string of thought. I whimpered again, looking up at Acanthus. *"I didn't get to the coven yet. Can you feed from the Hunter?"*

Acanthus lifted their head, looking around. I followed their lead. People were starting to come out onto their porches, and a car was slowing down. *"There's no time. The longer we linger, the more danger we're in. We don't know how much of that people may have seen, and will be questioning. Any Witches and Hunters in the area will be alerted as soon as the police arrive."*

They stood, adjusting their hood to further hide their face. They darted away, using their vampiric speed to grab my backpack from the tangle of bushes. They were back to my side in the space of a blink. I staggered to my feet, and Acanthus tilted their head towards the sidewalk on the opposite block. We began to walk away as humans started to chatter down the street.

"Did that guy get hit by a car?"

"Did anyone see what happened?"

"I didn't hear a crash, did you?"

Acanthus' eyes shifted back and forth and we walked quickly away from the scene, their breath thin and rattling. I struggled to keep up with them, my shoulder singing in pain as they continued talking, their anxiety deep and thrumming in our link. *"They'll likely have clean-up crews flooding in here any moment for damage control, and we need to be gone. Cypress; they're either going to arrest us and hand us over to Nekane, or they'll take us out without a second thought if we linger. Every public servant in Pennsylvania thinks I'm an armed and dangerous criminal, and I didn't disguise, before I flew to you. I wasn't exactly discreet."*

I whimpered, confusion clouding my head as I blurted, *"What about Benji? Can he help?"*

They were getting sullen, between hunger and anxiety. I'd been food insecure before, and I knew what it felt like to not know when your next meal would be. Guilt twisted my gut into knots. They shook their head. *"We are still under Nekane's jurisdiction. The Night Garden is a clandestine operation. He may be a free Witch, but she's a governmental figurehead, Cypress. If she gives the order, Benji can't just say no."*

They adjusted my bag and pulled the straps into the crook of their elbows, glancing around again. A siren kicked on a few blocks over and I tensed. *"Come here, Cypress,"* Acanthus' voice was urgent as they patted a shoulder. I jumped up, and they wrapped their arms around my waist. Before my next breath, we were in the air. My Wolf instinct was to flail around; I fought the urge. I thought, *Don't make things harder, Cypress.*

Guilt nibbled at the bottom of my heart until I couldn't stand it. *"Thank you, Acanthus. You're always rescuing me."*

"Pardon? I feel like that's the opposite case!"

"Not at all. You flew all the way here out of a dead sleep."

They laughed. "It was not a dead sleep."

"It certainly was. I could feel it through the bond. I was trying not to wake you. The net trapped me as a Wolf. If I had been human, I may have had a chance."

Acanthus' eyes narrowed as they responded, their voice taking on an edge once more. "Please allow me to change that."

I hated that they were right. I pictured them bleeding again, and gritted my teeth. I needed to get over this. *"Fine,"* I grumbled as we landed in front of the church. Acanthus didn't answer, and I hopped down from their shoulders. They swayed where they stood. *"Are you okay?"*

"Yes. Just tired." Their speech slurred, and they stumbled on their feet. I caught them on my back as they fell forward. They laughed incredulously. "Dammit, I can't deal with this right now. We need to figure out what to do!"

"What? What's wrong?!" I stood still, letting them lay on me, a strange sticky dryness invading my mouth. I smacked my lips before licking at my nose. It was like I hadn't drank anything for a week.

"I'm starved and drained in the daylight. I'm using my powers too much." I brought us to the church as I kept my ears perked, maneuvering us into a shaded spot. "We're sitting ducks, here. We can't go back into town."

"We've gotta do something. I can tell something's wrong." The dryness in my mouth compounded and my throat felt like sandpaper. Maybe I just needed a drink. Acanthus' voice was distant as their cheek plopped against my fur. "Pay it no mind. I can survive."

I whined, and tilted my head to look back at them. They promptly passed out, and my heart seized in a panic. *How long has it been since they've eaten? And they flew all the way to town and nearly squished a guy's head... Just how much does that take, what drives their power?*

My stomach was full of rocks as I shifted back into a human. Nakedness be damned, my friend needed me. I carried Acanthus upstairs, tucking them in, and backing out of the room. I didn't really have their permission to be in there, but I was a shout away. *I don't know what the fuck I'm supposed to do... How do we get out of this one?*

Acanthus had already looked me over, but I went to the bathroom to check my wound anyway. *Add to the canvas,* I thought bitterly. All the

Hunter had on him was a silver dagger and nets. They must've been aware that I was also here. Maybe Nekane wanted me alive. *What a shit-show...*

I cleaned the wound with some antiseptic, and growled at the sting. When it was adequately cleaned, I bandaged it and threw on the shirt. I was tired, but still extremely restless. There wasn't going to be much sleep today. Might as well make use of this energy and hit something.

I wrapped my hands to protect them from the bark, and went out to face the punching dummy as I waited for Acanthus to wake up.

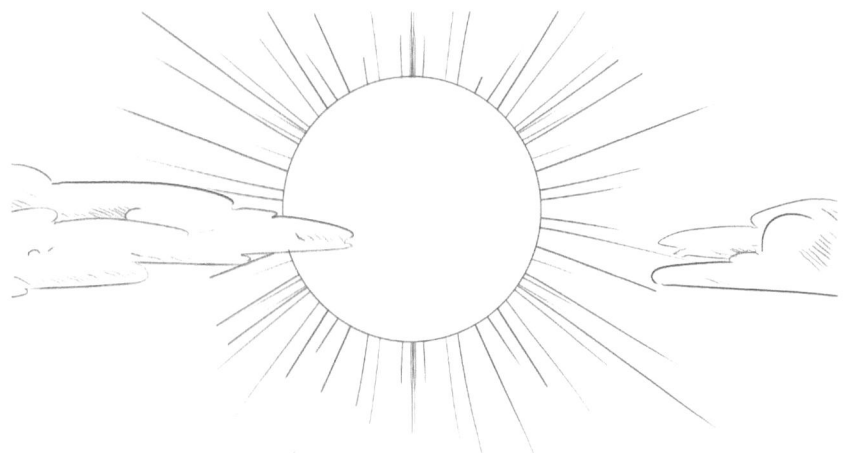

That Time I Lost Myself

Cypress

I was drenched in sweat as the sun set on the absolutely horrible day, my tank-top soaked through. My knuckles were bruised and sore, but already healing. I would've given anything for the soft, oiled leather of a punching bag, over this. I took a deep breath, and straightened when I smelled roses and a winding river in the wind. I turned to Acanthus, who was blinking sleepily in the doorway. "How long have you been there?"

"Long enough," they replied, their arms crossed. Their gaze danced across my skin, and I hugged myself to hide from them. "You have good form for offense, but not defending. You will never learn to punch a moving target from a punching bag."

So, we're back to *that* conversation. I gritted my teeth, averting my eyes. The constant pushing on that boundary was starting to get irritating, but they were right. My flesh crawled, prickling with the drying sweat. I knew their pushing was from a place of care, but it still bothered me. They were already struggling enough, and if I did something to hurt them, I wouldn't be able to handle it. Not to mention, a small part of me was scared that they'd be disappointed, if I couldn't keep up.

It didn't help that they were no longer being nice about it. Acanthus wasn't the best teacher, either, but they were the only one I had. "I'm aware that I need help training, Acanthus," I grumbled, fidgeting with the wrappings on my hands. "Did you get enough rest?"

"No," they said sullenly.

"Then go back to bed."

I leaned against the dummy, grimacing. I didn't want to be in this mindset, but Acanthus' irritability leeched like a poison into our bond. I had promised them that I would roll with their moods, and I was doing my best, but I was also exhausted and starting to feel ill. My throat hurt, the sandpaper and glass sensation returning. I wondered if I was starting to come down with something. Could Werewolves get strep?

"One moment please," Acanthus muttered before disappearing faster than I could see. The wind whooshed as they vanished. They were back in moments, dropping a lifeless squirrel into the bushes. I raised my eyebrow, though marveled at the fact that that sandpaper feeling had lessened. *Maybe I wasn't as thirsty as I'd thought.*

"By all means Cypress," Acanthus' voice cut through my thoughts. "Please go back to punching your log. I can get a better feel of where you need help then."

I matched their aloofness. "Are you waiting for me to invite you to spar?"

"I thought you'd never ask."

I rolled my eyes. The returning scowl I got was well worth it. "Okay, raccoon eyes, get over here then."

Their scowl deepened when they realized they still hadn't cleaned off the eyeliner. They still looked wonderful and beautiful, and— *focus, Cypress. Now is not the time to drool over your friend. They're starving, and you're sitting here bristling because they're being impatient with you. Give them some wiggle room.*

I blinked at them innocently as they huffed out, "We should lay down some rules, if you are ready to finally work with me."

"Of course. I thought that was a given."

"I do not expect you to pull your punches, or other attacks. If you are, you won't learn properly. If I catch you holding back, I'm not afraid to call you on it. When sparring, we'll use the word "hit" and that means everything stops. You landed a deathblow. I will manage my speed, to perfectly mimic the Hunters. Is that amenable?"

I nodded, still uncomfortable with the thought of sparring with them. The anxiety twisted my stomach into knots, but after what happened this afternoon, my hand was forced. I closed my eyes, picturing the razor sharp sting of the silver net and shuddering. I never wanted to be helpless, at someone else's command, ever again.

"Say you understand, Cypress," they pressed, and I gritted my teeth, tightening my fists and digging my nails into my sore palms.

"I under*stand*," I bit out.

"Good. Any rules on your part?"

"You'll have to tell me if I actually hurt you. The thought is devastating, Acanthus."

Their expression softened. They started to chew on their bottom lip, guilt barraging me from our link. I still wasn't used to feeling the emotions of someone else. And, every time it happened, I wore it like a wound, but it cut twice as deep. I blurted, "Can't we just go? Acanthus, I know I have to train, but I never wanted to fight a war. And, you're starving. There has to be another way."

The silence stretched for a moment too long, before they finally broke it. "Dear Pup, I know more than anyone how difficult this is. And I'm sorry that I keep asking you to fight. I…" They trailed off, before walking towards me and reaching to take my swollen hands. "I don't say this lightly. I am frightened. I ask you to fight because I don't want to watch you bleeding from the neck because of another Wolf again, or some Hunter, or whoever has a vendetta next. I will keep looking at our options. Maybe we can chance another move. But for now, let me help you train, Cypress. You won't hurt me, and if you do, you have my vow that I will tell you. I am not so fragile."

"Thank you." Their eyes were sincere, and their words rang true. I trusted them.

Clearing their throat, they nodded decisively and straightened their posture. "With that, let me see your form."

Acanthus

I knew that I was being quite hard on them when it came to training. My hunger was making me irritable, and sparring would certainly help with that — it'd burn off this restless anger, but it'd only serve to make me hungrier. I wanted nothing more than to rewind the last several months and undo them. *I should have asked them to stay with me*, the guilty part of my brain sighed, and the angry part responded, *To what end? It would have always ended up this way.*

Would it have? I used my irritability to steel myself. I was not going to hurt him, but I was not going to go easy on him, either. Going easy would just be a reason for a repeat of the afternoon, and I could smell the old blood from their wounds. My veins pulled, the copper and iron taunting me. I would need to go hunting after this, for something far more substantial than a squirrel, but I wasn't guaranteed to find much. I was terrible at hunting, clumsy and too impatient. It'd been centuries since I'd had to survive like this, and you couldn't exactly sweet-talk a deer.

Cypress was fidgeting. They still hadn't taken any form of offensive or defensive stance, and I was irritated by the pause. It shouldn't take this long to prepare yourself to spar. They blushed, before huffing, "Turn around."

That's right. "No, Pup. Human form first."

"Acanthus, come on," they crossed their arms. "Wolf form is hard enough against you, shouldn't we start with where I'm stronger?"

"The Hunter attacked you when you were human. I think we should train hand to hand first."

They didn't respond, instead glaring at me and crouching into a combative stance. His legs were spread and grounded in line with his shoulders, and arms up with fists curled, so that he could block or throw a jab easily. An acceptance and an opening, but I was pushing my luck. I wasn't sure if they were mirroring a combat style, or just working on instinct, but I took the opening and lunged, reaching for their chest, careful to keep my speed matching a human's. They went to block their neck and face, and I pivoted and touched their side, landing beside them. "Hit."

"Oh, come on!" Cypress exclaimed. "I had no way of knowing that'd be where you'd go!"

"Which is why we're doing this, Cypress. Again. Watch for my tells. You can see where someone is aiming by their movements. Like this."

I slowed my movement down for them to see. "Does that make sense?"

They muttered something in response, and assumed their pose again. We trained with Cypress in human form for an hour or so, and each movement left me murmuring, "Hit," followed by their frustrated huff. I broke down some more of our attacks step-by-step, but each time we went back to sparring, Cypress would lose. Rinse, and repeat. They lost their patience and went down on one knee, panting and exhausted. "Acanthus, I'm not going to beat you like this. Even with you moving at human speed, I can't land a hit. Can I please just shift?"

A bright sheen of sweat coated their limbs. The bandages on their hands were grimy and discolored, and the gauze pad on their shoulder had come unstuck on the upper left corner, lifting their tank top strap off of their shoulder. I considered their words. I could be cruel and say no, but what purpose would that serve? I found my eyes lingering on the gauze pad, and guilt gnawed at my ribs. *Patience, Acanthus. You can't push them this hard.*

I sighed. "This isn't over, we'll need to do far more of this. We can look at evasion methods another time. I need to put together a proper training schedule for you. But, you can shift."

I turned around, waiting to hear the soft whoosh of air from behind before I once again faced them, and this time, their wolf was crouched to strike. With a smile, I held my arm out. "Begin."

With a low, threatening growl, Cypress went up off of their haunches and lunged — and, I easily sidestepped, hearing them hit the ground with a skid behind me. Flipping around, my hair hadn't even settled before I had my arms around their neck in a choke-hold. "Hit."

"I'm well aware," they growled, their fur rippling under the skin of my arms.

"I'm only playing by the rules we have set, I'm not trying to mock. Set up again."

I let them go, and they bounded away, the anger blazing in their eyes. *Yes, get angry. Look for weaknesses.*

Maybe I should have kept that mental gate locked while I was hungry, but I didn't want to shut down all communication when we were training like this. They lunged again, and I sidestepped. This time they expected it, skidding and immediately running to lunge again. I listened to the footsteps and dropped to my knees, feeling the whoosh of air as Cypress soared over me. Reaching up, I touched their back leg. A small vicious part of my instinct wanted to grab and rip them out of the air. I could visualize them dangling by their rear leg, howling as I hovered, but I stamped it down. A Hunter wouldn't do that, and this was not a Wolf that was an enemy. I turned as they landed, touching their uninjured shoulder.

"Hit," I said calmly, and they growled.

"I GET it."

A spark of irritation ran through me and I snapped. *"Don't mouth back at me, would you rather I actually harm you?"*

"At this point, yes! It's so annoying!"

I laughed. "Don't be a sore loser. Again."

The growl that came from them this time was darker, far more threatening than before. They didn't like me goading them, but too bad. It was amusing. The night continued in that way — a series of growls, snarls, my own voice calmly saying "Hit."

We had been at it for at least another hour, Cypress trying different strategies and fighting styles, but they were still relying far too heavily on direct attacks. Hunters would expect the easy options. I could feel the anger rolling off of them in waves. They had yet to best me. "I'm growing bored, Pup."

"This isn't easy, and you're kicking my ass!"

Lemon Balm

"I hate to say it, Cypress, but I'm not even trying. Come up with new tactics. You're making your goal too direct and easy to see. Try something more subversive. Again, come on."

It was probably cruel to speak to them this way. I'd apologize later, when we were talking and I was nursing their wounds; not that I had wounded them. Rather, they were starting to hit the point of aggravating the one that they had. Cypress made a move as if they were going to lunge. I went to step aside, but they pulled back at the last minute, barreling straight into my legs. I fell backwards with a shout, and suddenly I had a very big Wolf with two paws bearing straight down on my chest. He was snarling in my face. All of the breath left my lungs and my heart sped into a chaotic thrum, and before I knew what was happening, they started excitedly tapping their feet on my chest. *"Hit."*

I laughed, relief making my arms and legs tingle. "Oh, you little bastard. Get off."

Cypress plopped down on me, laying across me and keeping me pinned. A vision went behind my eyes of a big stuffed wolf on my chest. Laughing again, I shoved them off, shaking my head. "Subverting expectations is a great choice. I suppose you had to celebrate that win. Are you done, or would you like to keep going?"

"A few more. We have a lot of night left."

"Are you certain? You haven't slept, and I need to hunt. You've been training for far longer than I've been out here."

They didn't answer with words, instead huffing and shooting me a look. I hummed softly. "Alright, Two more tries."

There was a floating feeling of agreement from them, and they went down on their haunches with a playful little snarl as I stood up. They ran at me, trying to catch me off guard again. Prepared for that little maneuver this time, I placed my hand on their shoulder and vaulted over them, confused and alert as a loud, pained yelp came from underneath me. I flipped, landing on my feet like a cat and skidding backwards. The air had taken on a dangerous, sharp tinge, and the ends of my hair stood up as my flesh erupted in bumps. "Did I hurt you? Are you alright?"

No answer came. Instead, a low, feral growl came from them, and they turned to face me, deep into their attack pose. Cypress was entirely gone — a wild Wolf stood before me, their eyes flashing forest green; one eye had a slash of icy blue through it, lining up with the scar Cypress had in Wolf form. I gasped, watching them prepare to lunge. "Cypress—"

They let out a roar, darting to the side. *That is NOT a Cypress move.*

I sprang into action, rising up above the jumping range of the Wolf. As he darted off, I lost sight of him in the underbrush and the trees. I whipped around. My breaths heaved and my heartbeat was in my ears, erratic in its hummingbird thrum. How fucking easy was it to lose a white Wolf in the middle of dark surroundings?

Pretty easy, as it turns out. I swallowed, slowly turning in the air as I scanned the forest floor. "Cypress?! Cypress!"

Hot breath hit my foot, and I pulled my legs up, shooting up higher into the air and just avoiding the clamp of teeth. Looking down, my mesmer switched on as I commanded the Wolf, "Stop!"

The Wolf fell to the ground, looking up at me in a daze. I kept my mesmer going at the highest strength I could muster, which was admittedly a mere figment of its true strength due to my starvation. I didn't know what was going on; this was entirely new. Cypress was nowhere to be found. *Did Cypress' wolf spirit just take over his body? That's impossible, isn't it?*

I stared, unblinking. I couldn't break eye contact, or I'd be attacked. This Wolf was ridiculously powerful, and I didn't want to chance a bite. ***"I am so sorry, Cypress."***

I floated down to the ground. My heart was bruising itself against my rib cage, but I took my time, willing it to slow. As I vaulted over Cypress, I must have put my weight on their injured shoulder. My stomach twisted into knots, but I still did not break eye contact with the Wolf. *Distraction is your doom, Acanthus, stay focused.*

Soft, subdued growls came from them, their chest heaving and their fur standing on end. "You are not to attack."

An open mouth snarl came in response, and I could feel the pressure of them fighting my mesmer. I knelt beside the Wolf with my arm out, close enough for them to smell, but just out of reach if they decided to bite. *I can't hold this for much longer. If I over-use my powers and faint, this Wolf will certainly kill me.*

I thought about going for the pressure point behind the Wolf's head, but to do so could be risking a bite from this angle. And, to move to a better one would mean breaking my mesmer and opening myself up to another attack. *What do I do? What about the silver in the church? No... That would break his trust, and I don't want to harm him.* I didn't know how else to subdue him without hurting him. We stood there for a long while in a standoff. At a loss, I begged past the lump in my throat, "Cypress, I need you to come back to yourself, please."

Cypress

I lost myself in the pain, and my instincts were screaming at me. *Kill him, and don't stop until his body is shredded!*

But I was screaming right back at myself. *This is Acanthus. Careful, calm, collected. They just put their hand down in the wrong place, it was an accident. They didn't mean it. Come on, Cypress, calm down. One, Mississippi. Two, Mississippi. Three, Mississippi...*

I was completely disconnected from my body, floating somewhere above my own head. Counting to thirty was helping me gain back my control, but through my attempts to self-soothe, my own growls pierced the night air. I wasn't even angry. *What's going on?! Fuck, fuck, fuck...*

Sometimes I surfaced and thoughts were cognitive, and I could almost reign in the snarls. Other times, I was fully submerged, and had no idea how deep the water was. My mind was a dark riotous ocean, and the waves kept coming. I don't understand what's happening, why can't I stop?

"Cypress, I need you to come back to me, please."

A life raft. A light in the dark. Whatever shitty comparison you want to draw between drowning and being rescued, it was me. I held onto those words, and swam upwards. *"Acanthus."*

The growls subsided and I blinked, stepping back into myself. I stomped my front paws, and shook my head. My entire body tingled, like a limb woken up from being asleep. Acanthus' eyes glowed with an intense fire, but I couldn't feel the strange fogginess of the mesmer. I stepped forward and set my chin in their hand, and they gasped and flinched. "How — ?!"

I didn't dare move, staring into their eyes. After a moment, the glow dulled and their shoulders sagged. They had dark circles dragging down their face. I whimpered, leaning further into their hand, and then huffed. Acanthus let out a shaky little sigh, closing their eyes. "Welcome back, Pup."

"Thank you for bringing me back."

"No, you did that. You were fighting against me so hard."

"That wasn't me. What even happened?"

Acanthus scratched my chin, and rubbed my cheek. "I don't know," they admitted, shaking their head. "Are you okay?"

What did they mean they didn't know? I thought about the strange feeling of bobbing in and out of water, and shuddered. One of the lessons from Nekane's camp came into my mind. *Your wolf spirit is a part of you and separate. Sometimes, you can lose yourself and your instinct will overtake. Is that what happened?*

Acanthus interrupted. "I didn't mean to hurt you, Cypress."

"You didn't." I stretched my neck out, showing them the wound on my shoulder. *"I was already wound up, and when you touched me, it hurt and it was unexpected. It must've triggered something in me, and I lost myself to it. I'm sorry if I scared you."*

They shook their head. "I'm just glad you're back."

Their forehead pressed against mine, and I kept my eyes closed, calmed by Acanthus' scent. *"Have you ever seen anything like that before, Acanthus? I wasn't in control at all."*

Acanthus shook their head, and my insides knotted. This Vampire had spent centuries fighting Wolves, and they hadn't seen something like that? I didn't know what to make of it. But, I knew that I definitely needed to work on keeping my cool. *"Please don't beat yourself up for this, Acanthus. I feel awful."*

I opened my eyes, leaning back and searching theirs. Their voice was the kindest it'd been all night as they replied, "As long as you're okay, I won't be too upset."

After the intense day and night, I wanted to sleep. There was so much that I needed to sort out about what just happened. There was a part of me that wouldn't have stopped if I'd actually caught them, and that thought made my heart twist and my head pound. *"If you need to look at the wound before I go to bed, I'll let you. But now, I'm fine."*

I sent them a thought of a stuffed wolf, the seam at the shoulder torn, with stuffing pouring out. They couldn't help but laugh."Okay Cypress. Okay. I'll stop worrying."

"Until I gain more control, that might be something we have to deal with. Please, if I ever lose control completely, do not hesitate to use whatever you need to stop me."

I started heading back towards the church. We'd managed to get a fair distance into the forest during our training. When I didn't hear Acanthus' footsteps behind me, I turned around to see them cross their arms, a deep frown marring their pretty features. "I will not harm you Cypress. I don't even feel the urge when you're snapping at me with intent to kill in your eyes. I don't have it in me. I felt bad enough sending you into a frenzy."

I sent the thought of a shrug through our link. *"Rabid dogs get put down."*

Silence. Then, I felt Acanthus' horror, strong enough to make my own stomach pitch and bile raise in the back of my throat. "You're…" Acanthus paused, and anger replaced the shock in their voice when they finished the thought. "Not rabid though. Don't ever say that again," their voice was made of acid and they were glaring at me, their eyes full of fire. "You are not just some dog off the street, and I refuse to think of 'putting you down.'"

I blinked at them. ***"I'm sorry? I won't say it again."***

They closed their eyes, taking a deep breath to calm themselves. "Can you just once, Cypress, think of yourself as important?"

My ears flattened against my head, looking as apologetic as a Wolf can. Acanthus had a point. They acknowledged my apology. We closed the distance between us and the church in silence. They turned around so I could shift again; my clothes on the patio where I'd left them. The moment I was a human again, I pulled on my basketball shorts and tank top. "Are you okay to look at my shoulder? I did the best I could."

I stuck my tongue out at them as they turned around and scowled at me, my earlier comment put aside and forgiven for now.

Acanthus

After cleaning Cypress' wound, I went into the forest and hunted for the rest of the night. Any irritation was locked firmly away, kept safely in a mental box for later. Their blood had me salivating, but I tamped that inner beast down harshly. *They smell so good, even from an old wound... I doubt I'd have been able to resist them when they were human.*

The thoughts bothered me, especially after the 'rabid dog' comments. Shutting down my mind, I focused on the forest around me, hunting for animals. I was out until the early dawn, but the only thing that I could procure was a skunk. *Blast this cursed existence.*

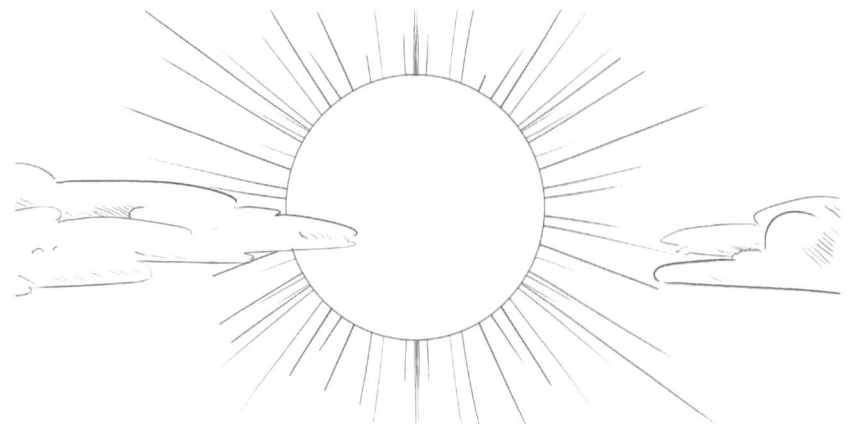

That Time I Lied To Cops

Cypress

When Acanthus was back from hunting, they were already starting to sway on their feet again. *Fuck, I can't keep sitting here and watching them starve.*

I smiled sweetly at them, already thinking up a plan. It seemed they couldn't stay awake much past dawn in this state. I wasn't sure if it was due to the rising sun, their hunger, or using their powers too much. Once they were asleep, it would be easy for me to creep out of the church, so long as I didn't step into their dreams or thoughts.

"You should get some sleep, Acanthus."

I reached for their hand, but they pulled it back and raised their eyebrow at me. "What are you thinking?"

"What do you mean?"

They eyed me suspiciously. "You have the look of trouble about you."

"Don't I always? Trouble is my middle name."

Acanthus yawned, tiredness dragging their shoulders down. The purple rings surrounding those beautiful eyes were even more pronounced, and their voice rasped as they spoke. "That is completely irrelevant."

I smiled, grabbing their hand and dragging them up the stairs. Acanthus was freezing. Touching them was like reaching into a refrigerator. I shivered, fighting the urge to pull my hand away. "Irrelevant or not, you need sleep. I'll stay out of trouble until you wake up."

They yawned again. "You will, huh? You don't cause trouble when you sleep."

"You're right. I sleep like a log." I pulled the blankets back for them, and they crawled in with no complaint, curling into a ball.

"I'm serious, Cypress. Stay out of trouble." They closed their eyes, sleep heavy on their voice. "I can't handle another frantic flight to the city."

My gut twisted, heart speeding slightly. *Did they hear my thoughts? No, they couldn't have. They just know me.*

They did cause me to second-guess myself, though. Hunters would be on high alert here, and I was clearly awful at being sneaky. Not only that, I was injured, sore, and exhausted. I was probably pushing myself past my limits. Not to mention, if I left and Acanthus woke up to find me missing, it'd stress them out a lot more. *What can I do?*

With a flash of insight, I remembered Benji's number was programmed into my phone. My heart rose with hope, light with excitement. *Bingo.* I waited until Acanthus' chest stopped its rise and fall before I left the room, grabbing my backpack and slowly closing the door behind me. I crept down the stairs, digging through the front pocket until I found my phone at the very bottom. *I hope this fucking thing has a charge...*

I pressed the button to turn it on, groaning with dismay when it flashed the 'I'm dead' symbol on the screen. *Fuck,* I thought. *I could give it time to charge, I guess.*

I dug through the backpack again, and a moment later, the charger was in my hands. I should've asked for Azalea's number when we were at the Yellow Rose. I plugged the device into an outlet in the kitchen. *This means I have to wait at least two hours for the battery to cycle. I could call when it boots, but that'll be a bit. What do I do until then?*

I was exhausted, but I didn't want to go to sleep before I had this figured out. I resorted to sitting in one of the wing-back chairs, drumming my fingers on the arm. I watched the window impatiently, urging time to move faster. It was about then that I heard a tone buzzing from nearby. *What the fuck is that?*

I stood, looking around the room. Considering my phone was in the kitchen, it couldn't be that. *That sounds like a phone, though. Is that how*

Acanthus has been speaking to Azalea? Where the fuck did they get a phone?

It was muffled, and clearly on vibrate. The sound was low, as if coming from a distance. I perked my ears, trying to follow the noise. It led me to an outlet behind the couch. An older track phone sat plugged into the wall, and I tensed. *Where'd that come from?*

The number that was lit up on the blue and yellow gradient screen was unsaved. This has got to be Acanthus'. *Should I answer?*

The fourth ring vibrated against the wall, and I lunged for the device. It could be help, and help was what I needed. *Fuck it.* "Hello?"

The line was quiet for a moment, before I heard a sharp inhale of breath. "Who may I be speaking to?"

The voice on the other line was cautious, but it sounded familiar. It was masculine, a smooth tenor with a lisp. I wracked my brain. Where do I know this voice from? "Uh…. This is Cypress. Who is this? Are you looking for Acanthus?"

The voice cursed softly. "Yes, I'm looking for the briar rose gardener," they said, their tone sharp. "This is Benji Walker."

I paused. "Benji… I take it you can't speak freely?"

"The situation is not ideal, no. My flowers are in danger of a blight. Listen carefully. Red and blue dogwoods are en route to the greenhouse. They're poisonous to the roses. You're going to want to relocate them. Purple dogwoods are invasive this time of year, and aren't far behind. Your briar rose is in danger."

My mouth went dry. I may not know the ins and outs of Acanthus' code, but I think I understood. "Okay…. Okay. Uh. Thanks. Got it."

The line went dead. My heart was pounding in my ears, and I dropped the phone back to the floor. "Red and blue dogwoods. Dogwoods… Acanthus said dogwoods are wolves… Red and blue, police? Fuck."

I glanced up the stairs. Should I wake them? What could we do in the middle of the day? I was so fucking tired. The sound of crunching gravel came from outside and my entire body was electrified with adrenaline. *Fuck, fuck, fuck, fuck! What do I do?*

The sound of a car door slamming echoed through the air, and I gulped, urging myself to calm. Another door slammed. Then, the sound of boots thumping up the stairs. I opened the door just as one of the cops was raising her hand to knock. "Oh!" I feigned surprise, my backpack slung over a shoulder. "Hello Officers. How can I assist you?"

Too cheerful. They see right through you.

I fought to keep the anxiety from showing. The female officer looked me up and down, thinly veiled surprise on her face. "Hello Mister…" She trailed off, eyeing me sharply, expecting an answer. I cringed at the honorific.

"Borne. Cypress Borne. How can I help?"

If I was smart, I'd have made up a name. *Jesus Christ, Cypress. You could've used literally anything. Victor Healseng, remember?!* My heart sped, and I fought to keep my breathing calm as my thoughts started to run away from me. *How could I just say my name to a stranger? These are probably not real cops. I'm an idiot.*

"Cypress," she said my name with a weighted tone and turned to look at her partner. His vest read *Det. Hudson Barke*. The female officer's name read *Claudia Marks*. "Do you live here?"

"Sure do, Officer. Is there a problem?"

"Well, Cypress," Claudia spoke. "Did you know you're a missing person?"

"I'm a…" I trailed off, dumb struck. How would cops two states over from my home even know who I was, and who on earth could call me a missing person? "What?" I tilted my head at her. "Well you found me," I said, giving an award winning smile.

Claudia was not amused. She looked at Hudson, and they seemed to talk without words. I tensed, swallowing. If they were talking without words, then these were absolutely supernaturals. *Fuck, what do I do?*

Hudson turned back to me with a tight smile, interrupting my internal freakout. "If you could come with us, Mister Borne."

"Wait, am I under arrest?" Any efforts I'd been making to keep calm went out the window. I'd never even gotten a speeding ticket.

His eyebrows shot up in surprise. "No, son. Your mother would love to see you."

"My mother? It's been a few months since I've seen her. Is she well?" Anxiety rolled through me, my skin tingling and my heart throwing itself against my rib cage. *If my mother knew where I was, was she at risk? What if Nekane figured out who's close to me and started to seek them out? My mother would be the easiest to find.*

"What's happening?" Acanthus' sleepy voice cut through my panic. *"Cypress, who's here?"*

"The police. Did you know I'm a missing person?"

"You're… What?" Acanthus' panic spiked through the bond and mingled with my own, but I didn't respond to them. However, I did start

to broadcast what I was seeing to Acanthus as I spoke aloud to the officers.

"I apologize, but I'd really appreciate it if you just forgot you saw me," I crossed my arms casually. "I'm not too keen to see my mom. Let her know I'm safe and healthy if need be. I'm living in the woods, contentedly, with my partner."

It was true, I was surprised my mother was looking for me. I didn't think that she'd care, and I honestly hadn't thought about reaching out. "Can you explain why your last known location was absolutely destroyed?" Hudson's voice was gruff.

Claudia piggybacked off of his question, backing up her partner. "The doors were busted down, the place was trashed. You were nowhere to be found."

"Well, to be honest, I didn't really have the money for the church. I bought it on a whim, and it needed a complete overhaul." Lying was beginning to get as easy as eating at this point. "I sold that church to a private buyer. There was too much upkeep. My partner had this place. I have no idea what happened to it, it's not my fault if squatters gained access in my absence."

I shrugged. Technically, it was true; I'd sold the church back to Acanthus before I left for Nekane's. They'd be able to see this if they looked into the property. They seemed to accept the answer. "Alright." Hudson grumbled. "Shoot your mom a text once in a while."

"Save us some trouble back at the department," Claudia agreed.

"Cypress?" Acanthus' voice was tight, panicked. *"Do I need to come help? They're absolutely a cleanup crew."*

My guts were tying themselves into knots. I sent an image of a stuffed wolf plush in a superman costume with a thought bubble that said, I got this. I definitely did not have this, but Acanthus would be recognized. I wasn't about to risk that with Nekane less than ten miles away.

I rubbed at the back of my head, feigning humility. "I've been pretty busy trying to figure things out and lost my phone, you see. My little Golf got in a wreck outside of New Jersey, and my phone was lost in the car. I've been too busy to replace it. I'll give my mother a call once I have a chance to get a new phone. I'm so sorry for the inconvenience, officers."

Claudia and Hudson glanced at each other, then nodded. Claudia spoke up, and I sagged in relief as she smiled. "Sorry for the intrusion. We'll let your mother know you're safe. Get yourself sorted, Mr. Borne. And, have a good day. Stay out of trouble, alright?"

I grinned at the officers. "Sure thing. Thanks, Officers."

Hudson smiled, and Claudia nodded. I watched as they made their way back to the car. They spoke together in low voices that I couldn't hear, and I shut the door, watching them leave the driveway through the window. As they pulled out, I sighed. *So much for being sneaky.*

Acanthus

I met Cypress on the stairs. My hunger added an edge to my anxiety over the interaction and I mindlessly braided my hair as I chewed my lip bloody. The taste was calming, though my stomach groaned, even with the earthy undertone and the sparse, sluggish flow that came from the damaged skin. He met me halfway, and we walked back up to the loft. I flopped into a chair, and he leaned against the railing, drumming his fingers against the wood. My voice was slow and deep, rough with sleep. "What did they say?"

"Nothing worth noting. My mother found the last church in the state we left it, and filed a missing persons report. They told me to text her or something." He tacked on a bitter thought. "Because now she cares."

I blinked, but chose not to push the subject. Cypress' mother was a point of deep pain, I had come to learn, but it wasn't something we had spoken about at length. I could barely hear them over all of the horrible noise; skittering, idiosyncratic heartbeats of the creatures in and around the church created a cacophony of sound. I was exhausted as if I hadn't slept at all, and my throat burned. *How long have we even been at this hideout?*

My time blindness was a blessing when I was forcing myself to go without, but I couldn't keep track of the nights. I was guaranteed to fall into a frenzy if I didn't get blood soon. The officers set me even more on edge, and Cypress' reassurance did nothing to touch my anxiety. Nekane had a huge network of Hunters and human aids. I could only imagine what type of influence she had over the local law enforcement and public servants. "Acanthus," Cypress frowned as they spoke. "What's wrong?"

I winced, my throat clicking as I swallowed. "If they didn't know anything before, they do now, Cypress. You gave them a lot of information. Did you catch their names? Hudson Barke? Claw-dia Marks? Those certainly are euphemisms. Not to mention, that could have been a thinly-veiled threat towards your mother."

Cypress was silent, their face falling to a contemplative seriousness that I didn't see in them often. Their eyes narrowed, and the frown was deep. "'My flowers are in danger of a blight. Red and blue dogwoods are en route to the greenhouse. They're poisonous to the roses. You're going to want to relocate them. Purple dogwoods are invasive this time of year. They're not far behind. Your briar rose is in danger.'"

Everything was both sharpened and fuzzy mentally, and it took gargantuan effort to ignore the dripping of the faucet in the bathroom, and the pulsing in my temples from my parched veins. Swaying in my seat, I inhaled quickly, then licked my lips. My skin was buzzing, and everything was touching me in too many places. "Where did you hear that?"

"Your phone. Benji called. I had to navigate your code without knowing any of it. What's it mean, Acanthus, do we need to go?"

So he found the phone. His voice held an irritated edge, but I guess the situation was more important than my secrets. "I'm sorry —"

"Don't," he cut me off, closing his eyes. "I'm upset you kept it from me, but we can talk about it later, okay? The cops scared me. You're clearly not doing well. Tell me what the code means and what I need to do."

I closed my eyes, repeating the phrase in my mind. "My flowers are in danger of a blight — sickness, or an attack. Red and blue dogwoods — police. Benji was talking about the Officers... The greenhouse is the hideout. They're poisonous to the roses, means me. I'm the briar rose in the Garden."

I closed my eyes, licking my lips again. My throat clicked painfully. "Human law enforcement is a powerful ally to have, and she certainly has them in her network. She knows where we are, and I'm too weak to fend off her pack."

Checkmate, I thought dully. "Let me take care of it," Cypress' response was immediate, and his voice was gruff and tapered off into a growl.

Their hands clenched the railing. I frowned, my eyes lingering on them. "Cypress.... I can't just let you literally throw yourself to the Wolves... We really need to be careful."

"Then we need to go, Acanthus," they blurted, then swore under their breath. I tensed, a spike of anxiety skewering my heart. They pushed off of the railing and walked over to the chair across from me. "If Benji called and used the code with me, then that means the Apothecary has eyes on it, right? Nekane didn't know where we were, but they're going to find us in a day or two. If those cops are her cleanup crew? That means we probably have hours."

I paused. Braid. Unbraid. Braid. Unbraid. They leaned towards me, their strong hands steady as they gently wrapped around mine. His heat nearly burned me. He shivered, and I pulled away, trying to protect him from my icy chill. I didn't have the energy to fight. "We can't leave until nightfall, Cypress, I can't go in the sun right now."

Lemon Balm

I trailed off and thought of the phone. I could try to call some of the Night Garden contacts. *Is it worth the risk, asking allies to get us out with Nekane so close? Could they even get to us in time with the heavy surveillance in these woods? I should've called for backup when Cypress was attacked. I don't know what to do.*

"*Merde*," I muttered. I swayed again. At this rate, I was going to be dead by nightfall. The starvation was at dangerous levels, and if I fell into a frenzy while we were running away, I could hurt Cypress. I swallowed, looking down to the floor. "There is a side of me that I fear. It may show itself soon and I need to feed before it gets to that point. I was in danger of it after the first attack in New York, but the sun damage to my body thankfully kept me too weak. The only thing that I can think of is running from this place. Perhaps we backtrack to Azalea's when the sun sets?"

"Do we have the time to wait for sunset?"

It was hard enough for me to admit that I was out of ideas. I didn't know what to do. I was a caged animal being poked with a sharp stick. Cypress panicked, their whole body snapping to attention. "Didn't we leave Azalea so that she wasn't caught in the middle?"

My brows furrowed. We had. "We have no other options than to return to the Yellow Rose. And, the odds are stacked against us. I must admit, I am at a loss."

I don't know when I fell back asleep, or how I did when the circumstances were so dire. I came into consciousness just past sunset with a red haze in my vision before I even opened my eyes. *Oh no.*

The skittering of creatures in the walls and their heartbeats clashed in a cataclysm, the half-formed nature of their thoughts echoing through the drywall. *Dig. Chew. Food.*

From across the hall came Cypress' thundering heart, both slow with the calm of sleep and terribly fast in my ears. Mice underneath the foundation, squirrels in the trees outside, bats and birds, worms in the earth, all creating a terrible and asynchronistic rhythm that threw me further into the haze. It was too much. It was all of me, and none of me, swirling in and out of connectedness like a horrible kaleidoscope of color, light, and blood. ***"No, no, nonono…"***.

I let out a rattling gasp as my fangs lengthened, totally disconnected from the sensation. My flesh tightened around my bones in a terrible constriction, my veins jutting out of my skin in thick cords, pulsing and writhing in time with the sounds around me. ***"Please, no,"*** I pleaded, while a baser side of my instinct screamed in response. *"BLOOD. BLOOD. BLOOD BLOOD BLOODBLOODBLOOD."*

My mind was both terribly present and unable to wrest control back from my inner beast. I worked so hard to avoid this monstrous state, and it caught me by surprise this time. I thought I had time. I wouldn't stay conscious much longer, losing myself to the desire to feed. *Cypress.*

Their animal musk, strong coffee and campfire scent layered in tantalizing overtones to the deep copper and iron liquid pulsing just beneath their skin from two rooms away. They were the closest to me, and their blood made me salivate even when I wasn't starving. *Eatchewfoodeatchewfood.* Every fiber of my being sang with thirst, hunger, and pain, and I snarled, my face contorting as my jaw dropped. My eyes flew open. I pictured myself lunging at my inner beast, screaming at it. *"Get out. Get out. GET OUT."*

My body crawled in disjointed movements out of the bed and across the floor to the bedroom door. I forced myself to focus, levitating into the air off of the loft and careening towards the front door, crashing through it and leaving it to hang awkwardly off its hinges as I flew at top speed into the forest.

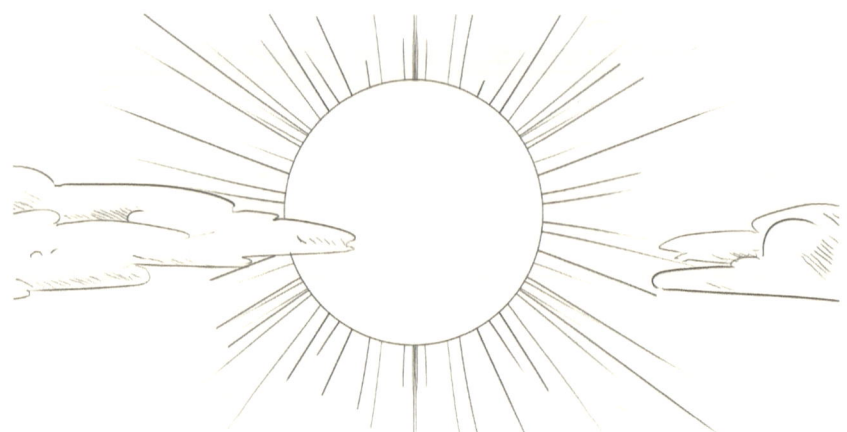

That Time Acanthus Fixed The Deer Overpopulation

Cypress

My eyes snapped open, my body instantly rigid with panic. *"Get out. Get out. GET OUT,"* rang loudly through my head.

"Acanthus?" My heart sped, my body cold even though I was coated with sweat. *"What's going on? Is it Nekane?"*

I heard the door crash open downstairs, and leapt from my bed as static began to pulse behind my eyes. *What in the hell? Are we under attack? Why weren't they answering me? God damn it all.*

Maybe Acanthus gave me what warning they could, but that didn't make sense. There was no further disruption, no commotion. *Fuck, we shouldn't have gone to bed after those cops came. We should've left during the day.*

I ran down the stairs in a panic, I couldn't see or hear anything wrong. Nothing smelled strange; no Wolves, or sweat, or the ozone burning of electrical equipment. The crickets sang their song, blissfully ignorant to the commotion. I stopped halfway down the stairs, staring towards the open door. "What... the fuck..."

It barely hung on by its hinges. The other side of the jamb was completely busted out. *"Acanthus?"*

Acanthus' gate clicked open in my mind, and my vision was tinged red. My throat and chest were burning, as though I hadn't drank any water in a decade. I hit the ground and rolled down the rest of the stairs, curling into a ball at the base. "Fuck, ow!"

My throat tried to convince me I'd gargled razor blades, and I coughed, winded. My lungs were empty and unable to fill. *What the fuck, this is worse than silver!*

As it dawned on me that my lungs were filling perfectly fine, it became apparent that this wasn't my pain. A heavy shove forced me out of the pack bond and back onto the floor of the church.

"Get. Out." Acanthus hissed icily. I shivered. I'd never heard that tone of voice from them.

"No," I growled back. *"Tell me how to help. I'm coming to you."*

"Stupid Wolf, do you have a death wish?"

I bit my tongue at the insult. Acanthus was not themself right now, and I know they didn't mean it. They'd likely be mortified at the thought. It was their voice, but something garbled and distorted. This couldn't be my friend. Stubbornly, I doubled down, trying to sound confident as I replied. *"Possibly. But I don't care. I want to help y —"*

"NO." The thought was screamed with such force that I flinched. *"Do not come near me."*

That sounded more like them. My face was hot with tears. I hadn't even realized I was crying until the drops started to stain the floor. *"Acanthus, let me fucking HELP."*

"If you help you will DIE, Cypress. I can't control myself."

"That's a risk I'm willing to take."

"Cypress NO," the command was sharper and less controlled. *"I am in a frenzy... I.. Can't..."*

Acanthus faded from my mind, a roaring cry dissolving into a manic laughter, with the mantra of *"BLOODBLOODBLOOD"* overlapping *"eatchewfood"*. I shivered, the chilling words forming ice in my veins. Acanthus shot further and further away from the church, and I attempted to connect again, my voice tight and small in our link.

"Acanthus?"

No answer. It was like they were there, but cloudy. Just a vague sense of energy in that direction. "Fuck," I growled, walking down the stairs. I shook my head, pulling my shirt off, and leaving a pile of clothes in the doorway. I hit the ground on all fours and ran, leaving the human realm behind.

I'd been searching for Acanthus for hours. If Nekane and her Hunters were in the woods, then I was risking more silver nets and knives in my limbs. I prayed to whatever deity I could think of that I didn't run into them. I didn't even want to think about Acanthus running into them. Fuck, I snarled. *How hard is it to find a Vampire?*

Almost as if summoned, I heard Acanthus' sad, whispery voice in the back of my mind, barely audible over the late summer wind. *"Cypress..."*

I stopped abruptly, my attention laser pointed to the East. *"WHERE ARE YOU?!"*

The question came out much more aggressive than concerned as I took off at top speed that direction. That was not my intention. I hadn't heard a THING from them since the start of their... Frenzy? I had no idea what they'd meant by that, but the circumstances scared the shit out of me. For all I knew, they were dying somewhere alone. I needed to find them.

They sent me an image of the lake to the East. I'd stopped there during my run to this church. I nearly stumbled when I recognized it. *"No fucking way. That lake is an hour away."*

I stared at it through their eyes. It was partially marred by a pink tinge and static surrounding the image, but I knew where that was and took off, projecting my path along the way. *"I'm coming."*

I ran as fast as I could, my legs burning. My paws ached, the constant pounding from the speed of my run sending shock-waves through my bones with every contact to the uneven forest floor. The rushing of wind in my ears was my only companion.

When I slowed to catch my breath, my hair stood on end at the distinct lack of any sound. The crickets had disappeared. The standard rustling and scurrying of animals was missing. It was eerie how lifeless the forest was. I was reminded of the first time I saw the woods in New York at night, when Acanthus and I met. Hackles raised, I scented the air, desperate for the smell of rose, oud, and sandalwood. I gagged; the pine-scented breeze was tinged with a dirty copper smell. I bit back bile as I adjusted course and took off running again. *"There's so much blood... Acanthus, please be okay..."*

The smell got stronger and sicker as I pushed forward. Two miles of my run were plagued with it. I slowed when I realized I was close to the clearing. The scent clung to my nostrils, and I soaked in the carnage, my heart pounding. A trail of gore lead towards the clearing. Everything was painted the dark, muddy brown of drying blood.

It had looked like anything Acanthus touched turned into a cloud of red mist, coating the leaves and the ground in a thick layer. At least, I hoped it was what Acanthus had touched. *What if that came from them, what if the Hunters found them?*

My stomach heaved, but forced down the bile in my throat. I tentatively put one paw in front of the other, trying not to pay attention to the slick grass. My paw brushed against something fuzzy. I looked down to see the mangled carcass of a rabbit. *"Oh my God…"*

Woodland creatures littered the forest floor, twisted in bizarre directions and partially hidden in the underbrush. Some were completely shriveled up from having life drained from them, and others left half drunk in preference for bigger prey. I don't think I've ever been so simultaneously relieved and disgusted by anything. Nausea rocked me, and my inner instinct was to run far away. I quashed the feeling down and did my best to continue forward.

I was fine until I caught sight of my paws. They were matted with blood, glistening and covered in gore up to my ankles. I shifted my gaze upward and kept walking. *It's just dew….*

It was nothing like dew; still warm, and way too viscous. *Thick, warm dew…*

When the forest opened up to the clearing, Acanthus was sitting in the glittering moonlight on the shore of the lake, petting a faun that looked like it was peacefully sleeping. The bite mark at its neck told me all I needed to know. The vibrations of a snarl bubbled up in my chest. Acanthus flinched and stilled, and I chastised myself. *Hush, you stupid beast.*

I forced my feet forward, against all my instincts, my heart breaking for them. They were a complete disaster. Their fangs were still out, blood running down their lips. Their cheeks were coated with tears and their hair caked and matted. "I'm a MONSTER. This is not sustainable. I can't do this."

I turned to look at them, whimpering. *"Hey, stop crying. You're being wasteful."*

I'd meant it as a joke. It did not come across as a joke. It was cruel and awful. A new wave of tears hit their cheeks. *"Hey, hey. I was kidding."*

I went to nudge them with my nose and paused. This was definitely a panicked situation, and I didn't have their express permission to touch them. I sat down on my haunches. *"I'm sorry Acanthus. That was heartless. I was trying to be funny. I don't know how to help, and... "*

I trailed off, remembering the thirst that absolutely floored me. Their thirst. *"You've dealt with a lot. I can clean this up. You should shower, or take a bath."* I looked over their matted hair. *"A shower might be better though. Would..."*

I trailed off again, terrified by their complete lack of reaction. With a bit more urgency, I asked, *"Is it easier for me to stay a Wolf?"*

They stared at me, unseeing. *"Acanthus?"*

If you say their name often enough, it begins to sound weird. Say it with me! *"Acanthus!"*

Nothing. Nada. No response. I stared at them for a long time, until the blood dried and pulled at my fur. The darkness against the white was starting to freak me out. I whimpered, shifting my gaze towards the lake. *"I need to wash this off... I'm just going to take a few minutes, okay?"*

There was no answer. My heart sank like a stone into the pit of my stomach. I stepped off of the bank, into the shallows of the lake, always angled to have the Vampire in my peripheral. Whimpering, I turned around to face them fully before I washed my paws off in the water. *There. Now it won't be so startling when Acanthus breaks from their daze.*

Then, we sat in silence for hours. At first I stayed by their side, laying in the grass with my head on their knee. It made me nauseous to sit so near the dead deer, but I forced myself to. I rambled to them as I sat, talking about anything and everything; making little stupid jokes and filling the frightening silence. I didn't know if I was comforting them, or me.

When I ran out of things to say, I stared at them. *"Come back. Please. Acanthus, I can't do this without you."*

There was no answer. Sitting still wasn't helping; my insides were compacted into a dense ball of stress. The lack of noise from around us, coupled with the lack of movement from Acanthus was driving me crazy. *At least no noise means that Nekane's not nearby.*

I busied myself by burying the dead animals, never straying too far. I started by gently dragging the deer out of Acanthus' hands. They didn't move, and somehow the sight of them with their empty arms and dull eyes made everything worse. I choked back tears as I dragged the carcass to the edge of the clearing and began to dig, always within sight of them. In case they needed me, I wanted to be within shouting distance.

As I dug, I thought about what I knew. The phone was behind the couch. If the Hunters raided the church while we were out here, then they'd find it. *Fuck, I should've grabbed that, or made a bag, or something.* I wasn't exactly covering my tracks in my panic. We'd run in the opposite way from the Hunters, but they could still easily look for signs of an animal the size of a lion crashing through the underbrush. Regardless, I think we needed to be gone as soon as Acanthus came back to me, sun or no. I didn't think we'd be going back to the church.

Burying the animals took me hours; by the time I was finished, the half-moon had set, and we were sometime in the silent hour right before dawn. I rinsed off one more time in the lake, and then took my place back at Acanthus' side. How did I know when they were coming out of whatever this was? They blinked.

My head snapped up at the first movement I'd seen in hours. They'd *BLINKED.* *"Acanthus?"*

The hope swelled in my chest, and every muscle in my body was tense, begging silently for an answer. Their head slowly tipped towards me, their eyes shifting down and darting over me. *"Cypress, you're…"*

I tilted my head at the thought as it trailed off. *"I'm what?"*

"Never mind."

They blinked slowly, as if seeing their surroundings for the first time.

We didn't have time for this; the sun would be rising soon. I wasn't sure if now was a good time for Acanthus to be caught in the sun. Not even taking into account the fact that it hurt them, the shadows of the pre-dawn morning hid the severity of the gore around us. I buried the bodies, but I couldn't hide the dried blood that misted over everything. I didn't want them to have to face the carnage they had caused. *"Should we go back to the church? The sun will be starting to rise soon."*

They looked down at their hands, still covered in blood. I couldn't help them by washing them, as a wolf. I hadn't thought about it. Fuck, so much from hiding the gore, I thought. They slowly panned their gaze up to me. Their hazel eyes were clear and focused, full of heartbreak and still tinged pink. Their voice was barely above a whisper, full of broken glass and sorrow. "Maybe you should go without me."

I recoiled as though I'd been hit, my ears flattening to my head. *"Go, what do you mean go?"*

Acanthus shook their head, slow and muddled. They looked like they were a video being played at half speed. Their voice was watery and thin, but no tears fell from their eyes. "This. Can't happen again. You seeing me like this. Me getting this bad. I'm a danger to you, I nearly ripped you apart. I think it'd be best if you left."

Confusion flooded my mind, and maybe now wasn't the best time to talk about it. *"Acanthus, let's talk as humans."*

"We don't need to."

I whimpered and looked down at my paws. There was no way in hell that I would leave them, but what could I do when they were in this state? I wasn't going to push them when they'd been catatonic for most of the night. I didn't answer; instead, I walked away from Acanthus for the second time. This time, by their choice; my heart crumbled to pieces as I walked to the edge of the clearing, and sat in limbo.

Acanthus

I waited for my soft, gentle white wolf to walk away from me, and looked up to the sky. Little did Cypress know, it didn't matter if they packed and went, or not. I was going to sit there until I turned to stone, shattering to ash under the heat of the day. *I'm done.*

My mind had been floating in thick, syrupy blackness most of the night. When I surfaced, all I could see was red; blood misting into the air. Animals turned to twisted, mangled remnants in seconds as I screamed at myself to stop. *I'm a monster.* The worst was when I surfaced into my mind to see my hands tearing a raccoon in half. The violence was senseless; I didn't even attempt to feed from half of the animals I'd killed. Nekane was right; I should be wiped off of the face of the earth.

I flopped into the grass, the wet soaking into my shirt. I don't know how long I lay there like that, staring up at the clouds. The slowly growing light was starting to become dangerous, but I couldn't bring myself to care. If the sun didn't find me, then Nekane and her Hunters would. *"Checkmate."*

My body was made of static. My skin prickled as the light hit the parts of me that were bare. A whine from the edge of the clearing alerted me to Cypress' presence. I should've known they weren't going to leave me alone that easily, but I needed to convince them to let me go. To let me disappear. *"I am dangerous. I am a monster. I nearly killed you* tonight, I don't know how I stopped myself from crawling to your room. I'm done, Cypress. Leave me."*

"But, you did stop yourself, Acanthus. You aren't a monster. Come on, we need to go. The sun…"

Numbly, I shook my head. My heart was empty, despite my full stomach. *"I'm done,"* I repeated. *"Let me go. You need to get away from Nekane. Go to Azalea's, she will know how to aid you."*

The Wolf threw their head back and howled several paces away. The pain was palpable in the noise. They turned to face me when they tapered off into whimpers. Tears welled in my eyes once more, and I shook my head again. *"Don't make it harder, Cypress, I cannot."*

"I will make it harder, dammit! You're my pack, Acanthus, please! I'm not leaving you. You're my only friend!"

The sun was coming up over the horizon, and the sky was slowly turning blue. Cypress came back to me, tugging at my sleeve. I shook my head. "Leave me to be in the sun. I'm done."

I shut the gate in my mind and locked it, picturing myself throwing away the key. This was surrender; defeat. They growled, their ears back and lips curled. When I didn't open the link, they jumped onto my chest, barking at me frantically, yelling in a voice I couldn't hear between us. Their eyes were wide and wild in their panic, tail tucked between their legs as they started to whimper in between their chaotic shouts. The image was terrifying, their teeth snapping inches from my face, while they covered me in slobbery licks. I watched through my wall of apathy before I closed my eyes.

I couldn't shut them out of my physical space, but I could ignore them. I pushed at them. "Go. Get off. Leave me."

The barks faded to heavier growls, and their weight on my chest was crushing. They way they were laying felt both like trying to get my attention, and trying to cover me from the danger. I could picture them banging against my mental gate. A pressure was building in my forehead, and I opened my eyes to see Cypress squinting theirs shut. The pressure built, and I shut my eyes again. *I'm done, I cannot handle this pain anymore.*

I was so tired. An audible *pop* rang through my mind, and their voice called through. They'd broken down my gate. *"Dammit Acanthus! For once, please think of yourself!"*

Why did that sound familiar? Oh yeah. I had said that to him several weeks ago. Blinking slowly, the tears finally began to flow. I sniffled, their form wobbling in my vision. *"I can't leave you,"* they continued, their own fat oily tears streaking down their fur. *"Please,*

Acanthus. Please. I'm lost without you. You are a light in the dark. Please."

I lost my resolve and wailed, sobbing into their fur as I threw my arms around them, broken. *I am so lost.*

The rest of the morning was a blur. By the time I had stopped crying, the sun was high in the sky. I tried in vain to cover my exposed arms and face. I allowed Cypress to carry me into the cover of the trees, and sat, despondent, in the underbrush. The forest was a void thanks to my frenzy the night before. *"Acanthus, listen to me. We need to get you covered, and the church isn't safe, right? Can you summon things to travel with from the church? We need to go."*

I didn't have the energy to speak aloud. *"Do you think Nekane has found it yet?"*

"I don't know," they whined. *"But your burner phone is still there."*

My heart stalled, and I whipped my head to look at them. That put the entire Garden at risk. *"What else do you need?"*

Cypress bristled and growled at me. *"None of this 'you' shit. We're getting out of here, together. Can you summon our stuff or not?"*

I didn't have the energy to fight, so I closed my eyes and nodded. Using my mental map of the church, I pictured our bags filling themselves with necessities. Our items were rolled neatly between the two backpacks and the duffel bag. The few shelf-stable food items left from when Cypress risked town were in the lunch tote.. I made sure the phone was in the front of my bag with its charger. The last thing I went for was my black travel cloak. I pictured the bags lifting and called them to me. In five minutes, they were in a pile in front of us.

I reached for the cloak, then stopped, the gore on my hands catching my eyes. Instead, I floated the fabric above my head, creating an umbrella. In the comfort of the new shade, I contemplated the decaying leaves on the forest floor. Cypress grabbed his bag with his teeth and walked into the forest, where I could no longer see them. When they came back, they were human, padding across the uneven ground barefoot and dressed in a tee shirt and jeans.

They knelt below the cloak and joined me in the shade with no complaints from me. If they wanted me to go along with them, then so be it. Gone was the person who would chide Cypress to take care of himself. Gone was the person who would care for myself to feel better. The frenzy, coupled with the circumstances, left me emotionally bereft and numb. That, coupled with the day, had me near catatonic. When I was full health, the day wouldn't affect me like this; all vampires slowed in the light, but the starvation and frenzy left me feeling my weakness.

Thunderous roars of laughter echoed in my ears, echoing memories of my Sire. I deserved to rot in that crypt. These moments, the moments where I gave up, were moments where his ghost won. They were moments where my own nature proved in shining, brilliant fact, that he was right. That we were monsters. That I should just give in to my nature and let myself be a cruel, sadistic thing of darkness.

It was eerily silent between us, though the link wasn't shut. There was nothing to say. I had broken one of my own inner rules and tried to push them away. I couldn't reconcile how kind they were with my own horror at my state. And yet, there they were, sitting with me when they should be running from Nekane. I stared at my flaking hands, and the dark part of my mind hissed, *"I deserve filth."*

The thought may or may not have floated between us. Cypress bristled. I could feel their heart twisting through our bond, but I couldn't bring myself to care. "What you deserve," Cypress' voice was thin and watery. "Acanthus, is to not feel like this."

A laugh I didn't recognize pierced the air, hollow and sharp. It echoed François' in my mind, creating a horrid discordant harmony. Monsters didn't care for feelings. Monsters ripped, and tore, and eviscerated. There was not much left to me. Slowly, images began to flood my mind— of the times I had healed Cypress, the times I had helped them, times I spent teaching them despite not fully knowing what Wolves needed. My eyes welled up again, and I closed them, shaking my head and trembling.

Cypress' hands clasped mine and I gasped. "Cypress, the blood —"

"How can you see yourself as a monster? You spend so much of your life healing."

The tears spilled over. The dried blood on my cheeks crackled as fresh blood spilled from my eyes and dislodged loose pieces of coagulation. I whimpered, a hollow husk of a sob barking out of my chest as if it couldn't stand to be within. *"Leave me."*

"No, Acanthus. Hey, maybe we should get you cleaned up? Getting rid of the blood might help you feel better."

I didn't answer, falling deeper into the numb indifference. Cypress wrapped their strong arms around me, their warmth infiltrating my chaos and making me feel safe. They carried me towards the edge of the lake, and I floated the cloak above us. "Come on, Acanthus, Please? I need you to try. Can you try?"

I blinked. What was the point of trying? We had lost. Nekane had found us. I killed everything in my path, and swept up everyone around me into a whirlwind of danger and risk. I twisted out of their hold, floating out to the center of the lake and lowering myself into the water, the cloak floating above. *Depths below, carry me to hell where I belong.*

Cypress

They didn't want to talk? That's fine. They also didn't have to look at me.

When I was growing up, my mom would stay out too late. Maybe someone would get too rough with her. The things she did to get her fixes were awful. I couldn't count how many times I had led her to the bathroom, vomit caked in her hair and dullness set behind her eyes. Once, when I was fifteen, she'd mixed alcohol with something she wasn't supposed to while we were on vacation at a beach on Long Island. One moment, she was slurring through a conversation with me, and the next, she'd passed out within the waves. I remember the panic, swimming to her and gathering her up. I remember gasping for air as I dragged her to the shore. I remember trying to steady myself and do first aid, a lifeguard stepping in when I couldn't keep the rhythm right.

A tear escaped my eye before I could stop it. *No, Cypress. This is entirely different. They don't have to breathe, for one.*

I watched the ripples in the water as Acanthus resurfaced with a small gasp. They turned to face me, eyes glowing. The light reflected off of the water in two pin pricks, and the waterline was just under their lips. *"You are not to blame, dear one. I can feel your guilt. Please, this is not your fault."*

I bit my cheek and didn't say anything to that. The water was a circle of red around them. It reminded me of a shark attack. I shuddered as Acanthus' voice echoed again in my mind. *"I have pushed you away again, and yet you're still helping me. Why?"*

My eyebrows knitted together. I was tired of sitting in our heads, and so I called across the lake, "What do you mean? You're my Pack, Acanthus."

They blinked. *"I'm so sorry."*

A stream of consciousness started to bubble through our link, regret and self hatred being the leading emotions. "Stop it," I said, my voice a razor edge as my heart sped. "You've self-destructed enough."

They dunked beneath the surface of the water again, and more blood clouded around them. The cloak slowly glided through the air, and they surfaced much closer to the shore. They started combing their nails through their hair. Love, appreciation, and relief radiated through our bond, and I sighed as I sat back. "I keep coming back, because I need you, too. I need you to think of yourself sometimes, Acanthus. Please."

Even with as vulnerable as Acanthus was, and as open as I was being with them, I couldn't focus too much on what I meant by needing them. I only knew that when I thought too hard about them being gone, my chest tightened. It was hard to breathe, and the world got significantly darker.

"I can't stop," they replied, breaking me from my thoughts as they stilled. *"The frenzy is the worst part of me. I'm sorry you had to see me this way, and I am happy you didn't leave when I asked."*

"Stop. Now," I repeated.

And oddly, they did. The tension that had been radiating off of them in waves lessened. They were still upset, but beating themself up wasn't helping anyone. The dead silence was deafening. It lasted for a beat too long before their voice cut through my mind, small and scared. *"What if this happens again? I cannot hold myself at bay if I cannot eat. I have been trying so hard."*

"So don't let it happen again," I spoke so seriously that there was no way to mistake my words for sarcasm.

"How?" The thought bit at me and I grimaced.

"I don't know, Acanthus. I'm not you, I don't know how to navigate your needs. I don't know how to set up supply lines, or create clandestine paths. I don't know how to make cool hidden getaways. You told me to go back to Azalea's. We said we'd go back to Azalea's together last night, but then this happened. If we backtrack, then we're out of the line of fire, right? That also gives you your supply lines back."

They didn't answer, dunking beneath the water again. I tilted my head towards the direction of the church. When they resurfaced again, the soft lapping of the water alerted me to their movement. I sighed. "You said you almost killed me, but I thought Werewolf blood made Vampires really ill, so, naturally and instinctively, you'd shy away, right? I mean, I still act on instinct when I see your fangs sometimes."

This time, they responded, parting their hair and flopping it behind their shoulders. *"No one knows what Werewolf blood does to a Vampire. But the legends have to come from somewhere."*

I scoffed. "Acanthus, how many legends have we disproven in the last three months? You're not even supposed to be talking to me mentally. I'm not supposed to be in a Pack with you. Who's to say there isn't some great Werewolf leader out there who just went 'I'm protecting our kind!'"

Acanthus let out a small laugh, and that made me smile. Laughter was good. Emboldened, I continued. "Look, all I'm trying to say is the legends might be full of absolute shit."

"Language", Acanthus automatically corrected me, but it was distant as if they barely registered what they were saying.

"There he is! I was worried I'd lost that pious bastard," I smiled as they ran their fingers through their hair.

"Stop, Cypress. What are you getting at?"

I shrugged, the light amusement from our conversation fading. It hit me that this was the most they'd moved since the frenzy had ended. My chest swelled with hope. They didn't push back on me when I started talking about the blood, either. Maybe they were ready to think about moving forward. *Maybe I can get them to pull out of this, after all. I thought they were going to die…*

Acanthus scrubbed at their face, their skin going pink. I chewed on my lip, stepping forward and sitting next to the line of the water. I didn't care about the wet seeping into my jeans. They'd said I was poisonous to them several times, but what if I wasn't? "What if I was a donor? We wouldn't find ourselves in this position again, and I'd be able to help. And, I guess the risk of me being killed goes down significantly if I'm horribly off the mark, and my blood is extremely toxic to you," I joked, and grinned at the scowl they shot me. "I'm just saying."

They were beginning to look more and more like my Acanthus rather than the shell of Acanthus they were a few minutes ago. I couldn't help the thought that slipped through. *"My Acanthus."*

It felt odd and possessive, and I blinked at them before shaking my head to clear it away. "I'm sorry."

The thought continued to rattle around in my skull, no matter how much I pushed at it, so I just let it linger a little bit longer. *"Mine."*

I don't know if it was the circumstances, or the way their eyes glittered, but the thought just felt right.

Acanthus

The possessive little word rattled between us and I blushed. Free from my dried gore, I walked along the bottom of the lake to where they were sitting, the cloak hovering over me. My clothes hung, sopping, from my frame as I knelt and clasped their hands. They brought their gaze to mine, and they murmured, "Look. I want a plan. I want to be able to avoid this ever happening again. And, if we plan, that means that you're looking forward. No falling into the void, Acanthus. I don't want to lose you, and I can't stand the thought of fighting without you here next to me."

I didn't answer as I pulled their right hand to my lips, kissing their palm. *"My Acanthus,"* ran through our bond again.

I tilted my cheek into their palm and nuzzled at the meat of their thumb, my affection leaking into the bond. I didn't have to say anything. I paused like that for a little while, savoring their warmth as I blushed. I couldn't quite meet their gaze. I wasn't sure what I was doing, and I wasn't sure what they were doing. "My Wolf," I whispered.

Once I was safely clad in tight black jeans and a thin, long-sleeved black shirt, I fastened the cloak around my neck.. Cypress had stayed by the lake, giving me privacy to change in the cover of the forest. When I stepped back into the clearing, he whipped around, tense, but his shoulders sagged as he saw me. "Hey," I greeted him.

"Hey," Cypress replied.

"I suppose it's time to stop wallowing and come up with a plan?"

Cypress reached for my hand, squeezing it. "Yeah. I think I've had enough wallowing to get me through the century."

I laughed at the joke, tilting my head to be on his shoulder. He watched the lake as I quieted. I didn't know where to start, but at least I wasn't throwing myself into the day. My skin prickled in the sunlight, and I tugged Cypress' hand as I jerked my head towards the line of trees. "Come on, let's go sit in the shade."

He nodded, and we walked hand in hand towards the trees. When we made it back to where our bags were sitting, Cypress took in a short breath before they broke the silence. "Excuse my language, Acanthus," they said, their voice low and careful, "But I'm pretty fucking tired of being in the dark. And I'm even more fucking tired of Nekane and her Pack chasing us. I don't know what I don't know. I can't ask questions if it feels like there are none to ask. And you keeping things from me has led us to this; you, half dead and looking to throw yourself into the sun, and me wondering once again what to do or where to go."

I cringed and lowered my gaze to the forest floor, shame coursing through me. Cypress' eyes were boring a hole into me, and he took my hands. I rubbed my thumb across his knuckles, chewing on my lip as he continued. "I don't blame you. I wouldn't know where to start with any of this either, in your shoes. But, I'm not going to run anymore. And neither should you. I want to know about the Night Garden, our resources, and how to fight back against this insane Wolf."

My breath caught in my throat, and I turned my palms up to touch his. "You are right. We cannot allow ourselves to be left in limbo like this. And perhaps, I should start doing what everyone around me thinks I'm capable of doing."

I pulled one of my hands out of his hold, closing my eyes and summoning the cellphone. When it fell into my hand, Cypress asked, "Where did you get that, by the way?"

"Azalea gave it to me. She said that I should keep in touch with the Garden. Before we left The Yellow Rose, I told her I wanted to re-join."

They blinked. I opened my eyes, unlocking the phone and scrolling the contacts. When I got to her name, I clicked the little receiver icon and put the device on speaker. Cypress' brow furrowed as the ringing echoed around the trees, and they glanced around us, tensing. The middle of the third ring cut short, and Azalea's cheery voice greeted us. "Yellow Rose Bed and Breakfast."

"Hello, my dear," I sounded far more confident than I felt. "I am inquiring about whether you have sweetbriars and silver dogwoods on your property."

I was restless and needed to move, so I pulled my other hand out of Cypress' and began to pace. I hovered the phone between us, and Cypress' eyes widened as they realized I was sharing the code. I kept my arms clasped around me as I waited for an answer. "None at the moment," Azalea responded. "Though, sweetbriars and silver dogwoods can be planted."

"Excellent. Expect a shipment late evening or tonight from the West," I cleared my throat as I turned on my heel. "The sweetbriars are sickly, and there are no local nurseries for their care. I fear shipments have been delayed, and my gargoyles are killing the roots. I'll need to replant them in more fertile soil."

"Certainly. Shall I have some plant food on hand?"

"Yes. I fear the sweetbriar has suffered a spotted blight. The dogwood is shaken, but we're looking to perhaps add two stars to the guiding path. Can you accommodate?"

"More stars are certainly needed, yes. Will there be a stand or a wagon?"

Cypress' face twisted in confusion, their eyes darting to me, but I answered smoothly. "Stand. Purple and lilac dogwoods are taking over the garden, so the less-beaten path is necessary."

"Understood. I'll be watching for your delivery. Have a great day!"

The line went dead, and Cypress stared blankly at the phone as it lit up, showing the call had ended. I floated it back into my bag as I paused in my pacing and dropped my hands to my side. "Did you catch any of that?"

"I know dogwoods are Wolves... And you told me you were a sweet briar. I figure colors mean something. But, I don't know much of anything else."

I pounded my fist into my palm with a decisive nod, assured. "Okay. I may not be able to teach you how to be a Wolf, but I can teach you about the Garden. Roses are code for vampires. Briar roses are vining. They are typically considered to be more weeds, but they grow in some of the harshest environments. My code in the Garden is specifically Sweetbriar, so that we do not give our names when we're overheard."

"Why roses? And, why is Azalea's Bed and Breakfast called Yellow Rose?"

I opened my mouth, extending my fangs, before retracting them. "Thorns."

Cypress tensed at the sight of my teeth, then relaxed, averting their eyes. "Okay. I can understand that."

I nodded. "A yellow rose in flower language is a symbol of friendship, joy, and optimism. The Yellow Rose was named to show her friendship with me, and her belief in the work that we were doing."

Cypress' eyes widened, and they gave a slow nod. "Does that make the purple and lilac dogwoods Nekane and her Pack?"

I nodded. "Dogwoods usually refer to wolves. Lilac was used for Hunters, before they were employed by the Nekane. So, Nekane's Hunters specifically are lilac dogwoods. Purple for an alpha or one of the Big Five, groves for packs and meetings."

Cypress tapped his fingers together, mouthing the colors as he tried to commit them to memory. I continued, pausing between each piece of code. "Red and blue for police, white and red for ambulances. We have other codes for Witches and their powers. So, what was said in that conversation just now, is that Azalea has room for us to relocate. I told her to expect us tonight or early in the morning. I also told her that I had a frenzy, our food supplies were cut off, and Nekane had guards closing in and choking us off. She'll have donors waiting for me at the Bed and Breakfast when we arrive, and I told her that we'll be traveling by foot through the forests and avoiding towns, covering our tracks."

Cypress blinked. "You said all that in a conversation about dogwoods and roses? Care to elaborate?"

"We should get going, Cypress, but once we're in safer halls, I will teach you more of the code. That was the other thing. The two guiding stars?"

He nodded, leaning forward. "I told her we were coming back into the fold. We'll be officially joining the Night Garden when we return."

He shook his head in amazement, before reaching for the bags. "No more running?"

"No more running," I confirmed. "I'd forgotten why I've been fighting for so long. You've reminded me. It's not about me. It's about things that are bigger."

Cypress nodded. "Wolf back or by foot, Acanthus?" I blinked, giving them a pleased little smile. They cocked their head. "What?"

They had grown so much from the scared, lost Pup that showed up on my doorstep three months ago. To relate the situation to a game of chess, Nekane still had us in check. But, I was wrong about being in checkmate. If I was king, then the Night Garden was queen, and perhaps, I'd moved my pawns back to reclaim it. If this was a war, then I was going to start fighting like I was in one. And, I needed to trust in Cypress, and fully open the door to our world. Being cautious had only proven to harm him, and I'd made a vow to protect him.

I reached to take the bags from Cypress. "Up for a run, Pup?"

They grinned. "I think I would've yelled at you if you didn't ask."

Cypress turned and jogged out of sight behind a tree, and a moment later, came back, his clothes gathered in his mouth. I grabbed them from him and stuffed them in his backpack. He lowered his head, and I hopped onto his back, adjusting my hold on the bags as I settled. He walked towards the mouth of the clearing, and I lowered my head, hiding in the hood of my cloak.

As he took off in a sprint towards the East, some hope sparked within me. For the first time in weeks, I felt light. I was looking forward to our next steps, and taking control back of my adventures. We would stop this war against me and the last remaining Vampires. And this time, I knew I wouldn't give up, and I knew I wouldn't back down. After all, I had Cypress by my side. We'd found each other amidst all the chaos, and somehow, that was enough to keep us going.

Author's Note
Thank you for reading!

Artemis here. Auden and I are independent authors, and we appreciate you taking the chance on our story! There is a second book about Acanthus and Cypress in the works. Thank you!

As independent authors, reviews are super important to us! If you enjoyed our story, please consider reviewing wherever you see fit!

As an illustrator, I also do all of the illustrations for the series. Some artwork is attached here at the end of the book. I'm also working on a set of two matching tarot decks; one centered on Cypress' focus, and one centered on Acanthus'.

Also you can check out more of my art and stories at:

https://www.vampireantihero.com

I'm a full time illustrator, and do custom illustration and concept artwork for books and TTRPGS. I also can do formatting services. If you need bookish art or design, don't be afraid to reach out! If you'd like more content surrounding the Night Garden, then consider following me on Patreon or Ko-Fi! Links can be found on my website.

If you'd like more behind-the-scenes and first-peek privileges, consider becoming a paid member on Patreon or Ko-Fi!

https://www.ko-fi.com/vampireantihero
https://www.patreon.com/vampireantihero

Lastly, if you want to chat about The Night Garden series, art, or writing, you can find us at our Discord, here:

https://discord.gg/dK7H6htPFt/

And, remember - no matter where you are, your voice matters. Your efforts matter. Our characters are rooting for you! Good luck out there.

With love and brightness,

Artemis Quinn and Auden Eris-Everen

www.ingramcontent.com/pod-product-compliance
Lightning Source LLC
Chambersburg PA
CBHW050516110726
47899CB00005B/1481